THE
PROPHETESS

A NOVEL

bancroft
press

Evonne
Marzouk

Poem on pages 18-19 by Jack Spicer.
www.poetryfoundation.org/poetrymagazine/poems/51258/any-fool-can-get-into-an-ocean

Author Photo: Natasha Kaufman Sheme, Natasha Anne Portrait Studio

Cover Art: Avraham Cohen, Avco Graphics

Cover/Interior design: Tracy Copes Creative

978-1-61088-504-1 (HC)

978-1-61088-506-5 (Ebook)

Published by Bancroft Press "Books that Enlighten"

410-358-0658

P.O. Box 65360, Baltimore, MD 21209

www.bancroftpress.com

Printed in the United States of America

Printed on 100 percent recycled paper.

For my mother, who always believed I could.
and
For my father, whose unshakeable love is a foundation of my life.

אלא הנח להן לישראל אם אין נביאים הן בני נביאים הן

Leave it to the Jewish people; if they themselves are not prophets,
they are the children of prophets.
Pesachim 66a

קרוב ה׳ לכל־קראיו לכל אשר יקראהו באמת

The Eternal One is close to all who call upon him
– to all who call upon Him in truth.
Psalms 145:18

PROLOGUE

Devorah

At the top of the steps, I hesitate, preparing myself for everything to come. I knock on the closed door. "Yonatan," I call.

I knock again. Down the stairs, I can see light shining in the common room; I hear the hushed voices of the others. Up here, all is silent and dark.

If he doesn't answer, it could mean the future I have seen is not yet certain. Or maybe there is more time than I understood. How I wish this could be true.

I knock a third time. "Yonatan." I lift my shoulders, prepared to turn away.

"Devorah," he calls, from within.

I don't allow my faith to falter. I open the door.

The room is plain, with wide plank wood flooring and bunk beds lodged against each of the four cement walls. Several of the beds are made up with sheets, white pillows, and army blankets. The men staying have stored their clothing, folded neatly, on the wood shelves between the beds.

But the space is not lacking in beauty. One empty shelf is painted with an explosion of flowers. A guitar case, artfully covered with stickers, pokes out from under a bed. Another shelf holds a much-used collection of Hebrew books.

Yonatan lies twisted in a rough brown blanket on a bottom bunk, staring hard out the window to the valley and mountains in the distance. At this time of year, the view is barren and dry.

I take a folding chair from the wall and settle my long skirt over my legs. The forlorn figure before me looks nothing like the nineteen year-old boy I met in Jerusalem when he first agreed to learn with me. His forehead is now lined with pain and sadness. In his dark beard, I can see the first strands of gray.

"Yonatan, I'm sorry," I murmur. "For you, for all of you. I'm so sorry."

His silver eyes aim like arrows out the window, hiding his anguish.

"I don't understand it," I say. "But the Ribbono Shel Olam[1] will bring good of it. Her memory will be a blessing, in the end."

A hawk soars across the sky outside, landing beyond our sight. Yonatan's

---

[1] Ribbono Shel Olam: A traditional Hebrew name for G-d, meaning Master or Creator of the World.

breathing is rough, labored. At last, he turns to face me.

"Why are you here?" It's a simple question, but his raspy voice turns it into a demand.

He already knows the answer. Shloshim, the ritual thirty days of mourning, is over. It's time for him to leave this place. But duty requires me to say it.

"Your time here is complete."

He meets my eyes and holds them. I understand how lost he is feeling; yet I know the strength of this man. He will find his way.

A breeze rustles blue and white flags on a distant hill as he turns back to the window. "I have nowhere else to go."

"You do now," I tell him. "A prophetess has been called."

His laugh is cynical. "You're asking me to teach someone now?"

"Yes." I rest my shaking hands on my knees. "She is the katanah."²

His shoulders give a little jolt, and I know he understands. The true test of a prophetess is in passing the flame.

"Devorah..." My name comes out as a moan. I glimpse his face, contorted with new sorrow, before his hands cover his eyes.

"Give her to someone else," he says. "Teach her yourself. Please."

I shake my head. "This calling is for you."

I know how hard it will be for him to untangle himself from his bed and become the person we all need him to be. But he will not be the first to go on in life when it seems everything is lost. Nor the last.

"Do not underestimate the resilience of the human heart," I advise him.

He uncovers his face. As we stare at each other, something sparks inside him—the flicker of a connection he'd imagined lost forever.

"Please," I say. "Do it for me."

His eyes turn upward, toward the unfinished ceiling. "For you," he repeats. "Devorah." His voice breaks on my name, as his gaze returns to meet mine. "I will do it for you."

---

² Literally, the small one.

CHAPTER 1

When I was a little girl, my grandfather would visit us on Friday nights. After dinner, my father and older sister, Beth, would disappear to their rooms, but Mom would hover in the kitchen, washing dishes, listening.

By the light of the candles my mother had lit, Zaide³ taught me Jewish wisdom. The Hebrew alphabet. Simple prayers. Hebrew words: *Shabbat* for Sabbath. *Shalom* for peace. *Siddur* for prayerbook. *Hashem* for G-d. He would never even spell out the full English word, so as not to risk taking His name in vain.

Stroking his white beard, Zaide told me about the town he had escaped before the Nazis came, where his grandfather was a great rabbi. His magical tales included holy people who spoke directly to their Creator, asking for wisdom, protection from plagues, or favor in the eyes of the government. In these stories, there was always a happy ending. G-d and His people always prevailed.

The silent end to his stories was never spoken—how in the great fire of the Holocaust, Zaide's entire world of Jewish Europe was swept away.

∞

The morning he died, my mother stroked my forehead with the tips of her fingers, waking me. "Rachel," she said, in her gentlest voice. I saw the expression on her face and knew he was gone.

Zaide was 87 years old, exactly 70 years older than me. He went peacefully, in his sleep. I guess I imagined he would always be there, walking more than a mile to our house on Saturday afternoons in his black hat and buttoned white shirt. He often frowned to find us using the dishwasher or the television, but still sat in the corner armchair as Mom brought him a cup of juice and a plate of cookies. He made loud, clear blessings in Hebrew over the food, not so much for himself, it seemed, but in the hope I might imbibe

---

³ "Grandfather" in Yiddish.

some Jewish tradition through osmosis.

Next to him in my shorts and T-shirt, I felt at least a world away. Still, his presence mattered to me. I loved the stories, the questions, the ancient Jewish traditions he shared. I was a Jew, if not a particularly good one. This man was my single link to a chain that connected me back to Abraham.

At Zaide's funeral, Mom, Beth, and I sat in the front row of the women's section of his Orthodox synagogue. Though it was August in Baltimore, we wore long skirts and long sleeves. Mom had given up her own Orthodox religious observance years ago, but to be respectful, we dressed like we fit among them. Over with the men, my father—in real life an irreligious psychology professor—wore a black velvet kipah[4] at Mom's request.

Mom's black dress was plain, and she wore a thin dark sweater over it. One of our aunts had ripped the sweater for her, in keeping with the tradition of tearing one's clothes when a close relative dies. Mom had tied her auburn hair under a black beret. Without her usual makeup, I could see dark cavities below her eyes, and shadows of frown lines along her cheeks.

After the funeral, we gathered for *shiva*[5] at my Uncle Zev's house, about five miles from ours on the other side of Pikesville, the Jewish community of Baltimore. I knew the house because we had sometimes joined them for Passover seder. The living room was large, but so crowded with family members, friends, and community members that people had to stand. Mom even had a few of her own visitors, from the dentist's office where she worked as an office manager.

Mom was the youngest of her family, so our cousins were older than Beth and me. They had come from Cleveland and Atlanta, Chicago and Los Angeles. Several of them gathered on the deck outside with babies and small children. You could hear them laughing from time to time.

"Excuse me," said one of my cousins, a tall young man wearing a black hat, with white strings poking out beneath his white shirt. The strings were *tzitzit*, as Zaide had explained to me; all Orthodox Jewish men wore them according to biblical command. I glanced up, encouraged he had noticed me—then realized I was blocking his way into the living room. He didn't

---

[4] Kipah: traditional Jewish head covering.

[5] Shiva: a period of ritual mourning observed after a close family member dies.

look at me as he passed.

I shouldn't have been surprised. Our cousins didn't want much to do with us since Mom had given up her traditional observance. Only Zaide continued to include us in his life. Mom even kept our home kosher so he could eat in our house. She used her mother's beautiful kosher dishes, which Zaide had given her when she got married.

I escaped down a half-flight of stairs to wander the house, and found myself in a den. The dim room had an unlit fireplace, a shag rug, overstuffed leather sofas, and shelves and shelves of Hebrew books. In the corner was a framed photograph of Uncle Zev's family, from when my cousins were still kids. One of the girls resembled Beth and Mom quite a bit, with hair Dad always said was the color of a burnt sienna crayon, and light blue eyes.

I had inherited my dad's hair, straight, thick, and so dark it was almost black. Dad's eyes were hazel, a color that hadn't made up its mind about what it was. My eyes were green.

Once, when Zaide was teaching me, he paused, looking at my eyes. "Your eyes are the color of light coming through emeralds," he said. "Like my mother's."

I had seen a photograph of her once, black and white of course, with hair like Mom's peeking out from under a dark kerchief. Her eyes were wide and kind. Until then, I had never known their color.

"What happened to her?" I'd dared ask, because he never spoke of her. I envisioned cattle trains, gas chambers, screams fading into silence. But Zaide only shook his head.

"I decided I didn't need to know," he said.

Shivering a bit, I turned from the picture to explore the books. Though I didn't know enough Hebrew to understand their meanings, they reminded me of Zaide's faraway lessons. He had taught me to say the Shema, the prayer that declares G-d's unity in the world. Even now, I sometimes said those few words if I was having trouble falling asleep.

Zaide taught me that individuals have the power to speak to G-d and G-d will listen, even to words in English. Even to the words of a young child. I was maybe seven years old then, and I believed him. In my childish voice, I would ask G-d to protect my family, or to make a friend better when she was sick. When I was scared or lonely, I asked Him for help.

Those Friday night visits had ended a long time ago, and I hadn't said much to G-d in years. Now I wished I could ask Zaide how you reconnect with G-d, when the person who taught you is gone.

It hit me then: I'd never be able to ask Zaide anything again. Overwhelmed with sudden grief, I sank to the ground, beneath the picture of a family that didn't look like me.

"Do you mind a visitor?" asked a hesitant voice.

I lifted my eyes to see Lauren in the doorway, one fingernail pressed to her lips. Her red hair was pulled back from her freckled face with a headband. Though we'd been best friends for ten years, this was one of the first times I'd seen her in a dress; she'd clearly worn it out of respect for my religious family. I appreciated the effort.

"No," I said, standing to welcome her. "Thanks for coming."

We sat together on the leather sofa.

"I'm so sorry about your grandfather, Rach." Lauren's eyes lingered on the picture of my Orthodox family. She gnawed the cuticle of her index finger. "I'm not sure I ever met him. Were you close?"

I shrugged one shoulder. "Kind of. We spent a lot of time together when I was little."

Two weeks ago, Zaide had come to our house. It was a sunny Saturday afternoon; Beth was at dance practice and Dad was at the university. I was only home because I had the day off from my summer job serving ice cream at a swim club.

Mom got him a glass of cold water, then drifted in and out of the living room while I sat on the floor beside the armchair he always chose. He asked me how things were going in school. When I pointed out it was mid-summer, he chuckled.

"That's right," he said, his voice still lilted with a European accent. "You're on a learning break."

I shook my head at him, feeling as usual he belonged to another place and time, where children always studied, and angels might come to visit when you least expected.

"I'm starting my senior year in the fall," I said, gently shaking him back into what I considered the real world.

"Be good," he said, and it was impossible to know whether he meant in the sense of morality, academics, or Jewish practice. Maybe all three. Now I wished I had taken the time to understand more of his world. I wished I'd asked what those final words meant.

Lauren pulled out a book peeking from my purse. "I'm glad to see you're using the poetry journal," she said. She flipped through colorful blank pages, each embellished with the shadow of a butterfly. I had been keeping notebooks for poetry since second grade; I already had stashed perhaps a dozen in my desk drawers. Lauren had given me this one for my birthday last May, but I hadn't begun using it yet.

"It's perfect now," I said. "Once I start putting words into it, it will never be the same."

I didn't really expect Lauren to understand this. She had spent the summer taking pre-law classes at Hopkins, trying to increase her chances of getting into Yale. To her, writing was a straightforward thing. But she set the book gently on the sofa, nodding in agreement. "Life is messy," she said.

After Lauren left, dozens of men gathered in my uncle's living room for prayers. Dad wasn't with them; I suspected he was using the opportunity to check email on his phone. Mom, Beth, and I stood with the women in the kitchen, which was hot from the oven and the bright August sun streaming through undressed windows.

"I'm going to have to duck out for practice," Beth whispered to me.

All summer long, Beth had been one of the dancers in *The Phantom of the Opera* being performed in downtown Baltimore—her first professional dancing job. Soon she would go back to college in California, to start her sophomore year in a competitive ballet program.

Beth had wanted to be a dancer since she was eight years old, but this summer had transformed her. The constant exercise and care with her diet had made her lean and muscular. She even walked like a ballerina now, light on her feet with head held high and straight.

"I'm sure Mom will understand," I said.

Beth put her arm around my shoulders. "You had a real connection with Zaide."

I looked toward the men praying in the living room. "Nothing like how *they* knew him."

"I don't know," Beth said. "You meant a lot to him. Remember all those Friday nights he'd stay and talk to you? He never did that for me."

"Only because you disappeared into your room so fast," I said.

She shook her head. "He never even offered to teach me. I mean, you're right, I wouldn't have been all that interested. But...he wanted to teach you.

And you wanted to learn." She smiled. "It was a really special thing."

"I don't think he ever saw me for who I really am," I said. "Only who he wished I would be."

"...Or who he hoped you might become," she corrected. "There's no harm in that."

⚭

Mom's friend Kay came to *shiva* on Thursday, bringing along my friend Maya, who had just returned from her summer with her father on Cape Cod. Kay and Mom had become friends years before in a JCC aerobics class, when Maya's parents were newly divorced. They started getting us together for playdates when we were ten. We'd been friends ever since.

Kay was a petite Asian woman. I'd heard from Mom she converted to Judaism to marry Maya's father. You could catch glimpses of her mother's heritage in the almond shape of Maya's chestnut eyes, her tanned complexion, and her luscious mahogany brown hair.

As Kay sat beside Mom, Maya and I retreated to the den. "I'm sorry I missed the funeral," she said, stretching on the shag rug. She wore hot pink lipstick to match her painted fingernails, and looked sun-kissed and healthy in her stylish new mini-dress. She always got new clothes when she was with her dad.

I shrugged. "I'm glad you came today. It's been kind of unbearable around here."

Maya raised her eyebrows. "No doubt." She frowned, plucking at my long dark skirt. It was one of four I owned, and I'd already worn it twice this week. "Do they really wear this kind of thing all the time?"

"Guess so," I said. "How was the Cape?"

She grinned. "I met a guy."

I laughed. "Why am I not surprised?"

Maya had dated perhaps a dozen boys since we started high school. Last year she joined the cheerleading squad and had dated every football player who asked her out. I'd once heard her say you have to try a lot of hay before you find your needle.

"He was so tall," she said. "And he knew just how to –" she broke off, blushing, looking up at the Hebrew books. "Well, I liked him."

"Will you see him again?" I asked.

She shook her head wistfully. "We agreed it was just a summer thing.

6

What about you, Rach?" she asked, leaning forward with her hands under her chin. "Did you go on any dates this summer?"

I shook my head, and she sighed. I had only been on a handful of dates in high school, two of which Maya had arranged. Sometimes I thought she considered my lack of a boyfriend a personal failure.

"You know what you need?" she said, stretching backward again. "A party. There's one at the Franks' tomorrow. Can you get out of here?"

I exhaled. "Yes, finally. We're done tomorrow night, when Shabbat starts."

"Perfect," she said. "I'll fix your hair and find something for you to wear." Her eyes twinkled. "I bet Chris will be there." The sound of his name had the usual effect: my heart gave a little leap, then I gritted my teeth.

I had no right to feel excited about Chris. We had been friends since his family moved in a few houses from mine when he was five years old. Of course, Maya knew I'd had a crush on him once. But she also knew he'd joined the football team in our sophomore year and dated half the cheerleaders since then. As for me, I'd given up any expectation we'd ever be more than friends. Her suggestion he would be at the party was both a tease and a longing hope she knew I couldn't afford.

I tried to keep my face even as Maya stared at me, willing me to admit I still wanted him. "That's nice," I said calmly. "It will be good to see him."

She kept her eyes on my face, grinning. "Yeah, I'm sure it will be."

CHAPTER 2

The party was a couple blocks from my house, in the backyard of one of Maya's cheerleading friends. Security lights streaked the yard like spotlights in the dark. Loud music played from a Bluetooth speaker set up with someone's iPhone. Citronella candles had made the air thick and faintly citrus.

Maya wore a strappy sleeveless shirt with short shorts, and deep purple lipstick matching her fingernails. "Have a drink," she said, handing me a Coke. I didn't drink caffeine, but I held the can like a lifeline.

As usual, I felt out of place in Maya's crowd. The girls had perfectly applied make-up and clothing like Maya's; even their toenails were manicured in their rhinestone flip-flops. Every now and then the cheerleaders would synchronize into an improvised routine, their long legs pointing, crossing, and turning at the same moment. Then they would break into babbles and giggles as they fell out of line.

The guys were tall and athletic, wearing graphic T-shirts with nice jeans. They gathered in packs, eating pepperoni pizza, glancing at the girls from under their baseball caps.

They were so different from my grieving Orthodox Jewish family, but they also wore uniforms and had their own language and codes. And in the same way as I had at my uncle's house, here too I felt like an outsider.

What would my cousins think of me, if they knew where I was tonight? I wondered. Then I shrugged the thought away. My coming to a party like this was probably already factored into their contempt.

Maya had done her best to dress me up tonight. I usually kept my hair back in a ponytail, but she had used some magical gel to keep it from frizzing, and brushed it out long so it hung halfway down my back. After tsking a bit at my closet, she chose a sleeveless blouse with khaki shorts. Then she applied her own makeup on my face: moisturizer, foundation, concealer, blush, mascara, eyeliner, and lip gloss.

When she was finally satisfied, she turned me around to face the mirror and admire her efforts. I had to admit I looked nice, but I would never spend that long getting ready for anything on my own.

Chris sailed past in the dark yard, surrounded by a small cloud of admiring girls. He had spent the last three weeks coaching at a kids' sports camp in Pennsylvania. Last night, he had texted me to say he was finally home.

I watched Chris stop in front of a blond cheerleader. She laughed, pleased by his attention. They joined hands, and he led her to the center of the yard, where some kids were already dancing. Chris looked so confident, touching her hands and releasing them. Their bodies brushed against each other, moving to the beat of the music. Her face was upturned, eyes closed, like she hoped he would kiss her. I wondered how long he had known her.

I had been watching the girl for several moments before I realized Chris was looking at me. He winked, grinning, before returning his eyes to her.

The moment reminded me of times in his backyard in second grade. He would swing and climb across the jungle gym as if I wasn't even there. And then, unexpectedly, he would look down at me. It was clear then it had all been a show: irrelevant without the audience.

Maya returned to find me still standing near the yard fence, holding my unopened Coke. "Come dance, Rach."

I shook my head. "You go on."

She looked uncertain, but I waved her away. Then I felt ashamed. All her efforts had been wasted. I didn't know what I needed tonight, but it wasn't this. I watched the cluster of teens dancing in the dark, wishing I could just go home. I set my Coke down on a lawn chair and pulled out my phone to check the time.

A hand rested on my shoulder; it was Chris, behind me. "Hey, Rach," he whispered into my ear, sending tingles down my neck. "Having a good time?"

I shoved my phone into my back pocket. "Sure," I lied, turning to face him. I reminded myself we were friends. Good friends. "Welcome back."

"I was sorry to hear about your grandfather."

"Thanks," I said.

His eyes explored my face. "Would you like to dance?"

I squinted at him. "Seriously?"

"Well, if you aren't sure," he said, taking both my hands and pulling me playfully toward the group. Several girls eyed me incredulously. Maya watched from a distance, eyes wide.

The music had changed; the new song had a slower beat. Chris spun me in a circle, then pulled me in close, his chin resting on my hair. I felt grateful for the few dance moves Maya had taught me the summer before.

"Having more fun now?" His arms felt warm on my back.

"Yeah." We passed the blond cheerleader, who glared at me. "I think your last girl is jealous."

He laughed. "At least you can enjoy that part."

Don't hope, I reminded myself. *Don't want it.* I knew Chris wasn't interested in me like this. He was just being nice. To comfort me, because of Zaide.

"Are *you* having fun?" I managed to ask.

He grinned. "Sure." He took both my hands, prepared to push me away.

Just then I heard it, a high-pitched whisper not far from my left ear; almost like a voice, but there was no one near me on that side. There was also a burst of light, like a shooting star, on my right. The dark yard whirled around me. I wobbled, losing my balance.

"Hey." Chris gripped my shoulder to steady me, then touched my cheek with his fingers. "Do you need some water?"

The dizziness evaporated quickly, but my cheeks burned. "No," I said. "I'm OK."

The music changed to something faster and louder. The other kids jostled us as they danced.

"I should head home," I said.

"Do you want me to walk you?" he asked.

I shook my head. "Can you tell Maya I had to go?"

He nodded, his concerned eyes following me out.

I closed the gate behind me before I looked back. Candles blinked like tiny stars, and one of the security lights shone on Maya dancing with a football player. Chris had picked up with another girl, a brunette with curly hair pulled into a perky ponytail, which bobbed as she danced. I felt humiliated and weary as I turned away.

He doesn't belong to you, I thought. *He never did.*

Because of the burst of light, I wondered if a migraine was coming on. I'd struggled with them since puberty. Two years earlier, I'd had a terrible string of them. I'd finally reduced them by cutting caffeine out of my diet. They still came occasionally, but I hadn't had one all summer.

I opened my purse, considering the little tablet I always kept with me just in case. Though a migraine was far worse, I didn't like how I often felt sick to my stomach after I took it.

This didn't feel like a migraine. There was no pulsing dart of pain above my right eyebrow, and the flashing lights had disappeared rather than gotten stronger. I felt better now, away from the loud music.

I took three deep breaths of the warm night air and closed my purse. I kicked a rock the rest of the way home.

When I reached our driveway, I found Dad getting out of his car. He had taken off the week to be with Mom, but had returned to work at his first opportunity.

Dad was tall, with a long, narrow face, and watchful eyes behind wire-rimmed glasses. A psychology professor at the University of Maryland, for the last several years he had also managed a research clinic that provided therapy for clients in the Baltimore community. He was also writing his first book. The multiple projects meant that, until we'd been moored together in my uncle's house for the week, we had hardly seen him all summer.

He stopped and grinned when he saw me approaching. "You look pretty."

I waved at my face and clothing, as if they required an explanation. "Maya dressed me up. For a party."

He tilted his head to appraise her efforts. "She did a nice job. Did you have fun?"

"I guess." I pulled my hair back from my face, wishing I had a rubber band to tie it back into my usual ponytail. "It was pretty different from the rest of the week."

He chuckled, rolling his eyes up to the sky. "I don't know if those people have ever been to a party in their lives."

"Doesn't seem like it." I released my hair; it cascaded down my back with a thump. He opened his arms and I melted into them, smelling his familiar Irish Spring soap. "How was work?"

"I had hundreds of emails waiting for me," he said. "To be honest, it was a nice dose of reality."

I hesitated a moment. "You've been so busy this summer," I said into his chest. "I've missed you."

He patted my back. "There are people out there who really need help, Rach," he said. "I'm just trying to give them what I've got."

"I know." I was proud of how my father helped people. "How's Mom?"

"She'll be okay," he said. "How about you?"

In considering my answer, I thought about my Orthodox cousins, the dizziness I felt while dancing with Chris, and Zaide, who would never tell me stories again. Then I looked up at Dad, relishing the warmth of his arms around me.

When I was younger, we used to go hiking on the Catoctin Mountain, just the two of us talking for hours on a Saturday afternoon. Then he hurt his knee, his job became more intense, and our hikes ended. We hadn't talked like that in years.

Was I doing all right? Probably. But if I wasn't, where could I even begin?

"I'm fine," I told him.

On Sunday evening, we ordered Chinese food and ate it together in the den, far from my grandparents' kosher dishes. It was our last meal with Beth before she went back to school.

Nine days after losing Zaide, Mom's face still looked like glass that had been shattered and hastily pasted back together. Her eyebrows pulled together into a sad little frown, and she kept pressing her palms together, rubbing one hand over the other, stroking her wrist with a thumb—little twitches that showed the effort it was taking to keep herself together. She picked at the shrimp fried rice that was normally her favorite. Dad sat next to her on the sofa, occasionally brushing her shoulder in support.

Beth sprawled on the loveseat with her long auburn hair spread behind her, eating her chow mein with chopsticks. I sat cross-legged on the floor, barefoot, eating pork lo mein at her feet.

"Are you excited to go back to college?" I asked.

"Yeah." She grinned. "It'll be good to get home."

"Beth," I said, a little hurt, "this is your home!"

"Oh, you know, Rach." She waved her chopsticks in the air. "Back to my regular studio, the shows, my friends."

She had spent all summer in a studio, dancing in a show, and seeing friends. But Beth was lucky. She was the kind of girl who could find home anywhere.

"She'll be back in her *real* home for Thanksgiving," Dad said.

Beth frowned and set her carton aside. "Why are all the times we get together about food?"

"It's only once a year," Mom said.

"It's not once a year!" Beth burst out. "It's Thanksgiving, Chanukah, New Years, Passover. Every time I come home!"

We all stared at her. She picked her carton back up and started picking again at her food with the chopsticks. "I'm just saying. It makes it hard for a dancer to stay the proper weight."

"You've managed it pretty well this summer," Dad said.

I agreed. "You look beautiful, Beth."

She shrugged, lifting a single mushroom from her carton and swallowing it. "It's not easy."

"I can make some low-fat things for Thanksgiving," Mom said.

Beth twisted her lips. "That might help."

"You've been a real professional this summer, Beth," Dad said. "Keeping in shape and in practice. And you even made money dancing!"

She looked up at them, shyly. "But you still think I need the double-major?"

This had long been a sore spot between Beth and my parents. Beth had gotten a scholarship for dance, but my parents only agreed to let her go if she also majored in something else. "Something you can make money with," Dad said. Beth's second major was in business, but it wasn't what she really wanted.

"Yes," Dad said. "Just in case dance doesn't work out as well as you planned." Mom nodded in agreement.

Beth sank a little in the sofa. She set her half-eaten Chinese food on the side table and took a sip of Diet Coke. Then, after a moment's reflection, she turned to me. "Rach, did I hear you were dancing with Chris Marino at the Franks' party on Friday night?"

Startled, I looked up, as my parents watched with bemused expressions. "Where did you hear that?"

She grinned. "When you dance with a hottie like that, it gets around." She turned the soda can around in her hands. "So are you finally dating him now?"

I felt my face flush red. "Of course not. We're just friends."

"Friends," Beth said sarcastically, taking another sip of her soda. "Whatever you say, Mrs. Marino."

From my spot on the carpet, I kicked her playfully in the shins. She held the soda can high to keep it from spilling on us.

"Easy," Beth said, giggling. "This body has a lot of dancing to do." She reached down to tickle me. I scooted away, then attacked her with a pillow.

Beth collected her soda and tossed her carton in the trash. "I'll be waiting for wedding news from California," she teased, as she headed back upstairs to finish packing.

CHAPTER 3

The mourning period for my grandfather had consumed my final carefree week of summer. Monday, Beth returned to California. Maya and I went to the mall to buy new school clothes. Dad's new semester started. On Wednesday, my swim club job ended, with a pool party for all the staff. Lauren and I received our new class schedules. The summer before my senior year came to a rapid close.

Lauren and I were taking a full load of Advanced Placement classes for our senior year, and we were continuing in the school orchestra together. Lauren was also vice president of the student council and captain of the school's Debate Club, which she had described as "essential" for a would-be lawyer. I signed up again for Poetry Club on Monday afternoons.

The morning school started, I found Mom alone in her bedroom, clutching an old siddur between her fingers. On the phone that night, Beth urged me to talk to her about Zaide. I wanted to, but I couldn't. When I thought of him, a world of questions I'd never asked burned inside.

According to Zaide, his grandfather had a miraculous ability to speak to G-d. When he prayed, the angels themselves would sing along with him. Sometimes, he would even receive divine messages. Yet he had not been able to protect most of his family from the Holocaust. Why? How had Zaide recovered from such a terrible tragedy? How could he still believe G-d was listening? Had *he* ever prayed in a way that the angels sang along?

That night, I opened the old children's siddur he had given me, a present on my seventh birthday. It had his scrawled handwriting in the margin.

For Rachel. May she grow into all of her gifts.

What gifts had he seen in me? I sighed, feeling I had disappointed him.

∽

On Friday afternoon at the end of our first week, Lauren and I came into the library, our arms heavy with books. She plopped hers on the table, sat, and rested her head on the pile. "I thought senior year was supposed to be easy," she groaned.

"Maybe that doesn't apply to seniors who take a full set of AP classes," I said, setting my books and bag on the table next to her.

Lauren sighed. Ever since we started high school, she'd single-mindedly followed her plan to become valedictorian, go to Yale, and get into law school. She wanted to use the law to make the world a better place. I felt less sure about my own aspirations. Naturally, my father wanted me to go to the University of Maryland, where he taught. But I had visited George Washington University over the summer and fallen in love with the hectic, purposeful air of Washington, D.C. I thought perhaps among the founding fathers of our country, I could find myself.

As Lauren opened her history book, I wandered toward the literature section. For the first session of Poetry Club next week, we were supposed to bring in a published poem that spoke to us. I wanted to find something that honored my memory of Zaide.

I was considering the table of contents of a poetry anthology when a burst of light pierced the air to my right. My fingers began to tremble. My book tumbled to the carpet.

Whispery and white, the light was like the streak of a camera flash that had not yet faded. I squinted, trying to see the light more clearly. After just a few seconds, it faded away.

My hands were still shaking as I leaned down to return my fallen book to its place. The titles on the shelves seemed incomprehensible. I pressed my fingertips against my forehead, staring at the books until words regained their meaning.

I thought I'd been away a long time, but Lauren looked up in surprise when I returned. She was still on the same section of the history book. "That was quick," she said. "Did you find anything?"

I collapsed into the chair. "No." I rubbed again at my forehead, though it wasn't hurting. "I just...I saw ...I..." I found myself incoherent and started again. "I saw some...flashing lights. Like before a migraine."

Lauren's eyes widened. "You haven't had one in so long. Do you have your medicine?"

I hesitated. "Yeah, but...I don't really think it *was* a migraine. I mean...it doesn't hurt or...anything."

"You don't want to mess with that," she said. "You always told me it was a mistake to wait till it hurt."

This was one hundred percent true. Lauren was the friend who had suffered with me through the worst of my migraines during our sophomore year. More than once she held my hand in the dark as I whimpered. When the migraines finally began to improve, taking the medicine at the first sign of a problem had become my mantra.

This felt different, though. Usually with a migraine, there wouldn't be a lot of pain at the beginning, but there would be something: a dull ache in my forehead or my teeth. Usually the light didn't go away but gradually got worse.

Lauren tapped her fingers anxiously on the table. "Maybe you should take your pill, Rach."

I slipped the pill out of one of the small pockets of my backpack. It looked innocent and helpful, but—migraine or not—I knew it would make me feel miserable.

"Do you want me to get you some water?" she asked.

I shook my head. *Better this than a migraine*, I thought, as the pill dissolved on my tongue.

She rested her hand on mine across the table. "Let me know if it gets worse, okay? We can head home."

"Okay," I said, pulling out my math book. It was a simple review of last year and should have been easy, but my brain felt sluggish. I struggled through it until Lauren finally took pity on me and drove us both home.

I spent all weekend looking for a poem. I searched online for poems about the Holocaust, but they were all so sad. After hours of research, I came across Rahel Bluwstein, one of the founding mothers of modern Hebrew poetry, who died in 1931. One of her poems reminded me of my feelings for Zaide, and I thought he might appreciate its use of my Hebrew name.

In poetry club Monday afternoon, I read:

Sad Song

Do you hear me, you who are
So far away from me, my dear?
Do you hear me crying aloud,
Wishing you were well, wishing you were near?
The world is vast, its ways diverse,
Brief meetings, partings long,
Men, with unsure feet, post on never to return, too weak

To find the treasure they have lost.
My last day drawing near
Of the tears of separation
I will await you until
my life leaves
as Rahel did her beloved.

After my poem, the teacher called on a junior named Jake. I listened with interest; Jake's poems were often the most interesting in our class.

Tall and lanky, Jake usually wore ripped jeans and a plaid flannel shirt. He hid his eyes and sandy hair under a baseball cap, which was forbidden during school hours, but he must have whipped it out after the last bell rang. When not reading poetry, he often stared out the window. Some days, he seemed to zone out, and I had the feeling he was using a bit more weed than was good for him. But when he read poems, his eyes always danced.

Today he read this, by Jack Spicer:

Any fool can get into an ocean
But it takes a Goddess
To get out of one.
What's true of oceans is true, of course,
Of labyrinths and poems. When you start swimming
Through riptide of rhythms and the metaphor's seaweed
You need to be a good swimmer or a born Goddess
To get back out of them
Look at the sea otters bobbing wildly
Out in the middle of the poem
They look so eager and peaceful playing out there where the
water hardly moves
You might get out through all the waves and rocks
Into the middle of the poem to touch them
But when you've tried the blessed water long
Enough to want to start backward
That's when the fun starts
Unless you're a poet or an otter or something supernatural
You'll drown, dear. You'll drown
Any Greek can get you into a labyrinth

THE PROPHETESS

But it takes a hero to get out of one
What's true of labyrinths is true of course
Of love and memory. When you start remembering.

As he finished the poem, he glanced up at the group, then quickly away. Was it my imagination, or had his eyes narrowed on me? I tilted my head, studying him, but he had already retreated beneath his hat.

CHAPTER 4

On the first morning of Rosh Hashanah, my parents and I walked twelve blocks to Zaide's Orthodox synagogue, a taupe-colored, box-shaped building with high ceilings, perched like an unwrapped present on a busy street.

For as long as I could remember, we had attended services here just two days a year: on the first day of Rosh Hashanah and on Yom Kippur. This year I'd overheard Mom and Dad discussing whether we would still come now that Zaide was gone. Mom insisted on continuing the tradition.

The service had already begun as we stepped through the metal front doors. In the women's section, Mom and I found our seats in the first row behind the *mechitzah*, a latticed wood decorative fence that separated the women from the men. When she was a child, Mom had sat in these seats with her devout mother. Dad sat toward the back of the men's section, a few rows in front of us. Zaide used to sit there beside him, but now a stranger sat in his place.

Though he came every year at Mom's request, religion wasn't Dad's thing. Once, while we were hiking, I'd asked Dad if he believed in G-d.

"I believe in people," he said, pausing to drink as we reached a lookout point. Below us, a river splashed over a series of boulders and a partially destroyed beaver dam. I bent down to tighten the laces on my hiking boots.

"People have the choice to be good," Dad continued. "But sometimes they need help. Maybe from therapy. Or maybe religion will help them."

I chewed my lip, not sure he'd given me a proper answer.

"What do you think?" he asked, as we continued up the tree-canopied trail.

Back then I still prayed, as Zaide had taught me. Before bed, I would often say the *Shema* prayer, then add the wishes of my own heart: protection for my family, health for a sick friend, a good grade on an upcoming test.

I always yearned for a sign G-d was listening. It was tricky, though. If I got the good grade, how did I know it wasn't just that I'd studied? If a friend got better, wasn't it just the medicine? I wanted to *connect* with G-d, but I wasn't sure how.

Of course, I couldn't share any of this with my father. "I think I believe in G-d," I said, hurrying to keep his pace. "And I believe in people, too."

"Just don't ever let religion turn you against people," he said. "Your god is in heaven, but the people who love and need you are right here."

Eventually, my nighttime prayers felt childish and trickled off. I hadn't tried to connect with G-d in a long time. But Zaide's death had awakened in me an old, half-forgotten longing.

I glanced over at Mom. In this synagogue the prayers were all in Hebrew, but she always knew how to find where we were in the service, even if the men were just mumbling quietly the way they were now. As I opened my book to the page she indicated, she closed her eyes and began to pray, words memorized so long ago she barely needed the book. Her fingers moved along the Hebrew like Braille.

When we stood for the silent prayer, I peered through the *mechitzah* to watch the men. Their seats were arranged around the *shulchan*, the table where the Torah[6] was read. Some squinted into their siddurs, lips moving as if reading a script. Others stood with eyes closed, rocking like trees swaying in the wind. Dad stood respectfully still, his siddur open but unused in his hands.

Before I could begin my own silent prayer, I noticed him.

The man stood on the left side of the men's section, several rows back from the *shulchan*, so I had a profile view of his face. His eyes were wide, his mouth open, as in a silent scream. His open hands lifted in supplication as he rocked feverishly back and forth.

The other men completed their prayers, sitting or standing patiently, waiting for the service to continue. But this holy man continued his fervent tirade. Though his intensity was alarming, it was almost beautiful. As his expression changed from rage to sorrow, I believed G-d was listening to him.

The main service had already resumed by the time he completed his prayers, stepping backward, bowing to the left and right, stepping forward again. His face seemed more peaceful now, a settling sea. I knew I should be reading from my own siddur, but for a long time I couldn't look away.

The service continued with the Torah reading and another long silent prayer. I prayed in English, trying to keep up with Mom. As often as I dared,

---

[6] Torah: the five books of Moses, written in a scroll and read publicly during synagogue services.

I peeked back through the mechitzah. The man I'd noticed was still immersed in his prayers.

What did he understand in all these words that I could not?

Gradually, I began to feel irritated. Hadn't we said enough? How many times could we hear the piercing blasts of the *shofar*[7]? Maya said the Rosh Hashanah service at her Reform synagogue took only two and a half hours. We had come late but still had been here almost four.

At last the service concluded, with a song led by a little boy from the *shulchan*. Through the mechitzah, I watched the holy man gathering his things. Before I could stop myself, I followed him into the lobby.

His face had creases I hadn't noticed from the distance: three crinkled lines stretching toward his temples from each of his gray eyes, and several frown lines in his forehead. His brown beard had strands of gray woven through it, like threads of silver. He had his own siddur – not one the synagogue provided – which he slipped into a coat pocket. Unlike the others who wore black hats, he wore a loosely knit, handmade blue kipah.

As he opened the metal front door, he took one long glance around, taking in me and all the other congregants in the hall with a wistful smile. I found myself walking toward him, but by the time I reached the exit, he had gone.

⚭

Maya pointed at a model in the fashion magazine spread out on her kitchen table. "You would look awesome in this, Rach."

The model wore a low-cut, sleeveless black satin gown and pointy black high-heels. I laughed. "In your dreams."

"It's perfect for your eyes and hair," Maya said, crossing her ankles on the tile floor. "You just need to lose ten pounds."

From what I could tell, Maya was always on a diet. I knew I wasn't fat, but Mom cooked well and had raised us to enjoy food. Though I gave half-hearted attention to her fashion advice, I tried to ignore Maya's comments about my weight. The one time I'd tried one of her diets, I'd gotten so light-headed I couldn't concentrate in class.

I shrugged. "Maybe I'll just stick with this weight and my jeans."

---

[7] Shofar: Ram's horn, traditionally blown on the Jewish holiday of Rosh Hashanah and at the end of Yom Kippur.

She rolled her eyes at me, closing the magazine and pulling her math workbook from her bag. The math workbook was the reason I was here. She had called the night after Rosh Hashanah to ask for help.

"What you have to understand," I said, "is that sin and arcsin are inverses. They cancel each other out."

I waited while she practiced on a few sample problems. Maya's kitchen was twice the size of ours, with granite counters and stainless steel appliances. Her mom had gotten their big, beautiful house in the divorce. Her cat Angel slunk by, and I reached out to stroke his soft white coat. He yawned and headed for his food bowl in the corner of the kitchen.

A shiver ran through me, as a bolt of light streaked along the periphery of my left eye.

Pure white, like a wisp of bright cloud, shining against the darkness of my closed eyelids. A dart of pain pressed into my left temple, like the point of a knife. My breath hitched in fear.

It was only a few seconds before the light vanished, but all my energy seemed to drain out as it left.

"Hey, can you check this?" Maya asked. I opened my eyes.

She passed me the problem set she had been working on. She had made two mistakes: one a simple calculation error, the second a misunderstanding of the concept. We settled back to work.

As we finished, Maya closed the book and turned to me. "You look a little pale, Rach," she said. "Feeling all right?"

I hesitated just an instant before answering yes.

DEVORAH

On the way home from the doctor, my feet find their way up the stone paths of the Old City. The voices of the prophets babble softly in the background, as always—unaware that everything is about to change.

The doctor's words confirmed everything I wish I didn't already know. I had hoped for more time – for myself, and for the girl whose future is forever bound with mine. But we don't choose when to die.

I was only a child when my family was confined to the ghetto. When they sent me away, my grandmother gave me one of her handmade blankets. "Something to hold onto," she said. It was taken, along with everything, after the train. But it may have saved my life those long cold nights in the forest.

I gather my courage.

"Let death be sweet," I pray. "May I not suffer. And let me know her. Please."

CHAPTER 5

On the morning of the fast of Yom Kippur, my family walked back to Zaide's synagogue. My stomach was already tight with hunger; we hadn't eaten since before sunset the night before. Mom and I wore white canvas sneakers, since leather shoes were not allowed on Yom Kippur. Dad wore his normal black dress shoes.

"G'mar tov, Elisheva," someone said to Mom, using her Hebrew name, as we walked into the synagogue.

The other night on the phone, Beth had reminded me Mom was always tense on Yom Kippur. This year without Zaide would be hard. "Try to take care of her," Beth advised, "if things get emotional."

I watched now as Mom nodded politely to the woman who had greeted her, maintaining her composure. I squeezed her arm as we hung up our jackets.

In the sanctuary, most of the men wore long white robes tied with a white sash belt. Zaide had taught me the robe was called a *kittel*; it was supposed to represent their angelic status on this holiest day of the year. Some of the women were also dressed in white, but Mom didn't worry about this the way she did about the shoes. I was wearing a green blouse with a navy skirt. Mom wore black.

Mom opened her book and began to pray in a fervent whisper. I opened my own book to the same page, then counted the pages until the afternoon break. More than a hundred. I sighed.

I gazed around the sanctuary: the many white-clad Jews lost in their whispered prayers, the mystifying Hebrew on the walls, and the small, high, stained-glass windows refracting colored light that never reached down to the congregants. I felt an aching pang for Zaide. Though I sat beside my own mother, I felt alone.

Without any instruction apparent to me, the congregation stood and began to sing aloud. The special cabinet at the front of the sanctuary, called the *aron kodesh*, was opened to reveal the Torah inside. The prayer leader called out the words of the Shema. My prayerbook provided the translation:

Listen Israel, the L-rd is our G-d, the L-rd Alone.

As the leader carried the Torah around the men's section, my lips moved, almost of their own accord. "G-d," I prayed.

Then I hesitated. We weren't exactly on a first name basis. I felt He was a friend of a friend; my only claim to him had been through Zaide. Now that link seemed broken.

Then the words came to me, and I uttered them without thinking. "Help me grow into my gifts."

Immediately I felt ashamed. It wasn't as if I was one of the faithful here. What right did *I* have to ask anything of *G-d*? As the Torah came to its resting place on the *shulchan*, I sighed again.

Through the latticed wood *mechitzah*, I again noticed the holy man I'd watched on Rosh Hashanah. His face was radiant this morning. He swayed from side to side, his hands open, as if begging G-d for blessings. His anger from Rosh Hashanah seemed to have washed away, replaced by faith and hope.

Fascinated, I continued to observe him. Today he wore a white kipah, knit with large strands of yarn. He wore glasses with a thin wire rim, which he took off periodically to rub at his eyes. His beard was brown and loosely trimmed, floating like a cloud around the bottom of his face.

My stomach tightened when the now-familiar light flashed across the side of my face. This time it was easy to know what to pray for. *G-d*, I begged, eyes squeezed shut. *Please, please, make it stop.*

Over the last month, these incidents had each lasted less than a minute. The light always disappeared quickly, leaving little in its wake.

This time, it didn't. The trembling overwhelmed me and I sank into my seat.

The city is silent except for the whisper of my footsteps in the darkness. A pale moon rises in the darkening sky; the moment of sunset has already passed.

"Come." I feel more than hear the word, a drumbeat against my heart. A cold breeze rushes by, and I wrap my shawl more tightly around me. My fingers grip the stone barrier in front of me. How creased and ancient they are: the hands of an old woman.

"Please," I beg.

A rush of wind is the only response. I gather my courage.

"Then let me know her," I whisper, as the sky falls dark.

I fell as if from a thousand feet to the sanctuary, awakening with a start.

In the men's section, they were still reading from the Torah. Beside me,

Mom's eyes were fixed on her book. I rubbed my fingers along my right temple, where a tiny echo of the light still radiated, like the dot of a laser.

The images from the dream were slippery, eluding me. *Darkness. The moon. Someone's voice, lost in the wind.* I sat trying to remember until I heard the rustling and singing that told me it was time to stand. They had finished the Torah reading. Still trembling a little, I got to my feet.

I glanced toward Mom. Had she noticed what had happened to me? Her eyes were focused intently through the *mechitzah*. Following her eyes, I saw the Torah held aloft by the same holy man I had been watching. As he turned, the scroll safe in his strong arms, I caught the intense joy in his eyes... and felt my own deep longing twist inside like a blade.

Yom Kippur is a twenty-five hour fast without food or water. For some people, like Dad and Beth, it wasn't very difficult. For me, it was always a struggle. As the service continued, I slouched in my seat, drained of energy. I stood for the second silent prayer, whispering it in English as best I could, one hand on the *mechitzah* for support.

The morning service ended around two-thirty. Tired, hungry and thirsty, I dragged myself home behind my parents. In our living room, I collapsed into the armchair Zaide often chose. A few hours must have passed when Mom placed her hand on my forehead, waking me.

I opened my eyes, still foggy with sleep. Her wide eyes held mine.

"Rachel," she said in a hoarse voice. "It's time."

Time to go back to synagogue. Or did she mean something else?

"Are you ready?" she asked.

I was not ready. I felt too weary for the long walk back to synagogue, and fully unprepared for whatever future awaited me.

But I clambered out of my Zaide's chair. In the hall mirror, I redid my ponytail and straightened my long navy skirt. I put the canvas-not-leather shoes back on. I followed my mother and father back to the synagogue.

We found the women's section sparse, though the front section was full of men. They had each spread ritual prayer shawls spread over their shoulders like angel wings.

Sweaty from the walk, starved both physically and spiritually, I gazed through the *mechitzah* like an animal through the wires of a cage.

The holy man was back in his seat. His face seemed to glow more, rather than less, as the day went on. It seemed to me he had traveled a long journey since Rosh Hashanah, from despair and anger to faith and confidence. Watching him gave me strength.

The sky behind the stained glass windows turned dusky, then dark. Our section gradually filled again with women. The prayers became more fervent, more tearful, as the congregation begged for G-d's forgiveness. I tried my best to sing along, still wishing for a sense of connection. At last, we listened to the long, solid blast of the shofar.

I felt desperate for some assurance my efforts had meant something. But mostly, I just felt relieved the service was over.

Mom tousled my hair as she collected my siddur. "You'll feel better when you get some orange juice," she said.

Dad met us on the stairs to the synagogue's chilly basement, where a break-fast meal of tuna fish, egg salad, crackers, and juice awaited. Dad squeezed Mom's hand, then rested his other hand on my shoulder; small acts of defiance in a place where men and women never touched. Mom pulled her hand away at the bottom of the steps.

The crowd waited as the rabbi recited a few Hebrew prayers. A young man raised the burning *havdallah*[8] candle. Mom waved her hands toward the flame before it was extinguished.

As if freed by an invisible rope, the men and women scattered to their separate tables. My family hesitated just an instant longer before splitting up.

At one of the women's tables, I poured orange juice into a small cup, drank it, and refilled it again. I could feel the juice carrying sugar and water through my veins. I found crackers at another table. As I stood in place, eating them, I spotted the holy man on the men's side, talking to the rabbi. The rabbi smiled and nodded, putting his hand on the man's shoulder.

I would have liked to talk to him, but what could I say? It didn't matter. He was over with the men. There may as well have been an invisible wall between us. Taking another sip of juice, I took a few steps backward and found myself pressed into a corner against the wood-paneled wall.

As I stood there – as if he had felt my gaze – he turned toward me, his

---

[8] Havdallah: a short service at the end of a Jewish holiday or Sabbath. A twisted candle is used during the service.

eyes shining silver. My heart gave an anxious leap.

Had he noticed me staring at him today? If not, why would he be looking at me?

I watched him take a cautious step forward, then another – like I was a frightened animal – until he was close enough to speak to me. His hands were folded behind his back. He cleared his throat.

"My name is Yonatan," he said. Though his voice was gentle, his eyes seemed serious.

"I'm sorry," I said quickly, "for watching you so much today."

He tilted his head. "Were you?"

I crushed my empty plastic cup in my hand. "Yeah."

"Why?"

I bit my lip. "I noticed you praying," I said. "You have quite a way of talking to G-d."

He studied my face. "Does that make you sad?"

I frowned, annoyed my emotions were so obvious to him. "Yes," I admitted. "Why?"

I couldn't stop myself from answering. "Because it looked like G-d would really listen to you," I blurted out.

His face was compassionate, but I looked away, wondering where my parents were. I spotted Dad eating crackers and tuna on the other side of the room. I didn't see Mom.

He ran his fingers through his beard. "The Holy One listens to your prayers, too," Yonatan said. "Every time."

I prayed so infrequently that it hardly seemed to matter. But I found myself thinking of my prayer from earlier that morning. *Help me grow into my gifts.* Was G-d listening then? Would He answer me?

Yonatan met my eyes, and I felt I could see into his shining silver eyes forever, through pain and anger to gentleness and love. How could he show me his truth so clearly? I wished I could learn everything he knew, enough that we could one day be equals, or friends.

"You remind me of my grandfather," I said. I watched as his lips formed a faint smile of satisfaction. "He died last month," I added.

Now his eyes softened. "I'm sorry for your loss," he said.

I waved away his condolences. "I'm not Orthodox," I said. "It's just – I guess – my grandfather used to talk about...being connected to G-d. You seem to be...good at that."

"If you'd like," he said, "we could learn together."

My eyes widened. *Learn together?* My father's voice rang in my head, cautioning me against brainwashing. But a part of me wanted to hear what this man could teach. Maybe it would be like learning with Zaide.

"I think," I said slowly, "I might like that."

"We could meet after services, on Shabbat morning," he said.

Come back here again on Saturday morning? I hadn't planned to be back for a year. But I told myself I could meet him one time. If I didn't like it, I'd never have to come back. "Okay," I said in a small voice.

His smile was like the sun bursting over the horizon at sunrise, filled with gratitude and faith. "Wonderful," he said. "I will see you then." He gave a strange little bow as he backed away.

My face felt radiant just from being in his presence. The weary exhaustion of the day had cleared. I stood there, flabbergasted, until Mom came to find me.

"Rachel," she said. "I've been looking everywhere for you."

"I've been here all along," I said.

She stilled, scrutinizing my face. "I guess you have." Unexpectedly, she hugged me; it was a hug that seemed to mean something. Was it an acceptance of the strange choice I'd made, to come back and learn with Yonatan? I hoped so.

"Let's find your father," she said. "I have chicken soup waiting for us."

I roused myself as if from a dream, to follow her home.

CHAPTER 6

I found Maya at her locker the next afternoon before cheerleading practice. "Got a sec?"

"Sure." She led me to the bathroom, where I watched her knit her dark hair into a braided bun.

"Um," I said awkwardly, "this Saturday morning, maybe ten a.m.? What are you up to?"

"Sleeping, probably," she said. She rooted around in her purse and opened a tube of fig-colored lipstick. "How about you?"

"I – I –" I pressed my hands together to take hold of myself. "I'm going to meet a guy."

"A *guy*?" She'd misunderstood me, but I knew it could only help my case. She capped the lipstick and stared at me.

"Yeah." I'd never done this before, and I felt ridiculous. "Can you cover for me? I mean, can I tell my parents I'll be with you?"

Maya raised her eyebrows, intrigued. "And where *will* you be, Rach?"

I looked down at the floor. "At Shomrei Emunah," I mumbled. "You know, the Orthodox synagogue."

Her eyebrows wrinkled into a frown. "Why there?"

This had to be done carefully, to strike the tone just right. "I started a conversation with a guy there on Yom Kippur," I said. "And I want to finish it."

Now her mouth formed a slow grin. "You started a conversation with a guy at an Orthodox synagogue on Yom Kippur? Wow."

I blushed. "It's nothing, really," I said, though I knew she wouldn't believe me. "I just need to talk to him." I let the urgency I truly felt color my tone.

Maya was getting excited. In her mind, I imagined, an Orthodox guy who would speak to me at synagogue on Yom Kippur might finally be the solution to my mysterious boy problem. Think Romeo and Juliet; she was already anticipating a star-crossed love affair.

"Of course you can tell your parents you're with me," she said. "But you have to tell me *everything*!"

"Okay," I said, though I wasn't sure I was telling her the truth.

After dinner that evening, I sat cross-legged in my bed, reading chapter two of my history textbook. We had a paper due on Monday, and if I didn't get a good start on it tonight, I'd be working on it all weekend.

I re-read the same paragraph over again, then turned to the meager outline I'd started.

I was distracted. Next to me on the bed was my poetry notebook, where I'd started a safety list for my conversation with Yonatan at the synagogue. The list had four items:

1) Don't let him get you alone.
2) Don't let him follow you home.
3) Don't go anywhere with him.
4) Find out if he's for real.

Most important, I needed to be sure he wasn't some kind of hallucination. Last summer Mom and I had watched *A Beautiful Mind*, a movie where the guy hallucinated a whole set of imaginary friends. It didn't seem likely, but how could I know, really?

Aside from questioning my own sanity, I didn't know how to judge the merits of what he might teach me. Except what I'd learned from Zaide, I felt so ignorant about Jewish tradition.

I traced my fingers across the paper, trying to reassure myself. I knew the first three items on the list basically conveyed the same essential message: Don't give him the opportunity to hurt me.

I didn't think he would hurt me physically, at least not if we stayed in the synagogue. But I knew there were other ways a person could get hurt.

I turned back to my history textbook. The paper had to be ten pages. I had a long way to go.

Saturday morning was gray and drizzly, but the air was warm. I dressed in one of the same long skirts I'd worn during the *shiva* period for my grandfather.

"Shabbat shalom," a woman said, walking by from the other direction. I looked up in hazy surprise. Without my mother, without our family baggage, I was just a stranger on the street, dressed like an Orthodox Jew. I wondered if I should respond, but the woman had already passed.

I opened the metal door to the synagogue building. From the lobby, I could hear the leader chanting in Hebrew. I hung my raincoat and took a siddur from the nearly empty shelf on the wall.

G-d, I thought to myself, but I hesitated. What to pray for? *Don't let him hurt me. Help me know if this is the right thing for me.*

I wondered if I should ask G-d *for* this to be the right thing for me, but I couldn't decide if I wanted that or not.

The service was near its ending as I entered, and the women's section was filled with women of all ages, all dressed in dark or muted long dresses and skirts. In keeping with tradition, the married women covered their hair, either with hats or wigs.

There was no space by the *mechitzah*, so I found a seat near the back. I couldn't see if Yonatan was here. What if he wasn't, and I'd walked all this way for nothing?

The service progressed to its conclusion, again with a little boy singing at the front of the room. *Who taught this little boy to do that?* I wondered. *Was a little girl ever angry she didn't get the chance?*

The women filed out of the room, heading toward the Kiddush downstairs. I sat paralyzed, too afraid to move. What would he teach me? Did I even want to learn? What if he wasn't even here? Was this all a crazy mistake?

Then I saw him lingering in the hallway by the entrance to the women's section. As the last woman left the room, he came into the doorway and stood there, gazing at me with his luminous eyes.

He was younger than my father, and taller than I'd remembered. He wore a white button-down shirt that showed an outline of muscles in his arms and chest. Under his colorful, loosely knit kipah, his hair was curly and dark. His face was friendly, with black wire glasses over his chipmunk-like cheeks, and a prominent nose. The few narrow wrinkles etched into his temples deepened when he smiled.

I stood, feeling young and shy in my ponytail and my *shiva* skirt.

As he had on Yom Kippur, he walked toward me carefully, as if I was a deer he didn't want to frighten away. Finally, he stopped in the row in front of me, lowered himself into a chair two seats away, and turned to face me.

"I'm glad you came," he said.

I took a big, deep breath before I sat back down in my own seat.

He folded his fingers together on the chairs between us. "After we talked,

I realized you never told me your name."

"It's Rachel." My words came out in a whisper.

He smiled. "Shabbat shalom, Rachel."

I hesitated, not sure how to answer him. "Shabbat shalom," I said finally.

"I've been thinking about what you said on Yom Kippur," he said. "About wanting to connect to G-d. You should know, you are already and always connected to the Holy One." He held my gaze. "You don't have to do anything to earn it. The connection is already there, through your soul."

My gaze drifted away, toward the *aron kodesh* at the front of the synagogue. "If I have one," I said.

He chuckled. "Not that you have one. You *are* one. A spiritual being, dressed in a physical body. Like all human beings."

His words, and the weight in his voice when he said them, reminded me so much of Zaide I turned back to face him. It was easy to think of *him* as a spiritual being. His eyes felt warm like flames on my face.

"The soul is a part of the Holy One," he said, "rooted in G-d, always receiving the gift of G-d's holy Light." As he spoke, I could almost feel it: a holy warmth filling my body. "This Light is the source of all the blessings of your life."

There was something trance-like about listening to Yonatan. As he spoke, the sanctuary seemed to fade into the background. I could only focus on his shining eyes.

"The Holy One wants to give you tremendous blessing," he said. "Though we struggle to understand, Hashem is always guiding the world to its destination. In the end, we will find that everything we experience is part of a larger story. All for a purpose; all ultimately for good."

His words danced like crystals in sunlight. Just for this one moment, I believed.

"Before you were born, your soul saw the world as it could be—all of its possible perfection. Then, your soul saw the world as it is. An angel asked you: 'What will you do in your life to help bring the world closer to perfection?' What you answered is your life's purpose."

Zaide's face swam in front of my eyes: his long white beard, his black hat, his earnest brown eyes. *May she grow into all of her gifts.*

I leaned toward Yonatan. "What's my purpose?"

He turned one hand upward, entreating, toward me. "I think that will be revealed to you," he said, "in the right time."

Gradually, I became aware of the sanctuary again. The rain had cleared, and light was streaming in through the windows near the ceiling. Who was he? How did he know all this? Could I really trust him?

His lesson complete, Yonatan took a handkerchief from his pocket, withdrew his glasses, and wiped his face. His eyes had a kind of shattered look to them, like broken windows revealing his heart.

"Remember, Rachel, we are all a part of G-d," he said. "Ultimately, there is nothing but the unity of G-d."

I looked around the room: the few men in the front section still praying, the high walls of the building and the stained glass windows at the top. The mechitzah, the chairs, the *aron kodesh*. The strands of silver in his beard, beneath his bright eyes.

"Nothing but G-d?"

The shattered look in his eyes passed like a cloud, and now his face was full of peace. "Nothing," he said.

CHAPTER 7

The next morning before lunch, I sat cross-legged on the squashy porch sofa writing in my poetry journal. I wanted to capture some of the beautiful wisdom Yonatan had shared the day before, but I was finding this difficult. I'd already scratched out half the words I'd written on the pretty notebook page.

Chris's bike whizzed up the street, past his own house, then soared back downhill toward his driveway, like we did as kids.

Once, when we were eleven, Chris took a curve too fast and slammed on the wrong hand brake. Still on my bike behind him, I watched his body fly over the handlebars and crash with a thud onto the street. When I reached him, he was a bloody mess. He couldn't put weight on his left leg. But he never cried out. Chris was brave even then.

We were a few miles from home, in an unfamiliar neighborhood. I banged on the doors of a half dozen houses until I found someone to call his mom. We went straight to the emergency room, where they pronounced his ankle broken. We didn't ride bikes the rest of that summer.

Now, six years later, he walked down the street toward my house, hands stuffed in his pockets. I closed my poetry journal and opened a math book instead.

"Hey Chris," I said, as he came up the porch steps.

He grinned down at my book. "Responsible Rachel," he said.

I rolled my eyes at him. "Can I help you?"

He chuckled. "I was just wondering...are you coming to the game this Friday?"

"I think so." Lauren and I often went together to the football games. She felt obligated as a school officer, and I liked to watch Maya cheer and Chris play.

He shifted his weight from one foot to the other. "There's someone coming from a school in Florida," he said. "To see me."

"Hey, that's great." I grinned up at him. "Good for you."

A little flush spread up his neck to his face. "So...it would mean a lot to me...if you were there."

"Okay," I said, processing his invitation. "Sure, yeah, I'll come."

He returned my grin. "Great," he said. "See you then."

Silly Chris, I thought. *It's me who will be seeing* you. It was never the other way around.

He reached out and tucked a loose strand of hair behind my ear. "Study hard," he said, glancing down at my Calculus book.

When we were kids, he would challenge himself by trying to jump down our porch stairs in as few steps as possible; but today he just took them one at a time. At the bottom of the steps, he broke into an easy jog back to his house.

I watched him all the way. He never looked back.

∽

Maya was ready for me when I arrived that Wednesday evening. She crossed her living room in three paces, examining my face for signs of love.

"How was it? Who is he? Are you going to see him again?"

I stepped back, unprepared for the barrage of questions.

"*Well?*" Maya demanded.

I wanted to answer her honestly, but her misunderstanding of the situation was key to her willingness to cover for me. "He's – nice," I said.

She frowned. "Do you mean ugly?" she said in a disappointed tone.

"No," I said. She settled into a kitchen chair and motioned for me to do the same. "He's different," I said as I sat. "From anyone I've ever met."

"Do you *like* him?"

I knew I didn't like him the way Maya meant. But I remembered the holy wisdom he had tried to teach me, about being a soul with a purpose; how listening to him felt like being in a trance I didn't want to end. The truth was, I couldn't wait to see him again.

"Yes," I said.

Maya popped a slice of cucumber into her mouth and chewed thoughtfully. "It's interesting," she said. "Because of your grandfather, I mean. Does he know you aren't Orthodox?"

I nodded.

"And he's okay with that?"

I nodded again.

She whistled low. "Wow," she said. "When will you see him again?"

"Saturday morning," I said. "If I can say I'm with you."

Her puzzled look turned into a smile. "Yeah. You should do this, Rach. Go see him again."

On Friday, Lauren and I climbed the stands near the forty-yard line. After years of effort, this season Chris was the star player of our undefeated football team. As the oldest of five kids, he was hoping football could help him get a scholarship to college.

I scanned the crowd, wondering who was scouting him. The old man in the baseball cap with an unfamiliar "F" logo? The middle-aged woman with the clipboard?

Maya was on the field too, warming up with the other cheerleaders. From my place in the stands, I caught her eye and waved.

In front of us, two sophomore girls were chattering about Chris. He was so cute. So muscular. So athletic. "What would it be like to kiss him?" the first girl wondered aloud.

"Become a cheerleader if you want to know," the second girl said. "He's already dated half the girls on the squad."

Lauren rested her hand on my arm in friendly consolation. Sometimes I envied her single-minded focus on school and her future career. She never worried about boys.

All week I had wanted to tell her about Yonatan, but I didn't think it would go well if I tried. Lauren and I had rarely spoken about faith. Her mother was born Jewish and her father was once Protestant, but now they were both sworn atheists.

I'd first asked her if she believed in G-d when we were about ten. She'd shrugged as if the question could not be less relevant to her life. "I don't know. I guess not."

"Why not?" I asked.

"Well...if G-d was real, why would so many terrible things happen in the world? And why wouldn't He punish bad people or stop them from doing what they do?"

Zaide would answer these kinds of questions by saying G-d has a plan far beyond human understanding, and that life isn't supposed to be easy so much as meaningful—that when bad things happened, they were opportunities to show kindness, or to grow. But I knew this wouldn't make sense to someone as logical as Lauren.

"I think my father is right," she said. "It's all a fairytale." I must have looked heartbroken, because her eyes softened. "I don't mean you can't believe, Rach..."

"It doesn't matter," I said.

We stood to cheer for Chris, who had plucked the pass from the air and was racing down the field to score his second touchdown of the game. In the end zone, he made the sign of a cross.

Ironically, in such a Jewish neighborhood, Chris was one of the most religious people I knew. His family went to a nearby Catholic church every week, and he always wore a gold cross around his neck. I wondered what he might think of Yonatan.

I closed my eyes. It was Friday evening, almost sunset. Yonatan would no doubt be in synagogue praying. What would he say if he knew I was watching football as he was welcoming Shabbat?

On the field, Chris intercepted a pass from number 14 on the other team, and again raced toward the end zone. Number 32, a huge player from the other team, tackled him just past the forty yard line. I winced as they hit the ground.

"Lauren," I said.

"Yeah?" She turned from the field to face me, as Chris shook himself off and stood to join his team huddle.

How could I tell her I'd met a stranger in an Orthodox synagogue and was planning to go back to see him again tomorrow?

"Nothing," I said, chickening out.

∽∞

The next morning, I dressed and hurried out before my parents could wake up. "Shabbat shalom," a young woman said, as we passed on the street.

"Shabbat shalom," I replied.

Because I'd arrived earlier than last week, the women's section was only partially full. I looked over someone else's shoulder to find the right page in my siddur. Then I peered through the gaps in the *mechitzah* to search the men.

Yonatan sat in the same place as during the holidays, his colorful kipah standing out amongst the black hats. When he glanced toward the women's section, meeting my eyes, a burst of energy rushed through me.

I continued to watch him as he returned to his prayers, but he didn't look back again.

Toward the end of the service, an elderly woman sat down beside me. She wore a velvet maroon scarf over her white hair, a long wine-colored dress with pockets, and black shoes with laces. When the service was over, she gave me a friendly smile.

"Good Shabbos," she said, and then blinked twice, as if seeing a ghost. *"Elisheva?"*

Shoot. Someone who knew my mother.

"N-no," I stammered. I could feel my face turning red. "I'm her daughter."

The woman's eyes widened. "You look so much like her."

I blinked at her in surprise. Beth was the one who looked like my mother. I was the one with dark hair and green eyes. But she had recognized me; our faces must be more alike than I realized.

"My name is Sima," she continued in a friendly voice. "What's your name?"

"Rachel," I said.

I heard her take a quick breath. "After your grandmother."

My grandmother had died so long ago I didn't really know much about her, except yes: I had been named for her. "Did you know her?" I asked.

"It was a long time ago," she said, a faraway look in her eyes. "Elisheva was just a few years older than you are now."

Naturally, I knew Mom had lost her mother when she was nineteen. But no one had ever pointed it out to me in quite that way.

"After she died, Elisheva used to come here and sit in the front row of the *mechitzah,* just like you're doing now." She sighed and shook her head. "A girl without her mother. It wasn't fair, what happened to her."

Mom had broken ranks with this tight-knit community. It always seemed to me she'd made the choice to wear what she wanted, eat what she wanted. It had never occurred to me she might have left with a broken heart.

Sima rested her hand on my arm. "It's beautiful you're here."

I shrugged awkwardly. "Thanks."

She stood to return her siddur, and I turned to see Yonatan standing in the doorway to the women's section. As the remaining few women exited, he leaned on the doorjamb, watching me. "Shabbat shalom," he said.

He came forward and sat in a chair a row behind me. Beyond us, I could hear the congregation filing downstairs for Kiddush.

My worries about what I was doing here, the anxiety and embarrassment of meeting Sima, all seemed to dissolve in his gaze.

I squeezed my palms together on my lap. "How are you doing that?" I asked.

"The Holy One wants to give us His Light," Yonatan intoned, and I began to understand this was the Light he was channeling toward me. I couldn't see it, but I could feel it, healing me.

"The Light is so pure that if we experienced it directly, we could not survive it," he said. "So the Holy One provides it in a form we can receive it, and give to others."

Yonatan spread his hands on the back of the chairs between us, and I noticed how calloused and rough they were. "When we receive the Light and give it to others, this brings us closer to the Holy One, so we can receive even more."

Once again, talking to Yonatan had me almost in a trance. The synagogue seemed to fade around us; his words and his face held my full concentration. I tried to take in the Light, as he had instructed.

Yonatan's face was suddenly concerned. "Rachel?"

My knees began to tremble as three streaks of light flashed at my right. *Not now,* I protested silently. But I could only wave my hand absently and rest it over my eyes before everything slipped away.

Spinning. The whispering of the wind. A stone courtyard under a milky blue sky.

Down stone steps in the silence.

When I recognize my name, I fall to my knees.

I didn't know how much time had passed, but I was back in the synagogue, the hard wood seat under me. As before, I could recall remnants from the dream. *Stone steps. The wind.* My fingers massaged my temples, though there was no pain.

When I opened my eyes, I found Yonatan staring at me with blunt astonishment. The sanctuary was empty. My breathing resounded in my own ears.

"I've been having...headaches," I said. It was almost a relief, to finally admit it aloud.

Yonatan's eyes widened. "Headaches?" he spluttered.

I nodded. "Migraines."

Yonatan's expression was a mixture of horror and awe. He lowered his voice. "How long has this been going on?"

I shrugged, looking toward the stained glass windows along the back wall of the sanctuary. "Maybe a month."

Yonatan exhaled. "A month."

I risked a glance back at him. "It hasn't been such a big deal until...recently."

Yonatan leaned back in his chair, studying me from a distance. "Rachel, that was not a headache."

My stomach fluttered; I wasn't sure I wanted to hear Yonatan's explanation of this mystery. "What do you think it was?"

He hesitated, his eyes filled with compassion. "It was a vision."

A vision? My soul seemed to lean closer, while every ounce of my father's logic and cynicism urged me to leap up and run from the conversation. This is where the brainwashing starts, I told myself. But I needed to hear what he would say.

"A vision," he repeated. "A holy communication from G-d."

I blinked at him, confused. "You're saying *G-d*...is trying to *talk*...to me?"

"Yes." He took off his glasses and met my eyes. "Rachel," he said in a quiet, reverent voice. "You're having visions because...because you are being called."

"C-called?"

He nodded. "G-d is calling you." He spread his fingers, palms up, on the chairs between us. "To be a prophetess."

Prophetess. The word rolled around and around in my head like a marble on a board. I knew the traditional Jewish view, that prophecy had ended and so there were no longer prophets after the beginning of the second Temple period.[9] Yet the mystical idea of prophecy had occasionally come up in my conversations with Zaide. He had spoken about prophecy as a closeness to G-d that brings light into our dark world. He taught me that some Jews could attain something close to prophecy, through piety and righteousness. He had never come right out and said it, but I'd sometimes wondered whether his own holy grandfather was one of those Jews.

"Prophecy," Yonatan said in the same reverent tone, "has been part of the secret mystical Jewish tradition, passed down through thousands of years." He leaned toward me, his voice only a whisper. "I am a prophet, and I have been called to teach this tradition to you."

---

[9] Source: "After the later prophets, Haggai, Zecharia, and Malachi, had died, the prophetic spirit disappeared from the Jewish people..." (Yoma 9b). See also: Babylonian Talmud, Sanhedrin 11a.

Behind him, the sun broke through the high windows at the back of the sanctuary, and cast a sudden, radiant glow upon the walls.

My thumb fidgeted with the siddur in my hands, flipping the pages nervously. I hardly met the standards of piety and righteousness Zaide had spoken of. What Yonatan was saying was hard to believe, but somewhere deep inside, I wanted to believe it.

"I can help you," Yonatan said. "If your visions are growing stronger, you need a guide."

As I stared at him, it dawned on me our first meeting hadn't been accidental. He said he had been *called* to teach me. He had planned this moment. He had been waiting for it. That's why he came to talk to me at the break-fast after Yom Kippur.

A twinge of fear rose up in me. What else did he know about me? Could I walk away from this synagogue and from him forever? Still, his words reminded me so much of Zaide. Possibly, he was an answer to my own prayer. Did I really want to stop now?

I remembered the prophet Jonah,[10] whose story we read every year on Yom Kippur. He had tried to run away from a call to prophecy, but had found there was no escape from the Master of the Universe.

"Is this just some trick to get me to be Orthodox?" I asked skeptically.

Yonatan chuckled. "If I only wanted that, I think I could find a simpler way."

We gazed at each other for a long moment. His eyes were bright, warm, and kind. I felt wary, but also...fascinated.

"What do prophets do?" I asked.

He folded his rough hands together on the chair between us. "We protect what needs to be protected," he said, his voice taking on the sound of a chant. "Save what G-d needs saved. Teach the words G-d has spoken. And bring G-d's blessing into the world."

I looked toward the sky beyond the windows. "Yonatan," I asked in a small voice, "why would G-d want *me*?"

I glanced back to see him staring at the *aron kodesh* at the front of the synagogue, his face a mystery of sorrow and faith.

"We never know," he said. Then he looked back at me, his expression

---

[10] Jonah is one of the prophets in the Jewish Bible. His story is traditionally read on Yom Kippur.

serious. "But you shouldn't doubt your worthiness, Rachel. You have powerful gifts."

Gifts. The word resonated in my mind. Was *this* what I had asked G-d for on Yom Kippur?

"You will be an extraordinary prophetess." The word was light on his lips, as if he had said it often before.

There was a silence as I tried to understand; the flashing lights and dreams weren't migraines, but visions, messages from G-d. Was this what he meant, when he was talking about my life's purpose last week? It seemed so preposterous I nearly laughed. But in the warm light of the sun streaming through the sanctuary windows, it was almost possible to believe G-d wanted me.

With all my courage, I met his gaze. His eyes shone a little brighter.

"As you develop your abilities, things will become clearer to you." He studied me for a long moment. "And the visions won't make you so tired."

Tired. I felt a few pieces of my puzzle slip into place as the fatigue I'd been feeling connected to the mysterious incidents I'd thought were headaches. It was true: After each one, I'd been exhausted.

"That would help," I said quietly.

"We can begin work on it next week," he said. He sounded almost eager. "It will be all right," he added, gently, watching my face. I wondered what he could read there, how much of my fear and uncertainty was apparent to this Orthodox Jewish man who considered himself a prophet.

He stood and led me to the lobby. When the metal door of the synagogue closed behind me, it felt strange to head back toward my house. The sun had come out, but I still found myself shivering.

Now that we were apart, everything he said seemed impossible to believe. What could he mean, that I was called to be a prophetess?

I wanted to run back to the synagogue and tell him I wouldn't return. That my parents wouldn't let me see him again. That I was obviously unworthy of anything he felt he could teach me. That I was going to see a neurologist, and we should forget the whole thing.

But I didn't.

CHAPTER 8

Iwalked home from synagogue chewing the fingernail of my thumb. There were trees up the hill in the distance, at this time of year a bright spectrum of oranges and yellows. As I stared at their simple, natural beauty, the idea I was destined for some divine calling seemed as unbelievable as being told I could fly.

Orthodox Jews kept hurrying by, their children in tow, wishing each other "Good Shabbos" as they passed. The men and boys all wore the same things: black hats, white shirts, and *tzitzit* hanging out over their black pants. The women added a wider variety of pink, blue, or beige; their long skirts and blouses covered their knees and elbows.

What would they say if they knew Yonatan had just called me to be a *prophetess*?

As I came onto my street, I watched two girls come out of the house across from ours. They were perhaps ten and twelve, their hair tied back in identical braids, each wearing a long skirt and a pastel blouse with a high collar. They were laughing about some joke I had not heard.

There were four other children in that house. Although we lived just across the street from each other, I didn't know any of their names. They didn't look toward me as they skipped away.

I tried to imagine Mom dressed like them. The woman at synagogue had made it seem as if she gave up being religious because her mother died, but I wasn't sure. I knew little about my grandmother. I'd seen pictures in Zaide's house, but Mom rarely spoke of her.

A few paces from our house, I stopped. Both cars were still in the driveway. I didn't want my parents to see me dressed in a skirt.

I stood hesitantly on the sidewalk, twisting my ponytail between my fingers. I could see Mom moving in the kitchen window. I waited, holding my breath, until she disappeared into the hall. Then I hurried up our walk, through the kitchen and up the stairs.

"Rachel?" Mom called.

I hesitated on the top landing. "Yeah?"

She appeared at the bottom of the steps, her auburn hair pulled back with a yellow headband, wearing a purple velour sweat suit and socks. She took in my skirt and dress shoes in one confused glance.

"Maya wanted to see this skirt," I said, scrambling for a plausible excuse. "Maybe for me to wear for Halloween."

She smiled faintly. "Did you have a good time?"

"Yeah." I shrugged awkwardly. "I'm going to change now."

"Okay," she said, turning away.

❦

In my dream that night, I walked barefoot on a beach, carrying a heavy weight on my shoulders. The whistling wind blew my loose hair into my face.

I looked up and saw, at some distance, Zaide.

He was just as I remembered him: thick white beard, white shirt, black pants, and black hat. Even in the sand, he wore the same black sneakers with dark laces. His hands were outstretched toward me.

I wore a sleeveless T-shirt, and my legs were bare beneath cut-off jeans. But I was so happy to see him, I didn't care.

As I drew closer, I heard him whispering over the sound of the wind. I stopped a few feet away, hanging back. I set down my burden at my feet.

He frowned as if I had done something wrong—a stern expression I had often seen during my childhood. It was always something I didn't *know* I wasn't supposed to do. His frustration and my ignorance. Neither were our fault.

Yet he was the kind of old man who would take a quarter and make it disappear from his hand; it would reappear in his hat, or behind my ear. Then he would give me the coin and encourage me to put it in a slotted metal can, for charity.

He could make you believe in magic.

I took another step toward him. Something shiny was in his hand: a key. The sunlight flashed in the ocean, bright like Yonatan's eyes.

"Go with them," Zaide urged me, his voice a little more solid in the wind. "Go as far as it takes you."

I took a step closer, but when I looked up again, he was gone. The key lay in the sand where he had stood, shining gold in the morning light.

I hesitated, listening to the sound of my own heartbeat. Kneeling to the ground, I picked up the key.

The next morning, I dug around in my jewelry box, looking for an old necklace with a Jewish star Zaide had given me for my Bat Mitzvah.

I found it at the bottom of a drawer, a bit tangled but otherwise perfect. The upper and lower triangles that formed the star were each doubled with white and yellow gold, so the star itself seemed to bring together disparate, complex pieces in a single unity. It dangled on a thin gold chain. It was prettier than I remembered.

I hadn't worn the necklace in years. But if I was going to continue down this path with Yonatan, I needed this gift from Zaide with me. I undid the clasp and put the necklace on under my shirt, so it was close to my heart.

Lauren and I were constructing a pulley Tuesday afternoon in Physics when I saw the next streak of white light. I stepped away at once, claiming I needed to use the bathroom. But once I was in the hallway – shivering hard, lights flashing so fiercely I could hardly see -- I only had time to duck inside a supply closet. Several brooms clattered to the ground as I fell.

Steps. The tight alleys, the silent city under the diminishing moon. The heavy metal door, engraved with a Jewish star.

Three flights in the darkness.

There is a key in my hand, but her apartment is unlocked.

A sliver of light under the door illuminated the brooms strewn on the cement floor. I couldn't remember much of what I'd seen. *Steps. A metal door with a Jewish star.*

My body felt heavy, as if my clothing had turned to lead. Despite the dust and the dirt, I wanted to curl on the floor and sleep.

It would be nice if Yonatan could channel some of G-d's Light for me right now, I thought as I dusted off my jeans. I felt like a sleepwalker dragging myself back to class.

When I entered the room, Lauren stood up, her eyes wide. I hadn't had the chance to look in a mirror. Was my hair a mess? Could she see how miserable I felt?

"Another migraine?" she said in a whisper.

I couldn't look at her as I lied. "I took the pill already."

"Rach, I'm so sorry," she said. "The good news is I got the results." She showed me her notebook. "Our experiment worked."

"Thanks," I said, pulling it toward me to copy her notes.

The next morning in Calculus, I held my breath as Dr. Davis handed back our first test. We had taken it the morning after Yom Kippur. After the fast, I'd forgotten to study for it. I turned my paper over and read the score: 76%.

Though I'd received a patch of Bs during my sophomore year because of the migraines, it was actually the first C I'd received in all of high school. It was a funny thing, being a good student: sometimes the grades seemed determined by a kind of magic rather than my answers. I stared at my score for a long moment, feeling my magic had somehow been broken.

When the bell rang, I stuffed the test into my backpack. Lauren approached my desk, grinning. "How'd you do?" she asked, resting her bag on my desk as I gathered my things. Of course we always shared these details, in a friendly, lightly competitive manner. Suddenly, the question felt intrusive.

"Fine." I stood up. "You?"

A few skinny lines appeared on her forehead, a slight sign of concern for me. "Fine."

Later that afternoon, Lauren and I walked home from school, crunching in brightly colored leaves spread under a blue autumn sky.

"Is that new?" she asked, pointing to Zaide's necklace.

I hadn't taken the necklace off since Sunday. Each morning I carefully tucked it under my shirt, but today it had escaped and lay exposed on my chest.

"I found it in my jewelry box," I told her, as we turned the corner to another tree-lined street. "My grandfather gave it to me. I dreamed about him the other night."

"Oh, Rach." She reached for my hand and squeezed it. "I'm sure he'd be glad you were wearing it."

A cool wind blew through the trees, scattering leaves around us. She caught a falling leaf and twirled it in her hands.

"I've been thinking about him a lot lately," I said cautiously. "He used to say some people might be able to receive messages from G-d, if they were worthy. If they were listening."

I had hoped this might be a way to begin to tell her about Yonatan, but Lauren raised her eyebrows skeptically. "Maybe, but how would they know it was G-d talking to them? Maybe it's just their own thoughts."

"Right," I said, looking away. I chastised myself for trying. Lauren was an atheist; how could she have any idea what I was talking about?

"Rach," she said, in a worried voice. "Have you been hearing voices in your head?"

I laughed, because the way she said it sounded so crazy, not at all like the wisdom Yonatan was teaching. "No," I said. "Of course not."

She caught a few strands of hair in her fingertips and pressed them to her lips. "Then what do you mean?"

"Nothing." I shrugged, ready to end this conversation just as she was trying to begin it. "Like I said, I've just been thinking of my grandfather. How he said people can talk to G-d."

"Sure people talk to G-d." She sounded relieved. "That's what praying is, right?"

"Yeah," I said.

She winked at me, smiling. "You're not crazy until you hear G-d talking back."

I kept my smile frozen on my face. "Right."

∽

"How did your second date go?" Maya asked, as we sat at her kitchen table Thursday night.

"Good." I pulled out my math notebook. "How did your math test go?"

She ignored my attempt to change the subject. "What does he look like?" she asked, resting her chin on her painted fingernails.

I didn't think describing his beard or his kipah would help. "He's tall," I said.

"Is he cute?"

I squinted, trying to assess this question honestly. Yonatan didn't seem to live in the same world with Maya and her boy obsessions. "I don't know."

"*Rachel*," Maya said, exasperated. "You don't *know*?"

"It's just – I'm not meeting him because he's cute," I said.

"Then why?"

I hesitated, trying to come up with an answer that would satisfy her. "I like listening to him talk," I said finally.

"Talk?" She rolled her eyes. "At this rate, you'll never get another kiss in high school. Come upstairs."

"Why?"

Without answering, she led me up to her bedroom, where she had spread out a pile of clothing for me to try on. It looked like she had robbed a Forever 21.

"You are going to wear something fabulous for the party on Thursday," she declared. "I know Brian Friedman is interested in you, and he's definitely coming."

Maya always hosted a big party at her house on Halloween. It was a chance for her cheerleader friends to flirt with the football players, and everyone else to watch admiringly as they danced. Class officers were invited, so I knew that at least Lauren would be coming to keep me company.

As usual, I didn't have a date. Maya had been trying to set me up with this Brian, the class secretary, since last spring. Until now, I had managed to avoid her attempts.

"Maya, nothing of yours is going to fit me," I protested. She had at least three inches on me, and weighed ten pounds less.

She shook her head, straightening her scarves and leggings with determination. "If we can't find something here, we're going to the mall. You need to wear something fabulous for the Halloween party, Rach, and it's not in your closet."

I sighed. No one could stop Maya when she got like this. She meant well.

She held up a pair of leopard-print leggings. We both giggled.

"Try them on," she said, tossing them to me.

I tried on everything on that bed, but in the end, those leopard-print leggings won out, under a stretchy black mini-dress. It didn't look like anything in my closet; that was for sure. But Maya reminded me this was a Halloween party. I wasn't supposed to look like myself.

"You don't have to sneak into the Orthodox world to find a boy," Maya said. "In that outfit, every guy at the party will want you."

Dad was working late again that Friday night. As we ate dinner at the kitchen table, Mom kept asking gentle questions about how things were going with school. I didn't want to talk about it, especially not the C I'd just gotten in math.

I was distracted by questions of my own. Why had Mom lit Shabbat candles on Friday nights when I was little? And why had she stopped? What had this tradition meant to her? Had Zaide ever spoken to *her* about prophecy?

But if we started talking about it, I was afraid I might end up revealing more than I intended. What if she forbade me to see Yonatan again?

When she stood to fill her glass with water, Mom stopped in front of me. She reached out and touched Zaide's star, which again had escaped from under my shirt.

"I haven't seen you wear that in a long time," she said.

"Zaide gave it to me for my Bat Mitzvah."

"I remember," she said, withdrawing her hand.

"I miss him a lot," I said.

When our eyes met, hers were wet. "I do too," she said. "I miss how he would tell us what to do."

I laughed through my tears. "But we never did what he wanted us to do."

She chuckled too. "We have to trust ourselves now," she said, squeezing my hand.

CHAPTER 9

The next morning I hurriedly silenced my phone alarm before it could wake my parents. I dressed in the third of my long skirts, pulling the star necklace out on top of my blue knit shirt. When I reached the synagogue, the service had only just started.

Following along in the siddur, I began to notice this service wasn't all that different from the high holiday prayers. I recognized the *shema*, followed by a long silent prayer, then the Torah reading. Finding a similarity in the structure reminded me I wasn't completely ignorant about this religion.

When we all stood for the second silent prayer, I closed my eyes. *G-d*, I prayed. *Please. Help me.* I didn't even know what I needed, but I hoped He would.

At the end of services, Yonatan appeared as usual at the door to the women's section. "Let's go for a walk," he said.

This suggestion directly contradicted safety rule number 3: *Don't go anywhere with him.* I fingered my necklace anxiously. In the dream, Zaide had told me to go with them, as far as it took me. Could this be what he meant?

"We don't have to." He backtracked, noticing my alarm.

"N-no," I said, as I stood. "It's OK." I hoped G-d had been listening to my prayer as Yonatan led me to the lobby.

It was a crisp fall day, the sun bright on the leaves falling to the ground. Yonatan took a deep breath of the fresh air. "Which way?" he asked. "You choose."

I led him in the direction away from my house.

As we walked, I kept glancing around, making sure we weren't alone. Along the main street there were plenty of Orthodox Jews walking in families and groups. We turned the corner onto a quieter street, but there were still several adults talking in the sunshine as the kids played in the grass.

"Rachel, do you pray?" he asked.

It was such a personal question I paused. "Sometimes," I answered finally.

"It's good to pray," he told me. "G-d wants our prayers."

"What difference could my prayers possibly make to G-d?" I asked.

He nodded slowly, as if listening to a higher voice inside of him before he responded. "G-d wants to be in relationship with us." He led me down a second street. "And I think you want a relationship with G-d, too."

The words seemed to come from deep inside of me when I said, "I do."

"Prayer is the beginning," he said. "Because when we pray we acknowledge how much we can't control, and how much we need. The Holy One created us lacking, so we would need each other and Him."

We continued down another street, toward a cul-de-sac at the end. Even here, a few children played outside with their parents.

"Yonatan," I said, "do you ever have...visions...at inconvenient times?"

He nodded, his fingers stroking his beard. "I know the visions can be disruptive," he said. "I'd like to help you become better at receiving them." We crossed a small footbridge. "It will help when you are able to meditate."

"Meditate?" I repeated, surprised. "Like Zen? I thought that was for Buddhists."

He chuckled. "Jewish meditation is a powerful and holy practice," he said. "It will help you."

We reached a small patch of green. Without another word, he sat down in the grass and leaned against one of the trees. He gestured to me to do the same. The grass was wet as I lowered myself to my knees. I folded my legs under my long skirt, keenly aware we were now alone.

His eyes closed and he spoke in a reverent chant. "Let's start with the *shema*," he said. "Do you know it?"

"Yes," I said.

He began to chant the familiar words. At first I repeated them a bit anxiously, trying to stay alert to my surroundings. But gradually I realized there was no danger here. Yonatan was almost in a trance. Following his example, I closed my eyes.

Shema...Shema...
Yisrael...Yisrael...
Hashem...Hashem...
Elokeinu...Elokeinu ...
Hashem...Hashem...
Echad...Echad...

As our words rang out, declaring the oneness of G-d against the background sounds of birdsong, I experienced – for the very first time – my soul.

It was an expansive halo, like a bubble of light around my body. It was bigger than I expected. A Light brighter and more real than the sun was flowing into it, from a source well beyond my view.

As we sat there, meditating together, I became aware too of Yonatan's soul, warm and safe, flickering towards me like a flame. At some level, higher and deeper than anything in the physical world, I experienced the truth that we were already connected.

In that moment, I understood him even more fully than the time after Yom Kippur, when I saw into his eyes and read everything there. I felt his love, his devotion to his calling, his selfless service. There was also anguish in his heart. There was not a hint of malice. The moment held such intimacy it might have been frightening, were it not so pure and holy.

When I finally opened my eyes, the air around us was shimmering, like the way light bends when it's hot outside. His eyes were open, too. He beamed at me.

"Everything in G-d's world is connected," he said.

Without his having to explain it, I understood what he really meant. *We* were connected, now and forever.

The shimmering heat around us faded as we left the trees and returned to the street. We were no longer two connected souls, but practically strangers. I felt almost embarrassed to think that anyone might learn where we had been and what we had done.

"The visions may become stronger now," Yonatan warned me, as he led me back to the main road. "You might see more. Try to embrace them."

"Should I try to meditate like we did?" I asked quietly.

He shook his head. "Not on your own yet."

I stared with bewilderment at the cars going past. They belonged to a different world than the one we'd just experienced.

"I'll see you next Shabbat," he said.

He turned back down the street toward the grassy area where we'd been. I wanted to ask to stay with him, but I turned back up the hill. It was a long way back to my house.

I walked in a daze, not even thinking as I opened the front door. In the kitchen, Mom was cooking for the week, surrounded by pots, pans, knives, and cutting boards. I was still wearing my long skirt, but Mom didn't seem to notice.

"Did you have a good time at Maya's?" she asked.

"Yeah," I said, remembering my story just a few seconds late. "She had a lot of instructions for the Halloween party this week."

I took a carrot from the cutting board and Mom looked up at me, her eyes clear and thoughtful. "I'm sure she did," she said.

<hr>

On Thursday evening, I showered and conditioned my hair, then dried it the way Maya had taught me. I put on the mini-dress, leopard leggings, and a pair of black boots. I pulled my hair back with a leopard ears headband Maya had found for me. On my face, I applied layers of makeup from the set Maya had given me for my birthday last year.

Downstairs, I bumped into Dad coming out of his office. "Whoa," he said when he saw me. "Isn't that dress a little short?"

"It's fine," I said, but I tugged it down a bit.

"Where did you get all that make-up?"

"Maya," I said.

He chuckled. "That girl really likes to dress you up, doesn't she?"

I laughed. "Yeah."

Dad studied me for a moment. I knew he must be thinking how *different* I looked. Thinking of all the other ways I was changing recently, I couldn't meet his eyes.

<hr>

Maya's cheerleading friends always looked like they had fallen out of bed gorgeous, with their straightened hair, plucked eyebrows, and slender muscular bodies. I tried to hold myself with the same confidence as I came into her living room.

About twenty of our classmates were already there, including Lauren, dressed as a witch with a pointy hat over her red hair. Maya wore a tiny black miniskirt with a spaghetti strap tank-top and high-heeled boots, showing off her long legs. Her hair was pulled back in an elaborate braid, with a tiger headband. Her lipstick and fingernails were blood red. She greeted me with an air kiss, then leaned in to whisper in my ear. "You look fabulous."

"Thanks," I whispered back. "Nice costume."

"Rawr," she said, making a clawing expression with her hand. "We're cats together." She winked at me before turning to greet some arriving cheerleaders.

"Hey Rach," Chris said, coming in from the kitchen with two sodas in his hands. His costume was a light blue jersey emblazoned with the name of a rival football team, which fit tightly against his chest. His cheeks were smooth, as if he'd shaved just before coming.

He gave me an up and down glance. "That's quite an outfit."

I blushed. "Well, it's Halloween."

"You look great. But it's not exactly your style, is it?"

I pushed my shoulders back boldly. "People change."

He laughed and then, to my surprise, kissed me on the cheek. "Yeah, they do."

I froze, speechless.

"Save a dance for me!" he called, as he headed back through the crowd.

Lauren nudged me from behind, grinning. "Well, that was interesting."

I attempted a casual shrug. "It was just a friend kiss," I said, as much to myself as to Lauren.

Maya's mother arrived with the pizza and the crowd focused on the dining room table. Soon the first three boxes were empty. When Lauren and I reached the table, only a box with pepperoni pizza remained.

Not kosher.

I reached unconsciously for Zaide's necklace, feeling a twinge of guilt. *I haven't made Yonatan any promises.* Shrugging away my doubts, I took two slices.

"Rach," Maya called, weaving through the crowd to us. She had Brian behind her, a blond kid with lots of freckles dressed incongruously as a gangster in a pinstriped suit. Lauren smiled wanly at him before patting me on the arm and drifting away.

I frowned after her. I had counted on her to save me.

"Nice to meet you," Brian said, over the chatter of conversation. He reached for my hand and shook it with a weak grip.

We chatted awkwardly over the music for a few moments, before heading downstairs to Maya's basement, where music was playing. I wasn't much of a dancer and neither was he, but we did our best through a few songs. Soon, the cheerleaders and football players took over, and Brian and I hung back, watching.

Chris was dancing with Maya, trying the type of dance maneuvers I hadn't been able to match last summer. It was fun to watch them together, swaying and spinning. They looked like they belonged on a TV show.

When sparks flashed in front of my eyes, I didn't hesitate. I released Brian's hand and fled up the stairs.

In Maya's living room, a half-dozen teenagers crouched on sofas, oblivious, making out. As the world spun around me, I vaulted up the second flight of stairs. I made it to the top landing before my knees gave out.

Moving in slow motion, his stomach tight with dread. Someone tries to stop him, but he pushes forward. He's too late. He can't be too late.

He's too late.

They have laid her face-up near the shattered car, her hair singed, her face scratched with glass, her eyes stony and blind. A low moan empties him.

Her hand rests on her abdomen, holding the baby they will never have.

Rocking like a little girl, hands wrapped tightly around my knees, I kept my eyes closed. This vision had been much clearer than any before.

The car. The woman. Dead. Who was she?

"*Nechama.*" Yonatan's voice, filled with misery, resounded suddenly in my head. In my mind's eye, I could almost see him: his own knees pulled to his chest, hands covering his eyes, on the floor in the dark.

"*She was my wife.*"

CHAPTER 10

I counted to ten, then took a long, deep breath. Then I counted to twenty. Was this what Yonatan meant by *stronger visions?*

At last, I opened my eyes. The beat from the music thrummed from two floors below. Down the stairs, I could see Maya's piano against the living room wall. In all the time we'd been friends, I had never seen anyone play that piano.

He was a widower.

No wonder he seemed so alone, without wife or family, especially in the Orthodox world where that was so unexpected. I had assumed it had to do with his calling. But there had been a wife...a pregnant wife.

Now I understood the anguish I sometimes saw in his eyes. The fury in his prayers on Rosh Hashanah. He had every right to be furious. To quit everything, the way my mother had. What was he doing here, trying to teach me about faith and trust in G-d?

I felt desperate to see him.

I dragged myself to my feet, and held the railing as I came down the steps. Chris startled me coming into the living room.

"Hey, Rach," he said, "ready to dance?" He put his hands on my shoulders, but I flinched and he lifted them away.

"I don't feel well," I said.

"Sick?"

I shook my head. "Just tired," I said, though the word hardly seemed to cover it.

"I'll be gentle." His warms wrapped back around me, sending tingles rolling across my shoulders.

A slow song I didn't recognize was wafting up from the basement. I rested my cheek on Chris's chest and let him lead me.

As the song ended, he pressed his chin into my hair, sending more chills down my neck. "That was nice," he said. He stroked his fingers gently through my hair. "Feeling any better?"

My cheeks burned. "Yeah."

"Are you coming to the game next week?" he asked.

I shrugged. "Probably."

"Maybe we could walk home from school together afterward."

My mouth opened. We hadn't done that since freshman year.

"We don't have to," he said quickly. "I just thought we could catch up a little."

"S-sure," I stammered.

∽

At home, I kicked off the leopard print leggings and huddled in my bed, furious with myself. The vision had weakened me. I was usually more careful with my heart.

For the one-hundredth time, I reminded myself that Chris had no idea the effect he could have on me. To him, dancing with a girl was no big deal. He had dated half the cheerleaders, after all. And a walk home was nothing to him.

My phone buzzed and for half a second, my heart leapt, hoping it would be Chris. But Maya's picture grinned up at me from the screen.

"I'm sorry," I said, before she could start.

"Do you know how long I spent setting that up with Brian?"

"I'm sorry," I said again. "He wouldn't have wanted to see me after I threw up." The lie came so naturally I almost believed it myself.

"You...what?" she asked.

"I got sick," I said. "Maybe the pizza, or just a stomach bug."

"What lousy timing," she said. "He was so hurt when you just left without saying anything. I don't know if I can fix it."

"It's really okay, Maya," I said. "I don't think he was my type anyway."

"You didn't even give him a chance," she said. "Is it because of Mr. Orthodox?"

I hesitated. *Was* it because of Yonatan and our spiritual journeys together? Or was I just rejecting every guy because deep inside I still wanted Chris? I certainly couldn't tell Maya how the night ended. She'd never let me hear the end of it.

"Yeah," I said finally. "Because of him."

She sighed. "I guess you have to follow where your heart takes you. Even if it's to some strange places."

Saturday morning was cold and rainy. I rooted through the hall closet until I found rain boots, which were at least a size too small, and a spring raincoat that wasn't really warm enough.

By the time I got to synagogue, I was soaked and shivering. I hung my coat and stood near the radiator in the lobby, warming my hands. How did the Orthodox Jews manage this? I wondered. But many of them seemed wet and cold, too. The women's section was noticeably emptier this morning. I settled into my seat, curling my toes in my boots, and stared through the *mechitzah*.

Yonatan never looked back at me, but I knew he knew I was there.

Something had changed since we'd meditated together last week. That vision about his wife was something I wasn't even sure he wanted me to know. Now, looking at him through the *mechitzah*, our connection felt almost tangible, a string of Light binding us together.

When the service finally ended, Yonatan appeared at the door to the women's section. For the first time since we'd met, he looked weary, dark circles under his eyes and thick creases in his forehead. He stood there a long moment, staring at me, before he came forward.

"I'm so sorry," I said, as he sat in the row behind me. I didn't know if I was apologizing for what had happened or for finding out about it.

He looked past me to the eternal light shining at the front of the synagogue. A few men still prayed at the front of the room. "None of this is your fault," he said.

"Why didn't you tell me?"

"You needed to trust me for other reasons."

I understood. He didn't want my pity. "But," I said, "how could you come here after that? How could you...do this...now...for G-d?"

A single tear slipped from one of his shining eyes. "It took something," he said in a thick voice.

"So you still have faith?" I asked incredulously. "Even after...?"

His eyes met mine, and they had that love and clarity and pain I'd seen so many times before. "It's not that I understand," he said. "It's that I know there's a story much larger than mine, in which it all makes sense."

His words made me think of Zaide. How he had continued to believe in G-d, even after surviving the Holocaust.

"Yonatan," I began hesitantly, unsure whether it was safe to ask. "Has something ...changed ...between us?"

He raised his eyebrows, impressed. "Yes."

"How?"

"I am helping you with your visions now," he said. "The spiritual link between us has strengthened."

"After the vision...I thought I could almost see you...on the floor. In a dark room. Was that really...you?"

He nodded. "We were very connected in that moment."

My eyes widened. "Does that mean you can see *me*?"

"Sometimes," he said. "When you need me." He took off his glasses and rubbed his eyes with two fingers.

"It must be hard," I said. "To have to watch over me like this."

Yonatan shook his head. "Helping you get through this is my mission, my responsibility. There is nothing more important in my life."

I stared at him, thinking about what it meant that his *life* was devoted to my becoming a prophetess.

"Thank you," I said finally.

"You were very brave this week," he said, with compassion. "I know it wasn't easy for you."

Rain pelted the small windows above us. I felt my throat tighten as I remembered racing up the stairs in Maya's house. The previous week, I had also been overtaken by two visions in school, both of them near misses where I managed to dart into stairwells to keep from being seen, then dragged myself to class late. One of the times I'd missed a history review, and yesterday I'd struggled through that exam.

I could almost see the Light Yonatan was channeling as he gazed at me, gradually restoring me. "The beginning is always difficult," he said, with regret.

"The thing is," I said, "I have responsibilities. School. My friends are worried about me."

"Prophecy will never get in the way of G-d's plans for you, Rachel."

I chewed my lip, wondering if G-d's plans would match my own.

"I wouldn't normally mention this so soon," he said, "but there is one thing that would help with the visions right now." He spread his hands on the back of the chair in front of him, palms up, and again I noticed his raw and calloused fingers.

"What?" I asked, perhaps too eagerly.

Yonatan hesitated. "It would help if you were more careful about what you are eating," he said. "Avoiding *traif* [11] foods would make your body a purer vessel. For the visions."

"You mean like – not eating pork and shellfish?"

He nodded once. "And other meat that isn't kosher."

I thought of the pepperoni pizza at the Halloween party. The pork lo mein I routinely ate with my family in the den while the kosher plates sat untouched in the kitchen. Dad always used to tease Mom about keeping kosher. Why should a god in charge of the whole universe care what's in my stomach? But G-d seemed...closer now.

He took off his glasses and looked at me with those bright eyes. "I know it's not what you want to hear," Yonatan said. "But eventually the commandments...matter."

My shoulders tightened. I didn't want the commandments to matter. Hadn't I made clear to him from the start that I wasn't Orthodox? I hadn't expected that keeping kosher – or any of the commandments – would eventually become part of the deal.

Yet, here was a man who had lost his wife and unborn child and picked himself up to come here, to teach me. What he was asking of me was nothing compared to what he had been through.

"I'll try," I said finally.

He pressed his lips together, and I knew he understood the sacrifice I was making. "It will help," he said.

We sat there a moment longer before I brought myself to ask. "Yonatan," I said, "could we meditate together again?"

He smiled, as if he'd hoped I would ask. "Yes." The rain was still pelting the windows outside. Yonatan looked around the sanctuary, as if wishing a forest would materialize. The doors to the women's section were open to the hall, and two men were still praying in their section near the front of the room. "I'm not sure this is the place, though."

I agreed. It wouldn't be good if the two of us were discovered meditating, alone in the women's section.

---

[11] Traif: a term used to describe food traditionally forbidden as not kosher, such as pork, shellfish, and other non-kosher meat. Note that the right margin on this footnote may be off, too.

"There's a library," he said. "It should be empty now, if you would feel comfortable."

I followed him out of the sanctuary. The library was a small room off the lobby, lined with more Hebrew books than the den at my uncle's, with just enough room for two tables with metal folding chairs. Though he left the door open a crack behind us, I still felt nervous about being alone with him. But Yonatan seemed oblivious to my concerns, and innocent of any ulterior motives. He sat straight in his chair, closed his eyes, and began to chant.

This time I didn't recognize the words he used. But sitting down across from him, I closed my eyes and began to repeat them.

Soon, I could feel my soul filling with light.

Through some spiritual bond, I became aware of Yonatan's soul, also radiant. Then I understood all of his physical and emotional scars, and all my weariness, terror, and frustration had not penetrated our souls at all. They were perfect, shining sparks of G-d.

Yonatan began to sing, a wordless melody that rang out from the depth of his being. I hummed along, swept along by the current of song, until the lights burst around me and carried me away.

The air is dry and hot under an unforgiving sun, and we've been planting seeds for many hours. There is little time to rest. But when the Light comes, it takes over everything. Trembling, I fall to my knees in the dirt.

When I awaken, I feel so weary I can barely move.

The other workers whisper above me. They think I've been broken by all I've seen. They may be right.

"Let me take her." It's that young man, the one who always comes. He kneels and strokes my dusty face, fierce devotion in his shining eyes.

"I'll finish the chores, Devorah," Noach says. "Take all the time you need."

"Rachel." It was Yonatan.

He began to chant again, his voice coaxing until I repeated the Hebrew words, until I recognized they were the rope to lower me out of the trance. I repeated his words again and again, losing track of how many times: until the room began to feel real, until I felt the pinch of my tight rain boots and the chill of the library on my still damp shoulders, until I could finally open my eyes.

Yonatan sat across from me at the table, his bearded chin resting in one hand. His expression seemed troubled.

"Sorry," I said.

His shook his head. "I just didn't know...you would enter the trance so quickly."

"Is that not...normal?" I asked.

He chuckled. "It's normal for you."

My stomach tensed. I didn't want things to move quickly. I wanted everything to slow down.

"Should I try to meditate this week?" I asked, hoping it might keep visions from coming in the middle of class.

He shook his head. "Not yet."

I twisted my lips, fearing I had done something wrong.

"With a gift like yours, Rachel...." As he trailed off, I understood. It had been hard to awaken and bring me back from that other, vision world. He didn't want me to get lost there without guidance.

He gave me a reassuring smile. "The kosher food will help," he said. "And I'll help you this week, as much as I can."

He stood. I got to my feet too, a little unsteady at first.

"Will you be alright getting home alone?" he asked.

I wasn't at all looking forward to the long walk alone in the rain, but I nodded. Despite everything, I was still clinging to safety rule number two.

CHAPTER 11

"Rachel?" Dad knocked at my bedroom door. I looked up from my copy of *Macbeth*. We had an English test at the end of the week, and I was behind in my reading. "Yes?"

Dad peeked his head in, grinning. "We're celebrating tonight. I finished my first draft on deadline." He waved the Chinese menu at me. "Pork lo mein as usual?"

"Um," I shook my head, "No, I think I'll go with...veggie lo mein tonight."

"As you wish," he said, humming as he went back downstairs.

After dinner, Dad turned on a football game, something he hadn't done all year. I stretched out on the carpet, still reading *Macbeth*. Mom was knitting a baby blanket for someone in her office.

"What should I make for Thanksgiving?" she asked us.

"Turkey," Dad said in a light voice, his eyes on the game.

She smiled indulgently at him. "Beth asked for low-fat choices," she said. "Just plain sweet potato will be healthy. And I can make roasted broccoli. The chicken soup is good – she can skip the matzo balls if she wants. Maybe some mashed potatoes?"

"You could make that spinach quiche," Dad said, his eyes still on the game.

Mom shook her head. "It's dairy," she said. This was all she needed to say. It was one thing to eat Chinese food in the den, but my mother wouldn't serve something dairy on our kosher plates with the Thanksgiving turkey. Not mixing meat with dairy was one of the rules.

Dad turned from the screen to look at her. "It would be all right," he said tentatively, "now that your father...isn't here."

I glanced up to see Mom shake her head.

He squeezed her hand. "It's been a few months now."

"Some promises last beyond the living," she said hoarsely.

I swallowed hard. Just a few weeks ago, I would have been on Dad's side, encouraging her to stop the pretense. It wasn't as if we were religious, I would have said. Zaide was old fashioned. We didn't have to keep following his rules.

But now I felt relieved Mom held the line. What would I do if she started cooking pork and expected me to eat it?

"You don't have to decide right now," Dad said.

I glanced up again, surprised to find Mom's eyes resting on me, as if she had guessed how important keeping kosher had recently become in my life. For one silent moment, our eyes met. Then she turned back to Dad, and I hurriedly returned to my book.

"No," I heard Mom say, her voice quiet but firm. "I can make the apple kugel.[12] It's low fat and I know Beth likes it."

∽

All weekend I felt on edge, watching for more streaks of light. By Monday afternoon at Poetry Club, I was on high alert, anxious to avoid a scene at school. I rushed through my reading of a poem I'd written after meditating with Yonatan, attempting to explain the feeling of the trance.

When our session ended, I zipped my backpack and rushed to the door.

"Rachel," Jake called from behind me.

Surprised, I stopped just past the doorway and let him catch up to me. His baseball cap was so low I could barely see his eyes.

"That was a nice poem." His voice seemed more alert and tense than usual. But not exactly sober, either.

My face flushed. "Thanks," I said, feeling more than a little embarrassed.

"I like the new ones," he said, scratching at his scraggly beard. "The ones about confusion and real life. That's what poetry is supposed to be about."

I paused; I hadn't realized the change in my poems was so obvious. "Yeah, I've been trying some new things," I said.

The corners of his lips twitched into a half-smile. "I have too."

I frowned; I hadn't noticed any difference in his poems.

"You're very pretty," he said, so quietly I wasn't sure I'd heard him right.

My eyes widened. "Yeah, okay," I said, taking a step back.

His lips curved into a fuller smile. *Was he teasing me?* I wondered.

"See you around," he said. He re-adjusted his baseball cap as he walked away.

---

[12] A traditional Jewish dish, usually made with potatoes or noodles.

65

"No migraine?" Lauren asked, when I caught up with her after Debate Club a few minutes later. It had become a common question from her. I knew she only wanted to take care of me, but I found it grating.

"No migraine," I said. "You won't believe what just happened." As she drove us home, I told her how Jake had complimented my poetry and then said I was pretty.

"He must have been high on weed or something," I said. "Don't you think?"

"Well, you are pretty," Lauren said with a grin. "But it seems a little weird to put it out there like that."

"He's usually so chill," I said. "Today he seemed different somehow."

"Maybe he has a crush on you," Lauren said.

"Yeah, right," I laughed, blushing. "I don't think he's my type. But he's a great writer."

"A great writer when he's high, or when he's sober?" she asked, pulling into my driveway. "See you tomorrow, Rach."

I might have stayed to discuss the situation with Jake, but a streak of light had just flashed across my field of vision.

"Yeah, tomorrow," I said hurriedly, grabbing my bag. At the top of the porch stairs, I unlocked the door with trembling fingers. I fled into the kitchen, through the living room, and up to my room.

The classical music played and his arms lifted, ready to swing her into the air. She too lifted her arms, prepared to fly. Ready to live the dream she had always prepared for.

At first, she was confused when the waxy wood floor rose up to meet her; then she realized she had fallen. Thunk. To the ground.

He cursed, cradling his sore wrist.

She will never stop hearing those words. Again and again, the rest of her days.

"No thank you," she says. "I had enough at breakfast."

The exhaustion rolled in like storm clouds as I opened my eyes in my darkening bedroom, where I was curled up on the wood floor. In the vision, there was another wood floor. *Music. A curse.*

It was lucky my mother was late coming home from work, I thought. That this hadn't happened in Lauren's car.

Luck? I wondered. Or could it be keeping kosher was actually helping?

⚭

"Are you still going to see Mr. Orthodox on Saturday mornings?" Maya asked, interrupting our math study Wednesday evening.

I nodded, and she sighed.

"I still can't believe you turned down a perfectly decent student officer for *him*."

"I don't know where it's going," I told her, my eyes still on the math book. "I just need to talk to him right now."

"Rach." She waited for me to look up at her. "Are you considering being Orthodox for this guy?"

"No," I said quickly.

She tapped her purple fingernails against her chin. "Well, since you're so interested in your Jewish heritage, I thought you might like this."

She pulled a paper from her binder and slid it across the table to me. It was a flier for a trip to Israel during winter break.

"I talked to my mom and she said I could sign up," Maya said. "The whole thing costs only three hundred dollars for almost two weeks. It's supported by some foundation that wants to bring Jewish kids to Israel."

I ran a shaky finger across the glossy page, printed with images of Jewish historic sites. Maya was looking out the window, making a great display of not caring about my reaction—a sure sign that, despite her confusion with my recent choices, she really wanted me to come.

"I'll ask my parents," I said.

⚭

Because Dad had finished his manuscript, he was making a big effort to come to dinners this week. Mom, grateful for his presence, was cooking his favorite meals. They both seemed relaxed and cheerful.

I waited until they were almost finished with their chicken the next night to bring out the rumpled flier from my pocket. "Maya gave me this," I said, spreading it on the table.

Dad reached for it first. "Two weeks in Israel, for three hundred dollars?" he asked. "Great deal." He passed the flier to Mom, who held the page by its edges like an ancient photograph.

"Who's sponsoring it?" she asked.

"Maya's synagogue youth group," I said. "You've been there before, right?"

Mom was unconsciously folding and unfolding the corner of the paper. "Yes. Before I met your father."

"So when you were just a little older than me," I said, to bolster my argument.

"It was a long time ago." Her eyes searched my face. "Maya gave this to you?"

I nodded, twisting my fingers together.

"I don't see why not," Dad said, studying the paper over Mom's shoulder.

"Do you want to go?" she asked, her tone more intense than I'd expected.

"Yeah," I said.

She stared back at the paper. "All right," she said at last.

"Thank you!" Impulsively, I jumped up to hug her.

Her arms wrapped tightly around me as she murmured Yiddish words I'd heard Zaide say to her, when he meant "You're welcome."

"*Mitn gantzn hartzn.*" With all my heart.

CHAPTER 12

I gripped the railing anxiously as Lauren and I wound our way up the bleachers for Chris' game on Friday afternoon. What if a vision happened *here*, in the middle of the game? One had come in the middle of the *Macbeth* study review yesterday, sending me racing out to the hall. I had made it through this afternoon's test, but I knew another could happen at any time.

We stood and cheered for the team as they came on the field. Chris was #23, but even without the number, I would have recognized the shape of his body. I watched him scan his audience. Was it just my imagination or was he looking for me?

Chris was at his best this afternoon, blazing down the field in the late fall sunlight. When the game ended, he had racked up another three touchdowns for our undefeated team. My stomach fluttered as Lauren and I followed the crowd out of the stands.

"He's just a friend," I said. I had told Lauren this at least a dozen times this week. "It's just a walk."

Lauren squeezed my shoulders. "It's going to be great."

Chris came out of the locker room dressed in jeans and a tight fitting long-sleeved shirt, his jacket over his arm. There were fresh comb marks in his wet hair. I took a deep breath as Lauren hurried away.

"Hey," he said.

I smiled. "You were great today," I said. "So what's it like to be the school football hero?"

He grinned, looking both pleased and a little embarrassed. "It's kind of an obsession," he admitted. "But I love it."

As we began walking, he reached for my hand, sending tingles through my fingers and up to my elbows. Then he turned to me with a dizzying smile. "What's new with you?"

I opened my mouth, and before I knew what I was doing, I was telling him about Yonatan. How we'd met on Yom Kippur. How he reminded me of my grandfather. That he'd told me I was called to be a prophetess, though I still hardly knew what the calling meant. The visions. The lessons. The kosher food.

Chris was the first person I'd ever told the whole truth. He listened patiently, not interrupting as Lauren had. When I finished, he touched the Jewish star on my neck.

"It sounds like G-d is calling you," he said.

"Doesn't it sound...kind of crazy that G-d would be calling...me?" I asked in a high voice.

He squeezed my hand. "What's it like, when he's teaching you?"

"Like connecting to something I knew a long time ago, but forgot," I said. "Like coming home."

Chris lifted a stray hair that had come loose from my ponytail and smoothed it back into place. "Sounds right to me."

We walked in silence for a few moments. The trees seemed to gather around us, shimmering gold in the last rays of the sun. A chill was rising in the air, but I didn't want to stop to zip up my jacket. I kept looking at our hands, entwined between us.

"Are you seeing anyone lately?" he asked.

My heart beat faster. "No," I said. "You?"

He shrugged. "A different girl asks me every weekend," he said. "I'm supposed to say yes to all of them, apparently. To be honest, they all kind of blur together."

I remembered the gossipy girls from a couple of weeks ago, saying how he'd dated half the cheerleaders. I looked up at his handsome face, little bristles of hair shadowing the surface of his cheeks. "You could have any girl you want," I said.

"You'd think," he said. "But when I'm out with those girls... I sometimes forget who I am. They think I'm just some football player." His thumb pressed a little tighter against my fingers. "The thing is, they make a big deal of guys using girls, but girls can do that too. They want to kiss me so they can tell their friends they did." He rolled his eyes. "I'm so sick of it."

"You don't have to go out with them," I said.

"Sometimes it feels like I do," he said.

The sun had slipped below the horizon, and the street lights began to turn on. I finally zipped up my jacket. We walked in silence, his hand still tight around mine.

"Would you really go all the way to Florida?" I asked.

"Maybe," he said. "With the right kind of scholarship." He looked at me.

"Are you still planning on G-Dub?"

I glanced up at him, surprised he had remembered. It was early in the summer when I'd mentioned that.

"Yeah," I said. "If they'll take me."

We had reached the edge of our neighborhood. A clump of trees stood tall above us, providing silent shelter. A cold wind blew through the branches and I shivered. Chris rested his hands on my shoulders, sending a different kind of chills through me.

His eyes looked so soft in the dark. Was he leaning closer? I only knew this was real when his lips reached mine.

His kiss was warm, confident, tender, just as I'd imagined it. Shivers rolled down my back, all the way to my heels.

After several precious moments, we separated.

My first thought was of Zaide.

Dating only Jews was one of his ironclad rules. What would he say if he knew I was here with Chris in the dark? More pressingly, what would Yonatan say? *Eventually,* he'd said, *the commandments matter.* If eating pork could make the visions worse, kissing Chris couldn't help matters.

I looked up and saw Chris' eyes, tight on my face, as if he could read the progression of thoughts I'd just had. I knew I needed to say something, but I couldn't open my mouth.

"I bet that teacher of yours wouldn't want you going out with a Catholic," he said slowly.

"Chris," I said, "would you seriously want ...to go out ...with *me?*"

He gathered me into his arms and held me tight in the darkness. "You're real," he said. "You remind me I'm real."

"I'm kind of a mess right now, actually," I told him, resting my cheek on his warm chest.

"I'll take it," he said fervently.

I looked down at the ground, trying to imagine myself in his life. Could he really commit to me, with all those other girls throwing themselves at him? Could I really commit to him, when my future was so uncertain and so...Jewish?

"I don't think I can," I said finally.

As soon as he released me, I wanted to slip back into his arms. In the darkness, I could barely make out his face. We walked the rest of the way to our block in silence.

"Chris," I said, when we arrived at my house. I wanted to tell him I loved him, that I had always loved him. I wanted to beg him to have me. But I couldn't.

He kissed me lightly on the forehead, and backed away in the darkness toward his house.

Upstairs, I huddled on the floor of my closet, knees to my chest.

What was I doing? Who was I becoming? I just wanted to be the regular girl I used to be. The one who didn't have tests marked with a C stuffed in her backpack. The one who would be floating with delight after a night like this with Chris.

I felt furious at Yonatan. Why had I ever agreed to learn with him? I hated everything he had taught me. I wanted to go out and eat a pepperoni pizza, tonight, Friday night, wearing shorts. Even though it was November.

Instead, I did the most mutinous thing I could think of. Sitting in the dark of my closet, hands clenched into fists, I began to whisper the words Yonatan had repeated in the synagogue library last week. More than any other rebellion, I wanted to lose myself in the world where he'd said I wasn't allowed to go alone.

I didn't know if I was saying the words right. I had no idea if they would work. I was prepared for it to take a long time, but the trance came suddenly, washing over me with the force of a storm wave, as if it had already been nearby, waiting to crash.

From his place at the top of a mountain, the ancient prophet clears his thoughts to meditate. But Devorah's face will not leave him. He has loved her nearly all his life.

The sounds of traffic. Pigeons. The smells of car fumes and trash. As they walk together down the curved service road, a black car pulls to a stop along the busy avenue. The security guard at the gate looks up.

...All the other men in synagogue are standing for prayer, but Yonatan sits, his forehead resting in his hands, a waterfall of Light pouring toward and flowing from his soul. "Rachel," he says. "Rachel."

Several moments pass before I remember this is my name.

Curled on the wood floor of my closet. Drained like a washcloth wrung dry.

With the little strength I had left, I whispered the holy words Yonatan had placed into my mouth. In some corner of my awareness, I could still see him, whispering those words in the middle of the synagogue, missing his own opportunity to pray to save me from myself.

DEVORAH

After the nightmare, I crept out of the tent and drew my knees to my chest by the campfire, sobbing softly in the dark.

"Was it a message?" Noach asked quietly. He stood at the entrance to his own tent.

I shook my head. "A memory."

"When you regain your strength..." he began.

"I've been here months now," I said.

"It will come," he assured me, coming closer. "The fate of prophecy rests with you."

The burden was almost too much to bear. I hid my face under the moonless sky. "You make it seem like I'm some kind of hero. But I can't do what you're asking me to do."

"You are a hero," Noach said. He smiled as I glanced up at him. "Gedolah Ha Dor, great one, teacher of the generation."

I shook my head. "You have to earn a title like that."

Noach held my eyes. "You will."

And all these generations later, she will too.

CHAPTER 13

I awoke early the next morning. Not allowing myself to think about what I was doing, I pulled on a skirt I'd already worn several times that week and went to meet Yonatan at synagogue.

The late fall air was warm, with a strong breeze taking the last of the leaves from the trees. I arrived to find the lobby congested with men dressed in black hats, black suit jackets, black pants. They paid me no notice as they filed into the men's section of the sanctuary. In the sparsely filled women's section, I stared blankly at the Hebrew words in my siddur.

Really I wanted to close the book, leave this building, and never come back. But what if I did? Would Chris even want me to give this up for him? And what about the visions? Wouldn't they just get worse without Yonatan's help?

By the time the service ended, the women's section was full. I sat by the *mechitzah*, my siddur still open to a random page. As the women disappeared into the hall, Yonatan approached the doorway, his face so kind and sad I looked away in shame.

"Oh Rachel," he said.

This time he sat in the same row as me, leaving just one seat between us.

I buried my head in my hands. "There's this...guy," I mumbled.

"The Christian boy."

I lifted my face, surprised. "You know?"

He nodded.

"How?"

He pressed his fingertips together in the air, then let them fall to his lap. "You remember," he said. "We're connected now."

It wasn't a fully satisfying answer, but I knew I wouldn't get a clearer one.

"He can't join you on your path," he said. "As you could see."

Through the *mechitzah,* my eyes caught on the eternal flame at the front of the sanctuary. I hated it, but I knew he was right.

"I meditated because I wanted to punish you," I said.

"I understand," he said wryly. "But it was a risky choice."

"If you hadn't helped, what would have happened?" I asked him. "Could I really have gotten lost...there?"

He closed his eyes. *"Ben Zoma glimpsed at the Divine Presence and was harmed. And with regard to him the verse states: "Have you found honey? Eat as much as is sufficient for you, lest you become full from it and vomit it."* [13] He opened his eyes and said, "If you had been without guidance, it could have been dangerous for you at this stage." His fingers knitted together on the back of the chair. "It's okay to be angry at me, Rachel," he said. "But it is important to say true to your path now. Your choices have consequences."

His tone had become stern, but I knew there was love in his rebuke. Gratitude for Yonatan surged up in me. How could I have been angry with him? He was the only savior I had.

"I'm sorry," I said.

He took off his glasses and clasped them in his large hand. "Some believe that a person can only be forgiven through suffering and sacrifice. But the Torah simply requires us to regret our choices and grow from them," he said. "Will you do it again?"

I shook my head. "No," I said gravely.

"Then the next step is to ask G-d for forgiveness," he said.

It felt awkward to pray aloud, but slowly I found the words. "I'm sorry," I said. "Please forgive me."

In that moment I could feel it, as if a tiny shard of light had been uplifted, restored, and made whole.

Yonatan leaned backward, satisfied. "G-d wants us to grow from our mistakes, not dwell on them," he said, in a softer tone. "Remember that."

I nodded.

He put his glasses back on as he stood. "One day you'll need this meditation," he said. "We will continue to practice until you are ready."

I followed him back to the empty library. There, surrounded by holy books, I repeated his words. As the sparks danced around me, I arose, arose, slipped into sleep and caught myself; awakening, awakening; pulled upward toward the Light, but falling...

I endured sparks, feeling I might be burned alive by the flames. There was a terrifyingly loud storm, and then silence. And then...

---

[13] Babylonian Talmud Chagigah 14b, translation from Sefaria. Prooftext: Proverbs 25:16. This is the key Jewish source that indicates mystical journeying can be dangerous.

I am standing in a stone courtyard.

An old woman leans on the stone wall across from me, her curled white hair wrapped in a yellow kerchief. Her shining eyes are blue: the color of a blueberry. The color of a bruise.

Then suddenly, I am the old woman, and I am staring at myself.

The girl is here, but not truly here. Behind her, the ancient Wall rises into the night. She is so frightened – more frightened than I would have imagined. Her green eyes burn like lanterns on her pale face.

Love and pity well up in me, as if she were my own child. "So young, and so brave," I murmur.

The girl stares back at me. "Who are you?"

"I am Devorah." I say it slowly and clearly, so one day she will understand.

Yonatan's voice was abrupt, commanding. "Rachel."

I was floating in a space with no pain or loneliness, and there was an old woman there – more real than anything in my life – who loved me. In her eyes, I had been unbearably young, innocent, frightened. Yet she had felt nothing but kindness toward me.

"Rachel," Yonatan said, his voice more gentle now. He whispered the words and as I found my voice, I repeated them, over and over, descending.

The cutting of my fingernails into my palms. The buzz of the radiator. My hands on the cold wood laminate table. The smell of the dusty books. The chair beneath me.

Yonatan's anxious presence.

At last, he told me to open my eyes.

I was amazed to find myself still sitting across from Yonatan in the library. It felt like I had been very far away. Was it my imagination, or did things look different now?

"Yonatan," I managed to say, "who ...was –" I broke off and tried again. "I ...saw a ...woman. Devorah?"

Yonatan closed his eyes. "Devorah is the Great One of the Generation," he said. "Gedolah HaDor[14], the leader and teacher of all the prophets."

"Then – she's – real?"

"Very real," he said. "She has waited a long time to meet you."

My eyes widened. "How did she – how does she even *know* about me?"

"Devorah receives the calling for the new prophets," Yonatan said. "She

---

[14] Literally, "great one of the generation."

assigns each one a teacher."

It hit me then. There were other prophets. One of them had *assigned Yonatan to me*. Someone else was out there in the world, caring about me, guiding me toward this world of prophecy.

My voice lifted a few pitches. "So you've been – talking to her – about me?"

Yonatan nodded. "It's not unusual," he said, glancing downward to his hands folded on the table. "Teaching a new prophetess is challenging, delicate work."

Maybe I should have been frightened. But after seeing Devorah, I wasn't. More than anything, I wanted to see her again. In just those few moments of meditation, she had become like the grandmother I had never known.

"Where is she?" I asked.

"She lives in Jerusalem," he said.

"I'm going to Israel this winter," I told him, feeling suddenly hopeful. "Do you think I could meet her there?"

Yonatan tilted his head; I had surprised him. "You're going to Israel?"

"Next month," I said. "With my friend's youth group."

A little smile spread on his face. "I will make arrangements to join you there."

A chill tingled down my back. What did he mean, *join me*? Would I be safe? Most importantly: Could I actually meet the prophetess Devorah?

"Have you been there before?" I asked.

"Israel is my home," he said, a wistful look in his eyes.

I chewed my lip.

"G-d has a plan for you," Yonatan said. "If He is bringing you to Israel, it's time."

❦

"You never told me what happened with Chris," Lauren said, as we sat together at lunch on Monday. She took a bite of her apple, waiting expectantly.

"It was kind of a disaster," I said.

She waved her apple toward me, still chewing. "What happened?"

"Well, we walked for a while," I began, "and then –" Unable to bear it, I rested my forehead in my hands.

"Then what?"

"He kissed me," I muttered.

She gasped. I looked up to see her grinning. "He *kissed* you? I knew it. He's –" She stopped, seeing my expression. "What's wrong?"

I shook my head, my chin still in my hands. "I just –" I shrugged one shoulder. "Couldn't do it."

"Rach," Lauren said reasonably, "you've had a crush on him for years. What do you mean, you couldn't do it?"

"I –" I broke off, looking at Lauren's puzzled frown. "He's not Jewish." She frowned at me. "So?"

My forehead slipped back into my hands. "I don't know," I said.

I could feel Lauren's eyes on me. After a long moment, I lifted my head.

"I didn't think that kind of thing mattered to you," she said.

I met her gaze. "I didn't think so either."

We stared at each other, a little crack appearing in what had previously been the tightest of friendships.

Finally, she shrugged. "He seems like a good guy," she said, taking another bite of her apple. "I'm sorry it didn't work out."

"Yeah," I said. "Me too."

∞

The day before Thanksgiving, I came home from school to find Beth's shoes in the front hall. I ran up the steps eagerly, but her bedroom door was closed.

"Beth?" I called out, standing on the landing at the top of the stairs. I knocked.

Her door was unlocked. Cautiously, I opened it.

She was asleep on her stomach, facing the wall. Her long auburn hair hung limply on the pillow. The rest of her body was wrapped tightly in a blanket. A crushed can of empty, caffeinated Diet Coke sat on the nightstand.

It must have been a long flight, I thought, creeping back to the hallway.

∞

Beth didn't join us for dinner that night, instead going out with her high school friends. When I heard her bedroom door open the next morning, I burst into the hall.

"Beth!" I shouted, too enthusiastically.

She looked tired. Not *I-just-woke-up-and-I'm-jet-lagged* tired, but *tired*, as if she hadn't slept properly in weeks.

80

"You're coming to the Turkey Bowl, aren't you?" I asked eagerly.

She took in my football team sweatshirt, my ponytail, my excitement. "Sure," she said. "What time do we leave?"

I waited while she brushed her teeth, showered, and dressed. When she finally reappeared, makeup had erased the weariness from her face. In tight black jeans, her legs appeared thin and muscular, each one like the trunk of a young tree. Ever the dancer, she seemed to float down the stairs in front of me.

"Do you want breakfast?" I asked, as we passed through the kitchen.

"Nah."

We reached Mom's car and she slid into the driver's seat. "How's college?" I asked.

"Good. Busy," she added. "How have things been around here?"

"Okay," I said.

I wanted her to look at me. To *see* me. I needed to know if I looked the same as I had last summer, or if she could tell the huge transformation taking place inside of me. I wanted to know what she thought about the fact that I seemed to be giving up everything that once mattered to me, to become a prophetess.

"School going okay?" she asked.

"Yeah," I said.

At a red light, she turned to look at me. "Senior year can be tough," she said. "Do you have Edmonton for Physics?"

"Yeah. We had a rough exam this week," I said. I didn't mention that the exam was rough because I'd cancelled a study session with Lauren after another unexpected vision on Tuesday.

She chuckled. "I could never understand a word he said. Some of my friends made a song out of his classes." Her voice took on a sing-song lilt: "*Diffraction, action-reaction, Newton's laws. Acceleration, objects in motion, sound and light waves.*" She grinned at me. "That's all I remember from his class." She shrugged. "If you're not going to be a physicist, I think you'll be able to get along without that stuff."

I grinned. Beth! It was so nice to see her. "Just as long as I get into college."

"Yeah, there's that," she said. "When are your applications due?" The light turned green and she turned back to the road.

"End of December," I said. "I have to finish them before I leave for Israel."

Her lips pursed in a little grin. "I heard you're going, lucky girl! I was surprised Mom let you."

"She's been there, you know. *Before.*"

I meant *before, when she was still Orthodox,* but Beth nodded knowingly. "Before her mom died," she said. "I think her mother got sick while she was there."

I frowned. "Really?"

Beth lifted one hand from the steering wheel, waving her fingers to count the evidence. "Well, she was there for the year after high school, and her mom died when she was nineteen. She died of cancer. So she must have gotten sick while she was there, right?" She glanced over at me, then back to the road. "I don't think she's been back since. It must be a big deal for her that you're going."

"How do you know all this?" I said.

Beth shrugged. "I asked."

I stared at her. *She asked.* Why hadn't I ever asked? The truth was, I had hardly wondered about my mother's childhood until now. "So why do you think she's letting me go?"

Beth shrugged. "I guess she didn't want her personal baggage to prevent a nice opportunity for you." She sighed. "I wish someone had invited me on a trip like that when I was still in high school."

"Maybe you could do it in college," I said.

She shook her head. "No time," she said. "This school is my one chance to make it as a dancer. I've got to give it all I've got."

At the field, Beth bumped into a few high school friends, and we found Lauren along with two of her brothers. Together, we found seats in the stands.

"You look great," Lauren said to Beth.

Beth shrugged modestly.

We all cheered when Chris scored his first touchdown. In the end zone, he kissed the cross dangling from his neck.

Just for a moment, because now I knew it could never happen, I allowed myself to imagine being his girlfriend. I would tell him I wanted him more than any calling, and G-d would release me from prophecy in service of *true love.* Chris would take me to parties, and kiss me whenever I wanted. The visions would stop, and I would forget everything Yonatan had taught me. I'd just be a happy teenager in love.

Lauren startled me from my reverie, passing a bag of salted almonds one of her brothers had brought. I took a handful and offered the bag to Beth, who passed it on silently.

"How's Mr. Marino?" Beth asked, following my gaze. "Are you guys still pretending you're friends?"

"Yep," I said sharply. "Still friends."

She waved her hands and leaned back, as if to avoid the fire coming out of my eyes. "Right," she said. "Friends."

Our team won 35-7. Chris never looked my way.

"Hi Rachel," a deep voice called as we came out of the stands. I turned to see him leaning against the wall, his baseball cap shielding his eyes, wearing a flannel shirt with sleeves too long, and the straggly blond remnants of an unshaven beard. Jake, the poet.

"Hi," I said.

"Who was that?" Beth asked, after we had passed.

"Just someone from Poetry Club," I said.

"*Oh.*" Lauren giggled. "*He's* the guy who said you were pretty?"

Beth raised her eyebrows, glancing back at him.

"It's a shame he's a stoner," Lauren said.

"I don't *know* if he was stoned," I said, embarrassed.

"He does look kind of sketchy," Beth said.

I knew they were right, but still I looked back. Standing with his open book, his face turned toward the sun, Jake looked almost beautiful. He waved at me, and without thinking too much about it, I waved back.

We turned into the parking lot and there was Chris, his tongue down the throat of a cheerleader named Emma Newman. They were leaning against someone's minivan, behaving as if a hundred people weren't walking by. Bile rose in my throat.

Silently, Lauren steered us toward the bicycle rack, so we could walk along the brick wall of the school. "It's okay," I muttered. "He has every right."

Lauren gave me a sad, knowing smile. "That's right," she said, soothing me. "And why would you want some guy who kisses girls in the middle of the school parking lot, anyway?"

I reminded myself what he had already told me. Those girls meant nothing to him. More importantly, I had already told him I could never be with him. So nothing had changed.

"I'm sorry, Rach," Beth said, as we climbed into the car.

I shook my head. "We're just friends," I said. But I hadn't heard from him once since Friday night. *Were* we still friends? Could we manage to stay friends at all?

CHAPTER 14

True to Mom's promise, she made a special effort to prepare low-fat dishes for Beth for Thanksgiving dinner. In addition to the kosher turkey, she roasted red potatoes in olive oil with rosemary, sautéed broccoli in soy sauce, and baked a low-fat apple kugel. She even made a special point to avoid serving matzo balls in Beth's chicken soup.

Dad had long ago established the tradition of spending Thanksgiving discussing what we appreciate about each other. So the conversation was light-hearted and warm, including appreciation for Mom's cooking and taking care of all of us, Dad's success with his book and the patients in his clinic, and Beth's efforts in college. Dad acknowledged me for my hard work in school, but with a growing stack of Bs and Cs crumpled in my backpack, I couldn't meet his eyes.

I ate several helpings, grateful everything was kosher, but Beth ate only the broth of the soup and a few pieces of broccoli with a small portion of turkey. She also drank a cup of wine, making jokes about the terrible beer she had tasted on campus.

For dessert, Mom served home-made baked apples, along with the usual pumpkin pie, which she also made from scratch. After watching Beth's paltry eating throughout the meal, Mom placed an apple on her plate without being asked.

"This looks so good, but I'm stuffed," Beth said. "I think it's time for me to go to sleep."

"Stuffed?" Mom spluttered. "You've hardly eaten –"

"I've eaten enough today," Beth said.

I might have protested, but at just that moment, a series of unexpected lights flashed in front of my eyes.

"Excuse me," I said, rushing for the hall bathroom. I heard Beth's light step on the stairs above me just before I collapsed.

The freight car rattles on, carrying more than a hundred souls to our final destination. There is no room to sit in the hot, foul-smelling darkness. I've had no water since we departed, and I fear some of the women near me are already dead.

Abruptly, I found myself on the floor of the bathroom, dread congealing in my veins. Though I'd seen the trains in movies, the Holocaust had never seemed so real.

My head was throbbing. For the second time that day, I covered my mouth and swallowed hard to keep from vomiting. Somehow, I knew it was the old woman Devorah in that awful freight car.

"Rachel?" Mom knocked from behind the door.

In the bathroom mirror, my eyes burned an otherworldly, incandescent green. I felt weak as a puddle on the floor.

"I'll be out in a minute," I said, sliding up against the wall to my feet.

***

"How are things going with your school applications?" Lauren asked, as we browsed for skirts at the mall the next morning.

"All right," I said, though I hadn't done more than download the questions into my computer. "Yours?"

She sighed, chewing a thumbnail. "Pretty well," she said. "I've finished almost everything for Yale. That one's due in just two weeks. But I want to apply to a few others, you know, just in case. To Maryland of course. I was also thinking of applying to GW, in case..." She glanced up at me and her intent was clear: *In case that's where you go.*

"That'd be great," I said, touched.

"It's a good school," she said, looking back at the skirts. "I mean, you know, I've always wanted to go to Yale. But if that doesn't work out...well, I'd like to be with my best friend."

I grinned. "Thanks."

We turned to a rack of dresses. "I don't know what people wear in Israel," she said. "Will any of these work for your trip?"

I shrugged, fingering a navy dress. "I don't know either." I wished I could have done this shopping with my mother, but it felt strange to talk to her about Israel, especially after what Beth had said. After much deliberation, I bought two skirts from the sale rack.

It was Black Friday, and the mall was packed with teenage boys in jeans and slides, harried mothers with whiny young children, and weary adults who had been there since opening. We took the escalator to the food court and waited in line.

I had just picked up an apple to go with my pizza when the lights swirled around me. It happened so fast I couldn't have escaped if I'd tried.

Flick at the lighter. Deep breath.

Snow. White crystals like shattered pieces of the white sky, reminding him of the first time he ever saw it. Four years old. Holding his mother's freezing fingers. The baby wrapped up tight against her chest, asleep.

They never went back.

My chest was burning. Flashes from the vision sliced through me like a knife.

Snow. A baby. A lighter. Fire.

It took several minutes before I noticed the anxious silence gathered around me. Had I been standing in line when — ?

"I called her mother." Lauren's voice was grave.

I opened my eyes to a crowd of people standing over me. A uniformed security guard was nearby, speaking into a walkie-talkie. My green apple had rolled a few feet away. Lauren crouched on the ground beside me, her face white as the snow in my vision.

∞

Mom rested her hand on my shoulder, waking me. Moments from the afternoon trickled back to me: Lauren's cold fingers on my arm. The sweet relief as the pain in my chest dissolved, leaving me like a wet rag on the tile floor of the mall. The clanging of my mother's keys as she approached; a dazed walk to her car. I barely remembered climbing the stairs to my bedroom.

Now, Mom sat perched in a chair beside my bed in the fading light of dusk, her hand warm on mine. Would she tell me anything I wanted to know, if I just asked? What would I have to tell her, in exchange? Right now, I only wanted to hide from her intense gaze.

"Lauren says you've been having migraines again," she said.

I looked away.

"You don't have to keep it a secret." Her fingers traced a circle on my palm. "How long has it been?"

Through my window, I could see the streetlights coming on. "A couple months."

She brushed her hand through my hair. "I wondered," she said. "These last a few weeks..." She shook her head. "We'll go to the doctor. It'll get better like before." She leaned forward and kissed my forehead. "Is it still hurting?"

"No," I said. "I feel better now."

"Have you been taking the Maxalt?" she asked. She had a pouch of the migraine medicine in her hand. She held it out, but I pushed her hand away.

"I don't like it," I told her.

"I know," she said. She set the pouch on my night table. "I'm sure the doctor will have something else we can try."

For just that moment, I pretended it was true; that I could go to doctors and they would make it all stop.

"Are you up for company?" she asked.

"Yeah," I said, sitting up. "Is Beth home?"

She shook her head. "She texted she'll be home late tonight. But I think you'll be happy to see who it is."

I heard his footsteps on the stairs, but my mouth still fell open when he came into view. He hadn't shaved and his cheeks had a shadow on them. My eyes caught on the gold cross hanging from his neck as he sat on the side of my bed and took my hand.

"Hey," Chris said.

There was so much to say, but I couldn't bring myself to say any of it. "Thank you for coming," I managed finally, my throat constricted with emotion.

He rubbed the back of my hand with his thumb, warming my whole body. "Lauren said you fainted at the mall?"

My cheeks burned. "It wasn't that big a deal."

He pressed his lips together, still stroking my hand. "I'm sorry I've been such an ass."

"Have you?"

"Kissing Emma in the parking lot." He lowered his eyes. "I was angry. It was stupid."

"Chris," I said, "I'm so –"

He stopped me, shaking his head. "You get to the point where you think you can have anyone," he said. "But you don't owe me anything, Rach."

"But I *am* sorry," I said in a small voice.

He touched the cross on his neck. "You shouldn't be." Then he leaned forward; I could smell peppermint on his breath. "I was wondering," he said, "if you fainted because of the ...thing ...we were talking about last week."

Of all people, how could I have told Chris? I wondered again. "Yeah," I said. "This week has been tough."

His eyes traced my face. "Is it because we – " He broke off before saying the word: *kissed.* Instead he finished, "I mean, because of our walk?"

My first instinct was to say no, but then I hesitated. Things *had* gotten worse since then.

"I don't know," I said honestly.

He reached forward to hug me. "You're going to be all right," he whispered.

"D-do you really think so?" I asked.

"Yeah," he said. "They were just talking about this at church on Sunday. When G-d calls a person, it can be a bumpy road. You need faith to get you through."

I marveled at how easy it was for him to talk about G-d. I'd never felt that kind of closeness with the divine.

"Yonatan says the beginning is always difficult," I told him. "I keep thinking if I can just get to Israel, maybe everything will make sense."

"I'll pray for you," he said.

"Chris," I said urgently, "you won't tell anyone, right?"

"Never," he promised solemnly. "How would G-d treat me if I screwed this up for you?"

"Thanks," I said.

More than anything, I wanted to kiss him again. But I knew I couldn't. Ever.

He stroked my cheek. "I'll see you," he said, and slipped out the door.

∽

In my dream that night, I was drowning. The pressure felt like a lead weight on my chest. I arched my back in a futile effort, struggling for air. *No.* My lips formed the word, but no sound came out. *No, not like this. Not yet.* I awakened gasping.

It was the middle of the night, but I lay awake for hours.

In the beginning, the visions had been occasional, painless, and brief. But since last Shabbat I'd had five of them, with worsening nausea, pain, even fainting. Now this dream of drowning. Could all of this really be explained by a divine calling? What if something terrible was happening to me?

Never had I wanted to meditate so much, but I held myself back, remembering Yonatan's warning: *Your choices have consequences.*

When the sky lightened, the first snowflakes of winter were falling from the gray sky. I walked in the slippery cold, wearing a new skirt meant for Israel. By the time I reached the synagogue, my legs felt numb.

I sank into my seat. But when I opened my siddur, I burst into tears.

I kept thinking back to Yom Kippur. Would I have agreed to learn with Yonatan then, if he had told me the visions would become so powerful, so painful, so debilitating? Surely I would have run in the other direction. But now it felt too late.

Maybe it was already too late by the time we met.

As the service progressed, I stared down at my book, avoiding the eyes of the women who came in. I waited until I heard the little boy singing, until I heard them gathering their sweaters and books, before I finally lifted my head.

Yonatan stood in the doorway, leaning on the doorjamb as he had when we first started meeting. I hadn't known then he looked so beautiful because of the mystical Light he was channeling toward me, but now I could feel it, restoring the broken pieces.

After several moments, he lifted his hand, beckoning me. "Come," he said, guiding me to the chilly library. Through the single window, I could see snow falling on an empty parking lot.

"I know how hard this week has been for you," he said quietly.

"Yonatan," I said slowly, trying to keep my voice under control. "I c-can't ...go on like this – it's too –"

"You're right," he said.

I stopped, surprised.

He pressed his fingers together in the shape of a circle on the table. "Human beings are vessels for G-d's Light. But right now, you are receiving too much – more than you can handle. The visions are overwhelming you."

A tremor seemed to pass between us. What if the visions started coming every day? What if I could no longer tell the difference between visions and reality?

"Maybe if I could just get a break?... from the visions...?" I said.

He shook his head ruefully. "Unfortunately, it is not possible to slow down," he said. "We need to increase your skills. To keep pace with your gifts."

"The meditation?" I guessed.

He nodded once. Then, strangely, I heard his voice, not aloud, but inside of me. *The meditation.* His eyes were gray and serious and I could see deep into them, to the place where they shone like silver, like the first day we met. We stared at each other for an intense moment.

Without his having to say it, I understood. Teaching me to meditate alone was a risk he had not wanted to take until we were in Israel. But there was no choice now. He had doubled his own connection with me just to make it possible. His whole being would now be devoted to protecting me, to make this work.

I felt ashamed I wasn't strong enough to do this on my own. "I'm sorry."

He shook his head. *"I am here for you,"* he reminded me, his unspoken words again ringing inside my mind.

I couldn't stop myself from asking. "Yonatan," I said, "is it …possible I have a brain tumor or some mental illness, and you're just…like a hallucination? I mean, you've never even touched me. What if you aren't even real?"

I was afraid he would vanish into thin air. Or laugh at me for asking the question. But he didn't flinch. "I understand," he said. "I know how hard it can be, to trust."

His presence was so calm and reassuring. Could a hallucination really make me feel this way?

"It's true, it hasn't been my practice to touch women," he said, hesitating only an instant before continuing. "But I will touch you now, so you'll know I'm real."

His hand reached forward, trembling a little. I realized he probably hadn't touched a woman since his wife. I held my hand out, not wanting to reach forward, but letting his hand come toward me. His large calloused fingers were warm and dry as they wrapped around mine.

I lifted my eyes from his fingers to his face. "Thank you."

"It's the least I can do for you, precious Rachel." He gently released me from his grasp.

I learned this from Yonatan. That G-d cared more about me and my sanity than the most stringent particulars of that law. That the practices of Jewish law could be compromised, just for a moment, just a little, to reassure a student in great distress.

This was one of the things that made me know I would follow him wherever he led.

CHAPTER 15

There, in the drafty library, against the discordant beats of the radiator, Yonatan taught me the secret words I was never to tell anyone. He explained about the fire, the storm, and the silence—the journey leading to the trance.

He explained that for those seeking prophecy without being chosen, this discipline might take years, or even a lifetime, before seeing a single vision. But for those called as prophets, the Light was so overwhelming that visions often came unsought, and with little warning, causing the problems I knew all too well.

"But the meditation can help," he said.

This time he did not say the words aloud. They came to me as a permanent impression on my spirit. I sensed his entire soul watching me as I entered the mystical space alone.

A breeze blows through the ancient stones.

"The calling may take more than a generation to return. The future of the world rests with the child who carries the flame of malchut.*"*

Zaide looks down at the infant, smiling though his eyes are filled with tears. "This one is called with the holiest gifts. And the younger will save the elder."

"Elisheva," he whispers. "Promise me."

With Yonatan's help, I repeated the secret words, again and again, until finally I opened my eyes. The details of the meditation were hazy but, as before, it seemed I'd traveled a great distance.

I knew Yonatan felt teaching me the meditation was risky, but I was eager to try again. "How often should I do this?"

"Once each day," he told me. Then his voice turned stern. "No more and no less. If you aren't able to enter the trance one day, just try again on the next."

I nodded in agreement.

"I will help you as much as I can," he said. "Will you be all right getting home?"

The snow was falling more thickly outside. With so much entrusted to Yonatan's care, it hardly seemed to matter anymore whether he knew where I lived.

"Could you walk me home?" I asked.

"Of course," he said.

Our coats were the only ones still hanging in the empty synagogue. Outside, the snow swirled down in eddies like fragmented pieces of sky. We walked together toward my house, our footsteps muffled in the frozen air.

"Did you have a job in Israel?" I asked him.

"I'm an artist," he said.

Now I understood his calloused fingers. "Really? What kind of art?"

"Blown glass, paintings, drawings, candles. I sell in Jerusalem in the night markets and other art exhibits. It's a good way to pass along a bit of wisdom when someone needs it," he said with a wink. "I never expected to be here now," he added, catching a snowflake in his bare hand. "But Devorah was right to send me. We're both...in transition. I'm glad not to be alone."

"Me too," I said.

As we came up my block, I was startled to see my mother sitting on the front porch in her jeans and winter coat. She stood when she saw us, braced herself and came down the steps.

"I'd like to meet her, if that would be all right," Yonatan said.

"M-meet her?" I spluttered. I stopped abruptly, but he continued toward my house. They met at the place where our path reached the sidewalk.

"Elisheva," he said. He was wearing a brown winter coat, his hood over his kipah, but I was suddenly aware of his beard, black pants, black shoes. Certainly to my mother, he was unmistakably an Orthodox Jew. She frowned up at him, tightening her coat around her in the falling snow.

"Surely you remember certain promises last through the generations," he said.

Astonished, I watched her eyes fill with tears.

"I've known for many years now," she said.

"Then go to peace, in blessing," he said. Without a word to me, he turned back down my street, disappearing into the snow.

I stood frozen in place until Mom came and put her arm around me, leading me back up the stairs and onto the porch sofa. "Sit with me," she said. "Have you been going to synagogue every week?"

I nodded, afraid she would be angry. But she only seemed thoughtful, gazing across the street at the snow-covered houses and cars.

"Why?" she asked.

"I like it there." At first, I thought I was lying. But as the words reverberated in my own head, I had to admit I did like it there. The cavernous sanctuary. The fervent chants of the prayer leader. The whispers of the praying women. Knowing Yonatan was there waiting for me.

She studied me another silent moment. "You must be freezing," she said, fingering my thin skirt.

"Yeah," I admitted.

"Leggings might help," she said. "I could pick up a pair or two, if you want."

I stared at Mom. I had been so afraid she would feel betrayed if she found out I was regularly going to synagogue. Now for the second time in a few weeks, it seemed like she was trying to help me.

"That would be great," I said.

"It might be best if you don't mention this to your father," she said. She smoothed the hair along the side of my face. "I'm glad you felt well enough to go, after yesterday," she said. "Head not hurting?"

I shook my head. "It's a lot better now."

"You should go inside and warm up," she said. She gave me a cautious smile. "Shabbat shalom."

Beth's room was much larger than mine, and still decorated with pictures of ballerinas, jazz dancers, and dancing movie stars. When we were younger, her room was often off-limits for me, so it always felt a little enchanting to spend time with her here.

Now her suitcase was open and half-full on the floor. She lifted it with surprising strength, given her thin arms, and dumped the clothing, then the suitcase, on the bed. I sat on her purple carpet as she folded things she hadn't worn and plopped them back into the bag.

"I brought the wrong kind of clothing," she said. "I forgot how cold it is here. Good thing my high school sweaters were still in the closet." She turned to look down at me. "Rach, did Mom say you *fainted* yesterday in the mall?"

I nodded. "I – I was just standing in line at the food court, and then – " I broke off, waving a hand. "I guess it's because of the migraines."

Her eyes softened. "Are they getting worse?"

I shrugged. "Maybe. I guess."

She came to sit next to me on the floor. "You've gotta take care of yourself," she said, running her long fingers through my tangled hair.

"You take care of *yourself*," I said, looking at her thin shoulders. "Beth..." I hesitated, then rushed ahead. "Are you eating enough?"

"Yes," she said firmly, meeting my eyes. "Look, Rach, Mom likes us to eat. But what she wants is not okay for a ballet dancer. Guys have to be able to lift me." She glanced away. "All the other girls eat like this."

I twisted my lips, uncertain. "Are you having fun dancing?"

Her face flushed with pleasure. "It's so...amazing," she said. "When I'm there on the stage – even in practice – and the music is playing, and we're all floating together like clouds – it's like a dream come true. This is what I've always wanted."

"I'm really glad," I said.

She squeezed my hands with her cold fingers, stood, turned on her toes and took a few light steps back toward her suitcase on the bed.

"I've missed you," I told her. "Will you please answer your phone when I call?"

She tilted her head, apologetic. "Sorry. Things can be crazy. I'll try to do better."

On Sunday morning, Beth sailed into the kitchen to give me a goodbye hug while I was eating cereal. Mom handed her a lunch bag she had packed for the plane. Dad was already loading her suitcase into the car.

"There's no time for you to eat breakfast," Mom said. "Do you want a granola bar for the car?"

Beth shook her head. "I'll grab something at the airport."

"I'll miss you," I said.

"Love you," she said. With a kiss and a wave, she was gone.

After they left, I locked my bedroom door. Sitting on my pillow on the floor, I whispered the words Yonatan had taught me, one by one, again and again in the silent house.

Meditation seemed to take much longer without Yonatan's guidance. *Was I doing it right?* I wondered. If I couldn't see anything, would I have to wait a whole day to try again?

Then, after a long wait...it all happened very fast: The shimmering, the fire. The storm. The silence.

...The guttering fire. Smoke. Flickering stars in the night sky. The smell of cedar trees. My own young hands cover my eyes. I creep out of the tent in a long, ragged nightgown and draw my knees to my chest by the fire.

"Was it a nightmare?" Noach asks, standing at the entrance to his own tent.

I shake my head. "Not a dream." My voice sounds like shattered glass. "A memory."

"Devorah," he asks gently, again, "were you in the camps?"

Gazing into his shining golden eyes, I admit it at last. "Yes."

Distantly, I became aware of Yonatan in the synagogue library, a Hebrew text unseen on the table in front of him. His attention was completely focused on me.

I repeated the words he had taught me, over and over and over, descending into my room. Gradually I became aware of my cold bare feet, my fingers clenched around the soft pillow. My back was tight from sitting so long, but there was no pain or exhaustion. Images from the vision flashed before me: *The flickering stars. The terror of the nightmare. The love in his eyes.*

When I opened my eyes, everything looked beautiful, sharply in focus, almost radiating with holy Light. I contemplated my own bedroom as if for the first time: my mirror and dresser, window and desk, bed covers matching the shaggy turquoise rug on the wood floor. I felt brightly, exuberantly alive.

I had done it. I had meditated successfully and returned in peace.

CHAPTER 16

After my first successful meditation, I made it a practice to turn off my bedroom lights each night, settle on a pillow, and whisper the holy words to enter a different world.

Some nights nothing happened. Other times I sat in the snow near a shallow, half-frozen stream, or lay in bed, looking up at the Jerusalem moon. I might see Beth dancing, or an old prophet praying in a house at the top of a mountain. The glint of a knife in the darkness. A long row of flags fluttering in the wind. Other times I would see trains and smoke and forests covered with snow in the dark. Some nights I was frightened by what I saw, but as I descended, the images faded, like dreams upon awakening.

Meditation wasn't like the unexpected visions, with their pain and terror and exhaustion. The experience left me invigorated. So I began to love the people I saw, their darkness and light, without really having any idea who they were.

Once I started meditating, the unexpected visions improved dramatically. Even Yonatan, who seemed to be constantly watching over me, was surprised how much it helped. As my skills improved, Yonatan began to meditate with me instead of guiding me, our souls journeying together into mystical worlds.

Without comment, Mom left leggings and a pair of warmer boots on my bed for my continuing pilgrimages to synagogue. In our lessons, Yonatan shared details about the prophets in Israel. Devorah was in the Old City of Jerusalem, near the Western Wall – which was called the *Kotel* in Hebrew. Other prophets lived in the holy city of Tzfat. He said prophecy and visions were often stronger in Israel, but assured me I was ready.

In our final meditation together, I watched his spirit step toward the large stones of the Kotel. He placed his hands, then his forehead against it. Flashes of light ignited his soul like a beacon.

What was he praying for? I still couldn't read his mind.

"Haven't heard about Mr. Orthodox in a while," Maya said as I climbed into her car, on our way to the mall the week before the trip to Israel. "It's been what, three months?"

"Something like that," I said.

"That's almost...serious," she said. She accelerated through a green light, her hands loose on the wheel. "Are you in love with him?"

My eyes widened. "In—in love?" I said. "No."

Maya's face softened. "Oh, Rach." I'd unintentionally given her the answer she feared. "Is he hoping you'll become Orthodox for him?"

"Maybe," I said.

She steered the car into the parking lot. "You don't have to," she said, pausing at a stop sign. "There are plenty of other boys. Maybe we'll find you someone in Israel."

I shrugged. The only man I planned to meet in Israel was Yonatan.

Mom and Dad brought me to the bus at the local Jewish Community Center early on the Tuesday morning before Christmas. I had been up most of the night, finishing my applications to GW and the University of Maryland.

Across the parking lot, I spotted Maya chatting with some of her youth group friends. Even this early, they were all wearing makeup. I ran my fingers through my wet ponytail, tucked into a baseball cap after a quick shower.

Dad pulled my duffel bag out of the trunk and wheeled it toward a pile of others. Mom reached into her purse and pulled out a dollar. "Give this to charity when you get there." I tilted my head at her, puzzled. "G-d watches over messengers of charity," she said.

Did she actually believe G-d would watch over me? What did she think about G-d? I still had no idea.

Mom set her coffee mug on top of the car and pulled me close. I could smell her lavender soap as she whispered, "Be safe."

I tried to put a lot of meaning into that hug: gratitude for the kosher food and the leggings and her permission to go on this trip. When I looked up, there were tears in her eyes, so maybe she understood.

Dad came back and slung an arm around me. "Have fun." He winked. "See you next year."

There were twenty-nine juniors and seniors on the trip, eighteen girls and eleven boys. "Lousy odds," Maya had commented when we received the participant list. But we had barely reached the airport when she started chatting with a cute guy in a navy sweatshirt. I didn't know anyone other than her, so I pulled out my phone and paced the long airport hallway, sending texts to Lauren, Chris, my parents, and Beth.

Though I knew I wouldn't find him here, I was looking for Yonatan. We hadn't made any plans for how or where we'd meet. *When was he leaving?* I wondered. What if, for some reason, he couldn't come?

I reminded myself I trusted Yonatan with my life.

Despite Maya's interpretations, I knew for certain I was not in love with him. He was grieving his poor wife, and he was more than fifteen years older than me. But I had no easy way to explain how desperate I was to see him right now. The feeling was similar to how Devorah seemed to have felt about her teacher so long ago: fascination, gratitude, and that twinge of fear I couldn't live without him.

The first leg of our journey was just a short flight to Newark. "Did you see him?" Maya said, as we buckled our seatbelts on the plane.

For one instant, I thought she might have spotted Yonatan. But she was gesturing with her head toward the kid in the navy sweatshirt, a few rows behind us. "His name is Matt. That's the boy I'm going to fall in love with."

"Good luck," I said.

"He has a cute friend," she added.

I shook my head. "Thanks, no."

On our second flight, from Newark to Tel Aviv, I waited until she was asleep before trying to meditate. Glancing around to be sure no one was watching, I began to recite the words. But I had only whispered them a few times when I felt a sharp bolt of pain in my chest.

I looked down, eyes wide, almost expecting to see a knife cutting into my heart. Then, powerless to protect myself, I endured the fire, the storm, the silence...and slipped away.

Russet-colored stones, dirty. Cigarette butts crushed into a storm drain. I am lying on the ground. Above me, a long blue rectangle of Jerusalem sky. My voice, ancient and weak, asks for help.

A hand reaches out to me. I hesitate, then grasp it with all my strength.

I awoke, gasping, twisted in agony, overcome by the pain in my chest.

The blue rectangle of sky. The dirty stones of the ground. The hand extended, the hand taken. The pain.

The pain. I massaged my fingers against my chest. It was even worse than the pain after Thanksgiving, before I started meditating regularly. I kept shifting in my seat, trying to find a way to contain it.

Yonatan had said prophecy and visions were stronger in Israel. Could this be what he meant? We hadn't even arrived.

I opened my eyes to the darkened plane. Next to me, Maya was snoring gently. She seemed small and young as I watched her sleep. At the front of our section, a map showed our location: somewhere over Europe. Behind us, a group of religious men gathered to pray, their jumbled words rough in the darkness.

I'd never felt pain with meditation before. But this pain had begun even before the trance. Did it have some kind of meaning? I listened for Yonatan, as I could often sense his presence after meditation, but I couldn't seem to find him tonight. Were we still connected while I was in the middle of the sky?

The pain was still with me when the plane lights turned on. Maya awakened, stretched, and went to the bathroom. Breakfast was served. She ordered decaf coffee for me, but I couldn't make myself drink. I stared out the window at an incongruous sunrise, my body still convinced it was the middle of the night.

I decided I would ask for a doctor if the pain continued. But just as we landed, it dissolved.

CHAPTER 17

Later that morning, our bus brought us to the Tayelet promenade, and we began our tour with a panoramic view of Jerusalem. Though my chest had stopped hurting, my fingers kept probing the spot where I'd felt the pain, as if it held the answers I was seeking.

I gazed toward the ancient walls of the Old City, the golden Dome of the Rock stretching into the sky. Until recently, I had never even considered coming to this city that was holy to so many. The previous summer, I had just been a teenager working at a swim club, looking ahead to nothing more than a fun senior year in high school, then college. Now, here I stood in Jerusalem.

"I'm here," I said into the wind. Was I speaking to Yonatan? The prophets? G-d? Maybe just to myself. "I made it here."

From her place on the promenade, Heather, the tour guide, began to describe the history of Jerusalem, a story that continued during our tour the next several days. We visited Machane Yehuda, the shuk with its many colorful stands selling wine, fish, spices, and vegetables, and we sampled sesame paste and dried fruits. We packed food baskets for the needy, and visited the Herzl museum, where we learned about Theodore Herzl's dream of a free homeland for the Jews. We ate falafel with fries, and schwarma[15] on pita with hummus. Every single restaurant we chose was kosher. I looked for Yonatan everywhere we went, but found him nowhere.

Every night, after the other girls went to sleep, I faithfully continued my meditations. The pain didn't come back, but I did notice the trance seemed to come more quickly here. As with my meditations at home, some nights the visions were sharply clear; others were like dreams that dissolved on waking.

⚬⚬⚬

She grips the phone. "Yes," she whispers, squeezing her eyes shut. Every promise has a moment.

---

[15] Schwarma is a common Middle Eastern food: roasted turkey or lamb, usually cooked on a rotating spit.

On Wednesday night, I awakened after meditation, my mother's voice resounding in my ears. *Yes.*

On Thursday afternoon, while walking the long, winding cobblestone streets of the Old City, I felt a wave of déjà vu.

Dirty brown stones, cigarette butts crushed into a storm drain with the shape of a lion embossed on it. Above me, a long blue rectangle of Jerusalem sky.

This was the place where she had fallen.

Who? I asked myself. *When? Was the vision even real?* Maybe it had taken place years ago, or was still far in the future. I stood still, disoriented.

"Rach," Maya called, from around a corner the rest of the group had already turned.

I scampered to catch up with them.

On Friday evening, Heather brought us back to the Old City of Jerusalem to pray at the Kotel. The sun setting behind us in the west, we stood at the outlook point at the top of the stairs, gazing down at the crowd of Jews gathered in front of the Wall. When Heather finished her lecture, we descended a long flight of stairs, through a metal detector, and into the courtyard.

A few feet into the plaza, I stopped, barely noticing the other girls walking ahead without me. I could feel the Light, a current of energy reverberating in my chest like music.

Drawn by the Light, I walked slowly toward the Wall. In the women's section, small groups clustered at the long mechitzah; individual women prayed silently in plastic chairs.

I felt pulled not only to this place but to this moment, through months and maybe years of my life. I put my forehead on the Kotel, and rested my hands on it. It was warm beneath my fingers.

For the first time in my life, I knew I was exactly where I was meant to be.

"G-d," I prayed.

The only answer was the sound of the wind, and the whispered prayers all around me. The Kotel was smooth as stone pressed beneath thousands of fingertips, and present like something alive.

"G-d," I said again.

I kept my forehead pressed against the Kotel a long time, feeling something I could barely understand: A bond not with the wall but with Something else. Something holy. Something real.

Forging, at last, my own connection with G-d.

A hand rested on my shoulder. "Rach," Maya said. "It's time for dinner."

Reluctantly, I lifted my forehead. Only a few solitary women remained in the chairs behind me.

I backed away from the Wall as I had seen the others do; it felt natural not to turn away from this Place. Beside me, Maya was also walking backwards. We turned from the tiled women's section to the stone courtyard, where Heather was waiting for us. I blinked, to be sure I wasn't dreaming.

Yonatan stood beside her.

He wore a navy suit with a blue tie and a colorful knit kipah. His silver eyes twinkled like lanterns in the darkness.

He dipped his head in a tiny nod. *"Nice to see you here."* His words reverberated in my mind.

My mouth opened but no sound came out.

"With your permission, Rachel," Yonatan said aloud, "I asked Heather if I could borrow you tonight."

"Sounds good," I finally managed to say.

"Yonatan will bring you back to the hotel after dinner," Heather said.

My mind was spinning with surprise and confusion. Beside me Maya gawked at the three of us. I gave her fingers a squeeze, to show I wanted this.

Yonatan spread his hands. "Ready?"

I gave a shy nod. "Ready," I said.

I followed him toward the Jewish quarter, glancing back once to see Maya still staring after us.

"Yonatan...where are we going?" I asked, struggling to catch up.

"To Devorah's."

Devorah's? He said it so simply, but my mouth went dry.

He led me up a set of stairs, past the Roman columns Heather had identified on a tour of the Old City the day before. We continued uphill along stone paths and narrow alleys through the Jewish quarter, past the place I had felt such familiarity the day before. Here I finally found my voice.

"Why did Heather let you take me?"

We turned into a dark alley of stone walls and he finally faced me, his eyes shining brighter than I'd ever seen before. "She understood," he said.

We came to a metal door engraved with a Jewish star. I drew back, astonished.

"I've seen this door," I said. "In a..."

He smiled. "In a vision? This is the entrance to Devorah's apartment."

Together, we climbed three flights of stairs, past children playing in hallways and mothers setting tables in apartments, smelling baked bread and chicken soup, to a door with a gold-plated mezuzah. Yonatan knocked before opening the door.

Devorah stood just past the doorway. *"Rahel,"* she said, turning my Hebrew name into a song with her gentle European accent.

For a time, I couldn't move past the threshold, staring at her round, kind face. I had seen her so many times in visions and meditation, I felt I was reuniting with an old friend.

Yonatan was always the one giving me Light, but it seemed Devorah and I were exchanging it. As my fear and confusion washed away, I also sensed her spirit being uplifted.

"Welcome to my home," she said, stepping forward to draw me in.

The apartment smelled of incense and fresh flowers. The small living room had a sofa draped with a colorful afghan, two old-fashioned upholstered wooden chairs, and an antique wooden coffee table with curved feet standing on a hooked wool rug. The walls were decorated with colorful paintings. Two lit gold oil lamps flickered beside an open window. In the corner of the room stood a walking cane with a quad base.

In real life, Devorah was small and aged, like an ancient miniature doll of the young and vigorous woman I had seen in visions. She wore a simple white blouse with a long, purple skirt, her white hair pulled back with a hand-dyed scarf of the same colors. Her fingers were crinkled like old silk. Her shining eyes were a blue as deep as the sea.

In the dining room, we stood around a polished wood table and sang "Shalom Alechem," the traditional song welcoming Shabbat. The melody reminded me of Friday nights spent with Zaide. Yonatan made Kiddush, the blessing over wine; then he showed me how to wash my hands with the copper washing cup in Devorah's sink. After the blessing over the bread, we ate challah[16] in silence.

---

[16] Braided rolls traditionally eaten on the Jewish Sabbath.

The moment was so perfect I feared I might do something careless to ruin it, like flick a light switch. For the first time, I felt embarrassed by my lack of Jewish observance. I wanted to immerse myself in the holiness of this place.

Yonatan and Devorah held each other's eyes. There was such wisdom and understanding in their shared gaze. Could that be possible for me, if I became the prophetess they said I was meant to be?

"You will grow into all of this, dear Rahel," Devorah assured me, standing up to bring in the soup. Like Yonatan, she seemed to know what I was thinking. She returned with a pot, but she let Yonatan serve the soup to us.

Her hand trembled as she lifted her spoon. "How have you found Jerusalem?"

I knew she wasn't asking about Heather's historical monologue or the tours. "Visiting the Kotel tonight was – special," I told her. "It felt like a moment I'd waited for...all of my life."

She pressed her warm hand on my wrist; as a woman, she had no concerns about touching me. "Indeed you have been called to this moment," she said. "And it is a marker on the road toward other moments."

I took a sip of the warm soup. "Until my grandfather died last summer, I never imagined I could be part of all this. I didn't even really know I wanted to."

Devorah tasted her soup, watching me carefully. "I knew your grandfather."

Carefully I set down my spoon. "You did?"

She straightened her napkin on her lap, smiling fondly. "Moshe. A bit of a troublemaker, he was, as a child." She stared into the distance. "Our mothers were friends. His holy grandfather was our rabbi." She held her fingers in a tight fist, then spread them wide. "But he escaped alone." Her eyes refocused on me. "He had a good life?"

I thought of my grandfather, the children and grandchildren and great-grandchildren, the hundreds of people who mourned at his funeral. And I remembered the dream I'd had, of the key he'd left and I had picked up.

"Yes," I said, "he did."

She smiled.

"He used to tell me stories, about his grandfather. Even about prophecy, but I didn't know they were true."

She chuckled. "Sometimes wisdom comes through stories, to children who can barely believe them," she said.

As Yonatan cleared the soup bowls, I thought of Zaide's holy grandfather, *my* great-great-grandfather. This was the man who had been Devorah's rabbi in Europe before the war. I watched the flickering flames by Devorah's window, feeling, for the first time, my own place in the chain of Jewish generations.

"What was he like?" I asked. "The rabbi?"

Devorah's eyes drifted away again, to the past. "He was one of the beloved ones," she said. "So deeply connected that simply to be in his presence was to receive abundant Light. Jews from all over Poland came to see him, to seek his blessing. He never turned away a single one."

"What happened to him?" I asked.

Her hands again clenched into fists, but her eyes remained unfocused as she answered. "They murdered him. He kept his faith until the end."

"But you survived," I said.

"Yes." She shook herself, returning to the present moment. "I survived, to discover how much beauty is possible in life, even after great darkness." She glanced at Yonatan, but he looked away. "You've been very brave these last months, Rahel."

I folded my hands on the table. "It's nothing compared to what you – " I looked up at both of them – "what you've been through. Still, if not for Yonatan ..."

Devorah smiled fondly. "Yes," she said, "what would we do without Yonatan?"

Now their eyes met again, that strange vulnerability and friendship. "And you, Gedolah," he said. "What would we do without you?"

As we finished the main course, I found the courage to ask the question that had been troubling me all week. "On the flight here, when I meditated...I felt this horrible pain," I said. "I wasn't sure what it meant."

"What kind of pain?" Yonatan asked.

"In my chest," I said, placing my hands to show them. "Like being stabbed. In the meditation I had fallen on the ground... It was daytime. We passed the place on our way here tonight."

As I spoke, both Yonatan and Devorah turned to stare at me. I looked from one to the other, suddenly afraid. "Is something wrong?"

"Take her to Tzfat next Shabbat," Devorah instructed Yonatan. "They need to see her."

"Are you sure?" he asked. "The others haven't –"

"I can't," I said. "My program –"

"They'll let Yonatan take you," Devorah said briskly.

Yonatan raised his eyebrows at her. "Are you sure?" he asked again.

She looked at Yonatan, then back to me. "Yes," she said. "It's time."

CHAPTER 18

E verything in the regular world seemed dim and mundane compared to Devorah's home. I collapsed onto a sofa in the hotel lobby after Yonatan dropped me off, almost dizzy with unanswered questions. How would we get to Tzfat? What would Yonatan tell Heather?

I'd tried to ask these questions on the way back, but he simply said, "I'll make the arrangements." His chin jutted high into the air, almost as if he was breathing in the stars. Or trying not to cry.

As I sat there, two teenagers fell into the sofa across from mine, kissing passionately. After a moment, I realized it was Maya, entangled with that boy Matt. Embarrassed for them, I hurried up the stairs to our room.

I was brushing my teeth when she finally came in, lipstick smudged, hair disheveled. "He kissed me," she announced.

I spat before turning to face her. "I know."

She sighed. "It was so romantic," she said. "We started after dinner, in one of the dark alleys of the Old City." Then she glanced at me. "How was *your* night? Who was that man you went with?"

I shrugged away the temptation to tell her *he* was the man I'd been meeting Saturday mornings. "A cousin of my mom's," I lied. "I think he leads tours around here sometimes."

"Hmm," Maya said, going to the bathroom to wash her face.

I climbed into bed, dodging any further questions.

⌒⌒

After Maya fell asleep that night, I crawled out of bed and sat against the wall, whispering the holy words. The prophets' world seemed to hover nearby. The trance came almost immediately.

"Her mother will need to give permission. For Tzfat."

He nods. "I'll arrange for it."

"She's bright and strong," I add, my ancient fingers stroking the afghan between us on the sofa. "When the time comes, she will be ready."

His agreement is like a soundless wail.

As I whispered the words that would return me to hotel room, I became aware of the carpeted floor beneath my fingers, the textured wallpaper against my back.

I had seen Yonatan and Devorah in her living room, but their Hebrew words were out of my reach. All I could remember was their deep sadness. *Was it because of me?*

Though it had only been hours since we parted, I felt desperate to see Yonatan again. It seemed impossible to wait a whole week.

⬯

We left Jerusalem on Sunday morning, heading south toward the Negev. Heather spoke to us about David Ben Gurion, the first prime minister of Israel, and we visited a kibbutz called Sde Boker where he had lived. Maya spent most of her time with Matt, but took the time to ride a camel with me.

That evening, over dinner in a Bedouin tent, Maya led Matt over to meet me. He had chestnut eyes, brown hair that hung loose around his ears, and a heartbreaking smile. He stood behind Maya, one hand resting on her shoulder, the other stroking her arm. Maya leaned toward him like a safety net. Watching them, I felt a grudging admiration for Maya. She knew exactly how to capture a boy.

⬯

The next morning, we awoke before dawn to climb Masada, a rock plateau in the desert overlooking the Dead Sea. Jewish rebels had lived here after the destruction of the second Holy Temple in Jerusalem, Heather explained.

We reached the fortification at the top just after sunrise, and wandered from ruin to ruin, exploring the signs of Jewish communal life, seeing the marks of destruction by fire. Their remains reminded me how many other destructions Jews had suffered and survived long before the Holocaust. Seeing how their memory had endured through history gave me a sense of peace.

Through a window in a stone wall, I looked down at the Dead Sea, sparkling in sunlight. Then the gleaming light of the sea turned to shimmering and I backed into a corner, shaking hard. As the others moved on, I slipped down the wall into the dirt.

The girls flutter like birds, legs and arms twirling as they complete their combinations. When the music stops, they hold still several seconds, as if in anticipation of applause.

109

A broken fingernail in the drain. Two mornings in a row.
"I could still stand to lose a few pounds."
Tall candles gleam in silver candlesticks on the buffet along the wall.
"Beth...?" My mother's voice.

A warm dry wind on my face. Fingers curled in the dust. *Beth.* In the vision, I had seen her dancing; I had heard my mother's voice calling to her. My stomach twisted anxiously. Was she all right?

I reached into my bag for my phone, but it was the middle of the night at home. I sent a text: *Love from Masada. Thinking of you all.*

Still trembling a little, I put the phone back in my bag.

After lunch, I pulled out my phone and dialed our number, hoping to catch Beth alone at home while my parents were at work. I just needed to hear her voice, to know she was okay. But no one answered.

I finally reached Mom the next night. "Howard, come to the phone. It's Rachel!" Mom said. "Where are you, honey?"

"We're in Eilat." I gazed through the window of my empty hotel room to the darkening sky. This morning we had visited beaches and the underwater observatory at the southern tip of Israel. "How's Beth?"

"She's good," Mom said. "Dancing every day. Busy with schoolwork and seeing friends."

A weight lifted from my chest. "I'm so glad."

"It's snowing here," Dad said. "Christmas Eve."

For the first time since arriving, I thought of Chris. When I was little, we often spent Christmas Eve at his house, their tree decorated with presents under it, his little brother and sister singing *Silent Night.*

"You can't even tell it's Christmas here," I said.

I told them about Jerusalem, Masada, the Dead Sea, Eilat, carefully editing out details about my visit to Devorah's apartment and my upcoming trip to Tzfat.

"They've been giving us a real education about Israel's history, too," I told them. "We're going to Tel Aviv next."

"Sounds like a great experience," Dad said.

"Has it been a meaningful trip?" Mom asked, her tone almost too casual.

I imagined her twirling a strand of her hair around a finger, listening for the significance beyond my words.

"Yes," I said.

In Tel Aviv, we visited Independence Hall, where Israel's Declaration of Independence had been signed, and Rabin Square, which memorialized the prime minister who had been assassinated decades before. On the bus, I took out my half-filled poetry journal and scribbled fragments of poems about the land of Israel, the heroes of Jewish history, and my realizations about the long chain of Jewish history stretching from past to future.

I had heard nothing from Yonatan, and as the days passed, I began to wonder if I had misunderstood. Was *I* supposed to make arrangements? Had the plans changed? Finally, on Thursday evening, I approached Heather after dinner.

"Heather, for tomorrow," I said.

"Right," Heather said, marking something on her clipboard. "Yonatan will pick you up at nine."

All the real world seemed to dissolve around me. "He will?"

"That's the plan," she said, squinting and gesturing toward me with a pencil. "You have family in Tzfat?"

"Yeah," I said, catching on quickly.

"You can leave your duffel bag with us, and just take what you need for Shabbat. We'll catch up with you in Tzfat on Sunday."

I swallowed. "Great," I managed to answer. "Thanks."

In my empty hotel room, aware of my heart beating under Zaide's star necklace, I separated my Shabbat things into my backpack and zipped everything else back into my duffel bag. Then I sat on the bed, staring at myself in the mirror. I was going to Tzfat with Yonatan. Tomorrow.

I didn't seem to have a choice. But, really, when had Yonatan ever given me a choice about anything? Yet hadn't I asked for all this, one bright and holy Yom Kippur morning, just four months ago?

It was hard to believe how much had happened since then. But I gathered my courage to continue this path, wherever it led.

CHAPTER 19

When Maya burst into the door, I looked up in alarm. Her face was flushed, her mascara smeared.

"What's wrong?"

"Nothing," she snapped, and rushed into the bathroom to wash her face.

Hurriedly, I joined her at the double sink. She dried her face, avoiding my eyes in the mirror as she picked up her toothbrush.

"What happened?" I asked.

She shook her head, blinking back tears. "Matt is just a –" My eyes widened as she let out a stream of curses. She slammed her toothbrush against the counter and stormed out of the bathroom. I followed her to her bed. She grabbed for her nightgown and pulled it on, then stood there, paralyzed with fury.

"We were in his room," she said. "He told the other guy to stay out late tonight. I think he was trying to be romantic. I mean he had music. But when I said I didn't want to..." she trailed off, staring out the hotel window.

"Did he hurt you?"

She shook her head. "He cursed at me. He called me..." She buried her head in her hands.

What could he have called her? Dozens of words ran through my head.

"Chink," she said, spitting out the word. "He called me an f-ing chink."

I gasped. It was true Maya's mother was Asian, but she had been raised a Jew her whole life. I was sure no one had ever called her that word before. "What the hell," I said.

"My mom's not even from China," she said. "Her family is from the Philippines."

She threw herself on the bed and grabbed a pillow, which she punched a few times before laying it across her lap. Then she threw the pillow back on the bed and lay face down into it. "I always pick the wrong guys," she said, in a muffled cry. "They only want one thing..."

I sat beside her, rubbing her back while she cried. I had never known this about Maya. I thought she liked the shallow flirtations, the purely physical relationships she had with the boys in school. I didn't realize all this time she had been hoping for something more.

"Thought he was...different," she said, beginning to sob.

"I'm so sorry," I said. I sat with her until the sobs evened out into heavy breathing. Finally, she fell asleep.

When I awoke the next morning, Maya was already up, knees curled under her nightgown on her bed. "I'm not going to tell anyone why we're not together anymore," she said, as if she'd been thinking about it a long time. "Let them come to their own conclusions. Help me avoid him this weekend, okay?"

"Um," I said. "Actually...it turns out I'm going away for Shabbat."

Her eyes widened. "You're...what? Where?"

"I'm going to stay with my mother's cousins in Tzfat," I said.

Maya tilted her head. "How will you get there?"

"Someone's picking me up this morning." I stood and hurried to the bathroom, eager to end the conversation, but when I came out, Maya was by the door. She watched as I pulled on the skirt I'd set out the previous night.

"Are they Orthodox?" she asked.

"I don't know," I said. "Maybe. Yeah."

She inhaled sharply. "Rach," she said in a warning tone. "Do you want to wear skirts for the rest of your life?"

I bit the inside of my cheek, feeling that, if I did become Orthodox, there might be greater difficulties than wearing skirts. But hadn't I decided last night I would go wherever this path took me?

Maya's mouth fell open as she watched me consider her question.

"Of course not," I said. I zipped up my bags and swung out of the room, leaving her still in her nightgown, staring after me.

My thoughts swirled as I walked down the stairs. Would Maya be okay alone without me? What if she told my mother where I was going? Was I really going to have to wear skirts for the rest of my life? Then I opened the door to the lobby and all my worries dissolved like salt in water.

There he stood, in jeans and a blue polo shirt, a colorful knitted kipah on his head. He had let his beard and hair grow longer than I'd seen before, and his eyes shone like tiny candles in the middle of the bright sunlit lobby. He handed Heather's clipboard back to her; it was clear he had signed me out.

"Good morning, Rachel," Yonatan said. "Are you ready?"

I nodded, speechless, and followed him outside.

Yonatan led me to a dusty blue Kia hatchback, with only two doors. He opened the passenger door for me and let me settle my backpack in the front seat before backing out onto the street.

Seeing Yonatan drive a car was a little like bumping into a teacher in a grocery store or movie theater. Until now, I'd only see him on Shabbat and holidays. I watched as he drove confidently on the Israeli streets. Was this really the prophet who had led me into the depths of meditation and could speak to me inside my mind?

As we turned onto the highway, the strands of silver in his beard caught the morning sunlight. A little smile lit his face, and he began to hum. I realized that – for the first time since I'd known him – he was happy.

"Do you like it there?" I asked, breaking the silence. "In Tzfat?"

"It's my favorite place in the world," he said.

The first part of the drive was northward, along the coast, but the climate changed as we turned east and began to ascend into the mountains. We closed the car windows, and Yonatan put on the heat. The sky turned cloudy and speckles of sleet splashed the windshield.

The trip took two hours. At last we drove into Tzfat, past the central bus station and up a curved road, past the ruins of ancient buildings and ice-coated cypress trees, to the residential area. Impervious to the gloom, Yonatan began to hum again.

"The other side of the mountain is the Old City," he said. "This neighborhood is called Ma'ale Canaan." The houses here were made of stone and marble, with long, distant views across valleys to other mountains in the distance, and long staircases leading down to entrances below. Yonatan parked the car.

My heart beginning to race again, I lifted my backpack and followed him along the wet street, past a water tower, to a large house with several entrances.

"This is it," he said. "The prophets' house."

The building looked like most of the others nearby. The walls were a combination of marble, stone, and cement. The building was set into the hillside so one could enter the upper level from the top, or the lower level by a side door. A long veranda, with tables and stacked chairs, stretched along the side of the house.

Yonatan led me to the side door. He hesitated just a moment, his closed hand poised in front of the door, before he knocked. When it opened, I nearly fainted.

Before me stood a man I'd seen only in visions: the young man from the kibbutz, the ancient prophet on the mountain. He was tall and thin, with a full gray beard that reached his chest. Silver wire glasses framed his bright, golden-brown eyes. His pleated forehead extended to a large, white, loosely knitted kipah, of the kind Yonatan often wore in Baltimore. His smile was warm as sunshine.

"Shalom aleichem[17]," he said greeting us.

"Aleichem shalom," Yonatan responded. "Rachel, this is Noach."

At first I thought they were going to shake hands, but Noach pulled Yonatan into a broad embrace. "Welcome home, *beni*[18]," he said. Over Yonatan's shoulder, his eyes met mine. "Shalom, *Rahel*," he said, calling me by my Hebrew name.

"Hello," I choked out.

"It's good to see you too," he said kindly, releasing Yonatan and turning back toward the house.

Yonatan beckoned me inside, to a large and uncluttered living room. There were colorful woodcut decorations on the walls, and an old wooden rocking chair with flowers painted on it. As we entered, two men and a woman stood up from brown leather sofas. Two more women came to the door of the kitchen, and three men hurried down the steps to greet us.

The men all had beards, but they wore a variety of head coverings: black, white, colored, a baseball cap, and in one case, a black hat like my grandfather's. The women wore dresses and skirts, blues and purples and dark reds. Some wore bright scarves covering their hair.

Yonatan approached his friends like a man moving toward a mirage in a desert. He embraced the men and greeted the women warmly in Hebrew, his fingers pressed behind his back to restrain himself from hugging them.

Noach cleared his throat to introduce me. "This young prophetess is *Rahel*. She will also join us for Shabbat." He gestured to the others one

---

[17] "Shalom Aleichem" (Peace be upon you) is a traditional Jewish greeting. The traditional response is "Aleichem shalom" and means the same thing (literally, "upon you, peace").

[18] My son.

by one, giving them names: Shoshana, Rena, Tirtza, Yechezkel, Yitzchak, Nehemiah, Michael, Moshe.

"Welcome, Rahel," said a woman from the kitchen doorway. She had wavy brown hair and caramel colored eyes, and wore a blue patchwork dress over a white blouse. "Would you like to freshen up? I'll show you downstairs."

I glanced at Yonatan, who was already engrossed with the others, speaking in Hebrew. The lines of tension around his eyes had disappeared; he looked ten years younger. He nodded approvingly and turned back to his friends.

"My name is Rena," the woman said, reaching out her hand. "Welcome to Tzfat."

She unlocked a door which led to an apartment separate from the main house. I followed her down a dark flight of stairs, to a room with fluorescent lighting and four sets of bunk beds. The walls were bare cement, but someone had painted flowers on them, giving the room a barren beauty. On the tile floor was a wool rug similar to the one in Devorah's apartment. Along one wall was a wooden bookshelf, overflowing with Hebrew books. A second bookshelf was half filled with books but also included a vase of dried flowers, several small pieces of pottery, and a mirror. There was a small kitchenette in the corner.

"This is where you'll sleep," Rena told me, setting a towel on a bed made up with white sheets, a soft brown blanket, and a pillow. She gestured to a door in the corner of the room. "And here's the bathroom."

"Thank you," I said.

"Have you come a long way?" she asked.

I hesitated. "Just from Tel Aviv this morning. But I'm from Baltimore. Devorah asked Yonatan to bring me," I said, as if in justification. "I didn't know I was coming until – well, really until last night."

She burst out a laugh. "He does draw out the mystery, doesn't he?" She rolled her eyes toward the ceiling as if she could still see Yonatan upstairs. "He could have given you some warning."

"No, Yonatan has been great," I said in his defense. "It's just ...when I saw Devorah on Friday night –"

"You saw Devorah?" Rena said eagerly, sitting down on the bed across from mine. "How is she? What did she say?"

I sat on my bed, absently folding and unfolding my towel. "She seemed okay," I said. "I guess. I'd never seen her before in real life."

"In real life," Rena repeated.

"I mean I..." I felt confused by how much Rena didn't know. Yonatan always seemed to know everything before I even said it. "I mean maybe I... dreamed about her," I said lamely.

"But why did she send you here?" Rena asked.

"She said...something about you all needing to see me," I said evasively, gazing around the room. There were four sets of bunk beds along the walls. Eight beds. All but mine seemed to be in active use. Could they all be occupied by prophetesses?

Turning back to Rena, I blurted out: "Are you a prophetess?"

She laughed. "Yes," she said, meeting my eyes. "Can't you tell?"

I bit my lip uncertainly. "No."

She sighed in mock exasperation. "Hasn't Yonatan taught you anything?! It's in the eyes." She widened her own as if to show me.

I looked more closely. I wouldn't have noticed it right away, but after a moment, I could see it. Her eyes were lit, like Yonatan's, as if tiny candles glowed inside them.

"Come here," she said, standing and gesturing me toward the wall. She stood me in front of the mirror so I could see my own face. "I always show this to the prophets *I* teach," she said. "Look."

There, in the mirror, I saw my own eyes as if for the first time. "Like sunlight coming through emeralds," Zaide had said. I'd spent so much time observing Yonatan's eyes, but had never realized the same Light was shining in my own.

"Have no doubt you belong here, Rahel," Rena said, as if part of an incantation. "Prophetess, you are one of us."

Slowly, it came together for me. The Light in our eyes. It was the same holiness that seemed to fill Devorah's apartment; the same power I had felt at the Kotel. The warmth I encountered when I spoke to Yonatan. The feeling of magic when I entered a trance.

The Light was in our eyes, filling this room, this house where the prophets lived, and flowing out into the world.

CHAPTER 20

Yonatan's beautiful artwork had been stored in a cabinet under the stairs when he left Tzfat. When I came back upstairs, he showed me colorful candles shaped into elaborate designs, and twisted glasswork formed into couples walking across bridges of water. Paintings of sunlit stone paths along a river. Drawings of people, including one lovely woman whose face seemed to be repeated often.

"She was beautiful," I said.

Yonatan picked up one of the sketches and cradled it in his arms. "Inside and out," he said. I watched his Adam's apple move in his throat as he swallowed. "She had an inquisitive heart. Like you."

I marveled at his words. Did he really think I had an inquisitive heart? All these months I'd thought of myself mainly as trouble for him. My visions coming too strongly, too quickly, the support I needed with meditation – how I always seemed to need more. I knew he was devoted to teaching me, but I'd never even considered what he thought of me. Whether he *liked* me.

He exhaled a little chuckle, as if he was reading my mind again. "And she could rarely see herself clearly," he said, rolling up the paper and putting it away.

In the kitchen, Rena introduced me to Tirtza, a young prophetess with long, straight blond hair. Now that I knew what to look for, it was easy to see her deep brown eyes also shone with holy Light. I watched her roll dough into thick strands and braid them into challah bread.

"Did you grow up making them?" I asked her.

"No," she said, shaking her head. "I grew up Christian."

My eyes widened. "Seriously? But how –"

"I guess the Merciful One had other plans," she said, winking.

"Is that what you call G-d?" I asked her. "Merciful One? I've always heard Yonatan say 'the Holy One.'"

She kneaded her fingers into the dough, rolling several more strands for the next challah. "My teacher taught me that each prophet finds their own ways of relating to Hashem. Sometimes I use the name 'the Merciful One,' because of all the kindness Hashem has done for me."

"Who was your teacher?" I asked.

"Daniel." I looked around, wondering if he was in the house, but she shook her head. "He lives in Boston."

"In Boston? But I thought all the prophets lived here in Tzfat."

"Oh no," Tirtza corrected me. "Only a few of us live here, and not permanently. The prophets are scattered around the world to serve."

I watched her braid her next challah, her fingers expertly shaping the dough. "How long have you been here?"

"Six months," she said, with a contented sigh.

I wondered if a time might ever come when I would be able to stay here that long. Would I want to? Would I have a choice?

"How long did you learn with Daniel before you came here?" I asked.

"Two years," she told me. "We met when I was in my sophomore year at Boston University. I was already working with a rabbi to become a Jew. I'd always felt a pull toward Jewish traditions. But I was pretty surprised when Daniel told me about prophecy."

"What did your parents say when you came here?" I asked.

She shrugged, finishing another challah and setting it gently in the pan. "They weren't exactly thrilled. But they've always let me make my own decisions. Last month they finally came to visit." She set the pan in the oven and turned back to the counter, where another batch of dough was waiting. "They could see it's special here."

"So do you...have visions?" I asked.

She grinned. "Sure. It's only been a few years, so I don't usually have to do anything about them, but..." She flipped the next piece of dough onto the counter. "Last month I saw this woman shopping in the Artists' Colony, over on the other side of town. There was a book on the shelf that was meant for her. I had to make sure she got that book." She shrugged, creating an intricate braid with her fingers as she continued the story. "It had something to do with Kabbalah[19], but she wasn't a prophetess. I never knew what she was supposed to do with the book. I hung around that store all afternoon, and *there she was.* In real life, looking just like I had seen in the vision! I followed

---

[19] Kabbalah: the Jewish mystical tradition.

her in and just picked up the book, held it for a while, and then said to her, 'You might be interested in this one.' When I left, she was still standing there in the middle of the store, reading it."

"And you just...knew what you had to do? It was clear from the vision?"

She shook her head. "Noach helped me put it together." She put another pan in the oven and washed the dough from her hands.

"The other day...I had a vision about my sister," I said.

She shook her head sympathetically. "It can be hard to understand them, especially when you're just starting out. For the whole first year, I didn't see anything but flickering lights."

I frowned at her, puzzled. Hadn't I moved past the flickering lights after just a few weeks?

"If you're concerned, talk to Noach," she said. "He'll be able to help."

Before candle-lighting, the seven other prophetesses gathered in the dining room, their eyes closed, lips moving in silent prayer. I could almost hear their thoughts: wishes for peace in the coming week, prayers for family and friends, and Light for all the prophets.

My grandfather's necklace was warm, like a hand resting on my heart. Through the open window, I saw that the clouds had partially cleared. The sun was low on the mountains, sparkling on the ice that had settled earlier on the trees. In the distance, I heard horns beeping and the thrum of car and motorcycle motors.

Now. This moment. In the cold breeze. Facing my unknown destiny with courage and, yes, apprehension. With the feeling of Shabbat approaching like redemption.

"Here I am," I said softly. "I am here."

The women came forward one by one to kindle lights in honor of Shabbat. Mirrors along the walls multiplied each small flame many times.

When I approached, the tray was already ablaze with light. I lit my match and touched the flame to two candles, then, like the others before me, let it drop to the tray to extinguish itself. As they had, I moved my hands around the flames and to my eyes.

The blessing was written in Hebrew on a laminated card tucked into the corner of the mirror: *Blessed are You, Our G-d, King of the Universe, Who Commands Us to Kindle the Sabbath Light*. This prayer was one of the few I already knew from my childhood.

There were other prayers written in Hebrew below the blessing. *Perhaps one day*, I thought, *I would know them too.*

Rena began to hum, and the others took up the tune, softly at first, then more strongly. Tirtza put her arm around me. We swayed in the light of the candles, singing together.

Boi kallah, boi kallah, the women sang, words to welcome the Sabbath. *Boi kallah, boi kallah, lecha dodi.*[20]

Together we walked outside and to the entrance on the upper level of the building, which housed a synagogue. This space was so filled with holy Light I could barely breathe. Rena led me to a seat at the front of the balcony. I found my place in the siddur. Enveloped by the Light, I opened my heart.

G-d, I prayed, as I had once before, *help me grow into my gifts.*

After services, Yonatan led me to a seat near the head of the dining room table, where Noach sat. Rena stood on my other side. I felt astonishingly alive, aware of the blood pulsing in my veins, the tingles the cool air sent across my skin, the rumbles of hunger in my stomach. We stood together to sing *Shalom Alechem,* welcoming angels to the table, and I could almost feel them descending to bless us.

Noach took a pewter Kiddush cup in his hands and chanted the blessing in his deep, resonant voice. Holiness filled the room like a presence.

A crescent moon shimmered brightly overhead. Through an open window, I heard other voices and other meals. The earlier motor sounds had evaporated beneath the darkening sky. The wind rustled in the trees. I sipped the wine.

Before I knew what was happening, sparks overwhelmed me.

A sweep of horror rushes through the prophets when I fall. "No," I whisper.

But it is too late. I place my hand on my chest, where the disease eats away at me, a bit more each day. Now they know.

Their voices ring out to me, filled with strength and courage in their sorrow, nothing less than I would have expected of them.

By the window, my two holy flames struggle against the breeze, casting

---

[20] A song based on a prayer traditionally said at the service welcoming Shabbat. The title of the song may be translated, "Come, my beloved, to welcome the Bride (the Sabbath)."

their flickering light on the gold tray beneath them. I try to draw courage from their unrelenting blaze, and from the crescent moon shining her narrow light across the sky.

"If only I could live a thousand years with you," I tell them, "I would."

Curled in a heap on the dining room floor, pain raging through my body, I opened my eyes to find their burning eyes upon me. Eyes flickering gold, blue and green, hazel, dark brown, violet, gray, and almost black. Knowing eyes filled with shock, horror, and disappointment.

"I'm sorry," I managed in a hoarse voice.

I looked for Yonatan. He would reassure me, wouldn't he? But his face seemed distant, like a stranger. I felt a jolt of terror.

"Please don't be sorry," Rena said. "It's only – "

"Take her downstairs," Noach said.

"Can you stand?"

Rena reached out her arm. It took all my strength to get to my feet. "I'm sorry," I said again and again. Downstairs, I sat on the bed she'd said would be mine, hunched over, my chest still ringing with pain. I was chilled by the look on Yonatan's face. Had I done something wrong?

"Do you remember the vision?" Rena asked, a note of trepidation in her voice.

"There were candles." I gasped as the pain in my chest flared deeper.

"I'm sorry, Rahel," Rena said. Her voice was anguished. "I think it might hurt a while longer." She put her arms around me. There were tears in her eyes.

"I'll stay with you," she said.

CHAPTER 21

At last, the pain dimmed. My sobs turned to whimpers, then faded into silence. I could hear Noach talking upstairs to the others, the deep strains of his voice resonating in Hebrew. Yonatan's calm voice floated over the quiet. The other prophets listened in what seemed to me a tense silence.

"Are you feeling better?" Rena asked.

She was channeling Light toward me, the way Yonatan did.

"A bit," I said.

"Ready to come back up for dinner?"

I covered my face with my hands. "I made such a scene."

"Tzfat is a holy place," Rena said, as if to console me. "Often when prophets come here, they have strong visions."

Maybe she was right. It had only been a vision, after all. Wasn't I among the only people in the world who would understand?

"Come back upstairs," Rena said, her hand a gentle pressure against my back. "It will be all right now."

Several prophets stood as I entered the dining room. Yonatan came toward me, his eyes warm again. He held out his hand, though I knew enough not to take it.

Maybe he never was angry, I thought. *Maybe I'd imagined the remote look in his eyes.* But then, why hadn't he been the one to take me downstairs and wait with me?

"I'm sorry," I said again.

"Visions are nothing to be sorry about," Noach said, coming up behind Yonatan.

Rena led me back to my chair. My chest still felt raw, but the soup was warm and comforting. Distant sounds of laughter and singing resonated from other tables in the holy Shabbat air.

Yonatan poured me more wine. Last week, in Jerusalem, the wine was dry and bitter-tasting, but this was sweet and light. Tirtza's challahs were delicious. Prophets and prophetesses brought fresh hummus and salads to the table. I drank another cup of wine.

The table conversation, carried on mostly in Hebrew, rolled over me like rain. As the lingering ache in my chest began to subside, I remembered what a blessing it was to be here, in the prophets' house.

There was singing at the end of the meal, and then a long prayer to thank G-d for the food. When I stood at the end of the meal, I felt light-headed.

I had the thought of being somewhere else. Another place where a stream trickled near a busy road. Or some other place where Shabbat lights were guttering out against the darkness of night.

Searching for the way downstairs, I came across a cluster of prophets in the kitchen, speaking quietly.

"This could change everything," Tirtza said.

"It certainly will," Noach said.

"She must have known this was possible," Rena said. "Did she want...?"

"No," Yonatan said, shaking his head. "But she felt you should know her."

Rena turned, noticing me at the door. I let her help me find my way back downstairs to my bed.

Awakening in the morning, it took a long moment to remember where I was. With a rush, it all came back to me: The prophetesses. The pain of the vision. The wine. I moved my hands along my chest, checking, but the pain was gone.

"Oh. Rahel," Tirtza said, stopping short as she came into the room. She gave me a strange, respectful gaze, different from the casual way she'd spoken to me yesterday. "I didn't realize you were still sleeping."

"No, I'm awake," I said, sitting up. "Where is everyone?"

"In the synagogue," she said. "Will you be joining us?"

"Yes," I said.

She waited while I dressed in the dim light and led me outside into the cool air. At the front of the women's section, Rena had saved us seats.

Everyone in this synagogue prayed in the same way Yonatan did: Eyes closed, chins lifted, hands open in supplication, talking to G-d. Their faces turned toward Jerusalem, like compasses attuned to true north. The men below us wore kipot in every color. I saw two men wearing black hats, and even one wearing a shtreimel.[21] I had never seen such a diverse group of Orthodox Jews in my life.

Dozens had come to pray, but now that I could tell the difference, I knew not everyone here was a prophet or prophetess. *Did the others know who was leading their service?* I wondered. Could they feel the Light filling the room? At first, it felt almost oppressive; then, as I allowed myself to melt into it, it felt like being part of a dream. The colors of the room took on a bright hue, and everything seemed to happen in present tense.

Just for a moment, I'm willing to give up everything—my family, my friends, Chris, and even my whole life in Baltimore—if only I could stay here with these holy people forever.

After services, we returned to the dining room for lunch, a fresh breeze lifting the white tablecloth as we stood for Kiddush. We washed our hands in the large kitchen, before Noach made a blessing over the challah. The plate of bread passed from hand to hand.

I turned to Noach. "I was wondering if I could ask you about a vision." Yonatan and Rena both leaned toward me to listen. "It was about my sister."

Yonatan exhaled a little "ah," but Noach's face remained serious. "The dancer," he said.

I was startled. Had he seen it, too? "It happened with my group, when we were on Masada," I said. "I didn't know what it meant but...I felt afraid. I wondered if it was some kind of warning."

Noach smoothed the edges of his gray beard. He turned to Yonatan. "How long has it been since you left for Baltimore?"

"Almost five months," Yonatan said.

Noach sighed. "So fast," he said. "You saw clearly. Your sister needs your help."

I sat up straight as my heart gave an anxious thump. "How can I help her?"

Noach hesitated. "The vision did not provide that guidance," he said. "But no one will know better than you, when the moment comes."

My thoughts whirled. This seemed much harder than what Tirtza had described. Hadn't she, after years of training, simply been required to give someone a book? And if Beth needed me, shouldn't I get clearer instructions?

---

[21] A fur hat worn by some Hasidic Jewish men on the Sabbath and holidays.

How could they ask me to do nothing but wait and hope to recognize the moment when it came?

Yonatan and Noach exchanged a glance. *What were they saying inside each other's heads, that I couldn't hear?* Finally, Noach shook his head.

"The Holy One requests this of you," Yonatan answered me gently. "When the time comes, you will be ready."

Noach pressed his hands flat on the table, rocking slightly in his chair. "Yonatan has spoken well," he said.

He pushed his chair back and stood. A silence fell over the table as the prophets watched him leave the room.

After lunch, Yonatan and I walked to the Old City of Tzfat. The winter sun shone on ancient stone steps and courtyards, but a cold breeze rustled in my hair. The skirt I'd brought wasn't warm enough for late December on this mountain. At least I had the leggings Mom had bought me.

I thought back to her strange meeting with Yonatan on our street, that Saturday afternoon in the snow. She had supported me in continuing to meet with him, even though she herself had given up being Orthodox. But what would she think if she knew I was with him here?

Yonatan and I climbed a long flight of stairs in the center of the Old City, which led to a pedestrian area. In a park at the highest point of the town, a lone artist sat smoking a cigarette on a bench. Nearby, two children played in the ragged, wet grass. A path wound through the park area, and we followed it to the memorial established for the soldiers who died in the War of Independence.

I spotted a narrow trail alongside the brick courtyard of the memorial and broke away from Yonatan. Hardly aware of what I was doing, I made my way through the overgrowth, following the sliver of worn grass, through the debris of an ancient fort, to a worn patch of land overlooking the city.

Here, the Light overpowered me and I fell to my knees.

Much younger, unbearded, Yonatan crouches against a stone broken from the fort. Across from him sits a young woman: long light hair, shining brown eyes. The ground is green with stubbles of grass. Wildflowers bob in the breeze.

"First we'll meditate together," he explains. "Later, I'll teach you to do it on your own."

She closes her eyes. Yonatan begins to whisper the words that will guide them but, after a moment, breaks off, caught by the beauty of her face.

"Yonatan?" she asks, eyes still closed.

"I'm sorry. Just give me a moment." He closes his eyes to still his racing heart...

Night. Shabbat. She wears a homemade-looking yellow dress, and they carefully pick their way along the path. Below them the city is hushed, streetlights twinkling. In the distance, other lights shimmer on faraway mountains. Above them, the sky is crowded with stars.

"I don't want to leave," she says.

"No one ever does."

They look out over the Old City, the silent homes and stone streets, the pedestrian mall with the stores shut tight, the artists' colony sleepy on the side of the mountain.

"I want to give them a blessing," she says.

Yonatan sweeps his hand through the air in affirmation.

"I bless them," she begins, "that they should always have peace, that war and terror never find their way here. That the mystics return with their holiness, and that everyone who comes here finds where they belong."

"Amen." Yonatan's eyes are focused entirely on her face.

"I feel like Hashem is watching over us tonight," she says. "Like He's paying close attention."

It is true. There is a pause as they experience it together. Then he tells her, finally.

"I love you."

She turns on him, surprised. "I love you too," she admits out loud for the first time.

He doesn't have anything to formalize it, not even a toy ring. Maybe it is the heaviness of the late summer flowers, or the sense of the Divine in the air. But he can't let her leave without asking her, without begging her.

"Nechama," he says. "Please marry me."

She looks stunned. Then, slowly, joy creeps over her face. "Okay."

Hunched over in the chilly wind. Hands and knees wet on the cold and muddy ground. I kept my eyes closed, savoring the moments of love I had seen.

She had an Australian accent. Her face was clear and smooth, like ivory. She kept her honey-colored hair loose and long. Her voice was deep, like the rushing sea.

When I finally opened my eyes from the vision, I found Yonatan leaning against a boulder a few feet away, one hand covering both his eyes.

"She was your student," I said.

He uncovered his face, blinking a few times as if to bring me into focus. His eyes seemed dim. "Yes," he said heavily.

All of a sudden, I could see him, how broken he was right after she died. *Lying on the bottom of a bunk bed, dressed in a dirty sweat suit, looking down the mountain of Tzfat.* Now I understood why he had been sent to Baltimore to teach me: It was the only way he would get out of that bed. I marveled at the strength it must have taken to leave here.

He heaved himself from the boulder and faced me. "Sometimes the burden of life itself seems greater than we can bear," he said. "And yet, we go on."

I studied him, wondering: Could I give him some of the Light he was always giving me? Where could I get it? How would I give it to him? But as soon these thoughts formed in my mind, I could feel a warmth starting above my eyes. Gradually, it descended upon us: a Light I was beginning to recognize.

I remembered what he had taught me: In order to receive the Light, we must be prepared to give it. I didn't want it for myself; I needed it for him. Maybe this was what he meant.

Somewhere inside my soul, I opened a doorway. Yonatan turned to me, surprised.

The Light came like a waterfall, filling the dark spaces between us, opening what had been closed. My own exhaustion washed away and I pulled myself to my feet, restored. I watched as a small flame sparked in his eyes.

"It's going to be all right," I said.

It felt very important that he understand me. As if the whole reason for coming to Tzfat was this conversation, in the shadow of the debris of an ancient fort overlooking the city and cemetery below.

"It's going to be all right," I said again.

Yonatan looked at me, his shining eyes reflecting the mountains beyond us. Very slowly, he smiled. "Yes."

CHAPTER 22

L ater that day, the women's section was nearly empty as Rena and I sat at the front of the balcony for the afternoon service. When it was time for the silent standing prayer, I stood and whispered it fervently. G-d's Light shimmered all around me: in this holy place where Yonatan had lived and loved and mourned and reclaimed his faith. Where I had learned some of my own gifts and responsibilities, and embraced them.

Sparks were shimmering all around me. At first I thought a vision was coming, but then I realized my prayers had opened a door for meditation.

Without hesitation, I whispered the words I had learned. It happened more quickly than ever before. I passed through fire and storm. I let silence overtake me.

A flash in the water reflecting his lighter.

The flame that passes from torch to torch.

The cane against the wall. Resolutely, she reaches for it.

You must find her. *Noach, seventy years younger, falls to his knees on a dirt road. "I can't." But he will.*

Devorah stands by the Kotel, leaning on her cane. The Wall is warm from the sun.

Toward the base of the mountain is an ancient cemetery, shining bright orange in the setting sun. "The true test is in passing the flame," Noach tells her, with the greatest regret. "You will."

As I descended, as I whispered the holy words Yonatan had taught me, I tried to piece together the scattered images I'd seen. *A flash of light reflected in water. A cemetery. Noach's face as a young man.*

When I finally opened my eyes, Rena rested her hand on my arm. The service was over; the synagogue empty. I had no idea how long she had been waiting for me.

I opened my mouth to apologize, but closed it.

☙❧

When the sky had turned dark enough to see stars, the prophets gathered back in the dining room and Noach recited the blessings of Havdallah to end Shabbat. Yonatan held the tall twisted candle, his eyes reflecting the shining light. Following the others, I held my fingers toward the flame before he extinguished it in the wine.

After some clean-up and changing of clothing, the prophets gathered in the living room, where the windows were open and small tables were arranged with candles and cake. Noach brought out a guitar, and another prophet, a violin, and together they sang Hebrew words I'd never heard.

After the music, in the reverberating silence, Noach closed his eyes and began to rock gently in his chair. "Long ago, I feared prophecy was over. We had lost so much in the Shoah.[22] My own visions became scarce and unclear. I couldn't find another prophet or prophetess anywhere. I came to the land of Israel, hoping, perhaps, that Hashem would have compassion on me here. I called myself Noach, because I was the one who survived.

"Devorah was so young then," he said, his voice breaking on her name, "but she carried so much power. I had never seen one called with her gift. When she was able to heal, to connect, to choose...a new era of prophecy began." His eyes opened, and he spread his hands. "For all of us."

The other prophets leaned forward, taking in each of Noach's words. Rena had tears in her eyes. Tirtza glanced at me, then quickly away.

"My friends," Noach said, rocking more fervently in his chair, "prophecy is not for us alone. In the coming generations, prophecy will rest on thousands and tens of thousands. A time is coming when everyone will know that Hashem is one. This is the journey we are completing." He lifted his voice, almost in a cry. "The end of this exile is now coming! When redemption comes, 'they will neither injure nor destroy in all of My sacred mountain, for the earth will be as filled with the knowledge of Hashem as water covering the sea.'"[23]

As with Yonatan, I felt Noach's words had brought me into a kind of trance. I could only focus on his shining eyes. The air in the room seemed electric as all the prophets drew strength from his holy words.

"Everything is for the good," he said. Then he began a simple wordless song, and we all sang together, passionately, the music drawing our souls together in the night air.

---

[22] Hebrew word for Holocaust.

[23] Isaiah 11:9 (Artscroll translation, slightly modified).

Later, as we gathered dishes to bring to the kitchen, Yonatan called me to the living room, where he sat on one of the old leather sofas. I settled on a folding chair across from him, still entranced by the music and the connection with the other prophets. "Thank you for bringing me here," I said.

"You'll have many more opportunities to come here." He pressed his hands against his knees and leaned toward me, staring at me that way he did, as if he could see through my eyes to my soul.

"Rachel," he said, "I am not coming back to Baltimore."

"You're not?" I stared at him, feeling a bit of my peace slip away. "Why?"

He glanced out the window. "Israel is my home. I have responsibilities here right now."

My eyes widened. "But – aren't I – one of your responsibilities?" I hated the childish sound of my voice. But I also wasn't sure how I could survive without him.

He met my eyes and put his hands out, palms forward. "You don't need me nearby now. Your training as a prophetess is nearly finished."

"Finished?" I burst out. "But I don't know anything! I don't know any of the rules!"

He gave me a wry smile. "Now you want rules?"

I flushed, looking away. "Will we still be...connected?"

"I will always be here when you need me," he said.

I stared around the sparse room, a yawning terror creeping into the space where only peace had been a moment before. "I'll miss you." The words hardly seemed to cover it.

Yonatan reached forward, his hand open to me. "I'll miss you too," he said. "But this is not goodbye. We will see each other again, soon, at the right time."

He ascended the stairs to the men's bedrooms where he had grieved so bitterly for his wife, and left me in the empty living room, alone.

By breakfast, he had already departed.

It was cold and cloudy as Rena walked me down the hill to meet my bus. She wore a dark green winter coat over her denim skirt, her long hair pulled back into a bun, the only sign of her gifts gleaming in her incandescent eyes.

In my ponytail, jeans and muddy hiking boots, I too felt disguised, as if my usual clothing couldn't account for the experiences of the last 48 hours.

As we stood awaiting the bus, Rena handed me a small package. "Yonatan asked me to give this to you," she said, her kind voice muffled by the cold wind.

I removed the brown wrapping and found a small, hardbound Hebrew-English siddur inside. I ran my fingers across the silver embossed pattern on the front. A picture of the Kotel was sketched on the inside front cover, with a long path winding away from it – or toward it, depending on your perspective. He had signed it with his name in Hebrew.

"Rena, why isn't he coming back with me?" I dared to ask.

I could see the tiny puff of her breath. "Devorah needs him here."

I stared down the empty road, feeling hopeless. Of course he wouldn't turn down Devorah, whatever she asked.

"This will be good training for you," Rena said. "Sometimes it helps to be on your own."

I tilted my head incredulously. "Even if you've only been learning for four months?"

Her sharp intake of air was as good as an answer.

I bit my lip in frustration. "Isn't there anything you can tell me?" I pleaded. "I'm going back all alone!"

Her bright eyes were full of compassion. "You won't be alone for long, Rahel," she said. "Devorah is the wisest woman I know. And she's being guided by the Eternal One. This too is for the good." A rumble filled the air; the bus was approaching. "Trust," she said, squeezing my hand. "It's all we have."

I sighed. The bus lumbered toward us, huge and out of place on the small mountain road, and stopped with a rumble and a loud squeak of brakes. I lifted my backpack onto my shoulders as the doors opened and a familiar group of teenagers tumbled out, chattering, tossing their paper coffee cups into a nearby trash can, stretching their legs after the morning's ride from Tel Aviv.

At first, I didn't recognize Maya among them. She was wearing an overlarge maroon sweatshirt over wrinkled jeans, clothing I wouldn't have guessed she owned. She wore no makeup, and her hair was pulled back into a ponytail under a baseball cap.

Seeing me, she came to the side of the road. Her brown eyes were as dull and lackluster as old pennies. "Hey Rachel," she said, without smiling.

I turned to introduce her, but Rena had already disappeared back up the hill. I could barely see the outline of her green coat departing, as if her pure soul couldn't intermingle with the rowdy teenagers from my tour. Beyond her, I could almost make out the citadel at the top of the mountain where Yonatan and Nechama had been together so many years ago.

"Friendly cousin," Maya said with a smirk. "How was your Shabbat?"

"Nice," I said. "Hey, I'm sorry for how we left things on Friday morning. I just –"

She shook her head and waved her hands, as if our argument couldn't matter less to her.

"Where did you get that sweatshirt and hat?" I asked.

"At a tourist shop in Tel Aviv," she said.

"Not exactly your style," I said.

She shrugged. "Sometimes it's better not to draw attention."

As we walked down the road toward the Artists' Colony, Matt and three of his friends stared bitterly at her. I understood why she felt the need to hide.

"Maybe you should tell Heather what happened," I said, though I knew she wouldn't.

She shook her head. "It doesn't matter. We're going home in a few days anyway."

That evening we left Tzfat for Caesarea. From the window, I watched the holy mountain disappear behind us. They had said I would be back, but I couldn't imagine when or how.

I thought again of the place at the top of the mountain where Yonatan had first fallen in love. I wished I had lived earlier; that I could have been his friend rather than his student. That I could have known him before he lost everything.

"Yonatan," I whispered. I knew we were still connected; I could feel his presence like a small sun shining on my soul. But I was still surprised when I heard his voice echo inside my mind.

"Have courage," he told me.

After all he had taught me, I knew he deserved my trust. "Thank you," I whispered. "For everything."

"Teaching you has been a privilege," he said.

I had feared going to Tzfat: that I would somehow get lost there and never make it home. And now, here I was with my group – safe and sound – but I felt my home was left there behind me.

CHAPTER 23

Our return flight left late Tuesday night. As the plane lifted from the ground, I stared through the window, watching the land of Israel shrink beneath me. I felt like a cut flower pulled out of water; how long would it take before my spirit dried out?

"Yonatan," I whispered. "Don't leave me."

Never, I heard him respond, but already I knew the distance between us was growing.

Beside me, Maya wrapped herself in a blanket and squeezed her eyes shut. The last few days had gone no better for her. She'd finally stopped wearing the tourist sweatshirt after spilling tahini on it, but continued to avoid everyone, folding into herself through the remainder of the trip.

Our group was subdued and groggy when we landed in New York. After so much Hebrew, it felt strange to see only English signs, familiar airport restaurants—a Starbucks. Maya flipped aimlessly through magazines on our connecting flight to Baltimore.

Though it was early Wednesday morning, Mom, Dad, and Beth were all waiting for me at the security gate. Beth's long hair was pulled back with barrettes, revealing cheekbones that were more prominent than on Thanksgiving. But her face seemed healthy, and she was grinning hugely.

First, I hugged Dad, smelling his Irish Spring soap and feeling his narrow chin in my hair. Then Beth pulled me into a hug. "Welcome home."

"Welcome home to you!" I said, squeezing her back. "Did you miss me?"

She laughed. "Desperately."

Finally, Mom held her arms open. "Did you have a good time?" she asked.

I nodded, looking up at her face. "Thank you for letting me go."

For dinner, we ate vegetarian lasagna, my favorite meal, in the dining room on my grandmother's kosher plates. I gave out presents: a dancing music box for Beth, a book on the archaeological history of Jerusalem for Dad, a decorative photo frame for Mom.

Dad put a new comedy movie on the DVR. Beth lounged on the loveseat and laughed along at the show. Mom twirled her fingers into Dad's hand. It felt almost like old times, before Beth had left for college, before Zaide died, before Yonatan. Just for an evening, I could pretend everything was the way it was before.

∽

Later that evening, I locked my bedroom door before sitting on my meditation pillow on the floor.

The gurgle of the nearby stream is the only sound tonight. The flame illuminates his notebook, his words scrawled across pages like blood. If he can turn his father's voice into a poem, the nightmares might spare him tonight.

In the distance, a grown man—blond, handsome, and well-dressed— walks toward me, his dark eyes shining in the night. No one I recognize.

"I survived only because of you," he says. "Thank you."

On the floor in my darkened bedroom, I whispered the holy words as I caught my breath. *The stream. The flame. The man walking toward me.*

Who was he? Was I supposed to help him? I didn't know.

Gathering my strength, I stood and faced myself in the mirror. In the darkness, my shining green eyes were my only proof of the journey I'd just concluded.

You will do whatever you need to, I told myself firmly, *because you are a prophetess.*

∽

When I awakened early the next morning, still on Israel time, I packed my things for school. I arrived early enough to catch Lauren before orchestra practice began.

Around us, the other kids were chattering, tuning their instruments, playing little chirps of notes. She reached forward to give me a hug. "I totally missed you!" She pushed her red hair back from her face. "Was the trip okay for you?"

"It was great," I said.

"Did you have migraines while you were there?" she asked.

I shook my head. No migraines: That was the truth.

Lauren exhaled. "That's wonderful." She grinned. "Do you want to see a movie Friday night?"

136

I hesitated. After the last two Friday nights with the prophets, was I really going to see a movie on this one? But it wasn't like Yonatan had told me I needed to observe Shabbat. If he was leaving me on my own, I had to find my own way.

"Okay," I said.

❧

Chris approached me on my way out of history class later that morning. "Happy New Year," he said. He wore a blue cable knit sweater and black jeans, his hair combed back, his cheeks shaved smooth. I fiddled with my ponytail nervously.

"To you too," I said. "Have you heard from Florida?"

He shook his head, chewing his lip pensively. When football season ended last month, our team placed second in the league. I knew he was worried this would hurt his chances.

"They have to take you, Chris. You were amazing this year."

He shrugged, then leaned closer to whisper in my ear, sending chills down my neck. "How was Israel?"

"It was...all...real," I said.

His eyes widened. "I knew it." He put his hand on my shoulder, his eyes so hot I might have melted into the floor. *Could he tell the effect he still had on me?* I stared up at his face, barely breathing. Wishing. Knowing it would never be.

❧

Beth seemed fine my first night home, but when I knocked on her door after school the next afternoon, she didn't answer. "Beth?" I said.

On the floor, unconscious. Barely breathing.

The image appeared and vanished, like the echo of a camera flash. Was it real? Or just my own frightened imagining? I knocked again, raising my voice. "Beth?" In panic, I turned the knob and opened the door.

Beth lay in bed, her long auburn hair splayed across her face, pillow and shoulders. Her laptop rested near her pillow, the screen dim. Her shoulders and back rose and fell with every deep breath.

Relief washed over me. She was just asleep.

Careful not to wake her, I tiptoed out of the room.

❧

THE PROPHETESS

From my bedroom window on Friday after school, I watched the haphazard parade of Orthodox men in black hats and dark coats making their way to synagogue to begin Shabbat.

My thoughts kept circling back to the prophetesses swaying and singing in the candlelight. The murmurings of the prophets speaking in Hebrew. The holy synagogue filling with Light.

Part of me wanted to follow the Orthodox Jews to Shomrei Emunah, but I knew I wouldn't find what I was truly seeking there. Anyway, how could I keep Shabbat the way they did? I didn't know the rules. What would my friends say? What about my parents? The truth was, I wasn't ready to become one of them.

Yet I wanted to mark this moment, the beginning of Shabbat.

I slipped down the steps to our living room and rooted around in the wall unit, opening drawers, until I found tea lights. I took a handful and a box of matches back upstairs.

In my bedroom, I pondered where to light them. My dresser and desk were wood. My eyes fell on an old ceramic plate I'd made years ago in Hebrew School, decorated with a Jewish star.

Outside, the sun shone gold against the bare trees, the final embers of a winter sunset. I put the plate on my dresser, near the mirror where the light would reflect. I took a deep breath, struck the match, and lit two candles. Then I said the blessing I remembered: *lehadlik ner shel Shabbat*, to kindle the Sabbath lights.

I still didn't know the longer Hebrew prayer the prophetesses had recited in Tzfat, but it would have to do.

CHAPTER 24

"What did you see in Israel?" Lauren asked as we waited in line for the movie.

I pulled out my phone and showed her pictures, beginning with the Old City of Jerusalem. Masada and the Dead Sea. The underwater observatory in Eilat.

There were no images of the prophets. So many of the special moments we had shared were during Shabbat, when use of phones wasn't allowed.

Of course, it was Shabbat right now, and here I was, out to see a movie. Still, I continued flicking through the shots on the screen.

There were pictures of Maya, dressed in tight clothing, sporting various colors of lipstick, and wound into Matt's arms. On the last day of the trip, I'd caught a single picture of her, staring unsmiling away from the camera.

"What happened?" Lauren asked.

"A boy," I said glumly. She rolled her eyes, but I shook my head. "It wasn't her fault. The guy was horrible to her."

"I'm glad you had fun," Lauren said. "I was so worried about you."

"You worry too much," I said, rolling my eyes at her.

As we approached the counter to buy tickets, my stomach tightened; I knew the rule against using money on Shabbat. I reached into my bag and pulled out a few bills, hardly looking at them as I passed them along the counter. Hastily, I tossed the change back into my bag.

"Do you want popcorn?" Lauren asked, as we passed the concession stand.

"No," I said quickly. I didn't want to pay for anything else.

Later that night, I wrapped my arms around my legs in my dark bedroom and closed my eyes, whispering the words of meditation as an antidote to all my confusion.

The evening had passed without incident; at least I hadn't had a vision during the movie. But as the superheroes fought their battles on screen, gradually it dawned on me that I didn't *want* to be watching a movie tonight.

I felt newly sensitive to the holiness of Sabbath around me, as if my experiences in Israel had awakened some spiritual sense I couldn't turn off. I didn't want to be riding in a car, spending money, or using my phone. I wanted to pray and eat with holy people, sharing discussions about visions, Jerusalem, and eternity.

It seemed harder to enter the meditation tonight. I continued to repeat the words, over and over again, desperate for answers. At last, the sparks began to flow and enter into me. I could hear the thunder of my breathing, rushing over me like wind. *Please,* I prayed. *Please.*

Finally the silence and...

Everything is white here except the flame, shivering along with him until he releases the lighter. Then the white eclipses everything again.

He loves the snow. The cleanness of it. And he likes the spices better, too. A better high.

But something is different today.

He doesn't sense the danger until the fire begins to rage in his chest.

Abruptly back in my dark bedroom, I clenched and unclenched my fists as images flashed like strobe lights upon me. *White. A flame. Snow. Fire... in his chest.*

I pressed my hands flat against my breastbone, where a fearsome echo of that fire still burned, and pushed myself to remember more. Where was he? *Who* was he? I squeezed my eyes shut, focusing hard in the darkness for a long time before the last detail came to me: A flannel sleeve.

With a flash of insight, I realized it was Jake, the poet.

The next morning, I huddled in my winter coat on the steps of our front porch, watching the Orthodox Jews on their way to synagogue. None were prophets, but I thought I could sense a trace of holiness in a few of them. Like those who attended the prophets' synagogue in Tzfat, they somehow reflected a glimmer of holy Light.

I imagined running down the steps to approach one of them. *I'm a prophetess,* I would say. *Could we pray together?* I wondered if they could possibly help me figure out the visions I was having about Jake. But I'd never heard anyone but Yonatan mention prophecy here. Even he had seemed cautious about talking about it at Shomrei Emunah. And my jeans and sneakers probably wouldn't recommend me.

When the parade started flowing in the other direction, returning home from synagogue, I went back inside.

∽

While in Israel, I had filled pages of my poetry notebook, but it all felt so inadequate as I came into Poetry Club the following Monday. How could any of the words I'd written describe what I'd experienced? As the others filtered into the classroom, I pulled out my notebook and skimmed the pages for something I might share.

I felt more than heard when Jake entered the room.

His light hair was tangled and hung down over his eyes. His flannel was ratty, with frayed sleeves that covered most of his hands. As he took his seat, he pulled on his baseball cap and retreated beneath it. No one else seemed to notice him, but after seeing him in my recent meditation, I couldn't stop looking at him.

As usual, we went around the circle, taking turns reading our poems and receiving comments from the group. I had found the most benign poem in my notebook. It was about the stars looking down upon Masada:

Did you watch all these two thousand years,
Dust piling over the stones,
The children missing,
The men praying
In a distant land –
Did you wait, did you wait
until the sun arose again?

When I finished, the group offered their usual bits of praise and advice. Jake didn't offer any comments. He seemed unusually jumpy today. He kept staring out the window, tapping a pencil on the table, shaking his knee under the desk. When the hour ended, he was the first one to leave.

Without really thinking, I tossed my book into my bag and hurried out after him. "Jake!" I called.

He was halfway down the hall but turned, squinting, giving me enough time to catch up. He kept tapping his foot, not that he was impatient, but more because he could barely stop moving it. I remembered Lauren suggesting that maybe he had a crush on me. By the time I reached him, I was flustered and doubting myself.

"I-I was sorry you didn't have a poem today," I said.

"Nothing worth sharing," he said. His eyes were focused not on my face but at the wall behind me. Self-conscious, I glanced backward. There was nothing there.

"Maybe next week?" I said.

"Maybe."

His eyes finally met mine, but my brain kept spinning in circles. What could I say to him?

"I just wanted to say – you shouldn't – you know, do anything dangerous right now."

He laughed. "Thanks. I'll keep that in mind." He pushed his baseball cap down, almost in salute, before turning back down the hall away from me.

That night, I knocked on Beth's door. "Hmm?" she called. "Come in."

She was sitting up in bed, her long legs curled under the blanket. Her hair was pulled back in a messy ponytail. Several empty bottles of Diet Coke sat on her nightstand. Her glazed eyes focused on her laptop screen.

"You look busy," I said.

"Yeah, Rach, sorry," she said, not looking up. "I've got to finish this for school."

"Aren't you on break?"

"Just a few things left over from last semester."

Look at me, I wanted to say. *Talk to me. Tell me what you need from me.*

She was still staring at her laptop. I gave up and slipped back out her door.

Maya opened the door barefoot, without any makeup, dressed in athletic pants and a tank top. I hadn't seen her since we returned to Baltimore. In her texts, she said she was recuperating.

"Hi, Rach," she said through the screen.

"Can I come in?"

She opened the door silently and let me walk past her to the living room. I sank into the plush sofa, sitting sideways, cross-legged, to pet her cat. But when Maya sat across from me, the cat abandoned me to curl into her lap.

"Sorry I got so...whatever...at the end of the trip." Without looking at me, she stroked the cat's fur. "I was angry, and – "

I broke in, reaching for her hands. "No one should ever call someone that, no matter where they're from."

"Yeah," she said, staring out the window.

"And he had no right to expect anything from you, either," I said. "He doesn't get to act like that just because you said no to him."

She shrugged. "I know."

"Have you told your mom?" I asked.

She shook her head. "It would only upset her."

Given all the things I'd hidden from my mother recently, I couldn't exactly argue with her. I frowned.

"She doesn't like it when I flirt with guys," Maya said. "She says I don't have to try so hard." Then, in a lower voice, she said, "She might be right." The cat stretched, hopped off her lap, and sauntered into the kitchen. "Anyway, not everyone is like...*him*."

"That's right," I said.

"So it's fine. I'm coming back to school tomorrow." Maya pulled a blanket off the back of the sofa and wrapped herself inside of it. "Did *you* have a good time on the trip?"

I nodded. It had only been a week, but the time in Israel already felt as distant as a dream. "Thanks for inviting me to go with you."

"So what did your *friend* say about your Shabbat with the Orthodox cousins?" she asked, a little twinkle starting in her eyes.

"Um," I said, startled by the sudden turn in the conversation. Despite everything, Maya still hoped I was finding some kind of love. But I had to be careful. She didn't realize I had spent my Shabbat in Tzfat *with* Yonatan. "He's gone," I said.

"Gone?" she asked, surprised.

"Yeah, he...he moved away," I said.

"Just like that?" She sat up a little straighter. "Where?"

I was sweating. "To Florida," I said, using the first place to come to mind.

Her eyes focused on me, sensing my discomfort. "Then you won't be seeing him anymore?"

I sighed. "I hope I'll see him again...someday."

Discarding the blanket, she leaned forward to hug me. "I'm sorry, Rach," she said, rocking me gently from side to side. "I know you loved him."

Not in the way she said, but I *did* love him, and I missed him more than I could ever explain to her. I buried my face against her shoulder and let her comfort me.

"We're both going to find better men," she said.

I sighed hopelessly in her arms.

CHAPTER 25

Beth had said we would hang out soon, but the days dragged on. I knocked on her door every afternoon that week, and each day found her burrowed in bed, her laptop balanced on her slender knees. She was dancing in the mornings at a nearby studio, so her hair was often damp from an afternoon shower. An ever increasing pile of empty Diet Coke cans was building up on her nightstand.

By Thursday afternoon, I ignored her polite head shake and barged in, plopping myself on her bed. "What are you working on?" I asked pointedly.

Beth stared at the computer for another moment, then, giving up, she set the laptop aside and faced me. "Economics."

"When is it due?"

She stretched her long neck and squeezed her wet hair through her hands. "Next Monday. I also had some math to finish. And a paper due for literature."

"Gosh, Beth," I said in a teasing voice. "Did you finish anything *during* the semester?"

"Yes, I did," she snapped. Then she sighed, pulling her knees to her chest under the blanket. "This double major is killing me."

Under the covers, she looked small and worn out, and I felt bad for teasing her. "Do Mom and Dad know how much you had left?" I asked. "Maybe if they knew how hard it is..."

She shook her head. "It wouldn't matter. At least the teachers are letting me finish this way." She sighed. "At first, I tried staying up nights during the semester...but I was so tired."

"Beth, how will you keep this going?"

"I'll be fine." She took a sip from the open can of Diet Coke on her night table, then closed the laptop and set it on the floor. "I guess it can't hurt to take a little break. How was Israel?"

"Great," I said.

She cupped her chin in her fingers, studying the pictures on my phone as I narrated. "I'd love to go to Israel one day," she said. "What was the best part?"

Looking up at her, I took a risk. "The last Shabbat. I spent it in Tzfat."

"Tzfat." She tilted her head sideways, thinking. "Where's that?"

"It's in the north," I said. "In the mountains."

She closed her eyes, breathing deeply as if she could taste the mountain air. "What did you do there?"

"I kept Shabbat...with some Orthodox Jews," I told her.

Beth opened her eyes with a puzzled frown. "What were you doing with Orthodox Jews?"

"I –" I swallowed. "They asked me to join them."

"The program let you do that?"

"Yeah," I said, thinking quickly. "It was kind of...part of it."

She chewed at a hangnail, still frowning. "So you didn't use electricity the whole day?"

I shrugged. "Well, they had lights *on*," I said. "And they made the food on Friday. We used things. We just didn't turn anything on or off."

Beth twisted her lips. Even as children, we had always approached Judaism differently. At services, I had struggled through the English words, trying to make sense of them, while she often brought romance novels to read under her siddur. I'd wanted her to understand how special Israel really was for me, but maybe it was a mistake to have shared with her about Tzfat.

"Well, I guess you can try anything once," she said, adjusting her weight under the blanket. "I bet Zaide would be proud."

I toyed with his necklace, which still dangled from my neck. "I kind of hoped so."

Late that night, I curled myself on my pillow on the floor. I hoped to see something more about Jake. But when the trance finally came, I slipped into another place entirely.

Gusts of wind distort the column of smoke rising to the sky. In the gulley, two children have been thrown from the burning car. Police are trying to prevent them from seeing their parents' bodies.

Yonatan turns off the television. Rena covers her eyes.

"Did you know of them, Devorah?" he asks.

I shake my head, and they both sigh.

I jolted awake, their images impressed on my mind. *Rena and Yonatan in Devorah's living room...those children and their parents...*

I wrapped my arms around my knees in the dark, horrified. What happened? *Had* it already happened, or could I do something to stop it?

I felt desperate to talk to Yonatan. I could feel his presence: a thin strand of Light maintaining our connection across the many oceans and miles. But I hadn't heard his voice once since coming back to Baltimore.

Though I was exhausted, I couldn't sleep. Instead, I searched online and found the news about the Israeli car, which had been firebombed on a road in the West Bank the previous day. The parents killed, the children thrown from the car.

My vision had been about something real, but it had come too late.

I covered my hands with my eyes. "Yonatan," I said quietly, "I don't know what to..." Tears began to pool on my palms.

I seized on the narrow beam that connected us, trying to follow it to Jerusalem. Could he even hear me? "Please." I waited, hoping he would carry me out of this world, into a vision, where he would explain everything. "You promised."

As I sat there on the floor, the screen of my phone the only illumination in my dim bedroom, I felt the Light flooding into me.

I couldn't hear his voice, but I knew Yonatan was restoring me. I took a gulp of breath, and then another. I wiped my eyes with a tissue.

Slowly, I began to think differently about the previous night's meditation. Yes, what happened was tragic. But wasn't it amazing I had seen it? Maybe one day G-d *would* warn me in time to save people. If so, that would be worth everything.

"Thank you," I whispered to Yonatan.

For the moment, this was enough.

On Saturday morning, I watched the Orthodox Jews from my bedroom window. Chris was stretching for a run in his driveway. After a few moments of unbearable indecision, I launched myself down the steps and out the kitchen door, into the cold sunlight.

"Chris!" I called, catching up to him as he finished his lunges.

He turned to me with an easy grin, his cheeks shadowed with stubble. I was suddenly aware I hadn't brushed my hair. I tucked my hands in my jean pockets, feeling shy.

"Could I – could I talk to you?" I said haltingly.

"Sure," he said. "Can we walk?"

"Let me just grab a coat," I said. I also grabbed a brush, and ran it through my hair before I came out.

"Is it about prophecy?" he asked, as we set off down the street.

"Sh-shh," I said. "It's a secret. Did you forget?"

He rolled his eyes playfully. "I'm not worried about the birds or the Orthodox Jews listening to me," he said. "What's up?"

A little breathless in the cold, I told him about the children who had lost their parents in the West Bank.

He stared at me, awestruck. "And you didn't know about it until the vision?"

I shook my head. "Not until I found it on the internet the next morning."

He whistled. "That's something, Rach. What did your teacher say?"

It felt too strange to try to explain how Yonatan had sent me Light yesterday morning. "He didn't say anything," I said. "He stayed in Israel. We haven't been able to talk since I left."

I hadn't shared this news with him until now. Chris studied me thoughtfully as we turned the corner and crossed a street. "Can't you call him on Skype?"

"I don't think it works that way," I told him. "I think I'm supposed to be – you know – learning to figure out this stuff on my own."

"But that's not fair," he said. "You only just started learning."

I twisted my lips. "I know." We turned onto a street lined with barren trees. "Do you think I'm supposed to do something?"

He shook his head. "Too late to save the people who died," he said. "When you're supposed to do something, I think you'll know."

We walked in silence for a few minutes, and I was uncomfortably aware of what had happened on that *other* walk. Maybe he was thinking about the kiss, too.

"There's a party next Friday night," he said casually. "At Alex Gleason's. You wouldn't want to – come with me, would you?"

"Um," I said anxiously, staring up at his face.

"Not like a date," he said quickly. "Just friends."

I shook my head. "I don't think it would be a good idea."

"Right, of course," he said.

We both took a breath, walking in silence for another moment. *Could he tell how much I wanted to kiss him?* Casting about wildly for a change of subject, I thought of something.

"I bet Maya is going," I said. "You could ask her to go with you."

"Maybe," he said noncommittally.

"If you do, she's – she's in a vulnerable place right now," I told him. "Just be nice to her."

He shrugged. "Sure."

CHAPTER 26

Despite my nightly meditation efforts, I wasn't able to conjure another vision about Jake. I hoped to talk to him more on Monday afternoon at poetry, but for the first time all year, he didn't show. It wasn't until Wednesday, when I was pulling books out of my locker between fourth and fifth period, that I turned to find him standing behind me.

He wasn't wearing the baseball cap, and his shaggy blond hair hung around his ears. His eyes were dark as midnight and trained on my face. His flannel button-down shirt was untucked. His hands were clasped tightly in fists, but I noticed stains on the fingertips of his right hand.

"I'm not really that scary," he said, seeing my expression.

His comment was so preposterous – I found him terrifying in so many different ways – I chuckled.

"I'm heading out," he said, gesturing with his head toward the door.

I frowned, confused. "Out?" It was the middle of the school day. "Why?"

"It's snowing," he said, as if this explained everything. "Wanna come?"

I stared at him, bewildered.

He put a finger to his lips. "See you later," he said, and backed away a few paces before turning to amble down the hall.

Staring after him, I noticed he had no jacket. Was he going out to smoke weed in the snow? Was he inviting *me* to join him? And how had he known where my locker was?

Beth finished her fall semester projects just in time for spring semester. On the Friday night before she was due to depart, we shared a family Chinese dinner after I quietly lit candles in my room.

As usual, I sat cross-legged on the carpet while Beth sprawled on the love seat, and my parents shared the sofa, their cups of wonton soup on the coffee table.

"Congratulations, Beth," Dad said, toasting her with a wonton. "Good work finishing your projects."

Beth was aiming for a casual pride, but the dark circles under her eyes gave her away. In response to his toast, she took a swig from her latest can of Diet Coke. She had already declared the soup too salty after a single sip. Now she was nibbling an egg roll.

"She worked the whole break," I said.

Beth glared at me. "At least I got it done."

"I know it's a lot of work," Dad said. "But you'll have to work even harder if..."

"If I want to be a professional dancer," Beth completed his sentence irritably. "Dad, I *know*."

On my chopsticks, I twirled a noodle from my vegetarian lo mein. This wasn't my favorite Chinese dish, but at least I had again managed to avoid eating pork. I kept wondering if Mom had noticed.

"Haven't heard about your poems in a while," Dad said to me, rolling himself a moo shoo pancake. "When do we get to hear one?"

I avoided his eyes. My recent poems were full of confusing religious images, bits of visions I had seen, and my own terrified reaction to seeing those firebombed dead bodies in the West Bank. "Um, never?"

"Nothing to be ashamed of," he said.

Mom put her hand on his. "It's OK if Rachel wants to keep her poems private."

"I'd like to read them too," Beth burst in. "I'll bet they explain what it was like to keep Shabbat with Orthodox Jews in Israel."

I choked on a noodle, as both my parents turned to face me. Mom's blue eyes were wide.

"You kept Shabbat in Israel?" Dad asked curiously.

"Just once," I managed to answer, shooting Beth an "I'll kill you later" look. She ignored me and nibbled another bite of egg roll.

"How was it?" Mom asked breathlessly.

"It was okay," I said, plucking the strands of the carpet to avoid everyone's eyes.

"Well, I guess it's a good idea to try something like that once," Dad said. "Were you stir crazy by the end?"

"Something like that," I said.

"Wouldn't want to live like that," said Dad, finishing his last pancake and collecting the trash from the coffee table. Out of the corner of my eye, I watched Beth toss half of her remaining egg roll into the bag.

Furious, I followed Beth up to her room.

"Why did you tell them?" I asked sharply.

She turned to face me. "You shouldn't become Orthodox under their noses without them at least knowing about it."

"It was one Shabbat!" I exclaimed.

"Yeah, and three weeks of lighting candles in your room on Friday night."

My blood ran cold. *What else had she noticed?* I took a deep breath to steady myself. "It's a tradition."

Beth put one hand on her hip. "A tradition Mom gave up her whole life to get out of," she said. "You think she wants you going back to the Middle Ages?"

My mouth opened, then closed. I'd never expected this from Beth. She was usually supportive of my choices. The stress from this winter had made her hard and cruel.

"Without Zaide here, Mom can finally do her own thing," Beth said. "The last thing she wants is a brainwashed daughter."

My stomach tensed. I thought Mom had some sympathy for the choices I was making. But if I was honest with myself, I hadn't told her myself because I still wasn't sure how she'd react. What if Beth was right?

"Thanks for telling me how you really feel," I said in a broken voice, leaving her alone to pack.

By the next morning, my anger at Beth had flared out. I remembered Yonatan and Noach saying I was supposed to help her somehow, and I knew I'd utterly failed her this winter. I felt distressed when she came into the kitchen the next morning, wearing an overlarge zipper sweatshirt, and declined breakfast.

"You haven't eaten enough this winter," Mom said. She was at the counter, making a cheese sandwich for Beth to eat on the plane.

Beth shrugged. "I could still stand to lose a few pounds," she said.

Mom and I both stared at her.

"I think you're thin enough, Beth," I said.

A pinched look came into her face. "Yeah," she said. "You're right."

I stood to hug her. She surprised me by hugging me tightly back.

"I'll miss you," I said. I didn't bother asking her to answer my calls, as I had after Thanksgiving. I knew she wouldn't.

"I'll be back for spring break," she said. Then she took a step back and her eyes focused on my face. She hadn't really looked at me since I got off the plane. "I miss you too."

I watched Beth roll her suitcase down the driveway and heave it into the car. Before she climbed in, she glanced back toward the window at me.

I put my palm against the glass. She raised her hand in a wave.

As she headed toward the plane that would take her thousands of miles away, I wished I knew what I was supposed to do to help her.

∞

After she'd gone, I sat on my meditation pillow, hoping for answers.

Freed from school early, he sits in the secret place, scribbling blurry ink into his wet notebook. Each day there is more to write; some days every face looks like his father's. His fingers are going numb.

Stuffing the book back into his bag, he pulls the lighter from his pocket, lights up...inhales...but it burns...oh...help.... like fire...

"Because of you, Rachel," the man says. "Because you came."

I awakened clutching my heart as the images flashed again before my eyes. *Snow. His wet notebook. The fire in his chest.*

I'd finally been granted another vision of Jake.

Because of you, Rachel, the man had said. What in the world did he mean? And what could cause the burning in his lungs? I knew weed didn't do that. Maybe it was a bad batch of something? Or maybe he was using something else.

∞

"Do you know how to help someone who's smoking too much weed?" I said to Lauren, as we sat in the mall food court the next afternoon. We'd spent the morning browsing new spring clothing, which almost felt uplifting until you considered the iron-gray sky and the dirty streaks of snow in the parking lot.

Lauren looked up from her cheeseburger, puzzled. "Who?"

I flinched. "Oh, just a guy I know," I hedged, and then, when she raised her eyebrows, I added, "from Poetry Club."

"*That* guy?" she asked. "Rach. You said he's not your type."

153

"I'm not talking about *dating* him," I said. "I just wondered if I could – help him."

She shrugged. "Do you know any of his family?"

I shook my head. "I don't really know him at all."

Lauren gave me a stern look. "He's not your problem."

"I know," I said.

But again that night in my meditation, he was.

The next afternoon in Poetry Club, I kept my eyes on my notebook to avoid staring at Jake's face. When he began to read his poem, in a voice full of ragged emotion, chills ran down my spine.

We never knew snow
In California
But it's
In the snow
I'm haunted
By your face.

Shadows and memories
Make impossible targets

For fists and rage.
Far as we run
From nightmares
There can be
No escape

Mid-poem, he glanced up and met my eyes—just for an instant—before he resumed his reading.

When the hour was over, I followed him out of the room.

"Thanks for sharing your poem," I said.

He shrugged, walking ahead of me. "It wasn't much."

"I'm sorry I didn't come out in the snow with you the other day," I told him.

He stopped abruptly, turning to face me. In the fluorescent light of the hallway, his face was sober, angry, and sad. "I wasn't expecting you to."

I drew back, stung. "Then why did you ask me?"

He shook his head and turned back down the hallway. Determined not to be left again, I rushed down the hall after him.

"Jake!" I shouted from behind. "I – I want to help you."

He turned back to me, outraged. "I don't need your help!"

I felt a crushing tightness in my chest as he walked away.

I thought the pain in my chest would stop after he left, but it worsened as I walked to my locker. By the time I packed my bag, I had to bend over to catch my breath. The lights whirled around me, unexpected, strong and fast.

I awaken gasping, struggling to breathe.

I know the time is coming, but...no. Not yet.

The young ones walking in the moonlight deserve this moment, but they will not have it. Rena stops abruptly in the stone alley, turning to Yonatan. "Something's wrong."

They have called 101 for an ambulance before they even make it back, unlocking doors and swinging into my bedroom, terror in their eyes.

I awakened slumped against my locker on the tile floor of the hallway, my hands clawing at my tight chest. I was alarmed by the unexpected vision; it hadn't happened like this since Israel.

I coughed hard and sat up, trying to catch my breath. *Couldn't breathe. And Rena and Yonatan...were coming to save me...*Who? Who?

The understanding came to me finally, just as it had with Jake. The person who couldn't breathe was Devorah.

DEVORAH

Beeping. The heavy sound of my own breathing. The soft babbling of faraway voices. The room is dim, lit by machines and the outside hall lights. A hospital.

They saved me. It almost seems too much trouble for an old woman, until I remember all that is at stake.

At the foot of my bed sits Rena, my constant protector. Yonatan is in the hall, soothing the girl. In Tzfat, Noach's eyes are focused out the window, to the dark abyss. But as always, his soul is focused on me.

What would have become of us, if not for his wisdom and unending faith?

"We will survive this," *he comforts me. But he knows I am not a part of that* we.

"I won't be able to keep the connection." *I admit this only to him, though I know it is his greatest terror.* "It will break, before the end."

"We are strong now," *he reassures me.* "And the girl grows stronger. I will guide her to restore it, when the time comes."

"But not yet," *I remind him. She is not ready yet.*

We both need to believe this. Because when she is ready, we know I will have to go.

CHAPTER 27

Back at home I curled into my usual meditation place, pillow against the wall.

"Yonatan," I whispered.

I was hoping he could send some Light to restore me, but I was surprised and almost confused when I heard his voice.

"Rachel."

I whirled around on the floor. It sounded as if he was right beside me, but of course no one was there.

"Yonatan," I cried out, tears streaming down my face.

"All is well." I heard his voice, comforting me.

"But what about Devorah?" I asked.

"All is well," he repeated.

As he began to channel the Light toward me, my lungs re-opened. I inhaled a strong, deep breath of air.

Of course everything would be okay with Devorah, I told myself. And it must be a sign of growth that my visions were getting stronger. Perhaps I wasn't as alone as I felt; maybe Yonatan really was watching out for me. Maybe I just hadn't needed him as much as I thought.

❧

Maya met me at my locker after the last bell rang the next afternoon. Though we had kept up a regular stream of texts, we hadn't seen each other since that afternoon before she came back to school. She wore pink lip gloss to match her fingernails, but I noticed she wasn't wearing her usual eyeliner or mascara.

"We need to talk," she said.

I felt a rush of concern, but her face seemed eager, rather than upset. I followed her to the nearest bathroom. She leaned back with one foot against the wall, squeezing her knuckles and avoiding my eyes. "It's about Chris," she said.

Chris had been far from my mind today. Still, my stomach fluttered as

I remembered our most recent walk. The shadow of a beard on his face in the sunlight.

Maya looked hopeful and almost guilty. "Rach. I always ...kept him off limits because of how you felt about him." I held up my hand in protest, but she shook her head, smiling ruefully. "It was obvious, kiddo."

I sighed. "It was never going to happen with Chris and me."

"It could have," she said. "But, Rach, we got to talking at this party last weekend and..." She blushed. "He asked me out, this Friday night. Would you mind? If you don't want me to – I won't."

"What have you done with my friend Maya?" I teased her. "The girl I know doesn't ask permission to go on a date."

She chuckled, but her face was serious. "Friends are more important than guys," she said. "I'm learning."

To hold her back would be selfish and pointless. I shrugged one shoulder. "Of course you can go out with him, Maya."

She fixed me with a hard stare. "Are you sure?"

I swallowed hard against the tightness in my throat. "Yes. I'm sure." I forced myself to smile. "Have fun."

⌒⌒

I had been trying to give Beth space at the beginning of her spring semester, but that night I could no longer restrain myself. I wanted my sister, the one who always had my back. I needed the one who always teased me about Chris to understand that, in the end, Maya was going to get him instead.

I dialed her number and pressed the phone to my ear. I shouldn't have been surprised when she didn't answer. "Beth, please call," I said, sniffling into the phone.

But of course, she didn't call.

In my muddled dreams that night, Jake exhaled fire like a dragon and Devorah walked barefoot through ghostly hospital hallways, haloed from behind as windows revealed the breaking of dawn. I watched her a long time, wishing she would notice me. But just as her gaze turned toward me, I suddenly awoke.

⌒⌒

That morning was frigid and cloudy. The snow began during Calculus, wet, thick flakes that stuck immediately on the cold ground. By History class, a thin coating of white lay on the schoolyard. We were in English when an early dismissal was called for the end of fifth period. The kids burst into applause.

I joined in their clapping, but something was nagging at me. An early dismissal in the snow. Had I – had I seen that recently – in a meditation? I struggled to remember.

⚭

"You've been scraping the bottom of that yogurt for ten minutes," Lauren pointed out at lunch.

"Sorry," I said, glancing up at her. "I was – just thinking about something."

"Care to share?" she asked, popping the last of her sandwich into her mouth.

I shook my head.

She tilted her head, curious. "Are you still worried about that poetry kid?"

That instant seemed to last a long time, as scenes from a recent meditation flashed before me. *Freed from school early, he sits in the secret place...*

Suddenly I understood. *Today, in the snow. Today* it was time for me to...

What? How? Frustration descended on me so powerfully, I felt almost dizzy. What was I supposed to do for him? Where was my clear instruction, my prophetic guidance? How could this be my responsibility? No one had answered any of my questions!

Just as rapidly, my frustration was replaced with fury, then desperation. I stood, ignoring Lauren's puzzled expression and the lunch tray in front of me. "I have to go."

"But we're not done till fifth period," she said.

I shook my head, grabbing my bag. "He's gone already."

CHAPTER 28

Outside, I wandered the streets, looking for him. The snow was already half an inch deep on the sidewalk. The frigid wind blew snow into my face, freezing my nose and cheeks. My fingers felt numb inside my gloves.

A stream ran under some of the roads in our neighborhood. That gulley where he hid had to be somewhere nearby. Half dazed by the cold, I walked several blocks in one direction before deciding it was the wrong way and turning back. Blinded by my own hot tears, I tripped several times, finally falling and twisting my left wrist.

Then I heard a low, terrible groan.

I froze, staring around me. "Jake!" I screamed.

Where was he? I waited, willing him to moan again.

"Ohhhhh." Then the awful sound of retching, and such a long and terrible cry I ran in his direction.

His baseball hat had fallen off. He wore no coat or gloves. His eyes were wide open, his body convulsing in some kind of seizure.

I stumbled downhill from the sidewalk to the stream, slipping a little on the snow. His shaking continued, spit and vomit dribbling from his mouth. I doubted he even knew I was there.

Ignoring the vomit, I knelt down next to him and grasped his fingers. They were stiff and frighteningly cold, but when I blew warm air onto them, he recoiled. Wincing a little at my sore wrist, I slipped off my gloves and put them on his hands.

"Help!" I shouted.

There was no answer, only a snowy silence. I was too late. What if he died right here? I thought of that time I'd rescued Chris after his bike accident, knocking on doors until I found someone to help. But I couldn't leave Jake here alone.

Hardly thinking, I opened my bag, tossing books and tissues into the snow. At last my hands closed around my cell phone, and with trembling fingers I dialed 911.

"It's an emergency!" I yelled into the phone.

When I'd finished giving the details, Jake had stopped shaking. His breath came in shallow gasps.

"Jake," I said, stroking his icy face with my cold fingers. "Stay with me."

I survived only because of you.

The words came back to me as if I was dreaming, but this was no dream. Jake lay unconscious, his body slowly being covered by the falling snow. Tears came rushing down my face, defrosting the tears already on my cheeks.

"I tried," I said, wiping my tears with my left sleeve so I didn't have to stop stroking his cheek with my right hand. "I tried. Please!" I screamed aloud. "Please, please." At last, I understood I was praying. "G-d, G-d! Let him live, please."

I prayed like that until finally I heard sirens approaching in the distance.

Lit by the revolving red glare of the ambulance, the EMTs rushed down the slippery hill in their sturdy boots, and lifted Jake onto a stretcher. They wrapped him in blankets and injected a needle into his arm. I watched from a distance, shoving my things back into my bag, until they shepherded me into the ambulance with them.

It was warmer inside, but my teeth still chattered. As the vehicle began to move, one of the EMTs turned to me.

"Are you high?" he asked. I shook my head. He grimaced, disbelieving. "Do you know what he's on?" I shook my head again.

He drew a sharp, impatient breath. "Listen, girl. I know you're scared, but his life might depend on it."

"I don't know what he's on," I said finally. My voice sounded very small against the background of the loud sirens. "I thought he smoked weed...but I think this was something different. I found him...after."

"I found a Spice packet," someone called from the front of the ambulance. "K-2."

The EMT cursed loudly. I shifted my arm and winced a little at my sore wrist. "Are you hurt?" he asked, a little more gently.

"Just m-my wrist," I said. "I fell when I was..." Tears started pouring down my cheeks again, unbidden. "When I was looking for him."

He studied Jake's immobile form under the blankets. "They can look at your wrist when we get to the hospital."

"Is he going to be okay?" I asked, unable to restrain myself.

The man gave me a pitying look. "Probably," he said. "This time."

◌◌

At the hospital, they rushed Jake away and left me in the emergency room. My teeth were still chattering, though I no longer felt cold, and new bursts of tears kept rolling down my cheeks.

When the triage nurse asked what had happened, I did my best to explain. "I knew he was out there in the snow," I told him. "I was worried what he might be...and when I found him..." I began to sob, overcome by the memory of him convulsing in the snow.

"Can I call someone to come get you?" he asked kindly.

"My mother." I didn't allow myself to wonder what she might think. I just needed her now.

◌◌

Mom was waiting in my little curtained area of the ER when I got back from the X-ray. Without a word, I began to sob in her arms. She stroked her fingers through my messy hair like when I was a little girl.

"Rachel, what happened? Are you all right?"

I had no answers for her questions.

The doctor who came to see us had curly brown hair streaked with gray, and her expression was friendly. She had good news: my wrist was sprained, not broken. She offered me a brace to keep it immobilized, and a prescription for painkillers. I took the brace, but refused the painkillers.

"No drugs," I said faintly. Then I looked up at the doctor. "Do you know anything about the boy I came in with?"

I ignored Mom's widening eyes, staring only at the doctor, who gave me a grim smile. "I heard you were quite the hero with him," she said. "I'm sorry, sweetheart, but I can't release any information. You should get in touch with one of his relatives."

A little sob escaped my chest. "Please," I said. My teeth had finally stopped chattering. "I just need to know he's going to be alright."

She hesitated. "Wait here a moment."

"Rachel," Mom began, as the doctor left, but I shook my head, staring at

163

the curtain. I couldn't speak until I knew what would happen to him.

After a few long moments, the doctor came back. "He's stable now," she said. "They're admitting him."

I slumped against my mother—spent, overwhelmed, but relieved. "Thank you," I said.

As the adrenalin drained out of me, my wrist began to throb. In the car, Mom drove carefully on unplowed streets, the windshield wipers pushing away sheets of falling snow.

It really wasn't safe to be out now. *What would have happened to him out there, if I hadn't found him?* I shuddered.

In the kitchen, Mom made tea and gestured for me to sit. I held the mug between my hands to warm them.

"Rachel," she said again. "What happened? Who was the boy you came in with?"

I took a deep breath. "He's just a ...friend," I told her. "From Poetry Club."

"But what were you doing out there with him in the snow?" She took a sip of her tea, waiting for me to explain.

I shook my head. "It wasn't – I mean – *he* was the one in the snow," I said. "I was just looking for him," I said. "I fell when I was trying to find him. That's how I hurt my wrist."

She frowned, pressing one hand against her own warm mug. "But why were you looking for him in – in this?" She gestured to the blizzard out the window. Outside, our car was already coated with a fresh layer of snow.

I stared at her a long moment, unsure how to answer. Finally, I said, "I just had a feeling he needed help."

She had been about to sip her tea but stopped, slowly setting it down on the table. "You had a feeling he needed help," she repeated slowly.

I nodded.

"What kind of help?"

"When I found him – " My voice broke. "He was having some kind of fit," I said. "I didn't know what to do. There was no one around. And then I remembered to call an ambulance..."

They have called 101 for an ambulance.

There was another ambulance. Devorah –

I felt suddenly disoriented, and I feared another vision was coming. But it seemed more a memory from an earlier vision that had overtaken me, like that moment in the snow when I heard Jake's adult voice reassuring me. Like that moment today, in the lunchroom, when I remembered about the early dismissal.

Was it a good sign I wondered, *that I was remembering these details?* Or a sign I was losing touch with reality?

Mom took another sip of her tea. "It sounds like you may have saved his life."

"I hope so," I said.

There was a short silence, as I tried to remember bits of the vision that had just flashed back to me, and Mom stared out the window at the swirling snow. Then she put her mug down carefully on the table. "Do you like this boy?"

I hesitated. "I think – I like the person he could be," I said.

She raised an eyebrow. "Be careful not to confuse that with the person he is," she said. "How's the wrist?"

I took a deep breath and slowly exhaled, "It'll be okay."

She wrapped her hands around her mug and studied me for a long, inexplicable moment. "When you're trying to save the world," she said finally, "don't forget to take care of yourself."

I sighed. "Yeah."

Mom had collected our mugs and was beginning to prepare dinner when Dad came out of his study, looking dazed the way he always did when he'd been staring at the computer too long.

"You're back," he said. "Where have you – Rachel, what happened to your wrist?"

I glanced at Mom. "I fell on the way home."

She forced a chuckle and rolled her eyes. "Sprained her wrist in the middle of a blizzard. We just got back from the ER."

"The ER!" he said. "Why didn't you call me? I would have come with you."

"There was no need to interrupt you," Mom said. "She asked for me." She said this with a quiet kind of pride.

Dad sat down next to me, taking my wrist and examining it gently. "How long will you need the brace?"

"Just a few days," I said.

Dad looked at Mom, who was beginning to chop carrots for a salad. "You should have told me," he said. "I would have wanted to be there."

I shrugged. "It wasn't that big a deal, Dad," I told him. "I know you're busy with your book."

Dad frowned, running his fingers across the stubble on his chin. Outside, it was getting dark. The snow fell harder, wind whipping the flakes into spirals on our lawn.

"The book is important," Dad said, "but you are much more important to me. I'm sorry if I haven't made that clear to you."

"Thanks, Dad." I appreciated the sentiment, but in reality his recent distraction had been almost helpful. "Really, I'm fine."

He reached for my good arm, and rubbed it gently. "Let's do something fun together soon, OK? Maybe a little hike, when your arm heals?"

Though I craved time with my father, his offer made me nervous. What would we talk about? I reassured myself he would probably stay absorbed in his book; it might be months before he remembered this invitation. I shrugged noncommittally.

"Sure, Dad," I said. "Whenever you want."

Lauren had left three voicemails and sent half a dozen texts by the time I checked my phone after dinner. Cradling my throbbing wrist, I put my phone on speaker to call her.

"Rach!" she said with relief. "Where are you?"

"I'm home," I said wearily.

"Do you want me to come over?"

"No," I said. "It's terrible out. You should stay home."

"What happened?" she demanded.

I sighed. "It's kind of a long story." I could picture her in her bedroom, chewing her fingernails, as I explained how I found him. The sight of him convulsing in the snow kept flashing before my eyes, like a vision that wouldn't go away. "He was...in pretty bad shape. But he's in the hospital now."

"*Hospital*," she said slowly. "Are *you* okay?"

"Basically," I said, fiddling with the brace on my arm. "I hurt my wrist, but it's no big deal."

"Why in the world did you go looking for him?" she said in an exasperated tone. "You knew how terrible it was out there."

Tears filled my eyes again. How could I explain that my meditations had given me no choice? "I couldn't just let him die," I said.

"Do you really think he would have died?" she asked in a whisper.

Through my window, I could see streetlights illuminating the snow, nearly a foot deep and still falling. "Maybe."

"Well, it's good he's in the hospital and other people are taking care of him," she said. "Now you can stop worrying about him and take care of yourself."

I wanted her to be right. Maybe I'd done all I needed to. But I couldn't stop seeing Jake's face.

By Thursday morning, the snow in our driveway had reached 30 inches. On the news, the broadcasters called the storm a "Snowtastrophe" and reported power outages, downed trees, and blocked roads. School was closed as the plows worked to clear the streets.

I called the hospital and asked for Jake's room, but I was surprised when he answered. "Hullo?" He sounded gruff, groggy.

"Jake..." I hesitated. During our last conversation, he had refused my help and stormed away. "It's Rachel."

"Rachel." In a more lucid voice, he asked, "Was it you?"

I hesitated. "Yes."

"In the snow?"

"Yes," I said. "I called the ambulance for you."

He cleared his throat. "Then...uh...thank you."

"You're welcome," I said.

"When I get out of here...maybe we could talk sometime?" His voice sounded suddenly young, and unexpectedly hopeful.

I set aside all the warnings I'd heard, as well as my own certainty he was more trouble than I could handle. I only answered to the man I'd seen in my meditations.

"Sure," I said.

CHAPTER 29

School was closed again on Friday. Lauren and I worked on our latest Physics packet together over the phone, avoiding further conversation about Jake. From my window, I watched Chris shoveling the snow from his driveway.

Our street was cleared in the early afternoon. An hour after the plow departed, Maya texted me. *Chris still wants to go tonight! So excited.*

I had forgotten all about their approaching date.

Great, I texted back, adding a smiley face to show my support.

⌒⌒

That evening, I lit candles for Shabbat, careful not to catch my wrist brace on fire. As I backed away from the flames, my eyes landed on the small siddur Yonatan had given to me in Tzfat, on the bookshelf from when I unpacked my bags from Israel.

Despite my regular meditations, I hadn't picked it up even once since then. But tonight – with my wrist still aching, deep uncertainty about Jake, and Chris on a date with one of my closest friends – I picked it up and turned to Shabbat evening prayers.

After months of attending synagogue, many of the words were familiar to me. I whispered some prayers in English, others in Hebrew, working myself into a fervor, pouring out my heart to G-d. I had always thought of these repetitive devotions as rote and foreign, but tonight I folded myself into them, as if they were a home I belonged inside.

When I reached the end of the prayers, I felt restored, almost as if Yonatan had been channeling Light toward me. As if G-d had been listening.

⌒⌒

Later that night, I whispered the mystical words, weaving them together like a dance in slow motion. Swirling sparks… Wind… Silence.

It is very late. In the front room of the Prophets' House, Noach is studying with several others, poring over the ancient books.

"The connection binds the prophets together and to the Ein Sof.[24]*The one we call great can access it, ascending to the level of Chaya, where all souls are already connected. One holds the space for the unity of all."*

Noach closes the book and takes off his glasses, rubbing his forehead. "When Shimon haGadol died in the Shoah, we were blinded. It was seven years before I found Devorah. It's taken decades to rebuild."

"Devorah," Yitzchak says, looking out the windows to the darkness below.

"Will she be ready?" Tirtza asks.

"She'll have to be."

The next morning, I called the hospital again, but Jake had already been discharged. Just as I hung up, Maya called. "How was the date?" I asked.

"Ama-a-zing," she said, stretching the word into extra syllables. "Rach! You never told me how *nice* he is."

I smiled ruefully. "Yeah. He's a really good guy."

"He brought me flowers, even opened my car door for me to get in. He listened to what I had to say, didn't just try to..." I could almost hear her grinning. "I really like him."

I pictured Maya sitting cross-legged on her bed, with pink lipstick to match her perfectly painted toes. This kind of enthusiasm about a boy wasn't all that unusual for her, but I hadn't heard her sounding this way about anything or anyone since we came home from Israel. "That's great," I said.

"Has he said anything about me?"

"No." With everything else happening, I hadn't texted him once this week.

I imagined her twirling her hair around two fingers. "I hate the part where you wait for him to call," she said.

"Why don't you call him?"

"Nah," she said. "Guys hate it when you're too eager."

I shrugged. Maya had a whole list of rules about dating and boys. "But you'd go out with him again, if he asked?"

"A thousand times yes," she said.

After we hung up, I texted Chris. *Date go ok?* I asked. As I waited for his answer, it felt as if not only Maya's happiness but also mine hung in the balance.

---

[24] Hebrew name for G-d, meaning "Endless One."

Finally, after twenty long minutes, he texted his reply. *She seems great.*
I swallowed hard. *Yeah,* I texted back. *She is.*

From my porch stairs, I watched the Orthodox Jews returning home from synagogue. It was a sunny morning and the air had warmed into the 40s. All the trees were dripping melted snow like tears.

"Shabbat shalom," Mom said, joining me on the stairs.

A family of seven rounded the corner. The mother pushed a double stroller, her winter coat open to reveal a long dress and round pregnant stomach. The father wore a black hat; white fringes hung from under his dark jacket. Two boys and a girl, dressed like miniatures of their parents, straggled behind.

"Was it like this for you?" I asked abruptly, gesturing to the family.

Mom smiled faintly. "Something like it," she said. "I was the youngest, and the only girl, so my mother often stayed home with me Shabbos mornings, instead of taking me to synagogue."

I fingered Zaide's necklace, trying to imagine him as the father in this family, with Mom one of the little children, observing Shabbat so long ago. "Was it...nice?"

"Some parts were nice," she said.

I turned to face her. "Then why did you leave?"

She exhaled a sigh. "It's complicated."

Frustrated, I turned back to the street. The children passed in front of us, the younger boy pulling at fringes sticking out from under the elder's shirt. The girl ignored them, her chin held high.

"At a certain...time in my life, I needed to find my own way." Mom hesitated. "And then I met your father." Her voice softened when she spoke about him, even though they had been married for more than two decades, even though he spent so much time burrowed in his office. "And we fell in love."

She hadn't been much older than me, I thought. Was her choice any crazier than the ones I was making right now?

"Was Zaide angry?"

She shook her head. "I think he felt guilty, more than anything. That he hadn't given me what I'd needed. But he said everything was part of G-d's plan."

"Do you ever...wish you hadn't given it all up?"

"Well, I haven't given it *all* up," she said. "We keep the kitchen kosher. We go to synagogue on the high holidays. Right?" She tilted her head at me, as if to make her point, that these things had at least made the traditions more accessible to me.

I nodded, chewing the inside of my lip.

Then she sighed, studying her fingernails. "There are some things I miss," she said. "Mostly the community. Orthodox Jews take good care of each other. But it was also...very restrictive. Don't eat this. Don't wear that. Don't think about that." She glanced back at the street, where the children were turning onto the next block. "I appreciate the freedom I have now."

"Do you ever feel guilty?" I asked.

She chuckled. "I don't know a person who doesn't."

My phone vibrated several times that afternoon before I found it under my pillow. I was surprised to see Beth's number.

"Hi!" I said brightly.

"Sorry I've been so hard to track down." She sounded tired.

"What have you been up to?"

"Working on a huge dance project," she said. "What's new with you?"

I could only share the thing I least wanted to talk about. I took a deep breath. "Do you remember my friend Maya?"

"The cheerleader? Sure."

"She went on a date with Chris last night."

"Oh," Beth said, in a voice that let me know she understood.

"It's all good," I said, hoping the little crack in my voice wouldn't give me away. "I mean, I hope they can be happy together."

"She shouldn't have," she said. "She knew you –"

"She asked my permission," I said. "I told her she could. Because it would never have worked out, for him and me."

She hesitated, probably deciding not to argue with me. "Don't worry," she said finally. "They say guys are like busses. If you miss one, another will be along in twenty minutes."

Despite myself, I laughed. "Really, they say that?"

"Yep," she said. I could hear her smiling. She had been so cold and distant over the winter, I'd almost forgotten how kind and loving Beth could be. "I'm coming home in April for spring break," she said. "We'll go for ice cream and figure out who the next guy is going to be. Okay?"

I giggled. "Okay. That sounds great."

Only after I hung up did I realize that Beth had offered to get *ice cream* with me. Ice cream was hardly on the diet she'd been so strict about this winter. Maybe she was back to eating more normally. Maybe she would sort it all out herself, without any help from me.

⚭

So many times recently I had meditated hoping to find answers, but that night I tried to release any notions of where I might be going. I simply allowed the sparks to lift me away.

The air is dusty and hot in the attic bedroom. The sleeping girl seems so young and beautiful, like one of his sisters. But she is not a sister; she is the enemy. His hand shakes as he lifts the knife, but it is steady by the time he plunges it down over the sound of her screams...

As I awaken from the terrible vision, two nurses rush into the hospital room. "Sedate her. She should not be agitated like this."

A babble of voices rises, then fades as sleep comes. But I need...to...Noach –

My bedroom door slammed open and there Mom found me, hysterical, screaming into my meditation pillow.

Mom held me tight, rocking me until I found my legs on the floor, my head buried in her shoulder. "It's OK," she said quietly. "Shh."

I couldn't stop seeing the girl, the blood, the knife. I whispered the holy words once, twice, again and again, until the spinning stopped, the lights stopped flashing, the images faded. I took a huge gulp of air.

Mom smoothed her hand through my hair. "Did you have a nightmare?"

I nodded. "Thanks...for...."

"I'm always here for you," she said.

"I guess I must have fallen asleep...here," I said, gazing down at the floor.

Mom helped me into bed and kissed me on the forehead. "Go back to sleep, Rachel."

⚭

But of course, I didn't. I pulled out my phone and searched the news. Who was she? Where was she? Had this terrible thing already happened? Or was it something I could stop? I found nothing, which frightened me even more.

I considered trying to meditate again, but Yonatan had always warned me to meditate only once each day. And of course, there was no guarantee I'd see the same thing this time.

Yonatan. In the darkness, I clung to the golden thread of spiritual Light still connecting us. Would he know what I had seen? Wouldn't he want to help me? *Yonatan.*

He didn't answer.

All night I lay awake, haunted by images of the young man with the knife, the girl's screams, the blood. Compulsively I googled words like "stabbing," "bedroom," "young girl," "murder." To my horror, I discovered more than one young girl had been stabbed to death just in the last year. But none of them were murdered in their bedrooms.

As the sky lightened outside my window, I read these reports obsessively, as if they held clues to the puzzle, when of course, any true answer was buried in my own head. Or, as Yonatan might say, "in my soul."

At last the weight of the long night overwhelmed me and I succumbed to nightmarish dreams: long shadows, shiny knives and Devorah's frantic, breathless screams.

∽

"There was a prophecy." Noach, increasingly desperate: "Did you see it? Did you? Did you?" "No." "No." "No."

"Devorah is sleeping. She must have...."

Tears in his iridescent eyes. "We have not been given the wisdom to save."

Terrified, I raise my voice. The weight of all prophetic consciousness shifts toward me, as I reveal what I saw. The girl. The knives. The blood.

"It is Rahel," Noach says.

"Too soon," Yonatan says.

"Better than too late."

CHAPTER 30

When Mom woke me late the next morning, I felt groggy and confused. Was it a dream, or had I actually sent a message to the prophets? I didn't know. Winter sunlight streamed into my bedroom. I clung again to the mystical strand of Light connecting me to Yonatan.

"Someone's here to see you," Mom said.

I squinted at her. "Who?"

She frowned. "I don't know. A boy." Eyeing my pajamas, she said, "You should get dressed."

He stood on the front porch, his hands stuffed in the pockets of his unzipped winter jacket. He had shaved – or maybe that happened at the hospital – and his chin was smooth as baby's skin. As usual, he wore a baseball cap over his eyes.

"Jake," I said, opening the door. Then I burst into tears.

He gave me a puzzled smile.

"It's so good to see you alive," I said.

As I came closer, I could see the whites of his eyes, streaked with red. His face seemed paler than usual. He squeezed his knuckles together. "I guess I should thank you for that."

Outside in the sun, the temperature was almost comfortable after the blizzard we'd been through several days before. Jake kept zipping and unzipping his jacket with trembling hands. We started walking up my street in the direction away from the synagogue. When we passed Chris's house, I couldn't help looking up, to see if he was in a window. He wasn't.

We walked past dirty gray snow melting into the gutters and dormant tree branches shining in the sun. As we rounded the corner, Jake swallowed hard and shoved his hands back into his pockets. "Wanted you to know...I haven't been on...anything since the hospital."

Studying his face, I found a mix of emotions: confusion, gratitude, fear. "I'm really glad to hear that," I said.

"Didn't want to waste all your efforts," he muttered. I watched him muster the courage to ask the question that must have brought him here. "Why did you save me?"

"Someone had to," I said.

He looked away, as if he hadn't expected anyone ever would.

"What the heck were you doing out there?" I asked.

"Sometimes the snow helps," he said. "With my writing."

I gave him a skeptical glance.

He sighed, looking down at the sidewalk. "I know. It was idiotic. But it seemed to make sense...at the time." His eyes fell on my wrist. "Did you hurt your arm?"

I shrugged. "Just a sprain."

As we continued walking, I found myself thinking of Yonatan. Would he approve of my walking with this strange boy in the snow? Had I finished the task called for by my visions, or was there more for me to do here? I felt again for the Light connecting us, and to my sudden alarm, I realized it wasn't there.

Yonatan wasn't there. I stopped on the sidewalk as icy terror rushed through me.

Jake turned back to me. "Hey," he said. "You OK?"

But then, just as quickly, it was there again. I exhaled slowly, trying to calm my sprinting heart. Jake reached out a shaking hand and squeezed mine.

"You look like you just saw a ghost."

The sun had slipped behind a cloud and the air around us suddenly felt cold. I shook my head. "I'll be fine," I managed to say.

He hesitated. "I wrote a poem for you," he said. "Do you want to hear it?"

"I'd love to," I said.

We sat down on the edge of the sidewalk, both of us shivering. He pulled a crinkled paper out of his pocket, unfolded it, and began to read.

Rachel.
Ghost of my dreams
Gift I didn't deserve –
Thank you.

When I believed
I was beyond help,
You appeared

In depths of darkness
To save me.

I cannot betray
Your noble action,
Cannot repay this,
Except by living.

As he finished, tears appeared in the corner of each of his eyes. He turned to me. "I know I've f****ed it all up," he said. "I hope it's not too late... to be better."

I put my hand on his. "It's not too late," I said.

He shook his head, gazing at the trees in the distance. "I don't know what happened last week. I've done spice a bunch of times before and it was never so awful." He shuddered. "But I know I have to stop...everything."

"Yes," I said.

"Last couple days have been rough," he said. "If you still want to help...I could use a friend."

Despite myself, I smiled. "Sounds good to me."

He looked at me more carefully. "What happened back there?"

Yonatan's connection was back: a tenuous strand of Light connecting me to Israel, the prophets, and all I had learned. I shook my head.

"Will you be okay?" he asked, more gently.

"I'll live."

"Hopefully we both will," he said.

∞

Back in the house, Mom hovered nearby while I ate a late breakfast, obviously hoping I would volunteer something about my conversation with Jake. As I finished my cereal, she sat down across from me. "How was your walk?" she asked pointedly.

"Fine," I said.

"Are you going to see him again?"

"Probably."

She hesitated, studying my face. "Rachel...Just be careful."

"Okay," I said. I knew she was right.

Chris came to my desk as I was gathering my books at the end of History the next morning. Even after everything, his presence could still make my heart beat faster.

"Did you have a nice date?" I asked, in as bright a voice as I could manage.

"Yeah." He cleared his throat as we walked into the hallway, keeping his eyes on my face. "I asked her out again."

"Good," I said.

I walked a little faster toward my next class, but he easily kept pace with me. "She talked about you," he said. "Said you were one of the best friends she has. It got me thinking..." He hesitated. "She doesn't know what happened...with us. Right?"

I shook my head. He exhaled in relief.

I made myself look at him, then forced myself to say it: "I think you should give it a try with Maya. You're both good people."

He gave me a sad, lingering look. "If you think so."

His voice echoed in my head as I continued down the hallway, like a door slamming shut.

Now that I was paying attention, I noticed with increasing alarm that my connection with Yonatan was weakening. The thin strand of Light seemed to fade several times a day.

Meanwhile, I continued to obsess over news websites, searching for a young girl stabbed in her bedroom. I was relieved each time I found nothing new, but couldn't help going back to check again.

Worries about Jake compounded my anxiety. He'd asked to be friends, but I didn't know where he lived or even how to contact him. In my meditations, I saw him unable to eat, struggling with nightmares, hiding his suffering from his family. When he didn't appear in school Tuesday, I walked to the little gulley where I'd found him the week before. I didn't know if I should be relieved or frightened to find the place empty.

He finally stopped by my locker on Wednesday between fourth and fifth period. The straggly hair was growing back onto his cheeks. His forehead was creased in pain.

"Headache?" I guessed.

He looked down at the tile floor. "Yeah," he said. "I barely slept last night." He shook his head, finally meeting my eyes. "I didn't think I'd have these detox kind of symptoms. Not from weed, anyway. And it's not like I was smoking spice that long."

"Do you think it would help to talk to a doctor?" I asked.

He shook his head. I noticed his hands were still trembling. "I've heard the first week is the worst."

"I hope you feel better," I said sincerely.

⚭

I took off the wrist brace Thursday morning. My arm felt lighter, but weaker than normal as I lifted my flute to my lips in Orchestra. First, I felt the music ripple around me, then the sparks—a boomerang of disorienting light.

The song continued as I stood abruptly, flinging my flute to the chair and hurrying into the hall. I wrenched open the door to the costume closet with shaking hands; the door slammed behind me as I fell.

"Come downstairs," she whispers. "Shh. Don't waste your strength."

We climb up steps and through dark alleyways, a strange procession in the middle of the night. At the top of the stairs, Yonatan opens the apartment door.

My legs sprawled on the dirty closet floor. Hands pressed against my face, I grasped for the thread of spiritual Light that connected me to Yonatan, but he was not there.

The bell rang.

Back in the Orchestra room, Lauren was waiting by my chair. Wearily, I picked up my flute and began to disassemble the pieces to put them in my case.

"Another migraine?" she asked quietly.

"Something like that." I snapped the locks shut on my flute case and picked it up.

"Rach?" Her eyes were wild with worry. "I just want to know you're okay."

How could I reassure her? I was definitely *not* okay. I was losing touch with Yonatan. Something was wrong with Devorah. Chris was dating Maya. I had no idea how to be the kind of friend Jake needed. If my visions were right, there was still a girl who was at risk of being brutally murdered, and I had no way to prevent it. And just now, an unexpected vision had nearly happened in a room full of people.

"I've heard I'm a good listener," she said.

I myself had told Lauren that many times. But now I was afraid. If I told her what was really happening, she'd try to talk me out of everything I knew to be true. And right now I needed, more than anything, to believe.

As I'd learned more than once, a vision was not a good way to start a full day of classes. After hours of observing my exhaustion, Lauren asked at lunch if I wanted to go to the nurse. "No," I said, so forcefully that she ate quickly and left with an excuse about School Council. For the first time in all our years of friendship, her absence felt like a relief.

All afternoon I kept checking for Yonatan's presence, but I felt nothing except my own growing sense of dread.

"Rachel."

I startled, nearly banging my head on the shelf of my locker.

Very gently, Jake put his hand on my back. "It's just me."

Blood racing, I turned to face him. He still looked miserable, his dark eyes sunken into a weary face. But he seemed amused by my reaction, and his genuine smile felt like a good sign.

"Don't do that," I said.

"I'm not your ghost," he said, lifting both hands to show his innocence. His gaze made me uncomfortable, as if all my secrets were written on my forehead, and he could read them. I turned away, grabbing a book in my locker and shoving it into my bag.

"You've made it the whole week," I said, aiming for a brighter voice as I turned back to him. "How are you feeling?"

He smiled wryly. "Sh***ty."

"Have you tried cranberry juice?" I asked. "I read it could help with detox."

He chuckled. "Thanks for looking into that," he said. "I'll give it a try."

"Are you planning to celebrate?" I asked, slamming the door to my locker.

"How about dinner?" he said. "Tomorrow night?"

"Y-you mean...with me?"

He held my eyes. "Yeah."

I stared at him in shock for a few seconds, but in the end I answered yes.

DEVORAH

On the way home from the hospital, Rena and I ride in the back seat next to oxygen tanks. I insist on taking each breathless step to my apartment. Rena's arm for support, as Yonatan goes ahead to unlock the door.

"Need...to get to...the Kotel."

"Another day," Rena suggests. I shake my head stubbornly. Today.

Finally the Kotel rises above me; I am here.

"Ribbono Shel Olam: Please, may it not be the last time.

"But more important than me, a young girl is in danger. The knives, the blood. Rachel has seen it. Please give us the wisdom to save."

I wait a long time, whispering the holy words, my face pressed against the smooth stones. Will I have the merit to save her? At last, the sparks descend.

The name of the settlement. The place of the breach. Lock doors. Tighten security. Tuesday at dawn.

I understand. It will be done.

CHAPTER 31

On Friday afternoon I picked through my closet and finally settled on an outfit I thought Maya would approve: purple sweater, stretchy jeans, short leather boots. I pulled out the make-up set she had given me and applied lipstick, mascara, and blush. Instead of my usual ponytail, I brushed my hair and let it hang long over my shoulders. I was ready more than a half hour before I had to leave. From my window, I watched the Orthodox men on their way to synagogue.

Since coming home from Israel, I had lit candles every Friday night, with tea lights and matches stashed in a desk drawer along with the Jewish star plate I'd made in Hebrew school. Last week, I'd finished my candles. When I opened the drawer, I realized I'd forgotten to get more.

I slipped downstairs to the wall unit in the living room, where I'd discovered them before. That time, I'd left only a few in the drawer, but tonight, I found a new box.

"Thank you," I whispered, not sure if I was thanking G-d or my mother.

Back in my room, Yonatan's presence hovered around me, stronger than it had been in days. I thought of Tzfat: the prophetesses swaying in the breeze of an open window. Longing rose up from deep inside me as I lit the candles and made the blessing.

Outside, the sun glowed orange against the bare trees. It was time to go. I pulled my grandfather's star necklace out from under my shirt, so it could be seen. And I left the candles burning in my bedroom, shutting the door tightly as I went out.

❦

Jake had told me to meet him at the Old Court Café, an old fashioned diner not far from school. When I got there, he was already in the front lobby, pacing along the maroon carpet from a car racing video game to a vintage Pac Man machine.

He looked better. His cheeks were clean shaven, his skin closer to a normal shade. He wasn't wearing his baseball cap, and he had combed his blond hair.

When he saw me, his face brightened.

"I didn't know if you would come," he said.

I raised my eyebrows. "If I came for you in the blizzard, I think I can make it to dinner."

I meant it as a joke, but he didn't laugh. Instead, he reached out to touch a single strand of my hair with his trembling hand, as if to reassure himself I was real. He kept glancing at me and away again, as if my face was the sun and he didn't want to stare too long at it.

"I tried some cranberry juice," he said.

I was surprised he'd considered my suggestion. "Did it help?"

He gave a little shrug and finally met my eyes. "I haven't slept much," he said. "But the headache is a little better."

"But you haven't – you know – tried anything since...?"

He shook his head. "No. Nothing."

"Is it hard?" I asked. "Not to?"

He took a deep breath and exhaled slowly through his nose. "Yes. It's hard."

The hostess assigned us a booth where ice water was already melting onto paper placemats. Jake took a sip of water and peered out the window at the darkening sky. I fidgeted awkwardly with my straw. I had never been good alone with boys. Except for Chris. Thinking of him made me wonder what in the world I was doing here.

It was because of the visions, I reminded myself. I clung to the Light Yonatan was sending me, afraid his presence would abandon me just at the moment I needed him most.

In the fluorescent light of the diner, Jake looked less than dangerous. He seemed more like a lost child trying to find his way home. "I'm doing it for my kid sister," he said suddenly. "She doesn't need a burn-out for a brother."

I reached my hand across the table and placed it gently on top of his. "No, she doesn't," I said. "How old is she?"

A smile played at the corners of his eyes, and I understood how much he loved this girl. "Twelve."

"Does she know? That you stopped?"

He shrugged. "I never officially started."

"You think she didn't know you were getting high?" I asked skeptically. "Why does she think you were in the hospital?"

He took a quick sip of water and glanced back out the window. "You're right. I should tell her."

That made two times he'd accepted my suggestions. Emboldened, I squeezed his hand, then released it abruptly as the waitress came to take our orders.

I ordered a grilled cheese with a side salad. Jake ordered scrambled eggs and a ginger ale.

"Scrambled eggs for dinner," I said, as the waitress walked away.

He fixed his gaze back out the window. "Helps with the nausea."

I looked up at him. "That's still a problem?"

"From time to time," he said.

There was an awkward silence. I found myself comparing this miserable boy to the man I'd seen in my visions. Was there really a shadow of that man in this kid? I worried I had misunderstood everything. But then I remembered his poetry.

"When did you start writing poems?" I asked.

He squinted back at me. "When I was seven, I think. I've had notebooks of them for as long as I can remember."

I flushed. "Me too."

"I liked your poem on Monday," he said, leaning toward me.

The poem I'd shared was one I'd started in Israel, on the bus when we were leaving Tzfat. *Ancient land, mountains, stars/ Find me in the distance/ Let me enter/ Where others departed* ..."Thanks," I said.

"You say nice things about my poems, but yours are good too," he said. "You should try to get something published."

I shook my head. "My poems are too private."

"Yeah, I always say that too. But no one knows what you *really* mean in a poem. They just hear their own stuff."

I shrugged. "Maybe."

When the waitress returned to deliver our food, I lifted my water glass to his ginger ale. "Cheers," I said. "To one week."

He grinned and clinked my glass.

I took a long moment pouring the dressing onto my salad, watching furtively as Jake nibbled at his eggs. He ate apprehensively, as if a bomb might be hiding in his food.

"I wrote that poem in Israel this winter," I said.

"I heard you went," he said, taking another careful sip. "What was it like there?"

I took a bite of my salad and chewed slowly. I hadn't really meant to talk about Israel. After all, this meal was about him, not me. But now that he'd asked, I wanted to tell him.

"Life changing," I said.

He looked up with interest, and I saw him take a more healthy bite of his bagel while his eyes were focused on me.

"I spent the Sabbath in a city called Tzfat. I –" I hesitated, then rushed ahead. "I met a lot of holy people there."

"Do you do that often?" he asked, taking another bite of his eggs. "Celebrate Shabbat?"

My eyes widened at the Hebrew term. "Jake," I said in surprise, "are you Jewish?"

He chuckled, swallowing another sip of ginger ale. "A bit," he said, waving his hand from side to side. "My mom had an aunt who was Orthodox. We stayed there for a few months..." He picked up his bagel and crumbled it slowly in his hands. "When I was little. She died...oh, maybe five years ago."

"My grandfather was Orthodox," I told him. "He died last summer."

He rested his chin in his hands. "That sucks," he said.

A laugh burst out of me, because it was such a strange way to say it and yet so true.

"I'd like to go to Israel one day," he said, a little wistfully. "Get my life changed."

"Careful," I said, rubbing at the corner of my eye. "You might not want it changed all that much."

"Anything better than this, here." He sighed and pushed his plate away. "Excuse me," he said, and stood to make his way to the bathroom.

After he left, I finished my salad and most of the grilled cheese. He had eaten less than half of his eggs, and most of the bagel was crumbled into pieces on his plate. *Was he throwing up in there?* I wondered. What a misery it was to detox from addiction.

Sitting in the booth, waiting, I wondered if I could doing anything for him. That one time in Tzfat, I had been able to channel Light to Yonatan. Jake was no prophet, and this was no holy land. But could I help him in that same way?

I breathed deeply, concentrating as hard as I could. A wave of Light began to build and wash through me, flowing out and – I hoped – toward Jake. Slowly, my wishes took form as a prayer.

G-d, please heal him.

The Light inside me burned stronger. With a twinge of alarm, I realized I didn't know how to stop or contain it.

My breathing came faster. My head began to throb. Then, all of a sudden, lights began to flash around me and it was too late to do anything but rest my head on the table before it fell.

Four flames flicker in the breeze of an open window in Devorah's apartment. Yonatan has cleared the table of the Friday night meal and washed the few dishes from it. It is late, but he has lingered in the front room, watching the candles burning.

He would arrange the candles for Nechama on Friday afternoon in their tiny apartment in Sderot. She always lit candles with a song.

How did he get here, alone? Some days it's so unfair he can barely breathe.

The burst of light catches him by surprise. Rachel: lost in the whirlwind and screaming. How did she even...?

But this is the kind of risk they took, leaving her there alone.

Knowing the danger to his own soul, he ascends.

"The girl has entered realms
Where she is not yet welcome, and
She is my responsibility
So I have come for her."

The form of an angel
Appears before him.
"Then take her back"
He says sharply,
Casting us both roughly
to the ground.

I knew I had done something wrong.

I had been in a place where everything was white. A holy place. But I myself was unholy, and unwelcome there. Straining to remember, I thought Yonatan had saved me. But his presence was gone now.

My head was throbbing; my throat felt tight and sore. My shoulders and knees ached. And of course, I felt shatteringly exhausted.

When I finally I opened my eyes I saw, to my dismay, that Jake was back in his seat across from me. He tilted his head curiously when I lifted my head.

"Did you have a good trip?" he asked sardonically.

I shook my head, almost too tired to feel the horror of what had happened.

I massaged my fingertips against my temples. He took another sip of his ginger ale and a few bites of food. I thought he looked a little better. Maybe my effort had helped him, a bit, before it took me to the wrong place.

When he had finished his eggs, he put down the fork and looked at me. "Are you going to tell me what happened?"

My voice sounded small and hoarse. "Maybe someday."

"Is it some kind of drug?"

I shook my head. "Maybe we could both use a...friend who understands?" I said.

He squeezed my hand back, and stroked the top of my fingers with his thumb. "Yeah," he said, his eyes locked on my face.

The busboy came to take our dishes: mine with the remains of grilled cheese I couldn't manage to eat, and Jake's with most of his bagel crushed into crumbs.

Back in the lobby, we watched through the window as snow flurries began to fall in the dark. I didn't want to drive. I didn't want to do much of anything, except sleep.

"I had a nice time with you tonight," Jake said. His voice was quiet but hopeful. He reached for my hand and held it.

"I did too," I said. "It's nice to know you a little better."

"Maybe we can do it another time," he said. "When you're feeling better."

"When we're both feeling better," I said.

He shrugged, as if his own ailments were of no consequence to him compared to mine. It seemed ironic that at this moment, I felt worse than he did.

"Do you need a ride home?" I asked.

He shook his head. "I live in the apartments just around the corner."

"I should go," I said, but we kept standing there. His hand felt like a tether, preventing me from slipping back to that place where I didn't belong and never should have been.

Unexpectedly, he leaned forward and kissed my cheek. "Have a safe trip home," he said into my ear.

All night we had been talking about being friends, but this seemed different. I turned in surprise, but he only squeezed my hand and released it.

"I'll see you in school," he said, and walked me out into the snow.

CHAPTER 32

It was not easy to drive home. My whole body ached and I was so tired I could barely keep my eyes open. When I came in through the kitchen, I was surprised to find Mom at the table.

"Rachel, where have you been?" There was an edge in her voice.

I leaned against the kitchen wall. "Out with a friend."

She stood, hands on her hips. "Who?"

"Jake," I said. "The guy from poetry."

"Oh." She seemed to wilt a little at my response. "On a date?"

I shook my head. "We're just friends."

She descended back into her chair, as if I'd sapped the energy from her. "I didn't...I didn't think you would take the car. On Friday night. Unless you really needed to."

I dropped into the chair across from her. "I probably shouldn't have."

She shrugged and waved her hands. "It's fine if you want to," she said. "I just worried...because I didn't know where you were."

I put my head in my hands. Mom stood and came over to me, resting one hand on my arm. As with Jake, her touch was grounding when everything around me felt surreal.

"You look tired," she said.

I looked up at her, and the mountain of weight on my shoulders overwhelmed me. "I'm so tired," I said.

"Then you should go to sleep," she said.

In my bedroom, my candles had burned out. I didn't turn on the light. With the last of my strength I pulled down the covers and fell into my bed.

By morning, my body was burning with fever.

⚭

Mom said it was probably the flu, and I let her believe that, because the symptoms were close enough. But I never doubted this was a spiritual punishment. I lay in bed, head throbbing, shivering; too sick to eat or read. I expected visions to come crashing over me too, but the reality was actually worse: no visions at all.

Trapped in the miserable present, I retraced every instant of the night before, trying to understand what I'd done wrong. Had it been trying to channel Light to someone like Jake? Or the fact that we were at a diner instead of at synagogue on Friday night? Had I revealed too much about prophecy in speaking about Israel and Tzfat? Was it a problem I'd held his hand, or that he had kissed my cheek?

I remembered months ago, when Yonatan first taught me to keep kosher. Eventually, he'd said, the commandments matter.

As Saturday wore on, I held back from checking my phone or turning on the television – actions traditionally forbidden on Shabbat. For one afternoon, I thought, I could resist. But without any distractions, the day dragged on interminably. Waves of nausea sent me hurrying to the bathroom. My head ached almost as badly as it did with a migraine. Mom gave me medicine, but it didn't help.

Finally, the sun reached the horizon. From my bed, I watched the light leave the sky, overtaken by darkness: the end of Shabbat. Nostalgia swept over me as I remembered my beautiful Shabbat in Tzfat. That astounding vision during the afternoon service. That one time my life made sense. Tonight, I could barely recognize that holy young woman from my memories.

When I was quite certain Shabbat had ended, I picked up the phone to check my messages...just as it buzzed.

"Hello," I said, my voice little more than a croak.

"That bad, eh?" Jake asked.

I cleared my throat. "Kind of." I hadn't recognized his number, and almost wished I hadn't answered.

"I've been known to have that effect on people," he said in a teasing voice. He sounded relaxed. Maybe even healthy. Had it been just last night we were together? I felt I'd traveled a hundred miles without water since then.

"Don't worry," he said. "They recovered in the end. I thought you might be sick today. You looked kind of awful by the end of last night."

"Thanks so much," I said.

"Any time," he said sweetly. "How are *you* feeling?"

"Better," he said. "I called to tell you something. I told my sister."

"Told her...?"

"You know." He paused. "About being clean. She was happy."

I held the phone in front of my face, as if I could see through it to stare at him. "That's wonderful," I managed to say.

"She told me to talk to a counselor," he went on. "They gave me some names, at the hospital."

"Are you going to?"

"I'm thinking it over," he said. "So how sick are you?"

"Fever's been a hundred three or so."

He cursed. "I didn't realize I was taking my life in my hands last night."

"You'll be fine," I said. "No worse than what you've already been through."

"Easy for you to say," he said. "Well, I guess this ruins my grand plan."

"Which plan was that?"

"To go running."

"Running?" I repeated.

"Yeah. For exercise. My sister suggested it." When I didn't answer, he explained, "I used to run track in middle school."

"Sounds great," I said.

"I thought you might want to run with me."

Again, I stared at the phone in surprise. He wanted *me* to go *running* with him? "Right now, I can barely walk."

He sighed. "That's what I figured. Maybe when you get better?"

"Don't wait for me," I said. "The exercise'll be good for you."

I could almost hear him rolling his eyes. "You sound like my sister."

"She sounds great," I said. "I'd like to meet her."

He paused, as if contemplating that meeting, and suddenly I worried I had pushed him too far.

"I mean, if you ever want us to," I added hastily.

"Maybe one day," he said quietly. "You better get back to bed."

"Never left," I said.

"I hope you feel better soon," he said sincerely.

"You too. Go running," I urged him.

"Good night," he said.

The next morning, when I was still too sick to get out of bed, I got a picture text from Jake, red-cheeked and doubled over in the bright sunlight.

Made it four blocks, he wrote. *Next week you're with me.*

If it *was* a virus, I knew I would start to feel better eventually. But I felt just as bad through Sunday. And into Monday.

Now that Shabbat was over, I tried to watch television, but it only worsened my headache. Maya had sent me a series of enthusiastic texts describing her Friday night date with Chris. I responded with happy faces, though I couldn't have smiled in real life. I texted Lauren to tell her I was sick, but couldn't bring myself to answer her phone calls.

Jake began to send me "get well" messages. Memes of puppies, kittens, cute babies – interspersed with his own silly updates about his day. He took pictures of his humble dinner – fish sticks with French fries – and of his pillow before going to sleep at night.

Periodically he wrote, *Just trying to distract you…let me know if too annoying.* But his texts *were* distracting, in just the right way. Maybe because he had recently felt so miserable, he actually seemed to know what would help.

On Monday night, I dreamed.

Through a barred window I can see the murderer pack his knife into a backpack and set out into the desert wilderness, that no man's land between the settlements and the territory. It is not a far distance: perhaps two miles, along forlorn roads in the darkness. At last he reaches the security fence; that one place where the barbed wire doesn't quite reach the ground.

He slips through, into the view of security officers, who received the prophets' warning. They seize him immediately.

Though she is some distance away, I am suddenly aware of the girl in her attic bedroom—safely asleep.

"This she has accomplished in her earliest days," Noach says, trembling before the angel in that holy place. "In light of this, may her punishment cease."

A long silence. At last, the angel nods assent.

When I awakened Tuesday morning, my memories of the dream were murky. Had I really saved the girl? Had Noach been praying for *me*?

I knew only one thing for certain. My fever was gone.

CHAPTER 33

On Tuesday evening, Lauren came by with our homework from the last two days. Instead of coming into the kitchen, she lingered on the front porch, speaking to me through the screen. Though I felt more certain than ever I wasn't contagious, I played along, keeping my distance from her.

After dinner I curled barefoot onto my pillow, touching Zaide's necklace for reassurance. I took a deep breath and exhaled slowly. Once, twice. Three times.

What if I got lost in the wrong place again? If I wasn't allowed there, how had I even gotten in?

Cautiously, I began to whisper the words Yonatan had taught me. Slowly, slowly...until the Light flowed around me...and everything real dissolved.

Voices flutter over me.

"His suffering continues."

"But he has done nothing wrong! "

"For lack of faith in the holiest places."

"For saving the katanah!"

"Unfair punishment for saving us all."

"In the world of Light, there are only lessons." Noach's voice carries above the others. "Through this, he will be purified."

Tears trickled from my closed eyes; I didn't bother brushing them away. I was better, but Yonatan was still suffering. As always, he was personally bearing the burden of my errors.

"Yonatan," I whispered, though I knew he wouldn't hear me. "I am so sorry."

∞

It was late, so I was surprised to find my phone blinking when I came back from brushing my teeth.

Seriously need a hit, Jake had texted.

My stomach lurched. I called, but he didn't answer.

Don't! I texted him. *You are doing so well.*

I waited anxiously for his response, feeling helpless. At last, it occurred to me there was one thing I *could* do.

"G-d," I prayed, head in my hands. "Please save them. Jake. Yonatan. Take care of them." My tears began to flow again, dripping onto my fingers. "Tell me how to help them. I want to. Please." I repeated the words until I couldn't anymore. I reached for a tissue and wiped my face.

I changed into my pajamas; I would be returning to school in the morning.

As I climbed into bed, my phone buzzed. I reached for it with trembling fingers.

Sister talked me through it. Still clean.

I took a long, shaky breath. "Thank You," I said quietly.

Proud of you, I texted him back.

⌘

"You look better," Jake said, his voice like a breeze on my neck.

I slammed my locker door as I turned to face him. "So do you."

He flushed, ducking his head. In truth, he looked better than I had ever seen him; his cheeks still smooth, his blond hair tucked behind his ears. The perpetual red streaks had faded from the whites of his eyes. Most importantly, he was grinning.

"I *slept* last night," he said, with an insomniac's appreciation for the luxury of sleep.

I grinned back at him, swinging my bag over my shoulder. "I'm glad your sister was there for you yesterday."

"Your texts helped too," he said.

"It's surprising how much something like that can help," I said, as we started down the hallway together. "Yours got me through the worst of this week."

"I'm glad they weren't too annoying."

I shook my head. "Not at all."

As we reached the front entrance, Jake said, "I'm going for another run this afternoon. Come with me."

"Um." I raised my eyebrows. "I don't think I'm quite up for that today."

He put a hand on his hip. "I thought you felt better."

I chuckled. "Not that much better," I said. "And it's only forty degrees out."

"You'll like it," he said. "We don't have to go far."

193

"You go ahead," I told him. "I'll join you another time."

<hr/>

Jake asked me four times before I finally agreed to run with him. By then, it was early March and the weather had turned warmer. Our first run was on a sunny Sunday morning, and we ran six blocks before I had to stop and catch my breath. Jake was a bit ahead, but he jogged back to me. "That was amazing!" He reached out to hug me.

I recoiled, not just because I was dripping with sweat. Yonatan never touched women, except that one time he held my hand. What if I wasn't supposed to touch boys anymore? Could hugging Jake somehow make things worse for Yonatan? I didn't want to add any further punishment to our shared account.

"M-maybe we shouldn't...for now," I said, taking a step back.

He backed away immediately, lifting his hands. "Right," he said. "OK."

After that, we ran together three times a week, and he never tried to touch me again.

<hr/>

Though I had recovered since the diner, the strand of Light that connected me to Yonatan had not returned. Without it, my meditations became murky: whispered voices, snatches of ballet music, an ancient sigh.

I had no way of knowing if the people I cared about were okay, and so for the first time in ages, I began praying regularly for them. The list started with Yonatan and Jake, but quickly grew. My mother and father. Beth. Devorah. Lauren, Maya, and even Chris. The other prophets in Tzfat, and all the prophets I had never met. The soul of my Zaide, in case he was somewhere listening.

I prayed every night, as if my words could protect them, or in some cases, perhaps call their protection upon me.

<hr/>

Jake was a good exercise partner. He ran a bit faster than me but would always glance back to make sure I hadn't fallen too far behind. He measured our progress with a fitness tracker his sister had given to him as a present. Each time we ran, we increased the distance we could cover. We reached a mile on our third Sunday.

We were running in a nice neighborhood on a damp and cloudy Thursday afternoon, about a half mile from school, when light ricocheted around me.

Despite Yonatan's absence, it had been more than a week since an unexpected vision. In a panic, I searched the manicured gardens and stairways for somewhere to hide.

Ahead, Jake turned to check on me. I waved my hands to encourage him to go on.

By then, I could only sink to the sidewalk as everything dissolved.

Nechama's translucent fingers reach out, her pale face always just beyond his grasp. Hallucination or vision, her ghost has devastated him anew. He wishes for death, if only to cradle her one last time in his arms.

Hands on his forehead. Water on the table beside him. The other prophets call, but they cannot reach him.

Devorah leans on her cane; I am only a figment of light. Our prayers are like a pillar rising up to heaven. Standing in the sunlight together at the Kotel, we feel the latch unlock.

"In your merit, Gedolah, and in the merit of the Katanah: Abundant healing Light to Yonatan ben Avichai HaNavi."

Yonatan has never been called in this way before. HaNavi—the prophet. His silent endurance has lifted him to a new level of holiness.

The Light is almost more painful than anything he has yet endured, as Nechama's apparition dissolves forever.

The restored connection felt like a gush of water in a parched desert: almost too much across the dry ground. Sharply, suddenly I was aware of just how ill Yonatan had been, for me. I felt desperate to apologize, to hear him explain. Eyes still closed, I shifted position on the ground, scratching my bare hands on the chilly cement.

"Rachel." I heard my name called, like a sigh. At first, I thought perhaps Yonatan was calling me, but then I heard it again – "Rachel" – whispered so softly, as if he didn't want to disturb me. I opened my eyes.

Jake sat across from me on the sidewalk, his knees pulled to his chest. If it had been Lauren, she would have already called my mother and an ambulance. But Jake looked more fascinated than concerned. I wanted to cover my head with my arms to hide from his curious gaze.

"Hi," he said.

"Hi," I mumbled.

I remembered he had already seen me awaken from a vision, that night at the diner. Maybe he had even been waiting for it to happen again. He hesitated, studying me, before asking, "Do you need anything?"

What I needed was to see if Yonatan would be all right now. To understand how Devorah and I had saved him. To beg for his forgiveness. But instead I sat caught, humiliated on the sidewalk, facing my new friend with all my secrets on display. I shook my head.

I wondered if he was going to ask, logically, if I needed to see a doctor. But he surprised me. "When you faint like that...the air kind of...shimmers around you."

My thoughts spun wildly. "It – it does?"

He kept staring at me. "How do you do that?"

I blew a gust of air from my mouth. "I don't *do* it."

"Then it just – happens?"

I pulled myself to my feet, avoiding his eyes. "Let's run," I said, and despite my own exhaustion and the weight of Yonatan's suffering on my shoulders, I bolted ahead of him as we ran back toward school.

Through some inner channel, I was aware of Yonatan beginning to drink, then eat. Dressed in jeans and a tattered gray sweatshirt, in a room no bigger than a closet, he reached for a set of charcoals and sketched Devorah's fragile face.

On the third day, he returned to the prophets' synagogue in Tzfat. Watching his fervent devotions, I remembered the first time I ever saw him, praying on Rosh Hashanah. How, in his fury and grief, he seemed almost to be yelling at G-d.

Now his prayers were more peaceful. His contact with darkness – his willingness to carry my suffering – had somehow opened doors to brighter light.

He never spoke to me. He didn't have to. I learned all I needed from seeing how, after everything, he chose to live.

From the porch, Dad clapped as Jake and I ran up my block. It was a warm and sunny Sunday morning, with a temperature close to sixty, but I was surprised to see Dad outside. He was finishing the second draft of his book, and had been so burrowed in his office I hadn't seen him for three days.

Jake and I slowed in front of my house. According to his tracker, we'd reached 1.4 miles today. "Nice one," he said, still panting.

I paced our front path, waving to Dad between gasps. "This is Jake," I said, and when his eyebrows arched, I added quickly, "my friend."

Dad took a few steps down the stairs. "I was just doing some revisions," he said. "Thought I'd get outside for a change."

"It's a nice day for it," I said.

"My final draft is due in three weeks," he said. "Then we can finally do that hike, you and me."

I was surprised to hear the hike was still on his radar. "Sure, Dad."

"Nice to meet you," Dad called to Jake. Dad looked back and forth between us, collected his laptop, and went inside.

After Dad left, I brought out two plastic cups from the kitchen and Jake and I sat on the steps, sipping cold water.

It had been more than a week since that vision occurred while we were running; since he'd said he saw light shimmer around me. Jake had not asked about it again, just as I never asked again about meeting his sister or why he never mentioned his father. I knew he was speaking to one of the counselors they had recommended at the hospital, and I never asked about that, either.

But the truth was part of me *wanted* him to ask me about the visions. *Would it be so wrong to tell him?* I wondered.

As we sat there in silence, enjoying the spring breeze and the cold water, a door opened across the street from us and four Orthodox Jews came out: a mother, an older girl in a dress and tights with a long braid, and two small boys wearing black kipot. On Shabbat they would have been walking, but today they piled into a minivan.

"We have some Orthodox Jews in my building," Jake said, leaning back on the porch as they drove away. "I see them in the elevator."

"Have you ever thought of being one?" I asked impulsively.

He chuckled, brushing his long hair from his face. "I doubt they'd let me in," he said. "But I think you'd be welcome."

I turned to him. "What do you mean?"

"Well," he said in a measured tone, "I can never reach you on Saturdays. I haven't ever seen you eat pork or shellfish." He shrugged, still staring at the now-vacant house across the street. "And you won't even let me touch your hand."

I was surprised these choices were so obvious. "My mother grew up

Orthodox," I told him.

"Why did she give it up?" he asked.

After all this time, I didn't really have a good answer. "I guess it wasn't for her." I hesitated, then admitted, "I went to an Orthodox synagogue near here a bunch of times last fall."

He tilted his head in surprise. "I didn't know you could just walk in."

"I guess you can," I said. "I wore a skirt. The weirdest part was when someone said I looked like my mother."

"Why did you stop going?" he asked.

Longing washed over me. How I missed Shabbat mornings in the synagogue! Struggling through the prayers and waiting for my simple, guided explorations with Yonatan.

I sighed. "What I was looking for...wasn't there anymore," I said.

"I know what you mean," Jake said, though I couldn't see how he could possibly understand.

CHAPTER 34

In past years, we often joined Zaide, aunts, uncles and cousins for Passover seder. But without him here, our Baltimore relatives were spending the holiday in Florida. Faced with the possibility of no seder, Mom chose for the first time to make one herself. She invited the dentist from her office, and suggested Dad invite a few of his colleagues from the university. She even invited Maya and her mother.

Cleaning the house of any leavened crumbs was a regular tradition in our house before Passover. In the past, Mom claimed her sometimes compulsive cleaning was so Zaide would be comfortable if he visited during the holiday. This year she made no such excuses, but progressively hung printed paper signs around the house to remind us not to eat bread in rooms that had been cleaned.

One Sunday evening, Mom and I were watching a movie in the den when Dad came out of his office. "Alicia," he said, holding up one of her signs.

"I cleaned your office this morning," she said. "I just want to make sure it stays clean for the holiday."

Dad might have brought out a thousand principled reasons for why this cleaning was both unnecessary and bordered on the obsessive. He had said these things to me himself in previous years. But tonight, he took a more pragmatic approach.

"I need to eat in there to stay awake," he said. "Until my deadline."

"You can eat carrots or something," Mom said. "Just no *chametz*."

We both glanced at her when she used the Hebrew expression for leavened bread. Dad raised his eyebrows. "Alicia," he repeated, in a warning tone.

"Howard, please," she said. "Let's just do it right this year."

Dad sighed and padded back to his office. He left the sign with us in the den.

⌒⊃

Three weeks before Passover, Lauren called as I sat on the porch, doing homework after school. "Rach," she said, "you won't believe it. I got into Yale!"

Affection bubbled up in me as I pictured Lauren's pink cheeks and red hair. We'd seen each other less often recently because I was spending so much more time with Jake. I knew she was spending more time with other friends from Debate Club and Student Council. I was touched she still called me first.

"Congratulations!" I said. "You deserve it so much, Laur."

"I-I'm just so relieved," she said. I could hear her pacing back and forth in her kitchen. "I didn't know...if they'd take me. When they deferred me in the winter...."

I glanced up at the trees at the top of my block, flowering in the spring. Last week we had both received acceptances to the University of Maryland. I still hadn't heard from GW.

"That was just a mistake they deferred you," I said. "You're so smart and responsible and good at everything. Why would they want anyone else?"

"Aw, thanks, Rach." I heard her pull out a kitchen chair and sit. "Connecticut isn't too far."

"Of course," I said. "And there are summers and winter break. We'll keep in touch."

∽◇◇

Matzo appeared in our house, wrapped in plastic bags and placed carefully in the cleaned den. Mom went to the kosher store to buy a shank bone for the seder plate. One day I came home from school to find her on the phone with one of my aunts – a woman I doubted she had spoken to since Zaide's shiva – writing down a recipe for *charoset*, the apple-nut dish that symbolically represented mortar for bricks during the seder meal.

Still busy with his book, Dad ignored all her preparations. I sensed he would have been happy to skip the seder altogether, but I knew he wouldn't. Just as he'd allowed her to keep the kosher plates, he wasn't going to fight her over this, at least not while he had a book to finish.

∽◇◇

"Nice run," Jake said, stopping in front of my house the Tuesday afternoon before Passover. He showed me his tracker: 2.25 miles.

"Great," I panted.

I never expected to run this far, but I could feel my body getting stronger. The exercise was helping Jake too. He had been drug-free for almost two months.

My phone buzzed in my bag and I pulled it out, inhaling sharply when I saw the email.

"What's up?" Jake asked.

"It's just – it's from GW." I backed toward the porch, still staring at the phone. "I just – I have to see this," I said. Jake came to sit beside me as I tried to access the website.

"OK, it's – four, eight, two, one," I said, entering my code with shaking fingers. I had to try several times before I got the numbers right. Finally the portal opened...and there it was. *Admission denied.*

"Oh," I said.

The world spun around me and for an instant I feared a vision. But really it was my future that had spun out of my grasp. I set the phone down and covered my face with my hands, hunched over like a person kicked in the chest.

I felt suddenly, unreasonably angry at Yonatan. I'd believed him when he told me prophecy would not get in the way of G-d's plans for me. *So what are Your plans?* I demanded.

"Rach?" Jake said. I turned to him abruptly and he leaned back, raising his hands. "I'm so sorry."

I sighed. "Me too."

We sat staring at each other in the spring sunshine, my phone between us on the steps. Then, without thinking, I leaned over and kissed him.

At first, he seemed almost afraid, and I wondered if he had ever kissed a girl before. His fingers cautiously touched my hand, then moved up my arm to my neck. Warmth spread throughout my body. I didn't think about Yonatan or prophecy or my future. Just for one moment, I needed this.

"Wow," he said, when I finally pulled away.

I closed my eyes, afraid something terrible would happen to both of us. But when I opened them, he was still sitting there, a bemused expression on his face.

"That was different," he said.

I blushed. "I hope you didn't mind..."

He reached for my left hand and squeezed it. "No," he said, studying my palm. "I guess...I just didn't think you'd want..."

My better instincts rushed in as I looked up at him. *What would Yonatan say?* I hated that everything in my life had to be measured by that yardstick. But I knew my actions also had consequences ...in a world with rules I didn't understand. With my right hand, I took my left out of his grasp. "It's... complicated."

Despair passed over his face like a cloud.

"It's not *you*," I said. He was staring into the distance like a child searching for a lost balloon. "Jake. Listen to me. I want to explain."

"Last fall," I said. I waited until his eyes found my face again. "I met a man ...at the Orthodox synagogue. He told me..." I faltered, but Jake held my eyes and I found the courage to continue. "He told me I was *called*... called for a kind of...Jewish prophecy. He taught me to meditate and connect with G-d...to understand things...that I'm supposed to do."

He stared at me as if seeing me for the first time. *He must think I'm crazy,* I thought. I hid my face with my hands.

"That's how...you knew...about me in the snow," I heard him say.

Slowly, I lifted my face and nodded. "It's not like G-d *speaks* to me," I said, rushing to clarify. "The visions are all confused. I don't always know what I'm seeing, what's happening..."

"And sometimes it happens at inconvenient times," he said, his voice filled with wonder.

I bit my lip, nodding again. "Yeah."

He frowned. "So then am I...like...a *project* for you?"

"No," I said.

He raised his eyebrows.

"I mean –" I broke off, rubbing two fingers across the corner of my eye. "You were," I admitted. "At first. But now..." I tried to smile. "Now we're friends, right?"

"Friends," he repeated, a little flatly. He leaned back on the porch steps, stretching his long arms behind him. It was getting late. Mom would be home from work soon.

"I like you, Jake. It's just –" I stopped, dropping my head back into my hands. "I'm *lost* right now. I don't know what I'm doing, I don't know the rules, I can't ..." I hesitated, lifting my face to meet his eyes. "I can't be *with* someone right now."

"Then why did you kiss me?" he asked.

I bit my lip. "Because I wanted to," I said in a small voice.

He pressed his lips together, concealing a little grin. "So what now?"

I shrugged uncertainly. The night Chris kissed me, I was so sure it could only end badly. Things felt more unclear with Jake. But in all my visions about him – past, present and future – I'd never seen a single image of us together. I'd always understood my role was to help him become the man he was meant to be.

"I don't know," I told him honestly.

He waited through a few breaths before asking, "Do you mind if we keep running while you figure it out?"

Relief flooded through me. "I'd love that."

He dipped his chin in a single, shallow nod. "Me too."

CHAPTER 35

Beth flew home the Saturday before Passover. My parents invited me to come to the airport, but I made excuses about schoolwork. I hadn't been in a car on Shabbat since the diner with Jake.

By the time the car pulled into our driveway, it was getting dark. A gust of her citrus shampoo entered the house with the breeze. "Beth!" I cheered.

Then I looked again, almost thinking they had brought the wrong girl.

Beth's long, beautiful auburn hair was cropped into a stylish pixie cut, long on the top but short at the back. The effect made her cheeks look even more hollow than in the winter. Her large eyes had dark circles carved under them.

"Your h-hair," I stammered.

"It'll grow back," she said, coming forward to wrap her arms around me. "Just wanted to try something new."

At least her voice sounded the same. As I hugged her back, her shoulder blades felt as delicate as bird's wings. "I missed you so much."

She pulled back to grin at me. "I missed you too," she said, running her fingers through my ponytail.

∞

Upstairs, I sat on Beth's bed while she unpacked. She wore a baggy gray sweatshirt over skintight jeans that made her thin, muscular calves look like tree branches. Though she must have lost at least five more pounds since the winter, she moved fluidly, heaving her suitcase up on the chair with strength. Sweaters, jeans, and warm pajamas came out of her suitcase.

"You know it's spring here," I said.

She shrugged, hanging a hoodie sweatshirt in the closet. "I'm always cold these days, except when I'm dancing."

"How are things going with the show?" I asked.

"Great," she said, turning back to put a pair of jeans in a drawer. "We're working night and day."

"I've never seen anyone work harder," I said.

Beth gave me a puzzled look, and I realized I only knew about her hard work through my meditations. But then she sighed.

"I've never worked harder in my life." She sat down beside me. Her body was so light, the mattress barely sank. She turned to me. "Hey, Mom said you didn't get into GW? I don't know what they were thinking, Rach. I'm sorry."

My chest tightened. "It was my fault." I shook my head, studying her purple carpet. "I let my grades slip last fall."

She chuckled. "*You* let your grades slip? What, to a 92?" she said teasingly.

"Something like that."

She put a wiry arm around me. "What happened?"

I wanted to tell her everything. But I remembered how she'd told my parents about my Shabbat in Tzfat, and knew I couldn't trust her with my secrets. I rubbed at my sore chest. "Just got distracted. Some bad migraines and other things."

She swiveled to face me, outraged. "They didn't give you a break because you were sick? Didn't you tell them about it in your essays?"

She was right; I should have written about the "migraines" to try to explain away the drop in my grades. But somehow in my daze last winter, as I prepared for my trip to Israel with Yonatan, I hadn't thought of it.

"You can transfer," Beth said. "One or two good years at Maryland and I'm sure they'll take you."

"Maybe." I knew this was what I should be planning for, but I couldn't get excited about it.

Beth pressed her forehead affectionately against mine. "What's the latest with Mr. Marino?"

I waved my hand. "In love with Maya."

Her eyes widened. "Seriously?"

"They've been exclusive for a month now," I said.

"That must be the longest either of them has ever gone," Beth said wonderingly.

"Not quite," I said. "Maya once dated a guy exclusively for three months. But I don't think Chris has ever been this serious about a girl." I shook my head, ignoring the increasing tightness in my chest. "I'm happy for them."

"That's the right attitude," Beth said, standing back up to finish unpacking. "So who are we going to find for you this spring? Mom said you've been spending time with a guy from school."

"We're just friends."

She studied my face thoughtfully. "Is that your call, or his?"

"Mine," I said reluctantly.

"So what's wrong with him?"

"Nothing's *wrong* with him," I said.

"Then why don't you want to be with him?"

It hit me like a punch in the stomach—how much I *did* want to be with Jake. To kiss him again. To feel his arms around me. Perhaps most important, to love and be loved by someone who knew my secrets. When I'd told Jake the truth, he didn't flinch. Yesterday at school, he had dropped by my locker the same as before, even though for all he knew I was insane. Or sent by G-d to save him.

I thought about confessing some of this to Beth, but when I looked up, her eyes were amused. She was teasing me, not trying to offer relationship advice. Disarmed, I grinned back.

"*Someday, my prince will come,*" I sang, playfully punching her on the arm.

"Of course he will," Beth said, kissing me lightly on the forehead. "That's the spirit."

At first, I thought the tightness in my chest was about college or about my feelings for Jake. But it lingered, worsening through the evening. By the time I sat to meditate that night, deep breaths had become an effort. I was worried; I didn't want to get sick and ruin my mother's seder. I whispered the holy words, spiritually reaching as far as I could, until the sparks filled my room.

Traffic. Pigeons. As Noach walks down the curved service road, a black car pulls to a stop along the busy avenue...

I awaken knowing this test is beyond me now. Nothing I can do will protect him.

It will depend on her.

Terror overwhelms me, and this connection — all I've held together for the prophets these many years — shatters like breaking glass.

"Devorah?" Rena calls from the living room. She felt it.

Prophets, hold tight. For the girl. For us all.

The vision ended abruptly, swirling away before I could grasp much. I whispered the holy words, aware immediately something was different. Wrong.

The prophets were gone.

Yonatan was gone. Devorah was gone. Even the tightness in my chest was gone.

I almost wondered if they had ever really existed. Could they have been just a figment of my imagination all this time?

I sat up on my pillow, seeking them, until I fell asleep, curled in a heap on the floor.

"Ready to work?" Mom asked, when I stumbled downstairs in my pajamas the next morning. She and Beth were already dressed.

The three of us spent the day in a rush of preparations. We sealed the cabinets with our regular plates and poured boiling water on the granite countertops before bringing out a new set of Passover dishes. "We got these for our wedding," Mom said. "It's about time we used them." She put us to work chopping vegetables as she began to cook.

"I think we need a break," I said finally, resting in a kitchen chair while Beth finished chopping a bunch of celery.

"It's no worse than dancing," Beth said. I watched her pop a celery piece into her mouth; it was the first thing she'd eaten since a rice cake for breakfast hours before.

That night I tried to meditate, but it was as if an iron wall stood between me and the spiritual world. Increasingly desperate, I repeated the holy words Yonatan had taught me, but nothing happened. No trance, no sparks, no Light.

I had been disconnected from Yonatan before, but this was different. Even the symptoms from last night had disappeared completely. I felt...like a normal girl. The kind I'd wanted to be when I'd kissed Jake.

Could G-d have changed His mind about me? The thought left me achingly sad.

I kept thinking my last meditation held clues, but I couldn't remember anything. If there had been a warning, I missed it.

"I missed running with you yesterday," Jake said, approaching my locker Monday afternoon.

"We worked all day," I said, putting a book in my bag. "My mom even took off work to finish up. But I think we'll be ready for seder tonight." Together we walked down the hall toward Poetry Club. "How did your run go?"

He grinned. "Two and a half miles," he said. "Beat that."

"Maybe next week," I said.

"It's on," he said.

As we turned a corner, his hand gently, probably accidently, brushed against mine. My stomach twisted again with that surprising yearning to kiss him. I glanced up involuntarily. Under his baseball cap, his dark eyes warmed my face. Alarmed, I pulled my hand away and stuffed it into my jeans pocket.

Once in the classroom, we headed for our usual seats, several chairs apart. Under my desk, I squeezed my hands together. This feeling about Jake was different from my crush on Chris. He had been out of reach so long I'd really never expected anything. But with Jake, my body and heart seemed to be making decisions without even giving me a chance to think. And I desperately needed to think, before I made a mistake that could ruin everything.

I never should have kissed him, I chastised myself.

What I needed, more than ever, was a conversation with Yonatan I could not have. I ran my fingers through my hair, dislodging my ponytail and retying it as the other students settled into their seats.

Jake's transformation had changed Poetry Club. Gradually over the last month, he had stopped retreating under his baseball cap. His insightful comments about the best poems had become a sign of respect. Before Mr. Keller had given Jake a wide berth on his poems, but now he sometimes even complimented him.

I made this difference, I reminded myself, by following a calling received entirely through visions and meditation. I hadn't imagined it; and if I was honest, I also hadn't had much help from Yonatan figuring it out.

But this desire to be with him was new. What if instead of something holy, it was dangerous? What if Yonatan was out there somewhere, desperately trying to restore a connection I had again damaged through my own carelessness?

Neither of us was due to read poems this week, and I was uncharacteristically quiet trying to sort all of this out. By the time Poetry Club was finished, I had decided. We were friends. That was all I could afford right now. It had to be enough.

"Have a nice Passover," Jake said as we left the room.

"You too," I said, aiming for a confident tone, as if nothing had changed between us.

CHAPTER 36

Mom had already finished cooking when I got home from school. Together, we placed the ritual items on the seder plate: egg, charoset, green herbs, shank bone, horseradish, and salt water for tears.

"Where's Beth?" I asked.

"Taking a nap," Mom said.

"Did she dance today?"

Mom chuckled. "Of course. She was at the studio for four hours." Then she hesitated. "I put out some candles for you." She gestured toward the wood buffet in the dining room.

I turned to the silver candlesticks, already set with tall taper candles. Their usual place was in the living room wall unit; I hadn't seen them out since Mom used to light them on Friday nights.

Though I'd been lighting candles every week, I hadn't thought of Passover. But there it was in my memories of seder with Zaide: a tray of candles lit by the adult women in the house. Mom was offering the continuation of this tradition to me.

"Are you sure?" I asked, moved.

She dipped her chin in a single nod. "It would be lovely if you lit them."

As the sun descended that Passover evening, I struck a match and lit each tall candle.

Then I joined Dad on the sofa in the living room, waiting for the guests to arrive. He wore a cream-colored button-down shirt with khakis, and had put on aftershave. For the first time all year, he was whistling. His book was finished.

"Did you have a nice nap?" I asked Beth, who sat on the armchair across from us. After her shower, she had spent a long time in the bathroom fussing with her new hairstyle. She wore black jeans and a pale blue sweater the color of her eyes. It looked huge on her.

I had on one of the long skirts I'd worn to meet Yonatan in the fall, as if it could call his presence back to me. Though the holiday had already begun in Israel, I'd felt not a flicker of spiritual connection.

Beth yawned. "Not really," she said, curling her arms around her knees on the sofa. This was a normal position for her, but she was so thin now it seemed like she was shrinking into herself. "I'm still jet lagged."

I looked at her quizzically. "Isn't it...like, four in the afternoon in California?"

She shrugged.

"Now that the book is done, we'll come visit you," Dad said to Beth, missing her slight look of alarm. "I have a conference in LA next month."

"Okay," Beth said. "If you want to."

"And we're going to go on that hike. Right, Rach?" he said, turning to me. "Maybe next Saturday?"

"I think I have plans for Saturday," I said quickly. "Maybe Sunday afternoon, after my run with Jake?"

"Sure, sure," he said, waving his hand as if his schedule was wide open, which of course it wasn't. He was still working several days a week at the clinic, and teaching every weekday.

When the doorbell rang, I jumped up, relieved to find Maya and her mother at the side door. I had forgotten how small Maya's mother was. Kay wore jeans with an orange V-neck blouse, and carried a generous bouquet of flowers that dwarfed her. "So good to see you, Rachel," she said, kissing my cheek before greeting my mother in the kitchen.

Maya wore a short navy skirt with a white cowl neck blouse, with pink lipstick and just a hint of blush. She leaned forward to kiss me on the cheek.

"Happy Passover," Maya said. "It's been too long. Look, both of us busy with our boys! I'm headed over to Chris's later," she confided.

The doorbell rang again and I opened the door to two of Dad's professorial colleagues, both men in their late fifties. "You must be Rachel," one of them said, reaching out to shake my hand. "I'm Roy Masterman. Ready to join us at Maryland next year?"

"Yeah," I said, in as convincing a tone as I could manage. "Can't wait."

Behind them came Dr. Olsen, the dentist from Mom's office, who had been taking care of my teeth since I was six years old. He was tall and overweight, bald on top and with a mustache, like a dentist version of Dr. Phil. "You've gotten so big, Beth," he said.

"Rachel," I corrected, as he gave me a hug and a kiss on the cheek.

After he ambled toward the living room, I covered my eyes with my hand. My house was filled with people who thought they knew me – and not one of them really did. But did anyone? Did I even know myself?

The pressure in my chest was back. *Because I was stuck going to Maryland?* I wondered. Because Dr. Olsen had hugged me without asking, when I wasn't even allowing myself to touch the one boy I wanted to be with? Or was something else happening in the spiritual world, that I couldn't feel except through my body?

I uncovered my eyes and watched the candles flickering on the buffet in the dining room. Were candles lit by prophets still burning elsewhere? Were they finishing a seder in Tzfat? Were they thinking of me?

<hr />

At last Mom emerged from the kitchen, wearing an apron over a dark blue dress, and invited us all to the table. Dad sat at the head, between Mom and Beth. I sat beside Beth, with Maya on my other side, and her mother at the end. The dentist and professors sat opposite us.

We opened our haggadot[25] and began with a brief review of the schedule for the evening – *"Kadesh, Urchatz, Karpas, Yachatz, Maggid, Rachtzah, Motzi, Matzah, Maror, Korech, Shulchan Orech, Tzafun, Berach, Hallel, Nirtzah"* – "Sanctify, Wash, Green Vegetable, Break the Matzo, Story, Wash, Bless, Eat Matzah, Bitter Herb, Sandwich, Dinner, Afikomen, Bless, Praise, Conclusion."

My father, the religious skeptic, stood at the head of the table, opened his *haggadah*, and recited the opening Kiddush flawlessly. I looked at him, surprised, as I drank my first cup of sweet wine. "That was great," I said.

He winked at me. "I practiced," he said.

I stood to help Mom with the ritual hand-washing. Mom filled a washing cup with water. My job was to hold a large bowl. Each participant poured the water from the cup over their hands, into the bowl. Having the water brought to them was meant to make them feel like royalty.

The professors and Dr. Olsen washed without comment, but Kay grinned at us. "I've never done a *real* seder before," she said. "This is beautiful." Mom beamed back at her.

<hr />

[25] Haggadah (pl. haggadot): book containing the text and instructions for the Passover seder.

We dipped parsley in salt water and ate. Mom broke the matzo and put a piece into a special cloth *afikomen*[26] bag. At my cousins' house, Zaide would hide the bag, after which the little children would search for it.

"Who's going to hide it?" I asked.

"I think that's you and Beth," Mom said.

I grinned at Beth beside me, but she didn't smile back. Her face was pale, with little beads of sweat on her temples.

"I think I...drank that wine a little too fast." She rolled her eyes, smirking at herself. "You might need to hide that afikomen without me."

"I'll do my best," I said, snatching the bag from the table and placing it on my lap.

At my cousins' seder, everything was in Hebrew and I had to read along silently in the English to understand anything. But tonight, we began in English, taking turns to read the story of the Jews' enslavement in Egypt and how we were freed. The rabbis who calculated how many curses the ancient Egyptians received as punishment. The miracle of the splitting of the sea. The many blessings received. The meaning and purpose of the Passover offering, matzo, and bitter herbs.

If I still felt connected to the prophetic world, I might have been tempted to meditate or felt afraid of a vision. But instead, tonight, I concentrated on the tradition of it all. Jewish families had been hosting seders like this for thousands of years, and here my candles still flickered against the wall. I was deeply proud of my mother for continuing the tradition in spite of everything.

Dad made a blessing on the second cup of wine. I drank mine without thinking much about it, then turned to check on Beth. She took a sip and quickly put her cup down.

As I knew from seders as a child, the time between the second cup and the meal is tricky. Everyone has had two cups of wine with little food. Some people start to look droopy, others silly. When I was little, I was always served grape juice. But tonight we were all drinking wine.

Mom and I stood again for the second round of hand washing. I took the *afikomen* bag and hid it under a sofa cushion in the living room, stumbling a little on my way back. Some guests were slower washing this time. Beth

---

[26] Afikomen: the final piece of matzah eaten at the Passover seder. Traditionally hidden to be found at the end.

poured too roughly, splashing both of us.

Dad blessed the matzo, and we began to eat. The bitter herb. Matzo sandwich with bitter herb and charoset. An egg dipped in water. Finally, chicken matzo ball soup. I grinned at Mom, so grateful for all her hard work. But instead of eating her soup, she was looking at Beth. I followed her eyes.

Under her perfectly styled auburn hair, Beth's face was white as a cloud. She sat straight up, breathing in strange, strangled gasps. Her open eyes were wide and horrified.

"Beth...?" Mom said.

In slow motion, we all watched her tilt off the side of her chair and fall, unconscious, to the floor.

CHAPTER 37

For one horrified second, no one moved. Then it was Dr. Olsen who leapt into action, his huge body darting around the table like an Olympic sprinter.

"Call an ambulance!" he roared, already down on his knees next to Beth, checking her pulse. I pushed back my chair to give him space. From the kitchen, I heard Mom shouting into the phone. Beth's breaths sounded distorted, like an animal's moans.

Slowly, like darkness encroaching after sunset, I realized the failure had been mine.

Your sister needs your help, Noach had said to me. I covered my eyes.

The tightness in my chest. Had it been a sign I'd missed? I'd allowed myself to become distracted, when I should have been focusing on her.

Mom pulled my hands from my face and crouched beside my chair. Dr. Olsen was still on the floor beside Beth. I heard sirens in the distance.

"Rachel," Mom said fiercely. I met her wild eyes. "We're going to the hospital. You – stay here. Finish the seder."

My eyes widened incredulously.

"Listen to me," she commanded. "Kay and Maya will stay with you. Finish the seder. *Do the mitzvah,*" she said. "It's important..."

The sirens grew suddenly loud; someone must have opened the kitchen door. Cool, moist air rushed through the house. Outside, an ambulance shrieked to a stop.

Mom hugged me. "We'll call when we know something," she said, grabbing car keys from a drawer. "Let Kay answer the phone."

Two paramedics rushed in. Dr. Olsen shouted to them, but I couldn't make sense of his words. Quickly they lifted Beth onto a stretcher. We all watched as they raced down the porch steps, my parents close behind.

Sirens again. Departing.

"Oh G-d *no,*" I moaned aloud, sinking to the floor. The room fell silent as someone closed the kitchen door. I covered my eyes again, but my prayers continued like screams inside my head.

No! G-d, no! G-d...I didn't know...She has to live, she ...
Oh G-d oh G-d...do not...do not...do not let her...die!

How selfish I had been, worrying about my lost connection to the prophets, indulging my own silly pride about GW, when all along I knew Beth needed me and I had done nothing.

Now I felt I would offer G-d anything if Beth could just be okay. *Even if I have to go to Maryland. Even if I never get to kiss Jake again...*Then it struck me.

Even if I have to be an Orthodox Jew without prophecy for the rest of my life.

Suddenly, I understood the Orthodox Jews parading back and forth on my block every Shabbat, the ones who observed every tiny mitzvah. They had no gift of prophecy, no divine messages, no certainty about what was right. Their prayers and their observance were the only ways they had to connect with G-d.

If prophecy was taken from me forever, would I be willing to do that hard work to build my own connection? Now that I knew it was all real... how could I do anything but obey?

In that moment of blind insight, it struck me that this was why Mom had told me to stay and finish the beautiful seder she had prepared. *Do the mitzvah.* The merit from this seder might be my one, last chance to save Beth.

Slowly, I uncovered my eyes. Atop my mother's buffet, flames still flickered atop the tall candles standing in silver candlesticks: signs of a tradition that had carried the Jewish people through thousands of years. A tradition still carrying us, with G-d's mercy.

Maya sat beside me on the floor, one arm tight around my shoulder. Dr. Olsen leaned against the wall, his face ashen. Dad's colleagues were still in their chairs, not speaking, staring across the table at me. Kay was pacing in the kitchen.

"My mother," I began hoarsely, and everyone leaned closer to hear me, "said we should finish the seder."

"You don't have to, Rachel," Kay said, coming in from the kitchen. "It's not..."

I nodded, pressing my lips together. "We do," I said. "Please."

Maya helped me back to my chair as the other guests began to move dutifully around me. Bowls of chicken soup were collected. Salad, mashed potatoes, and brisket came from the kitchen. The haggadot were collected and stacked carefully on the buffet. The meal was brief and quiet.

At last, Maya asked me where I had hidden the *afikomen.* "In the living room," I said. It didn't take long for her to find it. We all ate the final matzo of the meal in silence.

After we drank the third cup of wine, Maya opened the door for Elijah. I wouldn't have known what to do then, but Dr. Masterman told us he had learned to lead the seder in his Jewish youth group. He led us through the remaining Hebrew verses of praise, the fourth cup and the conclusion.

"L'shana ha-ba b'Yerushalayim," we sang at last. *Next year in Jerusalem.*

I rested my forehead on the table. "Thank you," I said quietly to the others. My head was spinning.

Please G-d, I prayed, *let it be enough.*

"We'll stay here tonight," Kay said, putting a blanket over my shoulders. She led me to the living room as the others took their things and left.

When the phone rang, I jolted upright on the sofa.

The lights were still on in the living room. Maya was asleep, wrapped in a blanket on the couch opposite me. From the armchair, Kay answered the phone on the first ring.

"Yes," she said briskly. "OK. Yes. Yes. OK." She waited a long moment, listening. "OK," she said finally. "I'll tell her."

At last, she clicked off the phone. "Beth is stable," she told me.

Tears sprang to my eyes. "W-what happened? Will she – will she be okay?"

Kay came to sit beside me on the sofa, her eyes full of motherly compassion. "Something went wrong with Beth's heart tonight," she said. "From electrolyte imbalance, your mother said. But they were able to stabilize her in the hospital."

I chewed my lip, confused.

"It can happen when a person isn't eating enough," she explained.

Now I bit down so hard on my lip I tasted blood. Kay put her arm around me and I buried my head in her shoulder. "I should have ...*done* something," I said.

Kay patted my back. "There wasn't anything *you* could have done, Rachel. But you can be there for her now." She squeezed my shoulders. "Your mother wants you to stay here and keep this holiday the traditional way," she said. "Maya and I will stay with you."

Mom had never asked me to observe a holiday in the Orthodox way before. But her instructions were clear and we all followed them. It was the least we could do.

The refrigerator was full of Passover food she had prepared, so we had plenty to eat. Maya was delighted to miss school, and asked no questions about why I was being so careful to avoid phones or televisions. I suspected she was sneaking social media posts in the bathroom.

Mom called Tuesday afternoon to tell us Beth was awake. The doctors had given her an IV to rehydrate her and rebalance her electrolytes. A psychiatrist had been in to discuss eating.

"Did she listen?" I asked Kay urgently.

Kay shook her head. "It was a private session. Your mother didn't know."

<hr />

Chris tapped on the kitchen door that evening, as we were eating a dinner of seder leftovers. Maya leapt up to open it, not even giving me time to brush my hair...or hide in the hall closet, as I might have preferred.

"Hey Sexy," she said, sidling into his arms.

"Hey Beautiful," he answered in a playful voice.

Staring down at my brisket, I heard them kiss.

Chris cleared his throat. "I – uh, came by to see if you needed anything."

There was a little pause before I looked up. His arm was wrapped around Maya's waist, but his eyes were on me.

"How's Beth?" he asked.

"She's doing better," Maya said, when I hesitated. "They have her on an IV."

"So you guys are just...hanging out here?"

"Only till tomorrow," Maya said. "Want some food? Rachel's mom is a great cook."

Chris shook his head, his eyes still on my face. He looked as if he wanted to ask me a question, and he may well have had a thousand: about the prophets, about this self-imposed religious retreat, and certainly about Beth. But of course he couldn't ask any of them here with his girlfriend and her mother in my kitchen.

He stared at me one moment longer, then nodded as if satisfied. He kissed Maya on the cheek, bowing slightly toward me as he turned toward the door.

"I'll text you later!" she called as he went down the steps.

After dinner, I tried to meditate, but Yonatan's words felt jumbled in my mouth. Was I even saying them right? The prophetic world had been absent only three days, but it seemed I'd sunk the spiritual equivalent of miles.

I finally gave up on the meditation and began to pray, first for Beth, then for my mother and father, who were with her in the hospital. For Yonatan and Devorah, wherever they were. For Chris and Maya: that I wouldn't get in the way of something good and right for both of them. At last, I prayed for myself.

Help, I begged. Of course, I heard no answer.

Downstairs, I found Kay asleep on the armchair. Maya's sofa was empty. I assumed it would be her when the porch door opened, but I jumped up when I heard my father taking off his shoes.

"Shh," he said, as I flew into his arms. "I'm sorry I woke you, honey."

I shook my head, my fingers wrapped tight around his waist. "I've missed you so much," I said with a whimper.

When I was a little girl, he would squeeze me so hard I could barely breathe. Then he would say that's how much he loved me – to the point of being breathless. But tonight his arms held me tenderly.

"I've missed you too," he said in a ragged voice. "Oh how I've missed you."

I rested my head on his chest in the dark kitchen, inhaling the leather of his jacket. "Is Beth okay?" I asked in a small voice.

He shook his head, stroking his fingers across my back. "She hasn't been okay in a long time."

"I know," I said quietly.

"I should have talked to her," he said. Somehow it was a relief to know he too felt responsible – that it wasn't just me who should have done something differently.

"I knew she wasn't eating enough," I said. "I just never thought...it could hurt her heart...like that. I should have –"

"You can't blame yourself," he said, interrupting me. "I'm just glad *you're* okay."

He met my eyes. I tried hard not to flinch.

"I'm sorry I haven't...been here," he said in a broken voice. "I've been so busy taking care of the kids in my clinic, working on the book...I haven't been taking care of my own girls." He squeezed me tighter. "I'm so sorry."

"It's okay, Dad," I said. In my heart, I knew he couldn't have changed much for either of us. There's only so much a father can do to protect a child from her own destiny.

"Mom's staying with Beth tonight," he said, releasing me. "There was only space for one of us to sleep in her room. I'll go back in the morning. Do you want to join me?"

I shook my head, alarmed by his invitation.

He shrugged. "Beth's been asking for you, but Mom said you should really stay here." He stared around the kitchen; Kay had washed the dishes and set them on the counter for tomorrow. "Maya and her mother are staying here with you?"

I nodded.

He kissed me on the forehead. We walked to the living room together, but he left me at the steps.

CHAPTER 38

Maya and I spent Wednesday afternoon on my porch, enjoying the spring sunshine. Because of the holiday dozens of Orthodox Jews were walking as families or in small clusters in both directions on my street. Two little girls in fancy dresses played on a tree swing in a front yard several houses away.

I will be one of them, I thought.

The idea was not as difficult as it had once been. The two days in the house had been draining but not impossible; if I was part of a community, and not terrified about Beth, they might even have been nice. If it meant Beth would be all right, it would be well worth it.

Still, I was looking forward to the end of the holiday. It would be nice to check my phone, and even to go to school. I was ready for mundane distractions.

"Did you have fun with Chris last night?" I asked Maya casually.

A guilty smile formed on her face. "I didn't think you would notice."

"Your sofa was empty most of the night," I said. "When did you even come in?"

She shrugged, still grinning. "About four, I think."

"Didn't he need to sleep before school?" I asked.

She winked at me. "There are more fun things than sleeping."

My eyes widened. "Wow."

"I love him," she confided. "And last night he told me he loves me."

"I'm happy for you," I told her.

She grinned. "And here's your guy now." Following her gaze, I saw Jake approaching, a lone figure in shorts and baseball cap, standing out from the Orthodox Jews. Despite everything, I was glad to see him.

"I'll give you some privacy," Maya said. The kitchen door slammed behind her as she went inside.

"I've been texting you for two days!" Jake called. He was out of breath; he had been running. "I heard something happened to your sister?"

I nodded as he reached the walkway to my house.

"Mind some company?" he asked.

I gestured toward the steps, inviting him to join me.

He settled on a step below mine, facing upward toward me. "What happened?"

I chewed my lip; there was still a small bruise from how hard I'd bitten it Monday night. "Something bad happened to my sister's heart during the seder."

"Her heart?" he repeated, surprised.

"Because she wasn't eating enough," I said.

He frowned. "So she just...needs to...eat more?"

"Yeah," I said. "If she'll listen."

He gazed up at the trees on the hill above my house, pink with flowers in spring. "She'll listen to you."

I shook my head. "She never has."

"But she will this time," he said confidently.

I shrugged.

He leaned forward intently. "Rachel, you saved my life," he said. "I'm sure you can help your own sister."

A rush of wind, soft on my face, came from the east. I wanted to believe him, but there was so much he didn't understand. About prophecy and how the now-missing visions had helped me with him. About Beth's stubborn streak. How I should have known this was coming, but still had failed her.

"Are you...Rach—are you—?" He had seen it coming before I did.

Sparks spun around me. I hardly understood what was happening, before everything real dissolved.

When the spinning stops, I am in that mysterious courtyard where I once met Devorah, like a ghost in her dream. I am quite real and completely alone now. From the overlook, I can see the Kotel plaza, eerily vacant.

"Where are they?" I ask.

There is no sound but the wind, gradually taking shape the shape of Hebrew words I cannot understand. At last, I hear my name.

"Rahel."

I fall to my knees, quivering.

"They are waiting for you."

My cheek pressed against a chipped wooden step. My knees curled up toward my chest. My thumbs pushed against my forehead, palms squeezed together as if I had been praying.

A vision! My spirits soared simply knowing G-d had not abandoned me. But where were the others in Jerusalem? Yonatan? Devorah? Rena? The other prophets? The other *Jews*? The final words of the vision provided the cryptic answer: *They are waiting for you.*

For *me*? I was waiting for *them*!

Yonatan? I asked tentatively, but he was as absent as he had ever been. The entire spiritual world was closed to me. Yet G-d had granted me a vision.

Cautiously, I lowered my hands from my face and opened my eyes. Below me on the steps, Jake sat unmoving, watching me like a fish in a bowl. Orthodox Jews continued to stroll up and down my street in the spring sunshine, greeting each other in Hebrew.

"I didn't want to interrupt you," Jake said.

I lifted my head. "Thank you for waiting," I said hoarsely.

He moved a few inches closer. "I could see the sparks of light shimmer around you," he said. "It's like nothing I've ever seen before."

I glanced away, embarrassed. "I didn't expect it ...just now."

He perched his chin on his fingertips, his eyes still wide. "Was there a message? Was it about your sister?"

His face was so eager, and I so desperately needed to share with someone, I told him the truth. "I was...in the Old City of Jerusalem. But I didn't understand why."

He stared at me, rapt. "It must have meant something," he said. "Were there any clues?"

"I –" I hesitated, trying to find the words to explain. "I was alone. I asked where everyone was," I said, frowning. "But they were waiting for me."

"Do you think it's something you're supposed to do?"

I shrugged. I knew I really needed a prophet to help me understand. But as in the vision, here in Baltimore I was hopelessly alone.

"Maybe another vision will explain it," Jake said.

I smirked a little, rubbing my sore cheek. "Hopefully not too soon."

But Jake was right. If G-d had a message for me, another vision would come. Right now, it seemed the only chance I might get any messages at all.

***

Maya swirled Mom's mashed potatoes on the glass plate. "You and Jake had a nice long talk," she said cheerfully.

I swallowed a piece of broccoli matzo kugel. "It was nice that he came," I said.

Maya winked. "I thought you could use some company."

Surprised, I lowered my fork. "You *told* him to come?"

"I just let him know where we were," she said innocently. She shook her head, smirking a little. "Something you might have considered before suddenly going all Ortho on us."

Despite myself, I bristled at her comment. "My mother *asked* me to do this. For Beth."

Maya raised one eyebrow in a skeptical glance. "Rach," she said, more gently than I expected, "I think it's time to call it what it is."

I stared down at Mom's turkey, feeling my face warm. Maya put her hand on my back. Outside the kitchen window, the sun was setting.

"If you *do* become Orthodox, we can still be friends," Maya said, still in that gentle voice. "Promise."

"When does the holiday end?" Kay asked, coming in from the living room.

"When we can see the stars," I said.

The phone rang as soon as the sky was dark. "I'm coming home to get you," Mom said.

CHAPTER 39

Huddled in the vast expanse of her white hospital bed, Beth looked tiny and defenseless. Her blue and white striped gown revealed bony shoulders, wrists, and clavicle. Tubes and wires poked out from her gown, and an IV led into in her arm. Heart monitor leads were pasted on her chest, and a monitor for oxygen squeezed her finger. A screen above her bed tracked the steady, reassuring beat of her heart.

She gave me a weak smile and reached out her hands to me. Her arms looked so fragile, but her hug was strong.

"I was wondering when you might stop by," she said in a breathy whisper, as Mom ushered Dad out to give us time alone.

"You look great," I said.

She laughed, a breezy and welcome sound.

"Well, you look alive," I amended, "and that's great."

She frowned at the IV. "They're feeding me against my will," she muttered. "You don't know what it will take to lose this weight."

My eyes widened. "Are you kidding me?"

She stared at me solemnly, then smiled cryptically. I couldn't tell if she was joking or dead serious. I sat in the chair beside her, astonished into silence, as she sat straighter in bed.

"How are you?" she asked. "Mom said Maya was staying with you for the holiday. Did you really keep it until now?"

"Mom told me to," I said. "I think she thought maybe it would help get you better."

"Yeah." She shifted in her bed, pulling the blanket to her chin. "Dad says it's all hogwash, but I *am* better. So who knows?"

I remembered Beth's frail, unconscious body on Passover night. "Beth." I reached for her bony hand. "You can't lose any more weight. It's time for you to start *gaining* weight."

She frowned back up at the IV. "I know." She sighed, plucking at the frayed white hospital blanket. "It's just I always said I'd do whatever it took to be a dancer."

"You can still be a dancer," I said.

Her hands perched like flightless birds on the blanket. "My freshman year, a senior sprained his wrist lifting me. He cursed at me, called me...horrible names," she said, shuddering. She threaded two of her fingers through a hole in the blanket, then slipped them back out and looked up at me. "He was an ass, but he was right, in a way. You have to be light to be a dancer."

I opened my mouth to protest, but she shook her head, looking back up at the IV. "It's so easy for the others. They can get by on a salad leaf. But at a certain point –" her eyes were frightened – "I mean, it felt good. Like I could live without eating at all."

"No one can live without food," I said.

"I guess," she said in a broken voice.

When Mom brought me home later that evening, I found myself sneaking glances at her in the car. Why had she asked me to keep Passover for Beth? Why didn't she keep the holiday herself? Did she really *want* me to be an Orthodox Jew? Still afraid to hear the answers, I let silence fill the car.

Lauren hurried up to me after Orchestra the next morning. "Where have you been? Why didn't you answer your phone?"

I held up my hands, as if to protect myself from her questions. "I'm sorry. It's Passover."

She frowned, pushing her hair from her eyes. "What does that have to do with it?"

I finished packing up my flute. "My mother asked me to keep the first days of the holiday," I explained, as we walked toward the hallway.

She squinted at me. "*Keep* the holiday?"

"Yeah." I pressed my lips together. "The traditional way. So I wasn't checking my phone. That part was actually...kind of nice."

Her mouth formed a little *o*.

"It was a tough couple of days," I said. "Beth went to the emergency room Monday night."

"Beth?" Lauren stopped walking. "What? Why?"

I turned back to face her. "Something bad happened...to her heart. During the seder."

She put her hand to her chest, shocked. "Gosh, Rach. What happened?"

"She just..." I pictured that horrible moment again, when she slipped off the chair, and a lump rose in my throat. "She just collapsed."

Lauren put her hand on my shoulder and met my eyes. "Are *you* okay?"

I considered the question. Despite being terrified about Beth, disconnected from the prophets, and at risk of unexpected visions at any time...I *was* okay. Beth was alive.

"Yeah," I said. "I'm fine."

∽

Beth came home that afternoon with a diet plan and a promise to gain weight. She had a dozen follow-up appointments scheduled: weight checks, heart checks, psychiatrist appointments, nutritionist check-ins.

Each night that week, I tried to meditate, still hoping to learn more about how to help her. But the trance refused to come.

In truth, there wasn't much any of us could do. The choices were all in Beth's hands. She was supposed to eat more each day, following a careful diet they had prescribed.

Dad was the most changed by what had happened. Beth said he checked on her nearly every hour. "I don't get why he's so *attached* all of sudden," she said to me one night, as I ate Mom's mashed potatoes, and she sipped a cup of apple juice.

"Because he feels so bad he wasn't there for you," I said.

She shrugged her thin shoulders. "It had nothing to do with *him*."

I wished she would say it had nothing to do with *me*, either, so I could overcome my own terrible guilt. But she had no way of knowing I'd had a warning months ago, and had utterly failed her.

∽

After Passover ended Tuesday night, we ate our first leavened bread products together in the den. Beth sat on the loveseat as usual, nibbling a bagel and drinking a glass of milk. I settled on the floor, savoring a blueberry muffin and the freedom of spring break. Dad was eating a poppy seed bagel. New creases radiated from his eyes to his temples, and his face was stubbly after a week of not shaving.

"I can't wait to get back to California," Beth said.

My stomach dropped. She couldn't really leave, could she? Wouldn't she just stop eating again? Mom leaned forward, her chin falling into her hands.

227

Dad's fingers tightened into fists.

"Beth," he said. "We've talked about this."

She lifted her chin stubbornly. "I'm *going* back."

"You can wait until next semester," he said.

Beth placed her plate and cup on the floor. The remaining piece of bagel and half cup of milk stood like silent witnesses of reproach. Dad and Mom exchanged glances.

"We've got the show next month," Beth said. "I'm losing too much rehearsal time here."

I set my muffin down and squeezed Beth's cold, thin hand. "Maybe they could find an understudy to cover for you."

"But then I wouldn't get to do the show," she said.

"Beth," Mom said, "there will be other shows."

She shook her head. "I can't afford to miss any opportunities, if I want to do this professionally."

I stroked her fingers with my thumb. "What you really can't afford is a heart attack," I said quietly.

She shrugged, looking away again. "I'll be more careful from now on," she said. "Keep the electrolytes in balance. That's the key, the nutritionist says."

"How are things going with the diet plan?" Dad asked pointedly.

We all stared at the unfinished bagel on her plate. Beth reached for it and took another small bite. "Whatever it takes to get back to dancing in California," she said, ignoring Dad's loud sigh.

⌇

Steps and more steps, the tight alleys, the silent Old City under the diminishing moon. The heavy metal door is engraved with a Jewish star. Three flights in the darkness. There is a key in my hand, but her apartment is unlocked.

Inside, everything is exactly as I remember: The polished wooden dining table. The colorful afghan on the sofa. The window open to the night sky.

"Devorah?" I call. At the far end of the room, a door opens.

The Voice I hear is as inscrutable as the wind, but I fall to my knees, bowing all the way to the floor on the threadbare carpet.

"What if I can't?" I cry out.

"You will."

Trembling, I returned to my bedroom floor, hearing again the fearful silence of Jerusalem in the darkness.

In the vision I had fallen to my knees in response to a Voice. *Was that the Voice of G-d?* I wondered. I had responded with panic and desperation, but the answer was kind, confident, and unyielding. *You will.*

The vision had come while I was dressing for school. I was still wearing my nightshirt over my jeans. I would now be late for Orchestra, but it hardly seemed to matter.

Cautiously, I unwound my arms from my knees and sat upright. "G-d," I said, voice shaking. "Please...please tell me what You want me to do..." My hands were shaking too. The message of my last vision came rushing back to me, still confounding. *They are waiting for you.*

CHAPTER 40

Chris knocked at the kitchen door that Thursday morning. I blinked twice – as if he were a hallucination or possibly part of a vision – before getting up from my cereal and joining him on the porch.

"Hi," I said.

A flood of thoughts rushed over me. What if I'd told him yes, back in the fall? What if I had never traveled to Israel? What if I had never met Devorah? Could I have been simply, happily in love with this boy? I knew I could not have, but still I sighed.

"How's Beth doing?" he asked.

I shrugged my shoulders halfway. "She didn't gain enough this week."

"Sorry to hear that," he said, frowning. "I've been praying for her."

"Thank you," I said. "I think she needs it."

He took a step closer. I could feel his body heat. Instinctively, I took a half step back.

"Are *you* okay?" he asked, a little breathlessly.

I knew I couldn't think too hard about my answer. "Yes."

"What happened with the prophecy?" he asked.

I hesitated. How could I tell him the truth without melting into a puddle of emotions?

"You don't have to tell me," he said quickly, "if you don't think you should."

His kindness broke me. Before I could stop them, tears tumbled down my face.

"I don't know *what's* happening," I admitted. "I...I'm...Oh, Chris." I leaned on the wall of the house for support.

Chris reached for my hand and squeezed it, then without asking permission took me into his arms. His body felt large, warm, and tense, like the body of a friendly tiger. I sagged toward him.

"Are you still having visions?"

I nodded into his chest. "But I don't understand them," I said.

"Oh, Rachel," he said, stroking my back. "What a heavy burden you've been carrying for your G-d."

Face still buried in his chest, I sighed again.

"Keep your faith," he said.

I lifted my head and stared up at Chris: his smooth tanned face, his strong chin, his liquid brown eyes. Why was he always the only one who seemed to understand?

"I don't know what I'm supposed to do," I said.

Chris traced his finger along my ear to my jaw. "He won't keep you in the dark much longer, I think," he said. With his other arm, he squeezed my waist and released me. I stumbled backward a few steps, but he leaned forward and kissed my forehead. "You wanted to be friends," he reminded me. "Don't forget I'm still here."

A spring breeze ruffled my hair. I shivered as he returned to his house.

That evening I found my parents in Beth's room, in the middle of a fight. Beth sat stiffly under the covers, bright pink spots standing out on her pale cheeks. Mom stood uncertainly by the foot of the bed, as if she had been pacing. Dad was in the corner with his arms crossed; the bristles poking through his chin made his face look silvery-gray.

"What's up?" I asked tentatively.

In response, Mom ushered me out of the room. "We had to do it. She lost two more pounds this week." She laced her hands together and pulled them apart, her face pinched with anguish. "The nurses told us to enroll her in an in-patient program." I squinted at Mom, confused. "It means she can't go back to school," she explained. "She has to stay here in Baltimore."

I exhaled in sudden relief. "She's not going back?"

She shook her head. "Not until fall...at the earliest. Dad and I talked about it for hours last night. If she's going to get better, she has to stay here." She ran her fingers through her hair, staring down at the hallway rug. "She's so angry," she said. "But we have to do what's best for her."

I hesitated. I agreed Beth needed to stay here. But would she be too angry to cooperate? "What about her dancing?"

"Dancing?"

"She wants to dance," I said.

Mom waved a hand. "She'll dance in the fall. There are more important things right now."

I shook my head vehemently. "Nothing is more important to Beth."

Mom gave me a patient look. "She needs to learn that her life matters more."

I frowned at her. "If she doesn't think she can dance, she won't get better."

"She has to," Mom said grimly.

The next morning, I came into Beth's room before breakfast. She was asleep.

My stomach was growling. I had a granola bar in my pocket and I took it out to eat, but then stopped, considering.

What if I didn't eat it? What if I tried never to eat again? How long would it take before I felt dizzy, before I couldn't think straight? How long before I gave in and ate?

It was really quite remarkable, what she had managed. If she could just direct her determination in a healthier direction, who knew what she could accomplish?

I gazed at Beth's small, peaceful form under her blanket. When we were little, I had watched her sleep like this countless times. Waiting for her to wake up, so we could watch cartoons or color together on a weekend morning. Those days might as well have been a hundred years ago.

Then – just as she always did when we were kids – she opened her eyes, dazed with sleep. "Hey Rach."

"I'm sorry," I said.

She blinked, still half asleep. "I forgive you."

A tear trickled down my cheek. I knew she couldn't really understand why I felt so guilty, but her forgiveness made all the difference.

"Don't die," I begged.

Her lips twitched, as if she was about to smile or speak, but she remained silent.

"Please don't die," I said again. "Stay and do the program. Get well."

Her eyebrows arched, then fell. Her words came out like a suppressed moan. "They won't...let me dance..."

"They – will – let you – dance," I said in a determined voice. "If you stay and get well, Beth, I'll make sure you're allowed to dance."

She shook her head. "If I don't finish the semester ..." she said, hiccupping back a sob, "they won't take me back....I'll never make it..."

"Then we'll find another program for you," I said stubbornly. "I'll make Mom and Dad understand."

She shook her head. "They think dancing is just a dream."

I had to admit she was right. Otherwise, why would my parents have insisted on the double major? They wanted her to be successful, but had never really believed she could be successful as a dancer. So why should she trust them, when they said she could dance some other year?

I hugged her skinny shoulders. "You're *going* to be a dancer, Beth," I said. "*I'm* never giving up on your dream."

◠◠

That afternoon, I googled the contact list for the dance department at Beth's school. I called each of the professors one by one, leaving messages in the various mailboxes.

After I finished, I felt frightened by my actions. What if I ruined everything by intervening now?

The house was quiet in the fading light. Beth and my parents were still at the hospital for one of her regular check-ins. When they left, Beth wasn't speaking to either of them, and her lunch sat uneaten on the floor of her room.

As the sun set through my bedroom window, I lit my candles and brought Yonatan's siddur out to the porch. I opened it to the Shabbat evening service and began whispering the words, mostly in English, pouring out my heart for my sister, for the prophets, for clarity about what I should do now. When the words were finished, I rested my head in my hands. I wished I could meditate, or that a vision would come and explain everything. But of course, I couldn't, and no vision materialized.

"Shabbat shalom," a voice called from the sidewalk.

It was one of the Orthodox girls from across the street. She was maybe twelve years old. Her light hair was tied back into a braid, her dress reaching past her knees and elbows. Her high voice was like the ringing of a bell.

I felt awkwardly aware of my jeans and T-shirt. "Shabbat shalom," I said.

She took a step toward me on the path. "I'm sorry your sister is sick," she said. "I've been saying *tehillim* for her healing."

I squinted at her. "Sorry?"

She pushed a loose strand of hair back from her face. "Saying psalms," she said.

233

"For Beth?" I sat back, surprised.

"She always seemed like a nice person to me," she said.

Chris's prayers were one thing, but I'd never imagined this young Orthodox girl praying for us. "Thank you," I said, hoping my words could convey just how much I appreciated it.

"Were you praying?" she asked curiously, tilting her chin toward my siddur. I nodded.

"I'm Batya," she said. She glanced behind her. "It's time for Shabbat dinner. Would you like to join us?"

I lifted my eyes to her house across the street. Light was streaming from all the windows. *Could* I just go there? I wondered. Could the holiness of Shabbat, the beauty I had experienced in Tzfat, really be right across the street?

"Really?" I asked.

She grinned. "Sure."

"Just let me change," I said.

"You're perfect the way you are!" she called out, but I was already hurrying through the dark kitchen, up to my bedroom to find a skirt.

The house filled with light was also filled with people. There were children of all ages, family members, and guests. Batya introduced me to each of them as "Rachel, who lives across the street." Her father, who had taken off his black hat and was wearing a black velvet kipah, greeted me with a stiff nod and smile. But the mother, tall and thin with a navy velvet snood covering her hair, reached out both hands to welcome me.

"We've all been thinking of your family," she said, shaking her head. "An ambulance, on the first night of Pesach! Is your sister feeling better?"

"Y-yeah," I stammered, surprised. "Getting there."

"She should have a *refua sheleima*," she said, and when I hesitated, she translated, "A complete healing."

"Thanks," I said.

As everyone stood around the table to sing *Shalom Alecheim*, welcoming angels to the table, tears pricked my eyes. This beauty had been here all along. All I lacked was an invitation.

"Come wash," Batya said, waving me toward the kitchen. She offered to help me through the rituals, but I found I didn't need much guidance. I remembered the details from Shabbat in Israel.

Course by course, Batya and her mother brought a procession of kosher food to the table. Matzo ball soup. Salad. Roasted potatoes and mushrooms. Noodle kugel. Baked chicken. They refused my help serving, but her mother paused to ask what my family needed. Food? Help with rides? People to visit Beth and give my parents a break?

I shook my head. "But thank you for having me tonight," I said. "Everything is delicious."

"We should have invited you a long time ago," she said. "I'm glad you could come."

After dinner, Batya walked me back across the street. I wanted to ask her if she knew about prophecy. Had she met Yonatan during his months in the United States? Could she and her family ever understand what I had experienced? Could they possibly explain the visions I'd seen? But I held back, afraid to ruin such a beautiful evening.

"Thanks so much for inviting me," I said.

She gave me a quick, unexpected hug. "Come over any time," she said. "Shabbat shalom, Rachel."

"Shabbat shalom," I replied.

In my bedroom, I curled into my pillow. But instead of attempting to meditate again, I whispered words of gratitude for the invitation to join the world of Shabbat, if just for tonight.

Prophecy was one thing – maybe quite a difficult thing – but G-d had shown me, once again, that faith, the long history of Jewish identity, and a beautiful community might almost be enough.

CHAPTER 41

I returned to school Monday for the final six weeks before graduation. By the end of the day, I had three messages from Beth's professors and her advisor. I whispered a little prayer before I called each one of them back. By Wednesday, I had reached all of them.

I wrote my findings on 3x5 cards, then typed them up, just as I was doing with my final History report for the semester. Finally, on Thursday – the night before Beth was due to move into the in-patient facility – I brought my parents into the den to discuss what I'd learned.

The tension in our house had only grown during the past week. Beth had rebelliously lost two more pounds. Mom and Dad were pinning their hopes on the program. My hope was pinned elsewhere.

"I wrote something," I told them, and drew the papers out of my backpack.

Mom took my report and sat on the loveseat. Dad sat beside her, reading over her shoulder. The report was five pages long. By the time they reached page three, Mom was crying.

I hadn't mentioned the details to her professors. I'd just asked each of them the same questions. "What is your opinion of Beth as a dancer? Could she make it as a professional? What stands in her way?"

I had quoted the teachers' answers. One said Beth was "brimming with potential." Another said she'd "never seen a student work harder than Beth." A third said Beth "would give up her life to dance" and had "the makings of a star." Even I had been surprised by how much her teachers believed in her. They also said she was held back by her obsessive perfectionism, her need to focus on a second major in addition to dance, and a lack of confidence in her abilities. Most importantly, one of her teachers had said she would consider Beth for her own company.

When Mom finished reading the report, she looked up at me through a haze of tears. Dad sat mute beside her. "We *can't* send her back there, Rachel," she said. "She'll dance herself to death."

"Not *now*," I said. I knelt on the floor beside Mom, taking the paper from her. "You just have to understand. This is Beth's *dream*."

Both my parents looked doubtful. "She did all this so she can dance," I told them. "She needs you to understand that if she's going to get better."

Dad's face turned pale, then red, and he began to cry with deep, choking sobs. I'd never seen him so upset. "I didn't know she was this good," he said. "I was just trying to protect her." He turned to Mom. "Do you really think she could make it?"

"If she could give up eating, she could do *anything*," I said.

Mom stared at me, and something seemed to pass between us.

And the younger will save the elder.

I began to tremble. "I-I just want Beth to get better."

Mom grasped my hand. "Thank you, Rachel."

⚬⚬

I visited Beth at the new facility on Saturday night, after Mom and Dad had shown her the report from her teachers. "I didn't know the teachers thought that," she said to me, her voice awed. "They were all so stern and serious with me."

"They were just pushing you to grow," I said.

She smiled wryly. "You wouldn't have heard that from the business professors."

"Well, clearly *that's* not your dream."

She giggled; it was the most beautiful sound I'd ever heard.

"Will you be okay here?" I asked her.

She shrugged her shoulders. "I guess. Some of the girls here are..." She raised her eyebrows and wiggled one hand. "Kind of crazy. I mean I don't really feel like I belong here but..." She shook her head. "I guess I do need...some help getting back to a healthy weight...so I can be healthy... when I dance."

⚬⚬

For more than a month, I had avoided discussing Jake with Lauren. She didn't seem eager to bring him up either, even when I went running on Monday afternoons with him after Poetry Club, rather than getting a ride home with her; and even when he sometimes caught me after lunch to pass me a folded note with a poem he'd written. But Tuesday afternoon, when Lauren found me laughing with him at my locker, it seemed she couldn't restrain herself.

"So...are you *dating* that guy now?" Lauren asked, wrinkling her nose as we walked into the library.

I shook my head. "We're just friends."

She exhaled. "Good." She opened up her Physics book, as if the conversation was closed, but I couldn't stop myself from protesting.

"You have him all wrong," I said.

Lauren looked down at her book. "Okay."

"He's really a good guy," I said. "And he's worked *really* hard to get himself together the last couple of months. Did you know we're running more than two miles? Three times a week."

She chuckled. "I never would have expected *you'd* be running three times a week."

"It's kind of fun with him," I told her.

She leaned forward curiously, fingertips on her chin. "Are you sure you aren't dating?"

I blushed. "Yes."

By the end of Beth's first week in the in-patient facility, she had gained five pounds. Though she wasn't allowed to dance while in the program, she was watching dance videos to learn about choreography and continue building her skills.

I had already visited her a few evenings that week. But more importantly, for the first time in our whole lives, Beth and I had begun to talk every single day. She would call me in the morning, to tell me how the night had gone, or after school while I was at the library with Lauren. If she didn't reach me, I'd call her in the evening after I finished my homework.

"Are Maya and Chris still together?" she asked one night.

"Yep." According to Maya, they were talking for hours every night, interfering with her preparation for her math final. Sometimes in school, I'd see Chris walking Maya to one of her classes, his arm wrapped tenderly around her shoulders. "It's the real thing for them."

"How are *you* doing?" Beth asked.

"I'm happy for them," I told her, and for the first time I really meant it.

The sparks began to shimmer in the corner of my eyes Sunday evening, while I was with Beth and my parents in her room at the in-patient facility.

Always before, the sparks had come suddenly, frighteningly, but tonight they came gradually, comfortably, like an old friend. Maybe if Jake had been there, he would again have noticed them before I did.

"Excuse me," I said. I hurried into the hall, searching for the meditation room I'd noticed earlier. As the lights began to spiral around me, I pushed the door open. Upholstered wooden chairs, a blue and gold painted mural...I slid along the wall to the floor.

The whisper of my footsteps in the darkness, beneath the moon shining in the milky blue sky. The Kotel stands in shadow, rising up above the small figures hunched in prayer below it.

At the top of the steps, I hesitate. The cool breath of morning frosts my skin. I grip the stone barrier in front of me and, when I look down, I'm startled how young my hands look. I feel as ancient as the earth itself.

The Voice rises from the distance, loud as eternity, though no one else will hear It. "L'chi Lach L'yerushalayim."

Above the Wall, the sun breaks through, illuminating the courtyard. A tear slips down my cheek.

"Come," the Voice says. "Before it's too late."

I awakened suddenly, my knees pulled to my chest. The wall was smooth against my back, but the carpeting was rough beneath my hands.

The Kotel. The sunrise. The command. *Come.*

When the door opened, I scooted instinctively toward the corner, as if to hide. Then I saw Mom in the doorway.

"Rachel," she said, her voice filled with compassion and dismay. She came in and sat cross-legged on the floor, facing me. "Were you praying?"

I shook my head.

One corner of her mouth twitched. "Why don't you tell me why you came in here?"

"I – I don't think I can," I said.

She pursed her lips. "You can." She reached for my hand.

So right there, on the floor of the meditation room, I opened my mouth to tell my mother everything.

"On Yom Kippur at Shomrei Emunah," I said, "I met Yonatan. He taught me...about Judaism, Jewish mysticism, and the prophets." When I said the word, I heard her inhale sharply. "He told me –"

"About the calling," she said.

My eyes widened. How did she know?

She reached forward, squeezing my shoulders. "Zaide told me I couldn't be the one to tell you. He said you'd need to come to it on your own."

My mouth opened. "*Zaide?*"

"Zaide ..." She smiled wryly. "He knew things."

I fingered the necklace he had given me, and remembered the inscription in his siddur: *May she grow into all of her gifts.*

"When you were born..." She stroked my cheek with her cold fingers. "He told me a time would come. That you would be called. I promised I would let you go." She tucked her fingers under her chin and shook her head. "I didn't think you would be so young."

"I think it all started when he died," I said.

She reached forward and I let her hold me, soaking in every drop of her love. "You've been through so much this year," she said.

I knew I'd have to tell her, now that I knew what the visions meant. But how could I say I had to leave? In that moment, I understood how Yonatan must have felt, staying behind in Israel when I needed him so much.

"I think I'm supposed to go back to Jerusalem," I said.

She sat back, searching my face. "When?"

I shrugged one shoulder. "I don't know. Soon. But –"

She took hold of both my hands. "Let me help you."

I stared at Mom, astonished. She pushed her forehead against mine. "Some promises last through generations," she said. Leaning back, she ran a finger along the edge of my ponytail. "Zaide said your gift had great power," she said. "Pray for Beth."

"I have been," I said, as we stood up. "Every night."

"Good," she said.

CHAPTER 42

Though my visions and dreams about Jerusalem continued over the next several weeks, telling Mom the truth brought a kind of calm into my life. Because I trusted she would help me, I was able to set my anxieties aside and focus on my final exams.

Lauren and I continued to study several afternoons each week, and Jake and I kept up our running schedule. I spent the remaining spare time I had with Beth.

After two weeks in the in-patient facility, she transferred to an intensive out-patient program. She began to dance again, at first just an hour a week. When we celebrated my 18th birthday, she ate cake.

I finished my last final exam on the last Thursday in May. That night, Mom came into my room. I set aside my poetry notebook as she sat beside me on the bed.

She handed me an envelope. Inside was an e-ticket...for a flight to Tel Aviv.

I stared at her, my mouth falling open.

"You finished your finals," she said. "Now it's time for you to go."

***

"You won't believe this," I said to Jake the next morning, as we sat on my porch steps drinking water before our run. "I'm going to Israel on Monday."

His mouth fell open in surprise. "*This* Monday?"

"I think G-d wants me to go," I said quietly.

Jake shook his head, biting his bottom lip with begrudging admiration. "When do you come back?"

"The Sunday before graduation."

I would have a total of twelve days in Israel. "You can come home earlier if you need to," Mom had told me. "Just change the flight. But Rachel," she said, wrapping her fingers around my wrists, "you *have* to be back for graduation."

I didn't question her instruction. Twelve days seemed more than enough. If I couldn't find Devorah in Jerusalem, maybe I could get a bus to Tzfat? I figured all I really needed was to find Yonatan, ask him to restore our connection, and come home.

∞

On the Saturday morning after Mom gave me the ticket, I told Chris about my upcoming trip. He turned off the lawnmower to listen to the story.

"You are an inspiration," he said.

I laughed. "Me?"

He rested one hand on the lawnmower, the other on his hip, studying me like he had never quite seen me before. "You, Rachel. You're like Abraham, following the call of your G-d."

I blushed, embarrassed. "It all happened so suddenly," I told him. "I don't even know what I'm doing."

He shook his head. "You don't need to know. It'll all make sense once you get there."

After Chris heard the news, it wasn't long before Maya texted me.

Going to Israel NOW??

Just a quick trip. I'll be back for graduation, I texted her back.

Will you stay with your cousins? she asked.

I had almost forgotten I'd said that about the prophets in Tzfat. Now I was glad I'd given her some idea of why I might go back.

I hope so, I replied. *Details still firming up.*

∞

On Sunday, Lauren had invited me to join her at her family's swim club, open for Memorial Day Weekend. I waited until we were sitting by the pool, eating ice cream, to tell her I was going back to Israel. She stopped her ice-cream mid-lick, lowering the cone to stare at me.

"So you're going...tomorrow morning?" she asked, her eyes wide.

"I'll be back in time for graduation," I said, trying to be reassuring. "My mother bought the ticket."

"Are you doing some kind of program?"

I shook my head. "I just...need to go."

Lauren studied me as if from a distance. "You've changed so much this year."

I knew she was right.

"All this Jewish stuff," she continued in a soft voice. "Was it because of your grandfather?"

"Maybe," I said.

My ice cream was melting on my hands. I wrapped my cone with a napkin and took a few licks, trying to salvage it.

"Are you happy?" she asked. "I just hope you're happy."

I seemed to have left simple happiness behind months ago. What I had now was more complicated: a sense of purpose and meaning, a trust in something beyond myself. I had to believe I was doing the right thing, following my path where it led. When I focused on that, a deeper contentment seemed to resonate inside of me.

"Yes," I said at last.

Lauren bit into her cone, her eyes meeting mine at last. "I'm glad," she said.

It was barely dawn, but the humid air felt warm on my face as Mom and I put my bags into the car. I wasn't bringing much, just some clothing and sundries in a duffel bag, and my backpack. Also my passport and my phone. Mom had tucked two one hundred dollar bills and a credit card in my wallet, in case I needed them.

I trembled as the car backed out of the driveway. It was Memorial Day. All the way to the highway American flags stood in doorways and gardens, waving in the morning breeze like a farewell.

For the first time in my life, I was going to be completely alone. How would I get to Jerusalem? Could I just take a cab straight to the Old City and find Devorah's apartment? What if she wasn't there? What if everything I'd envisioned had been a mistake?

I glanced over at Mom. Her face was stony and determined, her profile silhouetted by the rising sun outside her window. If she hadn't promised Zaide, would she be letting me leave like this?

"How did you convince Dad to let me go?" I asked.

She rested her hand on mine. "I think your father is...starting to understand he has to let his girls follow their own dreams."

In the last few weeks, I'd heard this same thing from Beth. He had stopped pressuring her to eat and begun to encourage her dancing. Together, they watched ballet videos so she could teach him the names of steps and demonstrate how they were done. While he still wanted Beth to have skills outside of dancing, he had relented in his long-held position that she should have a double major in business. Instead, he'd consented to a minor, which she had already nearly earned.

Thinking of this, I found myself smiling.

The airport came into view too soon. Mom was going to drop me at the door. "You'll check in at the American desk," she said. "They'll give you the Israel boarding tickets when you get to Newark."

She stopped the car and turned to search my face. "Will you be okay?"

Like everything related to prophecy, I'd had no choice about this trip. Yet when I looked past my terror, I could feel in my soul this was right. I wanted—no, needed—to go.

"Yes," I said, mustering all the courage I could find.

She reached for both my hands and squeezed them. "Call me when you get there," she said. "Come home for graduation."

I nodded.

She blinked and I saw tears in her eyes. "Promise me."

"I swear," I said.

She reached into her purse and handed me a five-dollar bill. "Give this to charity when you get there. Be safe." She kissed me on the forehead, both cheeks, and both hands, surprising me with her fervor. I had a momentary flash of her own mother sending her off, this same way, for a much longer time. The last time.

"Be safe," she said again.

I walked toward the airport with my backpack and duffel bag, feeling as if I was walking off this planet and into another reality. But when I looked back, I saw Mom still sitting in our car, staring upward, hands outstretched, her lips moving as if in desperate prayer.

Our plane arrived in Newark after an uneventful flight. Following the instructions for international travelers, I picked up my duffel bag and walked it through Customs. After a brief interrogation by an Israeli security guard, I dropped my bag back off, received my new boarding ticket, and waited in the line for security. Finally, I found my gate.

In the waiting area, I saw young families with many children, the women wearing long skirts, the men with black hats like Batya's father. There were even a few Chasidic men wearing side curls. There were also quite a few passengers who didn't seem to be Orthodox. Women and men wearing shorts. A small group of teenagers, younger than me, sat in a haphazard cluster on the floor. A single priest sat reading a newspaper near the jet bridge.

I sat in a chair near the window, anxiety threatening to overwhelm me. Where was I going? What would I do when I got there? How could they – my parents, the prophets, G-d – send me across the world all by myself?

I pulled my poetry journal from my backpack and began to scrawl my worries across the final page. *Alone. Frightened. What am I doing here? Is this really what G-d wants from me?*

He was just a few steps away when I finally glanced up.

His beard had grown longer in the last several months, and I could see more strands of silver twisted with the brown – matching his eyes, which were shining perhaps even brighter than I remembered.

Other than that, he looked exactly the same. Under his white shirt, I could still see the definition of his chest muscles. On his head, a colorful knit kipah covered his thick dark curls.

Yonatan lifted my backpack from the chair next to me and sat. I blinked several times. "Is it really you?" I asked.

"Yes, Rachel." His eyes probed deep into mine, that way they sometimes did, reading my soul. "It is really me."

DEVORAH

Noach has gone. Far from this holy land, to a city of bright lights and the lures of so many desires and temptations—a place where my weakened and fading spirit cannot reach.

Without him here, I feel more alone than ever.

We argued last night. He reminded me of the time Naftali protected the prophets, when danger pursued us. "If I don't go, he will not protect us again."

"The Ribbono Shel Olam protects us," I reminded him.

"I'll return by Shabbat," he promised. "Wait for me."

In Tzfat, a continuous rotation of prophets pray for him. I hear their voices day and night, but I cannot join in. Every drop of Light I have is for the girl.

If he dies, prophecy will not survive it. If he is threatened, I will not be able to save him.

Everything rests upon her now.

CHAPTER 43

Even with my face buried in my hands, I could still feel the warmth of his presence. Only now, with him here, could I understand just how much his absence had cost me.

"I'm sorry," I mumbled into my fingers. "I'm just...so happy to see you."

His sigh was a sound equal parts contentment and regret. "It's good to see you too."

I lifted my eyes to his face. "Am I – am I really supposed to be going to Israel?"

At that moment, the flight to Tel Aviv was announced on the loudspeaker. Yonatan chuckled, glancing at his watch. "I'd say right now you are *exactly* where you are supposed to be."

"But what are you doing here?" I asked.

"Bringing you to Israel," he said, as if this were obvious. "You gave me the opportunity to visit my parents. In New Jersey." As in the past, I found he was communicating more than just with words. I understood. After losing his wife, he was grieving too bitterly to go home, but this trip had given him the chance.

Three rows behind us, two small children were rolling a ball back and forth on the rough carpet. "Yonatan," I said, keeping my eyes on the children. "What happened? When I left Israel...you said you'd–" My voice broke with raw emotion. *"Always be there when I needed you ..."*

Yonatan cleared his throat. "I am truly sorry," he said, with deep emotion. "I never intended to leave you alone."

"Did I do something wrong?" I asked, my voice wavering.

"You did *nothing* wrong," he emphasized.

"Then why?"

"One day, I'll be able to explain it to you." He gazed at me with his bright eyes, transmitting holy Light, gently washing all my panic and betrayal away. I felt our connection, broken so long, knitting itself back together. It seemed almost strange how afraid I'd felt leaving home, now that I could see I was really coming toward him.

"I think we'll be able to stay connected now," he said. "And it will be easier in Israel. Holiness is easier to access there."

I found myself watching the children again; their ball had rolled away and they were hunting for it under some chairs.

"I needed you here," I said, my voice tinged with bitterness.

His eyes were still warm on my face. "Did you?"

I pressed my fingers against my forehead. I'd certainly *thought* I needed him. But maybe now, sitting here with him, I could admit I'd done all right on my own. I'd saved Jake; and really helped my sister. Despite everything, I was on my way to Israel. Guided by visions, and helped out by my mother, I'd made it to a meeting that was apparently my destiny.

I risked a glance back up at his shining eyes, and remembered my eyes were bright too; that I was a prophetess with all the responsibilities I had learned. It seemed like a long time since our lessons, but really it was not so long ago.

"There's so much I want to tell you," I said.

"I'm looking forward to it," he said, showing me his ticket. He had the seat next to mine.

I began by telling him about the visions that led me to find Jake in the snow. "Could you see that?" I asked.

"Yes," he said. "You were remarkable with him."

"Since then, we've become...friends," I said. "We've been running together."

"Running?" He scratched at his beard.

"For exercise," I clarified. "It's helped him stay off drugs."

Yonatan tilted his head. "Sounds like fun."

"Actually it *is* fun. And the exercise is good for me too." I folded my hands in my lap. "He's a good person," I said. "He just needed someone to believe in him."

He nodded. "Then it's good you were there."

I took a deep breath. "Yonatan? Were you punished, this winter, because of me?"

He pursed his lips. "I was punished," he said. "But it wasn't your fault."

"I'm sorry," I said anyway.

He shook his head. "In the mystical world, there are rules...but you couldn't have been expected to know them. And my punishment wasn't for your mistake."

"Then why?" I pressed.

"For lack of complete faith, in the holiest of places." His eyes, full of new-found humility, glistened with unshed tears. "Until I could find the strength to live without her."

Yonatan listened intently as I told him about our horrible seder night, and my mother's instruction to observe the holiday.

"Do you think I actually helped Beth by doing that?" I asked.

He took off his glasses and studied my face. "Your mother gave you wise advice," he said. "Mitzvot can add merit. It wouldn't have been good to ignore that in such a crucial moment."

I described how I'd helped my parents understand Beth and her need to dance. "I asked for G-d's help so many times," I told him. "I prayed, I cried, I tried to meditate. But in the end, I just had to try something."

Yonatan smiled. "Sometimes we don't even realize how our prayers are being answered," he said. "You did exactly what your sister needed."

For the first time in months, I let my shoulders relax.

"You have done *so well*," he said, as I wiped a tear away with a finger. "Even with such difficulty. You should be proud."

As the lights dimmed on the plane and others slept around us, Yonatan told me about the day Devorah came to him in Tzfat and asked him to come to Baltimore to teach me. He had only been given the name of the synagogue: Shomrei Emunah.

"On the day I arrived, I found a room for rent," he said. "By the second day, I'd met the rabbi, and on the fourth day I was at his house for Shabbat dinner." He stroked again at his beard. "That's how I knew the Holy One had not abandoned me."

"Didn't you have to work?" I asked.

He shook his head. "I sold a few special pieces before leaving," he said. "Of art," he said, when I looked puzzled. "Enough for food and rent." I was impressed to hear a few pieces of his art had paid for his time in Baltimore all those months.

When he arrived, Yonatan was broken, devastated, exiled from the holy land. On Rosh Hashanah, he was a lost prophet making peace with his own sorrow. Learning with me was part of his journey back to faith.

As the sky began to lighten, I couldn't stop yawning.

"It's a good idea for you to rest," Yonatan said. "You'll need your strength when we arrive."

I let myself drift into sleep.

Yonatan woke me as the plane began its descent. Through the window the city of Tel Aviv stretched below us, bright in the morning sun. Though I'd only slept a few hours, the spiritual energy Yonatan mentioned seemed to buoy me as we landed. Walking together into the airport, his holy presence strong beside me, felt like being inside a bright dream. I felt a jolt of excitement as we passed the sign in Hebrew and English: *Welcome to Israel.*

But soon, I began to feel...different. My breath was shorter than usual. A sharp pain twisted in my side as we walked through a long hallway with glass walls. I coughed, first quietly. Then I leaned over, gasping. I felt Yonatan turn toward me as the lights streaked across my field of vision.

There was nowhere to hide, and I had no strength to run. I felt the impact first in my knees, then my hands, as I fell to the ground.

A special armored car awaits them in New York.

Darkness presses in around him. It is very late. He tries to hear the prophets praying; he strains to connect with Devorah. But he hears nothing.

He came because he owes Naftali his life. And because this was no time to draw attention to the prophets' weakness. Yet now, alone, he feels something he hasn't experienced in many years: a tremor of fear.

My knees against the carpeted airport floor. The thrumming motors of airplanes. The hurried footsteps of passersby in the hall. Yonatan's watchful presence.

Breathless, shivery, achy to my bones, I lay crumpled against a glass wall. Yonatan sat inches away, guarding me.

"Is Noach in New York?" I asked.

A hint of alarm passed over Yonatan's face. "Yes."

"For how long?"

Yonatan leaned closer, his lips a few inches from my ears. "Just a few days. What did you see?"

Before, I thought he always knew what I'd seen. Was this a test, to see what I had understood? Or did he really not know?

Yonatan held my gaze, not giving me the answer.

"He was in a car leaving the airport," I said.

Yonatan seemed satisfied with my response. I wished he would send some Light to help me recover, but he seemed too shocked to realize I needed it. With enormous effort, I pulled myself to my feet. Yonatan carried my backpack along with his own as we continued along the hallway.

After a strong vision, I often felt as if I was walking underwater. But why did I also feel so sick? Ahead of us, through a glass wall, a waterfall flowed from the ceiling to the floor. I stopped to catch my breath, leaning against the pane.

"Rachel," Yonatan said protectively, "are you all right?"

I glanced at him. "Do you think you could – look at me that way that ...gives Light?"

His eyes widened, but he nodded. He led me to a set of chairs across from the waterfall. Gradually, I felt some of the exhaustion and terror leave me.

I'm here, I prayed. *I came like You told me to. Please, protect me.*

"Better?" Yonatan asked.

I nodded slowly. "I need to call my mother and tell her I'm here." I reached into my bag for my phone, but Yonatan handed me his before I could dig it out.

Mom answered on the second ring.

"Rachel? Where are you?"

"At the airport," I said. "In Tel Aviv."

"I'm so glad to hear from you," she said, a tremble in her voice. "How was your flight?"

"Good," I said. "How's Beth?"

"Beth is just fine," Mom said, in a tone that let me know her worries had shifted to me. "Will you be meeting someone there?" Her voice lifted a few pitches.

"Yes," I told her. "In fact, I'm already being well taken care of here."

She hesitated, and I wondered again: Would she ever have agreed to this if not for her promise to Zaide? "Take care of *yourself*," she said.

"I will," I answered, with as much confidence as I could manage. "Tell Dad and Beth I love them."

"Be safe," she said. "I love you."

"I will," I repeated. "I love you too."

I hung up and handed the phone back to Yonatan. Already, my chest was feeling tight again.

"Your mother is being very brave," he said. Then he looked at me more closely. "And so are you."

CHAPTER 44

Yonatan had slept less than me on the plane, but he didn't seem at all tired. He hummed as he carried my backpack toward the baggage claim. From there, he lugged both our bags out of the airport and into the damp summer heat of Tel Aviv. In the parking garage, he stopped in front of the blue Kia hatchback I remembered from our trip to Tzfat. He loaded my duffel into the trunk, then opened the passenger door so I could climb in.

"Is this your car?" I asked, finding my voice.

He shook his head. "It's Noach's."

I found a small basket with water bottles and snacks on the passenger side floor. A note inside read: *Rahel – Welcome to Israel! With gratitude, Rena.* *Gratitude?*

"Noach must have visited Devorah before driving to the airport," Yonatan said. Then he grinned, sheepishly. "Rena thinks of everything." He took a bag of Bamba from the basket, as I sipped from a bottle of water.

"Rena is with Devorah," I said. I had known that, in a meditation that seemed ages ago.

Yonatan glanced at me. He said cautiously, "Devorah has been...sick."

"I know," I said.

He turned onto the highway, a brooding expression on his face.

"Is she getting any better?" I asked.

Yonatan grimaced. "She'll be better when she sees you here," he said.

Ana Hashem, hoshia na. Ana Hashem, hoshia na.
Ana Hashem, hatzlicha na. Ana Hashem, hatzlicha na.[27]

Only when I startled awake did I realize I'd drifted back to sleep. The car was stopped at a red light; we had already exited the highway. In my dreams, I'd heard their mixed voices, intoning in Hebrew—the voices Noach couldn't

---

[27] Prayers for salvation and success.

hear from New York.

"Yonatan…" His name came out breathy and hoarse. I felt disoriented by the bright sunlight on the Jerusalem stones. The sky was a deep blue, just as in my visions.

"Yes, Rachel," he said. The streetlight flashed yellow, then turned green. The car accelerated.

"I heard voices," I said.

He glanced at me. "The prophets are praying for Noach."

A knot tightened in my stomach. "Is he in danger?"

Yonatan turned the car into a parking garage. He shook his head. "It's just a precaution."

"Can you hear them, too?"

He hesitated. "No." He parked the car in a space and turned off the ignition.

Yonatan lifted my bags out of the trunk. I followed him up a flight of stairs to ground level, then through an ancient gate into the Old City. The air was drier and cooler here than in muggy Tel Aviv. I sipped my water bottle as we passed tourists and shops. We turned left and downhill toward the Jewish quarter.

I thought we would go straight to Devorah's, but instead Yonatan knocked on a blue metal door. An old woman opened it. I leaned against the stone wall as he spoke to her in Hebrew. He scribbled something on a piece of paper and handed her some Israeli bills.

"This is a traveler's hostel. You'll stay on the second floor," Yonatan translated for me. "Get some rest. I'll be back later to check on you."

☙❧

The old woman carried my bags up a flight of stairs, then handed me a bundle of faded pink sheets and a thin blanket. "You – sleep – here," she said in English, pointing to a room with a half-dozen bunk beds, before heading back down the stairs.

I sat on a mattress by a dusty window and set the sheets next to me. Only one other cot had a sheet and blanket. When a toilet flushed, I turned, half-curious to see who I'd be staying with. Would she be old or young? Would she be Orthodox? My eyes widened as she entered.

"Tirtza," I said in surprise.

The young prophetess pushed a her long blond hair from her face,

255

kindness shining in her brown eyes. "Rahel," she said. "You're really here?"

I blinked, seriously considering the question. After all, how many times had I been in Jerusalem in dreams or visions? Could I be sure I was really awake this time?

"I think so," I said. "I mean, I flew in an airplane to get here."

She laughed and came over to hug me. "Yes, you're really here." Her warm hands were comforting on my cold skin. "Did Yonatan bring you?"

"He surprised me at the airport in Newark," I said.

"Rena always says he has a flair for the dramatic," Tirtza said, rolling her eyes. She sat down beside me.

I shook my head. "The visions told me to come to Jerusalem...and then I told my mother and...before I knew it...I was in the airport waiting for my flight, and he was there."

Tirtza frowned. "So you've been having visions? Wow."

I felt confused. "Don't we all...?" But she had become distracted, walking to the doorway to retrieve my bags.

"What are *you* doing here?" I asked.

"Rena sent for me." She stared out the window behind me. "I've been here a couple of weeks."

I took another sip of water.

"You look so tired," Tiztza said. "Do you want to rest for a while?"

I nodded. "Can you help me make this bed?"

"Sure," she said.

Ana Hashem, hoshia na. Ana Hashem, hoshia na.
Ana Hashem, hatzlicha na. Ana Hashem, hatzlicha na.

As I slept, their prayers filled my dreams, twisted with images of a lavish hotel room and New York City at night.

I awakened to find Yonatan kneeling beside me. Outside the window the sun had shifted; it was the middle of the afternoon. Tirtza had unpacked my bags onto a few shelves against the wall.

"How are you feeling?" he asked.

I wished I could tell him resting had helped, but if anything I felt worse. My joints and chest were aching, I felt cold and nauseated, and I still couldn't catch my breath. With all it had taken to bring me here, how could I have gotten sick?

"I'm sorry, Yonatan," I said.

"It's not your fault," he said.

"I'll get better soon," I said, lifting my face to meet his eyes. "Right?"

"Definitely," he said.

⌒⌒

Late afternoon sun blazing through my bedroom window.

"Worse than I expected."

"...Not the first time this has happened."

"But with Noach away, we need Devorah."

"Only a few days until he returns."

I sit up defiantly in bed. "Rahel doesn't deserve this." My voice breaks with emotion. "Noach needs her more than me now."

They bring water along with the pills. For her, I will sleep.

⌒⌒

In the hostel bed, I floated to the surface, momentarily awake.

"Tirtza," I said.

She approached immediately, and in a single moment of clarity I realized she had not come to Jerusalem for Rena or Devorah. She was here to take care of me.

"Don't let them drug Devorah," I said. "I don't want – I mean I can take it." I babbled on, unsure what I was saying, unsure what the dream had meant or if my words even would make sense to her. "Noach needs her, not me."

Tirtza bit her lip. "No one can change Devorah's mind when she's sure."

"But I can't help," I said, feeling my lucidity draining away. "I'm not – I can't..."

Tirtza rested her hand on my forehead, not as my mother would, to test for fever, but to soothe and ground me. I exhaled, drifting back to sleep.

"You can," she said. "We all know you can."

⌒⌒

They ascend on the escalator into the grand entrance hall. The room where the ambassador will give his talk is down the long hallway.

Ana Hashem, hoshia na. Ana Hashem, hoshia na.

Ana Hashem, hatzlicha na. Ana Hashem, hatzlicha na.

257

I slip through physical walls like a ghost, into the large assembly room where men and women – dressed in suits and wearing headphones – sit at long tables behind cards representing their countries.

From behind the Israel table, Noach's eyes shine holy Light into the room, though no one seems to notice. The ambassador sits stiffly in front of him, not receiving most of it even though he must have asked Noach to come just for this reason.

I remember Yonatan's teaching: "You must be willing to receive the Light and to give it." But none of these people have ever learned how to take this holy gift.

As the ambassador walks toward the podium, I drift toward Noach. I whisper his name, but he cannot hear me.

The ambassador's words start out fierce, requesting support but not really expecting it. Noach showers the Light toward him, filling the room, droplets scattering and touching a woman here, a man there. As beams illuminate the ambassador's face, his tone changes from anger to passion, from fear to hope.

In the end, it is an excellent speech. The other representatives break into applause as he returns to his place. Noach stands to shake his hand. "Well done, my friend," he says, in Hebrew.

There are many more speeches. Noach puts on headphones, listening, still filling the room with Light. The people here will not receive the full blessing, but they are receiving something. Tonight they will hold their loved ones with renewed gratitude and hope.

When at last the session ends, Noach turns in his headphones and walks with the delegation, surrounded by security and staff. The marble floors, the wide hallways of the United Nations. Down the escalator, past the security entrance, out into the sunlight.

The sounds of traffic. Pigeons. The smells of car fumes and trash.

As they walk together down the curved service road, a black car pulls to a stop along the busy avenue. Three men climb out to the sidewalk; their long lab coats are white, but their eyes are fierce, their souls dark. I tremble as they reach into their coat pockets.

Noach lingers a few steps behind the others as they reach the main gate. He is pleased by the results of this short trip. Casually scanning rooftops in the distance for snipers. Not understanding the risk right in front of him.

Ana Hashem. Ana Hashem. Please, G-d. *The prophets and their meditative chanting continue, never stopping even for a moment.*

From deep in her sleep, Devorah calls my name: Rahel.

For a moment, everything is still; one silent instant before everyone knows and everything moves fast and the bullets fly.

Rahel, *Devorah calls again.*

I remember when she said: "Noach needs her more than me." *And I understand.*

The prophets in Tzfat. Yonatan and Rena and Tirtza. Devorah in her bed in Jerusalem.

All the prophets across the world are waiting for me.

"Noach!" I scream his name, but no one hears me.

The car on the street pulls away. Noach takes a step toward the Israeli delegation. The security guard at the gate looks up. As if on cue, the three men pull out their guns. The guard draws his own gun, but a moment too late.

G-d, I beg. G-d. Please.

Then the words come to me:

"The calling of a prophetess is to intercede for her people. So please, may my words be heard. Protect Your prophets and Your people and save us."

My spirit leaps between the guns and Noach's body as bullets spray the group like rain.

CHAPTER 45

"Noach...!" I awakened gasping his name.

Outside the window, the sky was fading to summer dusk. The burst of bullets still reverberated through me, as if I had truly been there, blocking them with my own spirit.

Had I managed to save him? What if I'd failed?

Tirtza put her hand on my forehead, and this time I wondered if she actually was testing for fever. "Did you see Noach in your dreams?" she asked.

I stared at her. She didn't know. Did any of the prophets know? Was it real, or all just a horrifying dream? "I saw," I said, as everything whirled around me, "I saw them try to kill him."

Tirtza's eyes widened in alarm. "What?"

"The men...I tried to...stop them...warn him..."

Lights flooded in all around me. I was rising up and out; losing control of the vision-world, as Yonatan had always feared. Tirtza's fingers grasped my wrists.

"*Rahel*," she implored me. "Don't go. Stay here. Tell me what happened."

But I had already gone.

"For all the ways I've failed you, Elisheva," Zaide says, standing beside the hospital bed. "I'm sorry."

She shakes her head, though her eyes are wet. "Would you like to hold her?"

When he takes the tiny infant in his arms, he knows. After all this time, the youngest girl of his youngest daughter, like a birthright in reverse. Though he is no prophet, the words come unbidden: "This one is called with the holiest gifts. And the younger will save the elder."

He stares at his daughter. "Some promises last through the generations. One day, she will be called for greatness. Promise me you'll let her go."

Bright red blood oozing through his white shirt, Noach sags against the medic who comes to care for him. "A bullet grazed his shoulder," the medic says. One of the ambassador's bodyguards was also hit, in the knee. But the ground is littered with bullets that did not find their aim.

"It's a miracle," someone says in Hebrew. The entire group looks to Noach.

"Thank you, old friend," Naftali says.

Noach's face is white as his kipah. "Don't thank me," he says. It's a ritual, a requirement. "Thank Hashem." Then he slumps unconscious in the medic's arms.

⚭

The train: hours upon hours in that stuffy, foul-smelling darkness. I thought nothing could be worse than that terrible journey, until the doors opened. And, yes, there was something much worse.

⚭

"You plan to bring him on a plane? We can provide security here."

Noach clears his throat. He is a formidable presence on the emergency room gurney, his eyes alert and bright as the doctor lifts the curtain.

"Please patch up my shoulder," he says, his voice weak but clear. "I must return to Israel as soon as possible."

The doctor insists he confirm his name, age, the location, the date. When she leaves, he leans back on the gurney. "Devorah," he says softly, "you were right."

In Jerusalem, in a bed so far away, tears roll down her chalky white cheeks.

⚭

I'd been drifting so long I'd lost track of what was past, present or future... whether what I saw was real, vision, or dream. I floated like that until I heard Yonatan whisper my name.

I opened my eyes. Morning light streamed through the hostel window. Under my sheet, the jeans and T-shirt I'd worn on the plane felt crusty, as if they'd been drenched with sweat and already dried out. Yonatan knelt beside my bed, his eyes shining holy Light, restoring me. Tirtza stood beside him.

"Rachel," he said again, "we need to understand what happened...Noach called. He told us Devorah saved his life in New York. But Devorah...." He shook his head again. "Devorah said it was you."

Beside him, Tirtza gave a quiet gasp.

I tried to sit up, but my head spun. Tirtza leaned forward, propping me up with extra pillows. My body felt weak, as if my muscles had atrophied overnight. "I was in New York with him," I managed finally, "in a vision. When the men...shot...at them...." Yonatan's eyes widened. "I tried to...warn him," I said, "but he couldn't hear so...I prayed...jumped in front of him...to protect him." My eyes found Yonatan's. "Did he make it? Is he coming home?"

"Yes," Yonatan said soothingly. "He's on the plane now."

Tears of relief burned my eyes. "Thank G-d."

"Thank G-d," Tirtza echoed.

"Rachel." Yonatan's voice shook. "You can't imagine ... *Thank you.*"

"I just...I was just there," I said. "I don't know how I got there, I just...I just...."

"You did what needed to be done," he said.

"I have some questions...for Devorah," I said slowly. I tried to sit up again, but sank back into the pillows. "When can I see her?"

"Soon," Yonatan said. "When you've had a chance to regain your strength."

I frowned. I wanted to talk to Devorah *now* – to understand now.

"I'll be back later. Rest," he urged me. "You'll need it. And again," he said, his bright eyes searching my face, "thank you."

"I have some food for you," Tirtza said, as Yonatan strode back toward the stairs. "You must be hungry."

I hadn't eaten a thing since I'd arrived. "Yes, I am," I said. "Thank you."

Later that afternoon, Yonatan and I walked together in the summer warmth of the Old City of Jerusalem, to the silver door that had filled so many of my dreams and visions: the entrance to Devorah's building. Up three flights of stairs. Rena opened the door.

"Rahel," she said, taking me into her arms. "Baruch Hashem. Thank G-d you're here."

"Thanks for the water," I said. She looked at me quizzically. "In the basket," I said. "In the car."

She smiled. "Just a welcome after a long flight."

"How is she?" Yonatan asked, as Rena released me.

"Better," Rena said.

The apartment smelled sweet and sour, reminding me of my grandfather; that unique and particular scent of an old person. The small living room looked the same as it had in the winter: the sofa draped with an afghan, the decorative wooden chairs, and the coffee table on a colorful rug. Though it was only Thursday, two golden Shabbat oil lamps stood ready near the window. There was a new pillow on the sofa, embroidered with words in Hebrew. Rena's suitcase peeked out of a hall closet. The door to Devorah's bedroom was closed.

"Can we see her?" Yonatan asked.

"You'd better," Rena said. "She's been demanding to see you both. I haven't been able to get her to sleep since dawn."

Devorah's bedroom was small, crowded with only a full-sized bed and headboard, a dresser, and a cushioned chair in the corner of the room. The headboard shelf was laden with pill bottles. Behind the cushioned chair was an oxygen tank. A folding chair stood close to the bed. One large window looked out over the tops of the Old City buildings, to the cloudless blue sky above.

Devorah's white-gray hair was pulled back with a blue bandana, curly strands laying limp against the pillow. Her fingers were wrinkled and covered with liver spots, and her fingernails were too long. Her face seemed thin and pale.

A chill washed through me. In my visions, I had seen a younger Devorah, with smooth skin and a strong body. The woman before me was old and withered. I tried to remember: Had she looked this old when I had last seen her? Had it been just five months ago?

No, I answered myself. She was old then, but now she was also sick.

As I sat in the folding chair beside her, she shifted and sat up. She reached out her hand and I caught it in my own. I was hardly aware of Rena and Yonatan, standing in the doorway, watching us.

"Thank you," she said roughly, "for coming."

I squeezed her dry fingers. "Thank you for calling me."

"Not me." She shook her head, bringing my fingers to her face. "The Ribbono Shel Olam has called you here. And just in time."

"Devorah –" I couldn't contain my questions any longer. "Why did they attack Noach?"

She shook her head. "Wonder not why they wanted to hurt us, but why they were given the opportunity." She took a shallow breath. "It was a test," she said. "For all of us."

"Did we pass?"

A glimmer of pride shone in her face. "I think we did."

I was fascinated by her eyes, burning blue like the center of a flame. In them, I could see all the joy, pride, and regret of a lifetime.

"Will Noach be all right?" I asked.

She squeezed my hand and released it. "He's safe now," she said. "He's coming home."

"After I saved him...there were other visions," I told her. "I kept falling from one into the next...and I couldn't wake up, until Yonatan came."

She nodded. "You gave everything you had," she said in a shallow, breathy voice. "It can happen, when you come...to the edge of your gifts. But it gets easier...with time. And experience."

I remembered what Yonatan had told me long before, when my visions were slipping out of control, before I learned to meditate. *We need to increase your skills to keep pace with your gifts.*

"In one of the visions I –" I stopped, startled by a change in the air around us. A distortion, a shattering, revealing some other space beyond; a space both holy and completely unknown.

A splintering pain shot through me. I winced and bent forward, one arm wrapped protectively around my chest. I tried to release Devorah's hand, but she held me fast, with surprising strength in her fingers.

When the pain diminished, I opened my eyes. Devorah was also hunched forward, her pale lips pressed together.

"What...?" I managed to burst out.

Now Devorah's eyes carried only an endless sorrow. "I'm so sorry, Rahel." She squeezed my hand and released it.

Rena took a step forward. "You need to rest, Gedolah."

Devorah studied me a moment longer, then sighed. "All right," she said. "You'll come for Shabbat?"

"Of course," Yonatan said.

My chest was still ringing as Rena helped me to my feet. I glanced back at Devorah. I still had so many unanswered questions, but her eyes were already closed.

I followed Yonatan back through the alleys of the Old City, but as we came through a stone courtyard, I collapsed onto a bench. "Yonatan," I demanded, in as strong a voice as I could manage. "*What* is going on?"

He turned back to face me, his expression anguished.

"My chest hurts," I said. "I can't breathe, I....What's wrong with Devorah? What is...happening to...me?"

Yonatan hesitated, his anguish shifting to compassion. At last, he sat down beside me on the bench, gazing upward, to the blue sky above the stone buildings in the distance. "We didn't realize how bad it was for Devorah until...we saw how you're suffering," he said. "We never expected you would feel it like this."

Tears trickled down my cheeks. "So *I'm* not ...I'm not really ...sick?"

He shook his head. "Devorah's experience is your experience."

"But...why?"

"You have a special connection with Devorah," he said. I knew it was true.

I swallowed hard. "Then...is that how she knew...what happened with Noach?"

He nodded. "Devorah couldn't connect to Noach in New York. But through you...she was able to see."

"Through *me*?" I said in a high voice.

Yonatan pursed his lips, now studying the stone path beneath us. "It seems the Holy One wanted you to be the one to save Noach," he said. "As Devorah said, it was a test."

I raised my eyebrows, incredulous. "G-d was testing *me*...with Noach's *life*? What if I'd failed?"

Yonatan faced me, a flash of teacher's pride in his eyes. "Nothing happens by accident in this world," he said. "The important thing is you succeeded."

Tirtza invited me to shop with her at the *shuk* before Shabbat, but I encouraged her to go without me. After she left, I sat cross-legged on my hostel bed and pondered my situation.

Devorah was very sick, and Yonatan said I was feeling sick because of her. The good news was there was nothing truly wrong with *me*. That meant when she got better, I would feel better too. I must have been called here to help the prophets save Noach, while Devorah was sick. If all that was true, I might even be able to go home next week. I could see Beth. My mother and father. Jake.

For one moment, I let myself dwell on Jake's dark eyes, his pale pink lips, the growing muscles in his calves. How he could see the vision sparks coming even before I could. Had he been keeping up with his running? When would

I have the strength to run with him again?

I pulled myself out of bed and examined the shelves where Tirtza had unpacked my things. The little I'd brought looked like even less spread on the bare wooden slabs. A few skirts and shirts, a couple pairs of jeans, underwear, sneakers, a pair of sandals, soap, a razor, and a bottle of shampoo. There was the small siddur Yonatan gave me in Tzfat. Under it, I found the poetry notebook Lauren had given me last year—now battered and filled with words.

I took it down from the shelf and opened it.

The first poem was about Zaide. There was the safety list I'd written before my first meeting with Yonatan. Poems about my visions. About how I'd hurt Chris. A series of poems written in Israel, then verses about Jake – the visions that led me to save him, and all my efforts to help him stay clean. Scribbled stanzas about Maya and Chris. Poems about Beth, and then, because I'd had no other notebook handy, the notes from the teachers I'd called for her.

The final page held the words I'd written before seeing Yonatan in the airport.

Alone. Frightened. What am I doing here? Is this really what G-d wants from me?

There was just over half a blank page left. I reached back to the shelf for a pen, sat down on the floor, and began to write.

I don't know where I'm going
Or where I've been
Why I'm here
Or what to do now

You brought me, without clarity
I came because I was called
Led
Helped
Sent
Arrived without knowing
Served without instruction

In truth
I just want to go home.

But I remember
The agony of absence
No possibility of connection
Empty meditations
Your Voice resounding
"Come."

I know I'm here
For more reasons.
That I will not leave
Until all truths
Become true.

I'd had to squeeze the ending stanza into the margin of the last page. I closed the notebook, feeling my real story was just beginning.

CHAPTER 46

On Friday afternoon, I showered and put on a clean skirt and blouse for Shabbat. Downstairs, candles had been arranged for us to light. As the sun sank low in the sky, I followed Tirtza down stone pathways and steps, through parts of the Old City I'd never seen before, down another flight of stairs, until I stood there, feeling that ancient holy Power as I stared at the Wall.

A siren pierced the air and I froze, my thoughts scattering in alarm. *Would Noach really be all right? Would I have the strength to pass other tests? How many troubles had the Jewish people endured over the generations? How many tests had we passed and failed?*

"It's for the beginning of Shabbat," Tirtza said in a reassuring tone. I had forgotten the siren rang every Friday night here. She steadied me with her arm, and we continued into the Kotel courtyard.

As before, I walked trance-like toward the Wall, not stopping until I could rest my fingers, then my forehead, on the warm stones. I exhaled, finally feeling I'd arrived.

"Thank You," I whispered to G-d, "for helping me with Your tests."

Head down, fingers against the Kotel, a wave of holiness swept through me.

In the distance, I hear the sweetest singing. Hands of souls unknown rest on my forehead, whispering blessings. My body fills with Light. I hear my Hebrew name: Rahel bat Chaim v'Elisheva, and I realize the angels are singing to me, as Zaide once told me they could.

A warm breeze brushed my neck. Across the *mechitzah*, men were singing *Lecha Dodi*, welcoming Shabbat. Tirtza stood next to me, praying from a siddur in her hands.

I felt the angels' blessings upon me, a permanent imprint of light.

I opened Yonatan's small prayerbook and I whispered the words fervently, in English and in Hebrew, the best I could. Tears streamed down my cheeks. I don't even know what I said, but my soul was saying just one thing, over and over again. *Thank You. Thank You.*

Tirtza and I walked back up the many steps, through the darkening passageways, and into Devorah's building. At the top of the steps, the ancient prophet met us at the door.

His gray beard was long and straggly at the bottom, like loose strands of cotton. His shoulder was bandaged, but his face was a healthy, rosy color, and his eyes shone like gold reflected by the sun.

"Noach," I gasped.

Tirtza gave my hand a squeeze and disappeared into the apartment.

"Rahel," he said. *"Thank you."*

How could I accept his gratitude, when I'd barely understood what I was doing? The whole thing had happened almost in a dream. Then I remembered what he'd said, when they tried to thank *him*.

"Thank Hashem," I said, and felt relieved when he smiled. "I'm *so* glad you're all right." I ducked my head. "They hit your shoulder?"

He shook his head, touching his wound. "This part was for me," he said. "Punishment, for leaving at such a crucial time."

"Noach," I said tentatively, "why did you go?"

"Ach," he said softly. "Even prophets make mistakes. If you remember that, it will give you the courage to do all that needs to be done." He smiled at my perplexed expression. "I'll tell you more another day. Come inside. The others are waiting."

Devorah sat at the head of the table in the dining room. She wore a navy embroidered velvet robe, her hair pulled back with a dark blue scarf that highlighted her shining eyes. Yonatan and Rena sat on either side of her, and Noach took the seat facing her across the table. Tirtza sat next to Rena, so I found myself beside Yonatan as Noach recited Kiddush for all of us. Devorah's oil lamps glowed by the window, with Rena's candles alongside them. It was as if I'd slipped back into a dream. Was I really eating dinner with these holy prophets in the Old City of Jerusalem?

As we ate, Noach described his time in New York, noting the success of the ambassador's speech. Yonatan told us gratefully about his visit with his parents. Rena shared a few words of Torah she and Devorah had learned together, and Devorah added insights in a quiet voice.

Was Devorah getting better? I wanted to ask. She seemed stronger than yesterday. Her fingernails had been cut for Shabbat. I wanted to reach out and touch her hand, but we were too far apart.

After dinner, Devorah beckoned me to join her on the sofa. I sat on the bright afghan, my heart fluttering. Devorah's eyes probed into mine, as if she could see my soul in a single glance.

"If I could, I'd stay with you another thousand years. You know that, don't you?" She took a shallow breath, reaching for my hand with her ancient fingers.

I didn't want to hear what she was going to say, but there was no escape.

"Rahel," she whispered, "I'm dying."

I drew back on the sofa, childishly, resisting the impulse to cover my hands with my ears. *No.* But despite myself, I knew it was true. The bottles of medicine on the bed. The visions of...sunset. The *pain.*

"But I hardly got to know you," I said.

Devorah rested her hands on the new embroidered pillow on her lap. "You know me more than anyone ever will," she said. "That's the truth."

I was silent, remembering the visions of the horrors she'd seen in the Holocaust, and her journey to becoming a prophetess. The agony of her illness. In some of my visions, I had been almost like a part of her. But there were so many things I needed to ask her, and as with Zaide, I now knew many of those questions would go unanswered.

Devorah's fingers threaded through the colorful afghan. "My grandmother gave me a blanket like this, when I escaped from Poland. I want you to have this one."

A lump had taken shape in my throat. "Thank you," I said.

"You will see this was always how it had to happen, Rahel," she said. "The prophets. You. Everything happens as it should."

She leaned forward on the sofa with her hand outstretched, collecting a single tear from my cheek. There were so many wrinkles etched into her pale face, but her blue eyes flickered strong. I would remember this moment with Devorah for the rest of my life.

⟡

"Tirtza," I said, as we walked back to the hostel that night, "did you know about Devorah? That she's going to...." I couldn't make myself say the word.

She nodded. "Devorah wanted to tell you herself."

There, in the darkness of the Old City, I sank to the stone ground and broke into inconsolable sobs. How could any of us go on without the Teacher of the Generation? And when Devorah died, what would happen to me?

∞

The next morning, at the Kotel, my lips wet with salty tears, I pressed my head against the stones. "G-d," I prayed. "Don't let Devorah die."

I wanted a connection like the one I'd had the night before. If I could hear angels singing, if I could receive their blessings, maybe G-d would answer me this morning.

"Please, G-d!" I prayed. "Please."

But this time, I heard only silence.

∞

Devorah joined us again at the table for Shabbat lunch, but by now it was obvious to me how sick she was. Her pallid skin, her large burning eyes, her trembling fingers. Instead of rising to wash at the sink, she washed with a cup and bowl Rena brought to her.

After lunch, more prophets arrived. Some were dark-skinned, others pale and blond, and several others red-haired and freckled. The men wore black hats of different types and kipot of many colors, and the women wore dresses of all styles, many of them with their hair wrapped in colorful scarves. They had accents from every part of the world, and they spoke to Devorah in English, Yiddish, French, Hebrew. They were of every age.

How did they all fit in Devorah's tiny apartment? I didn't understand it, but somehow they did, sitting in chairs and on the floor, five prophets squeezed onto Devorah's little sofa, six around a coffee table I had been sure could only fit three. Then twelve around a table that last night had only fit six.

The women kissed Devorah on the cheeks and sat beside her on the sofa, on top of the afghan (*my* afghan, I had already begun to think). The men kept a respectful distance by sitting across from her, but they all seemed to be communicating in ways deeper than language.

I hovered near the kitchen, watching. From what I could tell, I was the youngest and newest of all the prophets in the room.

Toward evening, to a hushed room, Devorah spoke.

"My friends," she said in a gravelly voice. "Students. You've been my soldiers for Hashem's mission on earth, and I can't think of any greater honor than to have served with you. Thank you for all you've given."

She looked around the room, smiling at each, one by one. The prophets stared back with pure love. When her gaze hovered on me, hot tears blurred my eyes.

"The Ribbono Shel Olam keeps His promises," she said. "Keep your faith strong and cling to Hashem."

I feared Devorah would die right then, but she didn't. The conversation wandered to other topics, and Devorah participated, joyful when she heard about the boy who couldn't swim that Yitzchak had saved, or the musician Tirtza had inspired. Each time she heard about the goodness a prophet had brought into the world, her eyes seemed to burn a little brighter. I tried not to think about what would happen when the light in her eyes went out.

When it was dark, Noach recited *Havdallah* over a twisted flame. I followed Tirtza to the kitchen as the other prophets said their goodbyes. After cleaning up, Yonatan, Rena, Tirtza and Noach sat back at the table, speaking softly in Hebrew. Ignoring them, I knocked at Devorah's door.

I could barely hear her. "Come."

"Devorah," I whimpered, coming forward into her open arms.

She stroked my hair and kissed the top of my head. "Be strong, Rahel," she whispered to me. "You already have everything you need."

* * *

The pain woke me from sleep, lifting me out of dreams, into the darkness of night. Fire in my muscles. Knives slashing my bones. I lay paralyzed, my head filled with screams I had no strength to scream, and with whispers: taunting, halting, too distant to understand.

The pain erased everything. I drifted, powerless, into visions.

* * *

"Noach —" My voice breaks on his name. "I should have married you sixty years ago, when you asked me to."

"That was a long time ago," he says.

I grimace. "I was a fool."

"You were young, and angry," he reminds me. "We both were foolish and reckless. What we know now is more important than what we wanted then."

"I've never loved anyone the way I love you."

He dips his head and meets my eyes. "I know."

When I hesitate, he shakes his head.

"You don't need to ask, Devorah. I forgave you long ago."

✑

"When the time comes, you'll tell her?"
He shakes his head. "It's Noach's place."
"One day, Yonatan, you will stand in his place."
A humbled pause. "Together, then."

✑

"This is …Elisheva. Do you have my daughter?"
"Yes," Yonatan answers.
"May I speak to her please?" She wants to be firm, but she can't stop shaking.
"I'm sorry that's not possible," he says. "She isn't here with me right now."
Her hands tighten into fists. "When can I speak to her?"
"I'm protecting her with my life, Elisheva," he says. "With everything I have."
"I'm no Chanah[28]," she bursts out. "I didn't raise her only to give her away."
But they both know the truth. She did.

---

[28] See Samuel I.

CHAPTER 47

"Come downstairs," Rena whispered. It was the middle of the night.

The inside of my chest and stomach smoldered like ash, but the worst of the pain felt muted. Tirtza helped me into a robe and down to the street.

"Where's Yonatan?" I asked.

"With Devorah," Rena said.

"Devorah – " I gasped.

"Shh," Rena said. "Quiet now. Don't waste your strength."

They supported me by both arms, up steps and through dark alleyways, a strange procession in the middle of the night. When we finally reached Devorah's building, they practically carried me up the stairs. Yonatan opened the apartment door.

From the living room, we all moved together toward her bedroom. The afghan was still spread out on the sofa. They eased me into the folding chair beside the bed. Devorah's face was colorless as a cloud. Noach stood in the corner of the room, watching over us.

Devorah took my hand in both of hers. Her hands seemed weaker than last time. When was that? I had lost track.

"They gave me," she gasped, "something...for the pain. I hope...it helped you."

I bit my lip. "Thank you."

"It will be over soon," she said.

I shook my head, vehemently. Two tears rolled down my cheeks. "I don't want it to be."

"My time here," she whispered, "is ending. There are," she closed her eyes as a ragged pain cut through both of us, "...other realms waiting...for me."

I met her eyes and she touched my chin, now dripping with tears. Then he pressed her hands onto my head. "Rahel," she said. "*Chazak Ve'ematz.*[29] Be

---

[29] In the Torah, "Chazak V'ematz" are a part of Moses's instructions to Joshua before he dies. (Deuteronomy 31:23)

strong. And...have courage." Behind me, I heard the other prophets draw a collective breath.

"Amen," Rena said.

Devorah squeezed my hand, and closed her eyes. I saw her lips moving as she recited the words of the Shema.

Someone brought the afghan and wrapped it around me, as the others took their turns saying goodbye. I was too afraid to ask the others: What would happen to me when she died?

Just before dawn, I felt the shattering – the soul straining to escape the body, the agony of release. The air around us felt eerily warm, as if Devorah's energy had transferred from her body to the space around us. I sensed she was not in the bed but above us, looking down.

Her breathing came raspy, deep, slow. Slower. One last breath.

The flickering, shining flame gutters and dies out.

I wanted to wail, but I couldn't find a wisp of breath.

Noach hurried forward, tears running down his cheeks. "Go on, my most precious love," he whispered to her. "We'll take it from here." Then he recited a blessing, and tore at his shirt until it ripped.

⚭

Devorah died at sunrise. It was the third day of the Jewish month of Sivan, the 48th day of the Omer, just two days before the Jewish holiday of Shavuot.[30]

⚭

"You should eat something," Rena said.

I huddled on the floor, still wrapped in my afghan. I shook my head.

Prophets had been arriving at the apartment all morning. Some of them tried to speak to me, but I kept my head down; I didn't want to talk to anyone.

"Will she be all right?" someone asked. It took me a moment to realize the question was about me.

"Yes," Rena said, with none of the hesitation I myself felt.

Despite the rising heat of the morning, I shivered. Almost worse than the

---

[30] Shavuot (literally: weeks) is a major Jewish holiday marking the completion of the seven-week Omer counting period from Passover. Traditionally, it commemorates the day the children of Israel received the Torah at Sinai. (See Leviticus 23:9-21)

pain, which had departed with Devorah, was the numbness that followed. I felt lost, orphaned, cut off from everything and everyone.

Several hours before, Noach and Yonatan had left with the men who came to take her body. One of the undertakers wore a thick black velvet kipah; long tzitizis hung from beneath his white shirt. His eyes were a flat, dull brown; he was not a prophet. But when he heard it was Devorah who had died, his face crumpled with sorrow.

For reasons I could barely explain to myself, this was the only thing that had given me comfort all morning.

I thought perhaps Devorah's grave would be in the ancient cemetery in Tzfat, but Tirtza said she would be buried in Jerusalem. The funeral was scheduled for that afternoon, keeping with the Jewish tradition to bury the dead as soon as possible.

Tirtza brought me back to the hostel to change my clothing. I was sorry I didn't have something black to wear, but she said it didn't matter. So I wore something blue with a dark skirt, the first things that came into my hands, and we hurried back downstairs without even glancing at the mirrors to see how we looked.

A large crowd had gathered at the cemetery, all the more impressive because they'd had only a half day's notice to arrive. There were no chairs; everyone stood. I wanted to hide in the back, but Tirtza led me through the mourners to the front row, where Noach was still wearing the shirt he'd ripped. Yonatan gave me a grim nod of welcome as I approached. Tirtza and I took our places beside Rena; her shining eyes were streaked with red.

Noach gave the eulogy. He didn't speak of all Devorah had given to the prophets, or his own love for her. He simply offered a testament to a holy woman who had given her life to the world.

He had spoken for the prophets, but I was surprised when others arose to tell a different kind of story about Devorah. The single mother who had found in Devorah a free and loving babysitter while she went to school at night. The elderly man who had always found her ready to listen to his troubling life stories. The young man who spoke about the toys she'd brought him as a lonely child. One woman described how, in the darkest time of her life, Devorah had often invited her for dinner for no reason at all.

As the sun descended in the Jerusalem sky, these people came forward one by one. I stood motionless, drinking in the many gifts Devorah had given as a prophetess.

 ∽

Back in Devorah's apartment, the numbness still felt like wool around my heart. I re-wrapped myself in my afghan on the floor.

"You really need to eat something," Rena said again. She knelt before me with a sandwich, and a cup and basin to wash my hands. I looked away.

"To keep your strength up." She looked so desperate I took the cup, washed my hands, and bit into the sandwich.

I glared up at her, but I was distracted by a field of glowing, multi-colored stars; flickering blue and green, hazel, dark brown, violet, gray, almost black. Every prophet in the room was staring at me.

My anger turned to confusion as my eyes found Rena's.

"We're concerned about you," she said.

 ∽

I woke on the sofa in the middle of the night. Rena and Tirtza slept by me on the floor like guardians. Outside the window, a half moon hung large and white in the sky.

"*Rahel*," a voice whispered from behind. I turned, amazed, to see Devorah: her body small and white like a reflection of the moon. "Now it is time for me to go." Her voice was smooth and confident, reminding me of the vision when we'd first met.

"Please," I begged. "Don't leave me."

"It'll be easier after." She reached toward my cheek with fingers bright as light.

I wanted to look away, but Devorah's face was so bright and lovely, and so fleeting, I couldn't. Her eyes shone blue in the midst of her white face. "When they say you are great, believe them," she whispered. "Goodbye."

The moon curved tall and pure in the dark sky. She was gone.

 ∽

I awakened in the morning, alive.

There on the sofa – watching the rising sun – I found myself again a teenage girl. A healthy girl, who had been able to run two miles with Jake not more than a week before. A brave girl, who had made it to the Old City of

Jerusalem in response to holy callings, just in time.

Only now could I see how much Devorah's sickness had affected me. Not just in the last days. It must have started with the pain I'd imagined were migraines. For nearly a year, the suffering of a dying woman had insinuated itself into my own experience. And now, our spiritual connection had ended.

She was right. It was easier now that she was gone.

"You look a little better," Tirtza said tentatively, when she saw me awake.

"I feel better," I said.

When the prophets and other mourners came to the apartment to recite the morning service, I joined in their prayers.

CHAPTER 48

Back at the hostel that afternoon, I showered and changed into a fresh skirt. After prayers at the Kotel, nine of us ate at Devorah's for Shavuot dinner. They had to bring out an extra folding table: this time, we didn't all fit.

Rena had lit candles in Devorah's golden oil lamps. As I watched the flames flicker in the breeze, I remembered that other dinner with the prophets in Tzfat. How I had lost myself in a vision, and had to be led from the room. In the vision – it came to me now – there were golden oil lamps flickering in the wind.

Unexpectedly, I found I could reach back, into my memory of that vision. I hadn't understood it then, but I could see it now.

The sharp pain in my body, lying on the ground. The flickering of the Shabbat lights, casting their reflection in the gold tray beneath them, struggling against the breeze.

Devorah had already known it then. That she was dying. Did that mean the others in Tzfat also knew?

They found out that night, I answered my own question. *From my vision. They sent me from the room to talk about it.*

My fingers began to tremble. I remembered the pain, confusion and fear I'd felt these last months. Why hadn't they told me? Why hadn't anyone explained?

I turned to Yonatan beside me, but it was Noach who spoke.

"Rahel," he suggested, "let's take a walk after dinner."

I glanced at him, surprised. Around the table, the other prophets avoided my eyes.

"There are still many things to explain," Yonatan said.

I ate, no longer tasting the food. The others tried to change the subject, but no one sustained a conversation for very long. I kept noticing them sneaking looks at me.

At last, we said the blessing after the meal. Yonatan and Noach led me downstairs. The night air was warm and dry on my clammy skin. The moon lit the stones of the Old City as we walked down the stone paths toward the Kotel.

"The people of Israel are like the moon," Noach said. "We go from exile to exile, from persecution to persecution, but just like the moon, in our darkest time there will always be a rebirth."

Though it was late in the evening, the Jewish quarter was crowded with pilgrims visiting Jerusalem for the holiday. We walked past closed tourist stores and restaurants, past black clothed, bearded men walking, their hands folded behind their backs. Stray cats burrowed into the crevices of stone.

"Prophecy is also like the moon," Yonatan said. "You know, Rachel, after the Holocaust, when Devorah became the teacher of the generation, the world of prophecy had been devastated. The last teacher of the generation had been murdered. Noach was the only prophet in Israel."

As he spoke, another vision struck me.

Noach closes the book and takes off his glasses, rubbing his forehead. "When Shimon haGadol died in the Shoah, we were blinded. It took seven years until I found Devorah. It's taken decades to rebuild."

"Devorah," Yitzchak says, looking out the windows to the darkness below.

So many times in the past, these visions had been almost indecipherable for me. But tonight, months later, they all felt clear and available.

"When I found Devorah," Noach said, "she had been a prophetess for months without realizing it. She had terrible, uncontrolled visions. Everyone else thought they were simply remnants of the darkness she had seen. Before I met her, I wondered if prophecy was over."

Devorah creeps out of the tent and sits on a log by the fire, her knees drawn to her chest under her long, ragged nightgown.

"Was it a nightmare?" Noach asks gently. He stands at the entrance to his own tent, his hands folded in front of him.

She looks up to him, shaking her head. "A memory."

They led me down a flight of stairs.

"When I found her, she already had visions stronger than mine," Noach said. "She could sense prophets thousands of miles away. She held the gift of *malchut*, of G-d's consciousness touching earth. She was called to be the teacher of the generation. When she took possession of her calling, a new era of prophecy began."

We came to the courtyard where I'd first met Devorah, and like the other visions, this one came to me as well.

I am the old woman, and I am staring at myself. I have been waiting for her. She is so frightened – more frightened than I would have imagined. Her green eyes burn like lanterns in her pale face. Staring at her, I feel love and pity welling up in me, as if she were my own child.

"So young, and so brave," I murmur.

The three of us leaned on the stone barrier, gazing down at the Kotel.

"It took Noach a long time to find Devorah," Yonatan said. "We were more fortunate. When Devorah found out she was sick, we already knew who the next teacher of the generation was meant to be."

I felt relieved to hear someone new would lead us. Would it be Rena? She had taken such good care of Devorah. She was kind and wise and –

As the silence lengthened, I glanced up at Noach and Yonatan. They were both staring at me.

"Devorah was afraid your destiny would frighten you, as it did her," Noach said. "She insisted we wait until it was time."

I remembered the ghost-like Devorah I had seen last night.

Her eyes shine blue in the midst of her white face. "When they say you are great, believe them."

"Rahel," Noach said, breaking into my thoughts, "you were also called with the gift of *malchut*. The first in more than a generation."

I looked up in surprise. It was like a crazy joke, except they both looked so serious.

"*You* are the next teacher of the generation," Yonatan said.

"Me?"

Yonatan's eyes shone brighter than I had ever seen them, sending me an abundance of Light. "You were called for this," he said. "From the day of your birth."

Zaide looks down at the infant, smiling though his eyes are filled with tears. "This one is called with the holiest gifts. And the younger will save the elder. Promise me," he whispers.

My fingers clasped the stone barrier, dizzied by the revelation.

I grip the stone barrier in front of me and when I look down, I'm startled by how young my hands look.

"Visions brought you to Jersualem," Yonatan said. "Right?"

"Yes." Tonight they all stood before me with abundant clarity – the stones in Jerusalem, the number of steps from the Wall, the exquisite pain Devorah had shared with only me.

"Since Passover," he said gently, "few of the other prophets have even been able to see visions."

I frowned, confused. "What? Why?"

"One of Devorah's gifts," Noach said, "was to bind the prophets together into a shared consciousness. This connection makes prophecy possible. When she was too sick to maintain it, the other prophets lost their connection as well. Even those who could see visions –" he shuddered – "couldn't see much."

As shock and terror overwhelm me, this connection – all I've held together these many years – shatters like breaking glass.

I stared from one to the other. *This* was why I'd lost my connection with the prophets. Why they'd missed the warnings about Noach. Why I'd been the only one who could save the girl in the attic. "But –"

"But you –" Noach said, "even without that connection, had visions strong enough to bring you here. Strong enough to save my life."

I took a step back, one hand resting on my heart. "But I don't know anything," I said. "How could *I* lead the prophets...like Devorah?"

The two prophets turned to face me, silhouetted in the darkness, with the Wall behind them and the moon more than half full in the distance. Noach's beard was long and gray; Yonatan's shorter and still mostly dark. Their faces were earnest, confident. This conversation was fulfillment of a plan set in motion long ago.

"*You will,*" Noach said gently.

When he says, "The fate of prophecy rests with you," the burden is almost too much to bear. I sink back to my knees, weeping under the unforgiving Middle Eastern sun. "You make it seem like I'm some kind of hero."

Noach smiles. "You are a hero," he says. "Gedolah HaDor, great one, teacher of the generation."

I glance up at him, shaking my head. "You have to earn a title like that."

Noach holds my eyes. "You will."

I thought back to the night I first met Yonatan, after the long day of prayers on Yom Kippur. Could I have said no even if I'd wanted to? Each step on this journey felt predestined. I thought again of the prophet Jonah, running away from G-d. Did prophets ever really have a choice?

But they stood there, waiting for me to say something, and I knew I had to be the one to say yes. I had to choose this path, finally, for myself. I had to claim it as my own.

I looked down at the Kotel, up at the half moon, and toward these two men, teachers – guides – partners. I took in the velvet night sky and the moment in time: the first night of Shavuot.

"*Yes,*" I said, in as brave a voice as I could muster. "*I will.*"

Their smiles were like dawn breaking out of darkness, reminding me of Yonatan's smile when I first agreed to learn with him. Gratitude, faith, joy... relief. *G-d's will is happening as it is meant to be.*

I felt breathless, but not like when Devorah was struggling for air. "What do I need to do?"

Yonatan and Noach led me a few steps back from the stone barrier, toward a bench in the courtyard.

"The teacher of the generation connects all the prophets into a shared consciousness," Yonatan said. "You can create this connection now."

"It might help if you sit," Noach said.

I sat. They both remained standing.

"All human beings are connected at the deep soul level." As Noach explained, I sensed he had taught all this to Devorah many years before. "A prophet with the calling can activate that connection, so the community of prophets can use it."

"Begin with the meditation," Yonatan said.

Now I understood why I was sitting. I closed my eyes, preparing myself. I hadn't tried to meditate since arriving in Israel, and I was shocked how rapidly the sparks came; how quickly I entered into the trance.

Yonatan and Noach are here with me in the courtyard, shining waves of Light toward me under the bright moon. Their souls radiate awe, faith, and devotion. Against all the odds, we've made it to this moment. Everything else is destiny.

Try looking for the other prophets, *Noach suggests.*

I think of Rena first, and almost immediately I can see her; in Devorah's apartment, washing dishes after the meal.

Allow yourself to trust, *Yonatan advises.*

I remember how he opened himself up to me, that first time we spoke – completely vulnerable, with his entire truth – and I try to open myself up that same way, with all my fears and weaknesses, all my strength and love.

Deep breath. Please, G-d.

Rena, *I call, focusing not on her body but her soul.*

Rena, *I try again, with determination.*

At the deepest level, we are already connected. Rena.

The connection sparks like the burst of flame on a match.

Nearby, Tirtza lays fresh napkins on the table for tomorrow's lunch. Opening my heart, I look again for that connection deep within our souls. Appreciation flows through me for her generous care since I arrived. Tirtza, *I call to her.*

She pauses with a napkin in her hand, listening. Rahel. *I hear her response at the highest level of my soul.*

Now I regret I didn't learn the names of the other prophets staying for Shavuot, but Yonatan and Noach give them to me one by one. Daniel, Chava, Refael, Shmuel – four prophets in Devorah's living room, each connected to me – to each other – at the roots of our souls. Each answering easily when I call.

Yitzchak and Tzipporah, married prophets, are staying in an apartment in the Old City. In Tzfat: Shoshana, Ahava, Leora, Yechezkel, Nehemiah, Gedalia, Moshe. In Tel Aviv: Miriam, Leila, Yehoshua, Penina. In Modiin: Gavriel. In Eilat: Choni. Five in the United States. Nine across Europe. Two in Canada. As their names come to me, I call upon them. One by one, I can feel their souls enter our collective. The grief of losing Devorah, the long ordeal of her illness, has devastated them. But this moment fills them with awe and hope.

Prophets in South Africa, in Australia, in South America. Some of us had been sleeping, but now we are all awake. At some level, we were all connected already, but something new is being created: a collective built of devotion, faith, and love. A bond of commitment, to service and to holiness and to each other.

A ripple moves through our collective consciousness; several prophets have been called into a shared vision. The vision itself is like a crystal with many faces, which different prophets will see and understand in different ways. Together, we will understand the message more completely.

At last, I become aware of Yonatan and Noach, guiding me. Anticipating. Waiting. When I call their names, they enter, easily, into a renewed and holy community.

The many voices are a torrent of sound, but they feel familiar. Where have I heard them all before? Then I realize: I heard them every time I entered Devorah's mind.

Together, connected, the prophets are coming to peace and rest. We are one. We are healing. We can rely on one another. I never want to stop being connected to all of these holy people, who somehow are bound together by my own precious gift.

"Well done," Noach whispers, and despite all his certainty, his voice is filled with awe.

Back on the bench in the moonlight, I whispered the words that always ended meditation. I could still hear the prophets' voices, humming like bees in the distance. Very slowly, I opened my eyes.

The prophets continued, their souls, voices, and visions in the background. Their thoughts and feelings radiated within me, filling me with Light. And filling them as well.

I was their leader. The new Teacher of this Generation.

CHAPTER 49

Now that I could experience the other prophets through our connection, they didn't seem like strangers. They were friends and partners in our quest to bring holiness into the world. They had always treated me with deference, patience and love, and now I could finally receive it.

After Shavuot lunch, Daniel, one of the prophets staying in Jerusalem for the holiday, approached me. I remembered Tirtza said he was her teacher. He was younger than Yonatan, in his late twenties, with dark hair and flashing hazel eyes.

"I was able to meditate this morning," he said. He swallowed and risked a glance at my face. "I think – I think now I'll be able to manage my job. Thank you."

Simply by looking into his eyes, I could see everything in his heart. He was a middle school teacher in Boston, with a wife and a young daughter. But when Devorah's connection was failing in the spring, he had lost control of his own visions and had collapsed in front of his students. He'd had to take a leave of absence and come to Tzfat. Now he would be able to return to his life, and do all the good he was meant to do there.

"Don't thank me," I said. "Thank Hashem."

After Noach said the *havdallah* blessings to end the holiday, I turned to Yonatan and asked if I could use his phone. "I want to call my mother," I said.

He smiled. "That's a good idea."

Rena rested her fingers on mine. "He's been keeping in touch with her."

I was surprised. "Really?"

"Not all the details," Yonatan said. "I've just tried to keep her up to date."

I frowned. "Why didn't you tell me? I should have spoken to her."

Yonatan raised his eyebrows. "You weren't in any condition for phone calls," he said.

"And you needed to focus on your own journey here," Noach added.

I sat upright, trying to look like the leader I was. "You have to tell me things," I said firmly. Noach and Yonatan exchanged a glance.

"I mean it," I said. "Maybe you needed to keep things from me before, but not anymore. How can you keep secrets from me? I'm the *teacher of the generation*."

The other prophets smiled. Noach glanced at Yonatan, who turned to me. "You're right," he said simply. "No more secrets."

"Good," I said. "I'd like to use that phone now."

He took the phone out of his backpack, which had been left in a closet before the holiday.

"And I need to get this phone number," I said, remembering how hard it had been to contact him in the spring.

He winked, handing it to me. "I'll give it to you. But I doubt you'll ever need it."

∞

I stepped into the stairwell with the phone and dialed with shaky fingers. Mom answered on the first ring. Her voice sounded wary.

"Mom," I said. "It's me."

"*Rachel,*" she cried out, her voice breaking on my name. "Are you okay?"

I sat at the top of the steps, cradling the phone in my ear. "Yes. I'm good."

"Where are you?" Desperation and relief mixed in her voice.

"I'm in Jerusalem," I said. "But I'm coming home."

∞

Noach's car hadn't moved from the parking garage where we'd left it. It seemed strange to climb back into that car now, leaving the darkness of the Old City after a tranquil Shabbat. When we arrived, I'd felt so sick and frightened. Tonight, I felt strong and courageous. More importantly, I felt a hint of something I'd never experienced before in my life: inner peace.

I was using the return ticket Mom had given me, and would be home in time for graduation as promised.

In my backpack I carried another ticket – for my return to Israel. Noach had arranged for me to spend the summer taking classes in Tzfat, to learn at last all the rituals of Jewish life, and to begin learning Hebrew. In the fall, I would begin college at the Hebrew University in Jerusalem.

Over the last few days, Rena and Tirtza had begun transforming

Devorah's apartment for my use. Her bed would be removed, and the walls would be repainted. Noach was keeping her candlesticks, and some of the prophets were taking other mementoes she had bequeathed to them. But I had asked them to leave the incredible Shabbat table I'd seen fit so many. I hoped one day I too would be worthy of that kind of miracle.

Of course, the beautiful afghan was mine to keep. It was one of the few things I carried in my backpack for the plane ride back to Baltimore; I'd hardly been separated from it since Devorah died.

When the car pulled up at the terminal, I turned to Yonatan, my eyes blurred with tears.

"How can I leave here?" I asked him silently. I remembered Noach's error, separating himself from the prophets by going away to New York. I too had been disconnected in Baltimore. What if I was making the same mistake?

Yonatan shook his head. "You are fulfilling a promise to your mother," he said. Then he smiled. "Enjoy this time with your family."

"We will always be with you," he continued in my thoughts. *"Be safe and be well. Be strong and have courage, precious Gedolah."*

It was the first time any of them had called me this – *Gedolah* – the special title for the teacher of the generation. I blinked at him, moved, but he only opened the door, going to the trunk to retrieve my duffel bag. I took three long, deep breaths before joining him on the sidewalk.

"*Nesiah tova,*" he said. "Have a safe trip." Then, to my surprise, he handed me a few coins. "Give this to charity when you arrive."

I had only ever seen my mother do this; receiving money from Yonatan made it seem much more significant. I took the coins; they clinked in my pocket. "Thanks."

"With the help of the Holy One, I'll see you soon," Yonatan said one last time. "In Tzfat."

"In Tzfat," I repeated. I wanted to run into his arms and hug him, but instead I lifted my duffel and walked into the airport alone.

But not truly alone, I reminded myself, as the doors closed behind me and I entered the long line of other late night travelers. I was connected to the prophets now, wherever I went. And with Yonatan's blessings ringing in my ears, I was grateful to be going home.

❧

In that first call after Shavuot, Mom simply wanted to know I was all right. It was easy to reassure her then. But as my return plans came into focus, I needed to tell her the details, and our next call wasn't as easy.

"I need to come back," I told her.

"What about college?"

"I can do college here. And there's a summer program in Tzfat that will be good for me."

"You want to go back...this summer?"

"Mom...this is where I belong."

I knew she wouldn't stop me, but I winced when she began to cry.

∽∾

I was anxious about seeing my parents when I landed at the airport in Baltimore, but my concerns dissolved when I saw Beth there with them.

She stood waiting in a ballet posture, her narrow legs and feet placed in fourth position. My parents flanked her on each side, like bodyguards. Since Passover her auburn hair had grown to her chin, and there was new color in her cheeks. She grinned when she saw me coming.

I hurried straight for her, casting my backpack to the ground as I grasped her in a sobbing hug. She held me close with strong, slender arms, her lips pressed against my hair. "I missed you," she said.

I pulled back to examine her face. "How are you?"

She beamed at me. "I'm free," she said cheerfully. Then she glanced sideways at my parents. "Still have some work to do, but...starting classes at Maryland next week. I'm going to try to finish my degree...here...and then hopefully join my professors' company when I graduate."

"That's...that's...I'm so proud of you," I told her, hugging her again.

I turned next to Mom, whose eyes followed me as if I were an apparition. "*Thank you*." I held her eyes. "For everything."

I felt her body exhale as she embraced me. "You'll have to tell me what happened," she said as I drew back from her. I nodded agreement.

Finally, I turned to Dad. I thought he might be furious, but instead, he seemed almost afraid to touch me. I reached out to him, hugging him until his muscles relaxed and his arms came around my shoulders.

"I'm sorry you're not staying long." His voice sounded ragged in my ears, and I realized he was less angry than heartbroken. He'd been counting on more time with me as his little girl.

I had been prepared for fury, but his sadness choked my heart a little.

"I'm here now," I said. He only hugged me tighter in response.

Beth joined me in my bedroom as I unpacked from the trip. She wore a tank top and capri pants, revealing her bony shoulders and arms. She didn't seem comfortable sitting; she kept switching into various dance positions. But I had seen her eat a healthy snack of almonds and raisins with a glass of milk when we arrived back from the airport, and she had proudly shown me the brochure for the dance program here at Maryland.

I opened my backpack and spread Devorah's afghan across my bed; the colors were so bright it seemed almost otherworldly in my mundane bedroom.

"Did you buy that in Israel?" Beth asked, coming close to examine it. "It's so pretty."

I shook my head. "It was a gift."

She tilted her head curiously. "Who gave you a gift?"

I studied Beth, assessing whether I could trust her. Was this the same sister who had questioned all my religious yearnings earlier this year? Or was she the one who had always believed in me, before her own stresses had taken over? Her eyes showed me only innocence and love. I sighed and reached out to touch the soft yarn. "A friend," I answered softly. "When she died, she left this for me."

Her eyes widened. "Your friend – died? When?"

My eyes burned with unshed tears. "Tuesday."

"She died *Tuesday?*" Beth reached out to touch my arm, looking at me with compassion. "So – she died – while you were *there?*"

"Yeah." Tears tumbled down my cheeks and I cried onto Beth's bare shoulder as I thought again of all Devorah had been to me. Friend, soul-sister, a grandmother I had barely had the chance to know.

"I'm really sorry, Rach," Beth said, gently stroking my back.

I shrugged. "It's okay," I said, trying to take hold of myself. "She was... very old...and it was her time."

"Are you really going back there to live?" Beth asked. Her eyes were wide and wounded, like a healing child.

I swallowed hard. Beth wasn't the only one I'd be leaving. Already since arriving home I'd received a text from Jake: *See you at graduation tomorrow?* It wouldn't be easy to tell him I wasn't staying long.

"Yes," I answered.

"Why?"

"I...feel called...to be there," I said.

"In Israel?" She wrinkled her nose in confusion.

"Yes." I set my duffel bag down on the floor and sat beside it. "I've met... some other Jews there."

Beth sat down on the floor across from me, her skinny knees pulled up to her chest. "People like...your friend?" she asked, looking back up to the afghan on the bed.

"People like Zaide," I told her, touching the necklace that still dangled around my neck.

Her forehead creased into a frown. "Orthodox Jews, you mean."

"Yes. But...that's not why. They're holy people, doing good in this world," I said. "I want to be part of that."

She thought this over, holding my eyes. "Like what you did for *me*?" She leaned forward, resting her fist under her chin.

I hesitated. "Yeah."

She closed her eyes. "That felt like a holy thing," she said. "A gift from G-d."

"It was," I said.

"I'll miss you," she said, taking my hand in her fingers.

"You can come visit," I said.

She grinned at me. "I'd like that."

After Beth left, I contemplated my bedroom, making a mental list of the things to take with me. The plate I'd been using for lighting candles. The children's prayerbook Zaide had given me. And my flute. Maybe this summer I'd be able to play it with Noach and the others in the prophets' house in Tzfat.

Other than that, there were surprisingly few things I needed. Most of my clothing was inappropriate. As Maya had predicted, I would probably be wearing skirts for the rest of my life. But the idea didn't bother me the way it once did. I knew in Israel, the other prophetesses were right now making, giving, and buying me a new wardrobe of skirts and dresses.

I closed my eyes and reassured myself that my connection with the other prophets was still strong. It was important to stay focused. Yonatan had instructed me to increase my meditation to twice a day.

"Rachel?" Mom knocked at my door.

"Come in," I said.

She came forward and sat on my bed, her hands unconsciously stroking the afghan. "It's almost time for dinner," she said, looking at me again with that strange, wondering gaze. "We ordered from the Chinese kosher restaurant, for you."

"Thanks," I said, sitting beside her on the bed.

She waved her hands awkwardly. "He said you would need that," she said, in explanation.

"Did you talk to him a lot, while I was there?"

She shook her head. "We spoke three times," she said. "The fourth call was from you." She exhaled, looking troubled. "I kept asking why I couldn't talk to you," she said. "He said you were sick. I was afraid – they had hurt you, kidnapped you...but I just had to keep trusting them." Her eyebrows pinched together. "*Were* you sick?"

"Yeah. I was." I closed my eyes, remembering the horrible moments in the hostel, the trace of death I'd experienced in Devorah's bedroom. "But I'm really sorry I didn't call you."

"Do you *have* to go back?" she asked urgently. "What if you get sick there again?"

I shook my head. "I won't. It's different now."

"Maybe you could just stay here the summer," she said.

Staying with my family was such a tempting idea that I paused. But I knew the prophets couldn't wait for me any longer. "No." I shook my head again, more forcefully. "They need me there now."

She bit her lip, studying me. "Why does it have to be *you*?"

I wished I could give an answer that would make sense to her, but I could only tell her the truth I knew. "Because G-d asked me to."

"Are you sure it's really G-d asking?"

"Yes," I said.

She sighed. "G-d has never asked *me* for anything in my life," she said.

I reached out to touch her hand. "He's asked you for this."

CHAPTER 50

On Monday morning, my graduating class sat on the football field, wearing long robes in the sticky, humid air. Lauren and I sat with the orchestra, near a stage built on the 20 yard line. As the ceremony began, I lifted my flute. We played the Star Spangled Banner and the school fight song. It was lucky we were playing these easy, familiar songs, because I hadn't practiced in weeks.

My parents sat in the stands with Beth. As I watched, Dad kissed my mother on the cheek and she laughed. I had been home almost a day, but Dad hadn't escaped into his office once. Before jet lag finally sent me upstairs, he had joined us for dinner and even a family game of cards last night.

Jake sat a few sections closer than my parents. I wanted to wave, but knew he wouldn't spot me here with the orchestra.

When Lauren approached the podium to give her valedictory speech, I felt a rush of pride for her. She had done everything she had planned this year. Halfway through her talk, Lauren turned to the topic of friendship. "One thing I've learned this year is that life can change us," she said. "Our true friends are the ones who will be there no matter where or how the journey goes." As she glanced down at the orchestra, I knew she was talking to me. I gave her a little smile as she came off the podium.

The night before, Mom had given me my final report card: an unexceptional collection of Bs, and even a C—altogether the worst report card I'd ever had in high school. In another situation, I would have felt ashamed, but I didn't. The card was like a golden ticket in my hand; it was the sign G-d had been watching out for me after all. This fall I would also be where I belonged, in Jerusalem.

As they started giving out diplomas, I felt something shift in my connection with the prophets. A vision was coming. Anxiously I gripped my music stand.

"Focus on the connection," Yonatan whispered from afar.

From my place on the football field in Baltimore, I watched Daniel, the young teacher I'd met in Jerusalem, encounter this vision in his classroom in

Boston. Our connection was a shield of Light that strengthened him, giving him the moments needed to complete his lesson and dismiss his class. As he hurried to the staff room, I thought of all the times Devorah had protected me in this way, without my even knowing it.

A modern Orthodox boy, sixteen years old, in Sharon. His first vision will come during the afternoon service in school; a glimmer of light mistaken for pangs of hunger. His family will support him, but will never truly understand. Several years of training before being called to Tzfat.

Daniel descended, reciting holy words. Before anyone noticed he was missing, he was back in his classroom, looking up the boy's school, ready to begin teaching the new prophet.

❧

"Congratulations," the principal said. I took the diploma and smiled up toward the camera flashes in the stands.

After concluding speeches from school administrators, I lifted my flute to play the school anthem. Our caps flew to the air in a cloud. And just like that, high school was over.

"Glad you made it back for graduation," Maya said, coming up behind me. She had thrown off her black robe to reveal a yellow strapless sundress. Her lipstick was rose-colored, perfectly matching her blush and fingernails. She rushed forward to give me a sweaty hug. "I missed you, girl. How was Israel?"

I closed my flute into its case before responding. "Like nothing you could imagine."

"I heard you're going back," she said, but before I could respond, Chris had come up behind her. Under his open robe, he was wearing a white button-down shirt with a tie, and khaki shorts; he was still so handsome I took a quick breath.

He put his arm around Maya and she leaned toward him, giving him a tiny kiss on the neck. He kissed the top of her head. They both looked happier than I'd ever seen them.

"Yeah," I said. "I'm going back."

"Did you find what you were looking for there?" Chris asked meaningfully.

I held his eyes. "Yeah. I did."

I saw his fingers unconsciously reach for the cross under his shirt.

"Good," he said simply.

∽

My family caught up with me near the metal detectors. We exited the football field with the crowd, into the parking lot. My parents and Beth had already climbed into our car when Jake reached me.

"Hey there," he said in his deep voice. "Congratulations."

He had cut his hair shorter, and his arms were tanned, revealed by a short-sleeved polo shirt. His dark eyes searched my face, as if looking for gold. Warm currents washed down my spine. I blushed, grinning foolishly.

"Everything okay?" he asked. "During graduation, I thought I saw – something – happening with you."

"Could you even see me in the orchestra?" I asked, surprised.

"By the shimmering lights," he explained in an undertone, gesturing to the air around me.

How was it possible? I wondered.

He grinned, enjoying my confusion. "So," he said quietly, glancing toward my family in the car, "it was real?"

I held his eyes. "Yes. Real," I managed to answer. "I want to tell you about it, but not now. Maybe tonight?"

His smile turned warm. "I'll text you." He leaned forward, as if to hug me. But ever respectful, he held himself back. "I missed you."

A pebble seemed to lodge in my throat. "I missed you too."

∽

That evening, we walked the streets of the neighborhood at sunset. Jake had wanted to go for a run, but I told him I wasn't quite up to that yet. Then, in explanation, I shared everything that had happened in Israel.

I told him how I'd saved Noach in the midst of visions, and about what had happened to me when Devorah was dying. Then I took a deep breath and told him about the calling Noach and Yonatan had revealed to me on Shavuot. I felt pleased when his own face showed the same astonishment I had felt.

We stopped on a small footbridge over a stream, and I realized we weren't far from the place I had saved him, back in the winter when the ground was covered with snow. Now, near summer, the trees were abundant with green leaves. He turned to face me.

"You're going back," he said. It was not a question.

I nodded. "Yes."

He frowned. "When?"

"In a couple weeks," I told him. "I'm going to do a summer program in Tzfat, and then enroll at the Hebrew University in Jerusalem."

He pressed his lips together. "Is it what you really want the most?"

"Yes," I said again.

He glanced down at the water rushing beneath us. "I love you, Rachel."

I stared up at Jake. With his blond hair cut short and his polo shirt, his eyes bright with love, he looked more like that man in my original vision than I'd ever expected.

"I love you too," I confessed.

He leaned forward slowly, not wanting to surprise me. A thousand thoughts rushed through my head – *What if there was punishment? What about the prophets? What if I left and never saw him again?* – before I allowed his lips to reach mine.

I kissed him like I was tasting fruit for the last time. Warm shivers rushed through my body like lightning bolts in a summer rain. Finally, he put his hands on my shoulders, and gently pulled his lips away.

We didn't kiss again. Ever respectful, Jake kept a physical distance between us. But after that night, everything between us changed.

As the days of my time in Baltimore ticked down, we spent most of our time together. Watching movies in my den. Exploring the kosher restaurants we discovered in town. He told me about his summer job at a nearby bakery. He told me how things were going with his mother and sister. He even shared a few things he'd learned from the addiction counselor.

One night, as we were walking home from a kosher pizza restaurant, he told me he was considering keeping kosher. "Would that help?" he asked. "For us?"

It was the first time he had referred to us that way. The first time I was ever part of an *us*. I paused, looking up at his earnest face. "Would you really want to do that...for me?"

"Sure," he said.

I squinted, perplexed. "It's not that easy to do."

He shrugged. "I don't much like bacon anyway," he said. Then he winked.

"Can't be as hard as giving up an actual addiction."

"Um," I said, astonished. "Yeah, I guess it would help. But Jake...I still need to go back to Israel. Next week."

"I know," he said.

"And you're staying here, in high school," I said.

He looked away. "I know," he said again.

⁂

The Sunday before my flight back to Israel, Dad and I finally took our hike together. Dad wore a compression sleeve to protect his knee, but he kept pace with me. Because of all my running, I was in better physical shape than I had been in years. I wondered fleetingly who would run with me in Jerusalem.

Accompanied by birds and squirrels, we followed a foamy creek along lush green trees, up to a rushing waterfall. He stopped and leaned over to catch his breath. I took a sip from my water bottle.

"Your mother keeps telling me I shouldn't try to stop you from leaving," he said, straightening up to face me.

I bit my lip. "She's right."

He shook his head, staring at the trees across the water. "I thought you were with me on this religion thing."

"I once was," I said.

"So what happened?" he asked in a sad voice.

I so desperately wanted him to understand. But how could he believe me, when he didn't even believe in G-d? "I just started...looking for more," I said.

"More," he said, incredulous. "There's so much more." He spread his arms toward the beautiful nature around us. "Life is full of more. And you're going to miss it all if you let them cloister you in Israel."

I shook my head. "You don't understand," I said. "I'm not doing this because someone told me to. This is *my* choice. I need to follow my destiny, just like...just like Beth needed to dance."

He froze at the mention of Beth.

"She's doing great," I said encouragingly.

He smiled. "She is. I wish she would add a few more calories, but...the dancing is really something. I never realized...how good she is."

"Maybe there are things you never realized about me," I said.

He rubbed at his chin. "Like what?"

297

As I considered my answer, I thought about my grandfather and the calling he'd awaited for more than a generation. About the way I'd helped Daniel the prophet in Boston. But most of all, I thought about the inner peace and holiness I'd felt on the Shabbat before I left Jerusalem.

"I have gifts too," I said. "And there is a purpose waiting for me there. It's hard to explain but...this *is* what I've always wanted."

His eyes softened. "Will you be okay there?" he asked urgently, and I realized how worried he was. Things had turned out so badly for Beth when she moved away; how could this be a good choice for me?

"I'll be great," I assured him.

He sighed as we hiked past the first waterfall. I knew there were more waterfalls ahead; more streams and more mountains to climb. He reached out to help me up a steep incline, and though I didn't really need his hand, I took it. I knew it meant he would always be there.

The evening before I was due to leave, Jake met me on the porch and, for the last time, we walked through our neighborhood in the setting sun.

"I can't tell you to wait for me," I said, "because I'm not planning to come back."

"Maybe one day I'll come to you," he said.

I shook my head. "You have your family here," I said. "You have to stay for your sister."

"Sisters grow up," he said.

"This has been great, especially these last weeks," I said. I had already planned what I would say. I wanted him to be free to find his own happiness. I was afraid of what would happen to him, if he was alone and pining for me.

"I want to give you something," he said.

I started to protest, but he had already pulled a box from his jeans pocket. He opened it to reveal a silver friendship ring with a green stone.

"I know you have to go," he said. "And I don't know if I'll ever be able to follow you. I don't want to hold you back from anything." He took a deep breath. "I just want you to have this – to remind you. Of a possibility. With me."

I stared at him. Could he ever be part of my life in Israel, with the community of prophets?

"Please," Jake said.

The words came to me then, as if on the breeze; a memory of a vision, planted and plowed up at the right time. *I should have married you sixty years ago, when you asked me to.*

It wasn't that I expected to marry him. But if saying no to Noach was one of Devorah's greatest mistakes, perhaps she had revealed this to me as a lesson. Standing there in the sunset, I understood love was a possibility I might be allowed to choose.

I took the ring.

GLOSSARY
OF JEWISH AND HEBREW TERMS

Afikomen: the final piece of matzah eaten at the Passover seder. Traditionally hidden to be found at the end.

Aron Kodesh: the special cabinet at the front of a synagogue, where the Torah is kept.

Candle-lighting: a ritual traditionally performed by women marking the beginning of the Jewish Sabbath.

Challah: braided rolls traditionally eaten on the Jewish Sabbath.

Chametz: leavened products traditionally forbidden on Passover.

Ein Sof: Hebrew name for G-d, meaning "Endless One."

Kipah: (pl. kipot) traditional Jewish head covering.

Haggadah: (pl. haggadot): book containing the text and instructions for the Passover seder.

Hashem: a traditional Jewish term for G-d, which literally means "the Name."

Havdallah: a short service at the end of a Jewish holiday or Sabbath. A twisted candle is used during the service.

Jonah: one of the prophets in the Jewish Bible. His story is traditionally read on Yom Kippur.

Kabbalah: the Jewish mystical tradition.

Kotel: the Western Wall (sometimes called "the Wailing Wall") in Jerusalem.

Kugel: a traditional Jewish dish, usually made with potatoes or noodles.

Lecha Dodi: a prayer traditionally said at the prayer service marking the beginning of the Jewish Sabbath. The first words mean, "Come, my beloved, to welcome the Queen (the Sabbath)."

Machane Yehuda: also known as the *shuk*, an open air-marketplace where food and other products can be purchased in Jerusalem.

Mechitzah: the fence, wall, or other barrier separating men and women in an Orthodox synagogue.

Mitzvah: (pl. mitzvot): a commandment from G-d.

Passover: (Hebrew: Pesach) a Jewish holiday marking the exodus from Egypt in ancient times.

Refua Shleima: wishes for a complete healing.

Ribbono Shel Olam: a traditional Hebrew name for G-d, meaning Master or Creator of the World.

Rosh Hashanah: the Jewish new year.

Schwarma: a common Middle Eastern food: roasted turkey or lamb, cooked on a rotating spit.

Shabbat: the Jewish Sabbath (Saturday).

Shalom: peace.

Shalom Aleichem: (peace be upon you): a traditional Jewish greeting. The traditional response is "Aleichem shalom" and means the same thing (literally, "upon you, peace"). Also the name of a song traditionally sung at the beginning of the Jewish Sabbath, welcoming angels to the table.

Shema: a traditional Jewish prayer that is considered the most essential declaration of the Jewish faith. It is traditionally recited in the morning and the evening, before going to sleep, and at the moment of death.

Shiva: a week-long period of ritual mourning observed after a close family member dies.

Shloshim (literally, thirty): a period of ritual mourning traditionally observed by mourners of close relatives for thirty days.

Shoah: Hebrew term for the Holocaust.

Shofar: a ram's horn, traditionally blown on the Jewish holiday of Rosh Hashanah and at the end of Yom Kippur.

Shulchan: a table in the center of the synagogue, where the Torah scroll is read.

Siddur: prayerbook.

Streimel: a fur hat worn by some Hasidic Jewish men on the Sabbath and holidays.

Tayelet: a promenade in Jerusalem, from which the entire city can be viewed.

Tehillim: Hebrew name for the Book of Psalms, traditionally recited for healing or other blessings.

Torah: the five books of Moses, written in a scroll and read publicly during synagogue services.

Traif: a term used to describe food traditionally forbidden as not kosher, such as pork, shellfish, and other non-kosher meat.

Tzitzit: fringes (strings) attached to the corners of the tallit, the Jewish prayer shawl. These strings are also attached to a garment traditionally worn by Jewish men throughout the day. The commandment to wear tzitzit may be found in Numbers 15:38-41.

Yom Kippur: the Day of Atonement, the holiest day in the Jewish calendar.

Zaide: "grandfather" in Yiddish.

BIBLIOGRAPHY

The Prophetess is a fictional account of what it might be like if Jewish prophets existed today. The traditional Jewish view is that prophecy ended at the beginning of the second Temple period (approximately 500 B.C.E.) and will be restored in the future with the coming of the Moshiach (literally, anointed one).

To my knowledge, Jewish prophets are not currently being called into service and secret community as described in this book. However, the wisdom in this novel is based on the Jewish mystical tradition, and much of this wisdom is available to be learned today.

For those who may wish to learn more, in this section, I share some of my favorite resources on this topic. I've tried to incorporate some of their teachings in this book, though any errors are my own.

BOOKS

Seeing G-d by Rabbi David Aaron

In the Shadow of the Ladder: Introductions to Kabbalah
by Rabbi Yehudah Lev Ashlag

Inner Space by Rabbi Aryeh Kaplan

Jewish Meditation by Rabbi Aryeh Kaplan

Inner Torah by Miriam Milhauser Castle

The Well of Living Waters by Rabbi Avraham Sutton

Living Inspired by Akiva Tatz

TEACHERS

Rabbi Doniel Katz https://www.elevationproject.global/
Rivka Malka Perlman https://rivkamalka.com/
David Solomon http://www.inonehour.net/
Rabbi Avraham Sutton http://www.avrahamsutton.com/

DISCUSSION QUESTIONS
FOR BOOK CLUBS

1. During Rachel's journey of learning to be a prophetess, the prophets struggle with the tension of teaching her and protecting her. Do you think they were successful at finding the right balance? How might Rachel's story have been different if they were more or less protective? Now that Rachel has asked them to "tell her things," how might their relationship change?

2. Rachel's family and friends call her Rachel, but the prophets call her by her Hebrew name, Rahel. A similar dynamic exists with Rachel's mother, Alisha/Elisheva. How does the use of names reflect different aspects of a person?

3. Gifts play an important role in this novel. For example, Rachel enters the story with a necklace from her grandfather, a poetry journey from Lauren, and a make-up set from Maya. During the story, Yonatan gives her a prayerbook, Devorah gives her a blanket, and Jake gives her a ring. How did these different gifts help Rachel along her journey?

4. Rachel's journey teaches her both about Jewish tradition and about the mystical truths of life. Because of what she learns, she is left feeling the need to observe Jewish tradition even if prophecy were stripped away from her. Can you understand this conclusion? Do you think you would make the same choice?

5. Devorah and Noach have a unique partnership. Why do you think she refused his offer of marriage when they were young? Why do you think it took until her deathbed to admit her love for him?

6. Devorah, Noach and Rachel's grandfather each lived through the Ho-

locaust, but managed to keep their faith in the end. How were their post-Holocaust journeys similar and different? How did they each find purpose and the ability to have a good life?

7. In this novel, the prophets have the ability to support and uplift each other by channeling G-d's light. Have you ever experienced someone uplifting you in a similar way? Have you ever given "light" of some kind to another? What was the experience like? How was it similar or different to the descriptions in this story?

8. Yonatan rose from the depths of despair to teach Rachel, because he understood what was at stake. Devorah tells him, "Do not underestimate the resilience of the human heart." Can you think of other examples or role models for this kind of resilience, in history or in your own life? What lessons can we learn from this?

9. Chris seems to understand prophecy long before Rachel has the courage to tell anyone else. Why do you think the concepts of prophecy make sense to him as a Christian? What do you think of their friendship? Do you think their relationship will continue with Rachel in Israel?

10. Despite her hesitation, Rachel accepts a friendship ring as a gift from Jake before she leaves Baltimore. How does her relationship with boys evolve throughout the book? What future, if any, do you think is possible for Rachel and Jake?

ACKNOWLEDGEMENTS

This story has taken me more than twenty years to write. Blessed is Hashem for sustaining me, preparing me, and bringing me to this day. This book would not have been possible without the help of so many. I'm grateful for the opportunity to acknowledge them here.

I must start with thanks to my best friend and life partner, Jerry, for his never-ending love, encouragement, and partnership. Your support has made so many dreams into possibilities, including this book.

Thank you to Rafi, who always inspires me to be the best I can be, and to Coby, who has reminded me of the magic in stories and all of life. Thank you to my father, for always being there for me, for your loving gifts and your good advice. And many thanks to Fred and Vivianne for all you do to make our lives work and bring love into our lives.

My mother left us too early, but she made sure I knew how proud she was of all I'd done...and that there was much more I could do. Mom, as with all my happiest moments, I only wish you were here to celebrate this milestone with us. Thank you for everything.

Thank you to my beta readers, including Libby McKnight, Victoria Rothenberg, Ayelet Lederman, Elana Weinberg, Rosalyn Efron, Heather Shafter, Miriam Katz, Dr. Tina Rosenbaum, Esther Kustanowitz, Brianna Besch (who won the opportunity to be an advanced reader by donating to charity!), and long, long ago, Nigel Savage. A special thank you to Rob Eisen, who provided me with so much encouragement and several useful connections. Thank you to Faye Moskowitz, Sharon Freundel, Melissa Amster and Michelle Brafman for your wise advice.

Much gratitude to Rav Avraham Sutton, who has helped me understand I'm not alone in the Jewish mystical journey, and has provided so many important insights that have helped shape this story. And deep gratitude to my *chavruta*, Sheryl Grossman, for being willing to learn Jewish mysticism with me, and for all you've taught me.

When googling just wasn't enough, I was grateful to be able to ask questions of contacts in my extended network. Thank you to Asya Zlatina and Chelsea Brown for information about professional and undergraduate dance programs; Dr. Tina Rosenbaum for general medical advice and guidance; Kathryn Kline, for help understanding the psychology department at University of Maryland; Gabrielle Coleman, who provided advice on what it's like to be a teenage girl in Baltimore; Chris Biddix for guidance about drug abuse; and Bruce Taylor and Dr. Harry Brandt for helpful guidance about eating disorders. I appreciated your guidance and suggestions to help make this novel as accurate as possible, though of course any errors are my own.

I was privileged to develop my writing as an undergraduate in the Writing Seminars program at Johns Hopkins University. I am grateful to the professors and graduate students there for helping me develop the earliest drafts of this story. I offer special thanks to Stephen Dixon, my advisor, whose writing inspired me to apply to Hopkins, and to my professor Dr. Chaim Potok, z"l.

I am grateful to the course leaders, coaches, and graduates at Landmark Worldwide, for always standing for the extraordinary in life. You have taught me that anything is possible, including the publication of this book. My special, heartfelt thanks to seminar leaders Joan Sugerman, Jennifer Coken, Mark Stave, Chris Biddix, and Angela Wilcox for believing in me, and for all that you have taught me over the years. Thanks to longtime buddies Libby McKnight, Susan Clark, and Andrea Howe for always standing for the best in me.

I am blessed to live in a Jewish community that supports and inspires me on a regular basis, and one that has shared my excitement at every stage of this project. There are too many to name without forgetting someone, but dear friends of Kemp Mill – I love our community and I value our many connections.

Thanks also to the Jewish community of Pikesville for welcoming me and teaching me with open arms, and to Kesher Israel Synagogue, my first religious home. Special thanks to my first *chavrutas*, Devorah Friend and Miriam (Cohen) White.

I offer my "honor and courage, devotion and loyalty" to the members of Chavalla BBG, my first real Jewish community, especially our chapter advisor Judy Hirsch and lifelong friends Debbie, Chara, and Heather. Sending love also to Lori, one more lifelong friend who has been with me on this exciting journey, and to Joan Cohen and Tobe Dresner, who first encouraged me in my writing o long ago. And thanks to the many women who have stood in as mothers for me in my own mom's absence, including Shelly Lovenstein, Ruthie Feldman,

Rosalyn Efron, and most recently, Linda Krumm.

I cannot express enough gratitude to Lynn Schusterman, Sandy Cardin, Lisa Eisen, Justin Korda, No'a Gorlin, Elyssa Krycer, Talya Levin, and the entire ROI network for the micro-grants that made this book possible, beginning with my writing coach, continuing through the editing and beta-reading process, and even helping to pay for the beautiful cover art. I am so incredibly grateful to be part of the ROI network, which recognizes that individuals are worth investing in, even as their projects change.

Thank you to my writing coach, Kristen Moeller, who helped me realize I would never finish this book if I just kept editing the first fifty pages over and over again, held me accountable for a full first draft, and continued to provide good advice long after our official coaching relationship ended. And thank you to developmental editor Elizabeth Bartasius, for understanding the story I was trying to tell, and for the clear, wise guidance and good ideas that helped me tell it effectively. Thanks also to Jonathan Hawpe for his help with the first edit.

Thank you to Katherine Koman, Benji Gutsin, Tyler Jonas, and Madison Krchnavy at Bancroft Press who championed this story and provided me with such helpful feedback. This book is better because of you. I wish you much success in your future careers.

Thank you to Avraham Cohen for asking so many questions and putting in so much hard work to create such beautiful cover art.

And many thanks to Tracy Copes for bearing with all my perfectionism as you created such a beautiful cover and interior design.

My final thanks are to Bruce Bortz, who took a chance on me first in college and again all these years later. Your re-emergence in my life has confirmed everything I've ever learned about keeping all bridges intact. Thank you for taking me on, again.

ABOUT THE AUTHOR

Evonne Marzouk grew up in Philadelphia. While still in high school, she had two stories published in *The Apprentice Writer,* published a story in *Shofar,* and was awarded first prize in fiction in a contest by the Israel Programs Center, which won her a free trip to Israel.

She was an active member of the B'nai B'rith Youth Organization, serving as President of Chavalla BBG, Sisterhood Chair of Philly Region, and as an International Chair. She attended BBYO's International Leadership Training Conference in Starlight, PA in 1993.

Evonne attended the Johns Hopkins University and received a B.A. from the Writing Seminars program, with a minor in Religious Studies, graduating Phi Beta Kappa in 1998. While at Hopkins, Evonne served as co-editor of, and frequent writer for, *The Charles St. Standard.* From 1996-1998, she worked part-time as a book editor at Bancroft Press, editing *You Might as Well Laugh* by Sandi Kahn Shelton (1996); *Generation of Wealth* by Julius Westheimer (1997); and *Live by the Sword* by Gus Russo (1998).

In 1998, she was selected First Runner-Up in the *What Being Jewish Means to Me* Essay/Expression Contest of the American Jewish Committee. From 1998-99, she served as the COEJL Legislative Fellow in the Legislative Assistant Program at the Religious Action Center for Reform Judaism, representing the Jewish community on environmental issues on Capitol Hill.

She founded and led the Green Group at Kesher Israel Synagogue from 2000-2007, and also served as an executive board member of Shomrei Adamah (Guardians of the Earth) from 2000-2002.

Evonne founded and is the former director of Canfei Nesharim, an organization that teaches Jewish wisdom about protecting the environment. In 2004, Canfei Nesharim was accepted to Bikkurim: An Incubator for New

Jewish Ideas. For ten years, Evonne led Canfei Nesharim, working with rabbis, scientists, educators, and community leaders to create and distribute a wide range of materials demonstrating the depth of Jewish tradition on this topic, including Torah teachings on the environment for each weekly Torah portion, each Jewish holiday, and a comprehensive set of core teachings on the environment, which was later gathered into a book, *Uplifting People and Planet: Eighteen Essential Jewish Lessons on the Environment,* available in e-book format on Amazon.com.

In 2008, Evonne was invited to join the ROI Community, an international network of Jewish activists, entrepreneurs and innovators. In 2009, she was selected as one of *The New York Jewish Week*'s "36 under 36." In 2011, with ROI's generous support, Evonne launched and led the team to develop Jewcology.com, a web-based portal to support resource sharing and collaboration across the Jewish-environmental community. From 2007-2014, she also led Maayan Olam, a Torah-Environment committee in Silver Spring, MD.

Evonne began work for the U.S. Environmental Protection Agency in 1999. In 2001, through an IPA agreement, Evonne worked as a program associate for the Center for a New American Dream, where she conducted outreach for a project called Turn the Tide, to engage individuals and organizations to take simple steps to reduce their impact on the environment.

In 2002, she was the youngest person on the United States delegation to the World Summit on Sustainable Development in Johannesburg, South Africa.

She has played a key role in work on the North American Agreement on Environmental Cooperation, the Minamata Convention on Mercury, and the Global Alliance to Eliminate Lead Paint.

She also manages a number of other communications and website projects for EPA's Office of International and Tribal Affairs.

Through her work at EPA, she was awarded a Bronze Medal for Commendable Service, for diligent and exemplary contributions to the 14th Session of the Commission for Environmental Cooperation in Morelia, Mexico on June 26-27, 2007; the International Affairs Award (2009), for enhancements to quality of work and dedication to developing core values for the office; OITA Communicator of the Year (2012-2013); the Russell Train Sustainability Award (2015 National Honor Award), for significantly advancing the work of the Lead Paint Alliance towards its goal of eliminating lead paint globally by 2020; and a Bronze Medal for Commendable Service, for efforts in support of United States participation in the Second UN Environment Assembly (2016).

Evonne continues to serve as an executive board member for Canfei Nesharim and as a steering committee member for Greater Washington Interfaith Power and Light.

She blogs on Medium at https://medium.com/@evonnemarzouk and continues to speak and teach in the Jewish community about Torah and the environment, among other topics.

She lives in Maryland with her husband and sons.

The Prophetess is her first novel.